Passion's Beginning.

Alura heard her father call for her. Strength flooded back into her. She came to her feet and ripped the sodden headdress off, freeing her hair. Looking back to see her father watching, Alura stepped toward the man on horseback. Fate had sent this man to her at this particular moment in time, and no matter who he might be, she would make use of him. She could not see his face in the shadows as he swung down from his saddle, but that mattered naught.

"Take me, sir knight," she said loudly as he turned toward her. "Use me as you will."

And with that, she threw herself into his arms, lifted her face to his, and kissed him with all the passion she could muster.

Jove titles by Elizabeth Hallam

ALURA'S WISH
SPIRIT CATCHER

Alura's Wish

ELIZABETH HALLAM

JOVE BOOKS, NEW YORK

MAGICAL LOVE is a trademark of Penguin Putnam Inc.

ALURA'S WISH

A Jove Book / published by arrangement with
the author

PRINTING HISTORY
Jove edition / August 1999

The Penguin Putnam Inc. World Wide Web site address is
http://www.penguinputnam.com

ISBN: 0-515-12566-0

A JOVE BOOK®
Jove Books are published by The Berkley Publishing Group,
a division of Penguin Putnam Inc.,
375 Hudson Street, New York, New York 10014.
JOVE and the "J" design
are trademarks belonging to Penguin Putnam Inc.

PRINTED IN THE UNITED STATES OF AMERICA

10   9   8   7   6   5   4   3   2   1

For Mary Nelson with thanks

for letting me borrow some

knowledge of medieval times

Prologue

◦◦◦

Long, long ago, in the ancient and honorable island kingdom of Azlon, somewhere off the coast of Persis (later known as Persia):

The man and woman were running so hard as they entered the throne room of the palace that their feet almost slipped out from under them on the highly polished floor. The man grabbed one of the heavy, gold-plated doors and said, "Give me a hand with this!"

The woman took hold of the other door and began shoving it closed. "This is all your fault!" she shouted at the man.

"My fault?" he practically howled as he pushed his door closed with a loud clang. "You're the one who said a wizard shouldn't marry!"

The woman's door crashed shut. "I said a wife might distract Sharrahz from his duties to us, his king and queen. I never told you to send his beloved off to marry the Emir of Kaffiristan!"

The man, who was the king of Azlon and who was known to his subjects as Zahir the Merciless, Zahir the Mighty, and Zahir the Scourge of the Known World (or at least so Zahir himself preferred to think), took hold of a table carved from the cedars of faraway Lebanon and, grunting and straining, pulled it in front of the doors to block them. He wiped the back of his hand across his brow under his green turban and said, "Who knew the girl would throw herself from the ship and drown rather than graciously accept the edict of her king?"

"You fool!" Zahir's queen, the beauteous Radiya, snarled at him. "She loved Sharrahz. She preferred death to a life without him. Only a man could fail to understand such a thing!"

"Well, we're safe now," said Zahir as he looked around at the luxuriously appointed throne room. "Even if the palace guards are afraid to face the wizard's wrath, these doors will stop him."

"Zahir!" Radiya grabbed her husband's arm and jerked him out of the way just as the golden doors exploded open. The terrible force splintered the fine hardwood table and sent shards of it flying across the room to stick like darts in the thick cushions of the thrones on the dais.

The king and queen stumbled backwards, away from the broken doors, their faces etched with terror. A man strode through the opening. He was clad in robes of silver and wore simple sandals on his feet. Medium-sized, with a shaven pate and compelling but not overly handsome features, he possessed such an air of power about him that he might as well have been a giant. He gazed at Zahir and Radiya with eyes grown dark from sorrow and anger.

"You two have ruined everything with your meddling," he said, and though his voice was but a murmur, the king and queen heard the words as clearly as if he had shouted. He lifted his hand slightly and continued, "I should remove you from the face of the earth."

Zahir flinched, but after a second he straightened and grasped Radiya's arm to thrust her partially behind him. "I did what I thought best for Azlon," he said, summoning up a shred of defiance and dignity. "I . . . I regret the girl's death, but there is nothing that can be done about it now. Not even you, Sharrahz, the most powerful wizard in all the eastern lands, have the power to restore life."

"True," said Sharrahz, "but I can take yours."

Once again the royal couple flinched, until the wizard continued, "But I will not."

Zahir blinked. "You won't?"

Radiya, more suspicious, asked quickly, "What will you do, then? Will you forego your revenge?"

A bleak, thin smile curved Sharrahz's lips. "Nay," he said softly. "I will forego nothing. My revenge on you shall be long, and sweet."

He strode across the room, the power of his presence forcing Zahir and Radiya to shuffle to the side and stay as far away from him as possible.

Sharrahz reached one of the ornate chests where the riches of Azlon were kept and threw it open. He plunged his hand into the piles of jewels and coins and came up with a heavy golden bracelet connected by a chain to a golden ring made in the same fashion. At the points where the chain connected bracelet and ring were simple sittings in which glowed a pair of magnificent fire opals. Sharrahz turned toward Zahir and Radiya with this slave bracelet in his hand.

"The two of you have always been so proud of your baubles," he said mockingly. "Now, this one shall be your prison."

"No!" exclaimed Zahir.

"I shall transform the two of you into djinn. You, who have ruled this land and been catered to and served by thousands of slaves, shall be condemned to an endless life as magical spirits confined to these jewels, able to emerge only to do the bidding of your human masters, whoever they may be who come into possession of this trinket."

Radiya's lovely face was pale with shock. "You . . . you cannot do this to us, Sharrahz. We have made mistakes. . . ." She swallowed hard at the look of fury that passed over the wizard's face but hurried on anyway. "We have made mistakes, but surely we do not deserve an eternity of such an existence."

For a moment, Sharrahz was silent as he considered her plea. Then, surprising both the king and the queen, he nodded in agreement. "Not an eternity, then," said Sharrahz.

Zahir heaved a sigh. "How long?"

"A suitable period of time." Sharrahz nodded again. "Because of the two of you, I have lost my love. She would have been my wife, and we would have been happy sharing a life together. So, as I transform you . . ." He raised his hands and gestured, and smoke seemed to spring up out of nowhere, curling around the figures of Zahir and Radiya. They both cried out in horror as Sharrahz went on, ". . . I charge you to bring together men and women who truly love each other, so that their happiness may in some small way balance the pain you have caused me."

Zahir and Radiya clutched each other as their bodies blurred and began to fade. The smoke swirled more thickly about them. Zahir cried out, "When we have done this, you will free us?"

"The curse will be over," said Sharrahz, "when you have brought together enough happy couples to ease my loss."

"How many?" asked Radiya. "How many couples?"

"How about . . . a thousand and one?" Sharrahz smiled again. "Yes, I like that number. A thousand and one couples it is."

Zahir shrieked, "But we will never—"

His voice was gone before he could finish his protest, as was his body and the body of Radiya. Now there was only the thick gray smoke, and as Sharrahz performed another elegant gesture, the billowing cloud split into two.

Sharrahz held up the slave bracelet, and with a sound like the howling of the desert wind—though there was no wind here in the throne room of the royal palace of Azlon—each pillar of smoke was drawn into one of the fire opals. The gems seemed to glow even more brightly for a moment, and then the radiance faded.

"Enjoy your new homes," purred Sharrahz as he looked down at the slave bracelet. "You will be there for a long, long time."

Then he cast the bracelet aside, turning away as it clattered on the floor.

This place held nothing for him now. No one would dare stop him. He would make his way to the mainland and from there spend the rest of his days wandering the world, looking for that which he knew he would not find.

And in Azlon, with the king and the queen gone, destroyed by the vengeful wizard for all the populace would know, civil war would undoubtedly rage.

Zahir and Radiya had left no heirs to assume the throne. In the chaos, there was no way of knowing what would happen to the bracelet and the ring where the royal couple were now trapped, no way of knowing into whose hands they might fall.

But sooner or later, that person would rub those fire opals, and then he or she would be in for quite a surprise.

One

The heat seared a man's soul as well as his body, stripping away any weakness that was to be found there, leaving behind only a hard, dried husk.

Despite the cool sea wind that blew in his face, Connor still felt the heat where it mattered most: inside.

God, would it never go away? Would it be with him always, the soul-killing heat that blazed down from a yellow sun and harshly limned the horrors he had witnessed? The horrors in which he, God save him, had participated?

"Sorry, milord! I swear, I wasn't expecting that gust of wind just now, else I never would have chosen to empty that bucket. . . ."

Connor looked down and used his boot to scrape the potato peelings over the side of the ship. They had been tossed at his feet by the wind when Jeremy had emptied the scraps from the galley.

"T'was an accident, lad," Connor said. "No harm was done." He frowned. "But you are a squire, my squire, a knight in training. You should not be performing such menial chores."

"I know, milord," said the young man. "But I was listening to the stories told by old Balthazar, the cook, and it seemed only fair that I lend him a hand. He has been many places and done many things, you know.'' Jeremy looked down shyly at the deck. ''And bedded many women, too.''

The corners of Connor's mouth moved slightly, but no one would have called the momentary change of expression a smile. Jeremy was of an age when the coupling of men and women interested him greatly. Connor could remember being that young and enthusiastic himself.

A thousand years ago, it must have been. At least, that was the way he felt. . . .

''You will find that those who speak of all the women they have bedded sometimes have very active imaginations,'' Connor advised the young squire, ''while those who keep their own counsel have often known even more of the world and its pleasures.''

Jeremy looked up at the towering figure beside him at the ship's rail and thought, *Then you must have coupled with ten thousand women, milord, because none is as closemouthed as you, Sir Connor.*

Wisely, the boy kept those musings to himself as he went back to the galley, swinging the empty scraps bucket in his hand.

The ship had set sail from Acre several sennights earlier, bearing home a score of knights who had followed Richard Lionheart into battle against the Saracens. In the Holy Land itself, Richard was now negotiating with Saladin, trying to bring an end to the war over Jerusalem and the other holy shrines.

But for Connor and the other knights on board this ship, the war was already at an end. The injuries they had suffered in battle were too grievous to allow them to take the field again.

At least he was returning to his homeland relatively whole, Connor thought as he sat at the table in his cabin that night and tried to summon up an appetite for the food Jeremy had placed before him. Unlike some of the men who had lost limbs, Connor still had a full complement of arms and legs.

It was just that one of them would no longer work the way it should.

He pushed the plate aside, the food on it having barely been touched.

Connor looked down at his right hand and tried to clench the fingers into a fist. They curled slightly, but that was all. He strained until beads of sweat popped out on his forehead, but the hand would not close. He moved on to the next step in this nightly ritual, bending the arm toward him from the elbow. It moved a few inches, then stopped. Again, no matter how much effort Connor made, the arm would move only a certain distance and no more.

He tried to raise it above his head, but he could not reach even the level of his shoulder. Connor's lips pulled back from his teeth in a grimace.

"You're doing better tonight, milord. You really are."

Connor heard Jeremy's words of encouragement only vaguely. With a curse hissed between gritted teeth, he dropped his right arm back into his lap. It was nothing to him now but a thing. It might as well have been carved from wood instead of being comprised of muscle and bone and blood. No longer was it a part of him, the part that had wielded a sword and a battle-ax almost effortlessly.

"You've improved a great deal since we left Acre, Sir Connor," Jeremy said. "In time, no one will ever be able to tell that you were wounded."

"You lie," Connor said in a near-growl. "Scars may have covered the wound, but the sinew underneath will never mend."

"You don't know that, milord," insisted Jeremy. "Why, Balthazar talks of having seen men hurt even worse than you who regained all their strength—"

"Balthazar is a lying old bag of wind!" Connor scraped the bench back violently and stood up. "By God, what ever possessed the captain of this vessel to bring aboard a Spaniard to serve as cook?"

Jeremy nodded tentatively at the plate of nearly untouched food. "The meals are quite good, milord. . . ."

Connor swung away with another growled curse. He was a menacing figure in the candlelight, tall and muscular in boots, hose, and an open-throated tunic. He was clean shaven, unlike most of his countrymen. Thick dark hair fell around his shoulders. His features might have been quite handsome, had they not been cured to the color of saddle leather by sun and wind and sharpened by his experiences until his expression matched the wolfish grace of his body. He reached down onto his bunk with his left hand and withdrew the sword from the sheath that lay there.

It still felt odd to grip the sword with his left hand, even though he had been practicing since before the ship had left Acre. He lifted the weapon. Its weight was no strain on muscles grown strong from carrying a heavy shield into battle. What bothered Connor was the sheer awkwardness of it. He swung the blade slowly from right to left, frowning not with effort but from the concentration needed to control the sword.

The slow swings became slashes as the blade moved faster and faster.

Candlelight glinted on the shining steel. Connor brought the sword up, then down, then thrust out with it as if impaling an imaginary enemy. He drew back quickly, parried a phantom stroke, lunged again. Sweat stood out on his brow.

"Very good, milord!" Jeremy exclaimed, unable to hold in his enthusiasm any longer. "I'd wager my coins on you against any knight in the lists."

Connor lowered the sword and rested the point on the deck, leaning on it as he tried to catch his breath. "Then you would lose your coins," he said harshly, "just as I would lose my life if I were foolish enough to enter a tournament against a true fighting man. I'm slow, Jeremy, slow and weak."

"Not true, milord. . . ." The squire fell silent as Connor pinned him with a glance.

" 'Tis true, and we both know it," Connor said quietly.

"But you've gotten better, both fighting with your left arm and using your right again. The time will come when you're as good as you ever were, Sir Connor."

"I hope you're right, lad . . . but I fear you are not." Connor picked up the scabbard with his clumsy right hand and slid the sword back into it.

Jeremy leaped to his feet to take the sword and put it with Connor's other weapons in a corner of the little cabin.

—

"Shall I take the food away?" asked Jeremy. "Are you going to sleep?"

"You can take the food," Connor told him, "but I am not yet ready to sleep. I believe I will go up on deck."

But he would not go alone. He knew that even if he ordered Jeremy to remain here in the cabin, the young man would slip out and come up on deck to keep a watch on him. Jeremy feared that he was so despondent, he might actually plunge far enough into the depths of gloom to do away with himself.

Suicide was a mortal sin, of course . . . but so was murder.

And he already stood condemned for that.

A man could burn in the fires of eternal damnation but once, Connor told himself wryly as he slipped on a surcoat and a cloak. He left the cabin without bothering to order Jeremy to stay behind. It would have been a waste of breath. Using his left hand to brace himself, he climbed up the steep, narrow stairs and emerged through the hatch onto the deck of the ship. The wind immediately caught his cloak and whipped it out behind him.

It was a dark night, with swiftly scudding clouds covering the moon and most of the stars. Connor's keen eyes adjusted quickly to the darkness, but still the shadows were quite thick, almost impenetrable. A faint phosphorescence came from the sea itself, however, and guided his path to the rail. His steps were sure; he had long since grown accustomed to the tossing and heaving of the ship. He had that much for which to be thankful.

He put his left hand on the smoothly polished wood and gazed out over the waves.

Connor had no idea how long he had been standing there, still as a statue, when someone behind him rasped, "Wot're ye doin' there?"

Instantly, Connor turned, letting his instincts take over. His left hand shot out and clamped around the throat of the man who had come up behind him. The man was almost formless in the night, a deeper patch of darkness in the shadows, but Connor struck unerringly anyway. The corded muscles in his shoulders bunched. The man's feet came off the deck, and he flailed at Connor's arm as he fought for air. He might as well have been lashing out at an iron bar.

Then Connor drew a deep breath and forced his fingers to relax. The man slipped out of his grasp and dropped the couple of inches to the deck. He went to one knee as he gasped and pawed at his throat. Connor hoped that he hadn't crushed the man's windpipe.

After a moment the man began to recover. When he had pulled in several great lungfuls of air, he stumbled to his feet and croaked hoarsely, "There was no need to be doin' that, milord. I meant ye no harm. I didn't recognize ye when I saw ye standin' there at the rail."

"The only passengers on this ship are knights recovering from their wounds as they go home," said Connor. "Who else could I have been?"

"I know that, milord," the sailor whined. "But the cap'n, he don't like nobody wanderin' around on deck in the dark. He's afeared one of ye will . . . fall off."

"Jump, you mean." This sailor was just like Jeremy, thought Connor: worried that he would end his life so that he would not have to face long years as a pitied cripple.

That was a legitimate worry, Connor supposed. He had heard some of the other men grumbling about how it would be easier to take a poniard and slit their own throats, as they had slit the throats of so many Saracens before their injuries had laid them low.

But the captain and the crew had little to worry about where he was concerned, if only they would believe that. He had already been to hell.

He had seen the desert sands soak up rivers of blood until they could drink no more. He had seen his best friend cut down, butchered like a hog. And even before that, before the crusade that had taken him to the Holy Land, he had faced tortures the likes of which no imp of Satan could have devised. No, only a man could have come up with the hellish indignities Connor had endured.

Apologies did not come easily to him, but he said to the sailor, "I should not have attacked you." That was as far as he was prepared to go.

It was enough to mollify the man. He rubbed at his sore throat again and muttered, " 'Twas me own fault. Had I known 'twas ye, Sir Connor, I would have stayed far away."

The implication was plain enough, at least to Connor. Those who dared to be close to him came to bad ends. If Jeremy had had any sense, if he had not been blinded by hero worship, he, too, would have abandoned Connor. It was the reasonable thing to do.

Suddenly the night was pressing in on him as closely as the walls of the cabin had been earlier. He might as well be down there as up here, he decided. He could lay in his bunk and toss and turn for an interminable time before exhaustion finally claimed him.

"Good night," he said gruffly to the sailor as he turned away.

"G'night, milord," the man called after him.

Connor saw a shape drop through the hatch as he approached. That would be Jeremy, scurrying back to the cabin so that he could pretend he had not observed the entire incident with the sailor. If it was that important to him, Connor would allow him to believe that the deception had succeeded. He lingered a few moments longer on deck.

Down below, Jeremy snatched up a cloth and a piece of the jewelry Sir Connor was bringing back from the Holy Land. He had no real reason to fear the knight: Sir Connor had always been a kind master, never cuffing or beating him the way some knights did with their squires. But Jeremy did not want him to know that his orders had been disobeyed, either.

Trying to look busy, Jeremy swiped the scrap of cloth over the fire opal set into the bracelet he held. A ring with another fire opal in its setting was attached to the bracelet by a thin chain. The gold from which the ring, bracelet, and chain were fashioned was dull with age. There was no telling how old this piece of jewelry was.

Suddenly, as Jeremy began to polish the second stone, a huge thunderclap shook the small cabin. At least, it seemed so to Jeremy. He fell back against the bulkhead, gazing up in shock and amazement at what was occurring right before his disbelieving eyes. He had dropped the bracelet and ring, and now smoke was rising from the two gems. The smoke swirled and spun, and it grew and stretched until it took on human shapes. A man and a woman in strange clothing seemed to stand before Jeremy.

He screwed his eyes closed and jammed his fists against them. "Go away, go away, go away," he chanted. "Whatever is happening, I wish it would just go away and I could forget that it ever happened!"

When Connor entered the cabin a few moments later, Jeremy was sitting cross-legged on the floor, a small wooden chest in his lap. The lid of the chest was raised, and the squire was holding a piece of jewelry. Jeremy was polishing the golden bracelet with a soft cloth he held in his other hand.

"Fussing over those trinkets again, I see," said Connor.

Jeremy looked up at him. "They are not trinkets, milord. You are returning to England with a great treasure in gold and gems. You will be a wealthy man in your own right."

"But the estate and the title will still belong to my brother."

The piece of jewelry over which Jeremy labored was a slave bracelet, a thick golden circlet with a ring attached to it by means of a slender chain adorned with golden leaves. The wearer would slip the ring onto her finger first, then thrust her hand through the bracelet. Where the connecting chain met the bracelet, a beautiful fire opal was set into the golden circlet. The ring had a stone, too, a matching dark-red fire opal that threw back the light so brilliantly it seemed almost alive.

Though plunder was not the reason Connor had joined King Richard in the Third Crusade, he had picked up a few such items in his perilous travels through the Holy Land. Some of the knights were interested only in the gold and gems they could loot and the women they could rape. Connor had kept the things like the slave bracelet that had struck his fancy, and he had taken women as well, but only when they were willing. Not one had been forced to pleasure him at the point of a sword. Honor was a damned foolish thing, he had thought more than once, but he could not avoid its constraints, even though his companions insisted that chivalry need not extend to Saracen women.

"Put that away," he ordered Jeremy just as the squire hesitated, an odd frown on his face, with the cloth poised over the fire opal on the ring.

"But milord, I've not had the chance to polish these gems since you obtained the bracelet in Acre—"

"They shine brightly enough," snapped Connor. "Put it away."

Jeremy replaced the bracelet in the wooden chest and lowered the lid. He pushed the chest underneath the bunk with the rest of Connor's things.

Connor tossed his cloak and surcoat onto the table, then removed his boots and hose. He waved away Jeremy's offer to help. "Blow out the candle," he said. "I would sleep."

"Yes, milord."

The darkness that engulfed the cabin as soon as Jeremy puffed out the candle was complete. This was what the pits of Hades must look like, Connor thought as he rolled into his blankets. Eyes open or eyes closed, the stygian blackness was the same.

He heard faint noises that came from Jeremy as the squire settled down in his own blankets on the floor on the other side of the cabin. That was a hard bed, but so was this bunk. Truth to tell, both of them had slept in worse places. At least there were no sharp rocks poking into their flesh here.

After a few moments of silence, Jeremy whispered, "Milord?"

Connor sighed. He had known the young man was not asleep; he had been able to tell that from the sound of Jeremy's breathing. "What is it?"

"What are we going to do, Sir Connor? When we get back to England, I mean."

This wasn't the first time Jeremy had asked that question. "Someone will need an old soldier to train their men-at-arms," Connor said.

"You're not old, milord. Only twenty and six."

Only twenty and six . . . If the lad but knew how old that could truly be.

"Perhaps your brother might have a place for you," Jeremy went on.

"I want nothing from my brother," Connor said coldly. "And I would not be welcome at Stavebrook. Morvyn made that quite clear when I left to join Richard."

"But perhaps Lord Ridglea has relented—"

"No," Connor Warrick said, and his tone made it clear there was no room for argument. "If I never see Morvyn alive again, that will be best for both of us. . . ."

Two

The cold wind blowing through the drafty chapel plucked at Lady Alura de Gabin's dark mantle. She wrapped it more tightly around herself, shrinking into the hooded garment and trying not to shiver as she listened to the echoing tones of the priest intoning the mass for the dead. Flanked by her father and mother, Alura stood before the stone sarcophagus of the man she had been pledged to marry.

Outside, the late winter storm dropped handfuls of sleet on the churchyard, but the weather had not prevented a large number of mourners from putting in an appearance today. Morvyn Warrick, Lord Ridglea, had been a wealthy, powerful man. Lords and ladies from neighboring estates, along with large numbers of vassals and serfs, had dared both bandits and the elements to come today to pay their respects to him and honor his passing. In truth, few if any of them had reason to bear any genuine affection for Lord Ridglea, but they were here nonetheless.

A shudder passed through Alura. Her mother put an arm around her shoulders and hugged her. "Be strong, my darling," she whispered. "Morvyn would have wanted it that way."

Alura took a deep breath and controlled the reaction she

felt. Her father reached over and patted her hand awkwardly. Herve de Gabin was known as a warrior, not a comforter of young women, even his own daughter, but he tried. Alura acknowledged his touch with a weak smile.

"Will that blasted priest never finish his gabbling?" muttered de Gabin under his breath.

"Herve!" his wife protested, also in a whisper.

"Blessed priest. I meant blessed priest," de Gabin growled.

Alura felt as if she were teetering on the edge of the grave herself, although in reality quite some distance separated her from the burial ground behind the church. And speaking figuratively, she was far from the grave, too, since she had known this life only ten and nine years. But Morvyn was only thirty and one and should have had a good many years left to him, and he had been struck down by the capricious hand of fate. It could happen to anyone, at any time.

But, truth to tell, Morvyn *had* contributed somewhat to his own demise, Alura supposed. . . .

The burial mass was finally over, and Alura's parents led her away from the chapel as the rest of the crowd began to disperse. She heard bumping and thumping behind her as serfs wrestled the sarcophagus toward the crypt where it would stand for a time, covered with a silken cloth and surrounded by burning lamps and wax candles. With each grunt of effort from the men, Alura's mother tightened her arm about Alura's shoulders, as if to give her daughter added strength to endure the final moments of this ordeal.

The family had ridden from Brynclair, the de Gabin castle and estate. Alura's father helped her and her mother onto their horses, then stepped back and said to the captain of his well-armed guards, "Return to the castle."

"You are not coming with us, Herve?" Katharine de Gabin asked.

The old warrior shook his head. "I must speak to Mossgrave."

Alura had no idea why her father would want to have a discussion with the seneschal of the Warrick family. Any pending connection between the Warricks and the de Gabins had been severed with Morvyn's death. Yet she knew better than to demand an answer from her father. Herve de Gabin was not accustomed to having his decisions questioned by the women in his family . . . or by anyone else, for that matter.

"Have my horse brought from Brynclair for me later," de Gabin added to the captain, who nodded his helmed head. When de Gabin had turned away, the horses were heeled into a steady walk. Two of the guards led the animals ridden by Alura and Katharine.

"Why does Father wish to speak to old Mossgrave?" Alura asked her mother.

Katharine could only shake her head. "I have no knowledge of what your father thinks, and but small knowledge of what he does. He keeps his own counsel and always has."

Not unlike other members of the family, thought Alura. Her parents seldom if ever knew what she was thinking, and all things considered, it was probably better that way.

It was a bit less than two leagues from the church back to Brynclair, and by the time Alura and her mother had covered that distance on this cold, drafty day, both of them were thoroughly chilled. As the party rode through the gate in the outer wall and started across the outer bailey, Alura looked forward to the warmth that would come from the fire in the great hall. In a matter of moments, the riders were through the town that had grown up around the castle Brynclair and had reached the moat surrounding the keep. The drawbridge was down and the portcullis was up, awaiting the arrival of the lords of this particular manor. Alura frowned slightly. No one was expecting trouble, of course, but with the gates wide open like this, outlaws or even an invading army could have strolled into Brynclair and made it their own, had they so desired.

Women were not supposed to concern themselves with such matters, of course. The defense of a castle was best left to males, or so the conventional wisdom held. But Alura had a sharp eye, and her father knew it. She resolved to speak to him about the laxity of precautions taken recently.

She knew what her father would say. Herve de Gabin would sigh heavily and proclaim, "Peace! It dulls a man's keen edges!"

He would have liked nothing better than to follow Richard

Lion-heart to the Holy Land for the Third Crusade. Even though Richard's army was comprised mainly of Normans from across the Channel, de Gabin would have fought alongside the Franks willingly. A sword in his hand, the weight of armor upon his breast, the smells of smoke and blood . . . those were the things Alura's father had lived for all these years.

Alura and Katharine entered the great hall a few moments later. Katharine headed straight for her apartment, saying over her shoulder, "I am truly exhausted." She paused at the bottom of the staircase that curved along the wall to the upper floors. "Will you be all right, child?"

"I'm fine, Mother," Alura told her. "Please, do not concern yourself with me."

"But you've had such a great loss. . . ."

Alura bowed her head. "With God's help, I shall be strong enough to stand the pain."

"Very well. But if you need me—"

"I shall find you, Mother."

Katharine nodded in acceptance. Alura had always been a rather strange child, keeping to herself, sharing little of the pain—or the pleasure—of growing up. But Katharine had always believed that God must have a purpose for Alura, otherwise He would not have allowed her to survive when all of Katharine's other children had not lived past infancy.

When her mother was gone, Alura took off her hooded mantle and went to stand before the fire. She unfastened her wimple and stripped it from her head, allowing thick braids of hair the color of flame to fall freely. Even though she knew she'd have to cover and rebraid her hair again, she unplaited the long braids and ran her fingers through her fiery hair, enjoying the sensuous feeling of freedom that gave her, enjoying as well the waves of heat from the fire that broke over her. The chill was soon driven away as she stood there, eyes closed. Her lips moved soundlessly.

Finally, finally, she could offer up a prayer that expressed what she had been feeling ever since word of Morvyn's death had reached Brynclair. She'd had to hide those emotions for too long a time, and chief among them were two that were closely related: thankfulness and relief.

Now she would not have to marry Morvyn Warrick, and Alura was so happy about that fact that she could have sung like the birds of spring that would soon be arriving once again in England. . . .

Whistling! Her father was actually whistling an airy melody as he strolled into the great hall of Brynclair several days after the funeral mass of Lord Ridglea. Alura tried not to stare at him. Sir Herve de Gabin was not a man to display happiness so openly.

She hoped he was not ill.

"My dear Herve," Katharine said, equally puzzled, "what are you so cheerful about? 'Tis not often we see you in such a fair mood."

"Are you saying that I am naught but an unpleasant old man?" demanded de Gabin. He slipped his hand into the vertical opening of his surcoat to caress the hidden purse beneath.

Alura and Katharine were sitting near the fire, mending clothing. Outside the keep, a slashing rainstorm was making life miserable for nearly everyone else. Even inside, it was fairly cool and drafty.

Katharine put her mending aside and said, "I never claimed you were an old man, Herve."

"But I *am* unpleasant."

"Nor did I say that. It is simply . . . unusual . . . for you to be so demonstrative about your feelings."

"I have petitioned Prince John to grant me title to Stavebrook, and I have every reason to think that he will do so," de Gabin said smugly.

Both Alura and Katharine stared at him.

After a moment, de Gabin frowned and snapped, "Why are the two of you looking at me in that fashion? I've done nothing wrong. In a matter of sennights, Stavebrook would have been ours anyway."

"It would have still belonged to Lord Ridglea," Katharine pointed out.

"But Alura would have been married to him."

Alura said, "I am not married to Lord Ridglea, nor will I ever be. He's dead, Father, in case you have forgotten so soon."

The frown on de Gabin's face deepened and his features began to flush with anger and impatience. "Of course I have not forgotten. But the two of you were to have been wed. I had already paid the dowry, which remains in Stavebrook's coffers to this day. Warrick had no heirs. It seems clear to me that Stavebrook should go to you, my dear, and I am certain John will see it the same way."

"Only if the bribe accompanying your petition was sufficient," Alura said.

Her father did not bother looking shocked at the suggestion that he would stoop to a bribe. When dealing with John Lackland, Richard's brother who sat on the throne in the true king's absence, bribery was an accepted means of doing business. De Gabin removed his hand from the hidden purse, stalked heavily across the room to warm his hands at the fire, and as he did so, said confidently, "It will be." He looked into the flames and muttered, "It must be."

"You are not the only one who will covet Stavebrook now that Lord Ridglea is dead," said Katharine. "Nor are you the only one who knows that Prince John's favor can be purchased. Why are you so sure he will favor your petition, Herve?"

De Gabin waved a knobby-knuckled hand at his daughter. "Why, because of Alura here, of course. She was Warrick's betrothed."

"But the marriage never took place," said Alura.

Her father looked away, staring into the flames as he muttered a response that was unintelligible.

Katharine was closer to him, however, and she must have understood some of what he said, because she stood up and demanded in a taut voice, "What did you say, Herve?"

With a fierce glower, de Gabin swung around toward his wife and daughter and snapped, "I implied in my petition that Warrick and Alura perhaps did not wait for the actual ceremony before, ah, consummating their relationship."

"What!" Alura exclaimed as she came to her feet. The

clothes she had been mending fell from her lap, completely forgotten.

Her father cleared his throat loudly, then went on, "I, ah, perhaps even implied that an heir might exist, if only in a, ah, fledgling state. . . ."

You told Prince John that I was with child by Lord Ridglea?" Alura could not believe what she was hearing. She knew that her father coveted the neighboring estate of Stavebrook; that was why her marriage to Morvyn Warrick had been arranged in the first place. She had not wanted to marry Morvyn, but she'd had little choice in the matter. Herve de Gabin was that set on someday owning Stavebrook. But she had never suspected that he would . . . would ruin her good name simply to strengthen his claim to the estate he wanted so badly!

Only the fact that he was her father kept Alura from flying at him and clawing his eyes out. Her mother was equally furious. "How dare you do such a thing, Herve?" Katharine demanded. "You've done horrible damage to your own daughter's name—"

"Bah!" de Gabin broke in. "I've done nothing of the sort. Think you that anyone will care if Warrick tumbled her before they were wed? God's eyes, woman, half the brides in this land have swollen bellies within a month of their wedding and deliver the little brats a few months later."

"But it's not true!" said Alura. "Morvyn never touched me!"

De Gabin snorted. "That doesn't matter, as long as Lackland thinks it may be true. His power is shaky; he won't risk a dispute in which he could be shown to be wrong. That's why he will grant title to Stavebrook to me, as the grandsire of Lord Ridglea's sole heir." The old knight's eyes narrowed in thought as he looked at his daughter. "If you were to get yourself with child in short order, it might be a good thing, Alura. No one would ever have to know the babe was not Warrick's. You're a comely lass; I'm sure one of my men-at-arms would be glad to oblige—"

That was all Alura could stand. With an angry cry, she threw the pincushion she had almost forgotten she was holding in her hand. Her father let out a yelp of surprise as he threw up an arm to ward off the missile. Alura bent and snatched up the stool on which she had been sitting, and she would have flung it at her father's head as well if her mother had not hurried to grasp her arm.

"Peace, child," Katharine said to Alura. She looked over her shoulder at her husband, who wore an expression of mortally offended dignity. " 'Twould do no good to try to dash his brains out. He has none."

"How dare you, woman!" roared de Gabin. "I'll not be talked about in such rude fashion in my own keep by any female, not even my wife."

Katharine turned on him. "I shall speak of you in any way I please, you old dullard! To imply that our daughter is not chaste and pure, simply to gain title to an estate—"

"I did what I thought best!" De Gabin flapped a hand at Alura. "True, a maiden's virginity is highly prized, but in this case, the sacrifice seemed well worth it."

Alura was not sure who was more angry, her or her mother. Both of them were fairly trembling with rage as they stared at de Gabin. They were silent now, but the intensity of their gazes was such that de Gabin began to shift nervously back and forth.

"At any rate, 'tis done," he finally said. "There is no point in arguing about it now. My petition and a letter explaining the, ah, delicate circumstances are even now on their way to London. Within a fortnight, we should have Lackland's response."

"Write another letter," Alura said. "Tell Prince John that you were mistaken."

Stubbornly, her father shook his head. "I cannot do that. My petition stands."

Alura looked at Katharine. "Mother . . ."

With a sigh, the defiance seemed to leave Katharine. "There is nothing we can do, daughter," she said without looking at Alura. "If your father's mind is made up—"

"It is," said de Gabin.

"—I am afraid his decision is the final one."

Alura looked from one to the other of her parents. Katharine was right: ultimately, the power lay with Alura's father.

Women were little more than chattel, to be taken, bartered, and used as men saw fit. The rightness of it might be open to debate, but the reality of it was not.

But she was not totally powerless, Alura realized. She could still control her own fate.

"Will John grant your petition, Father," she asked, "once he has heard that I have left Brynclair forever?"

Katharine cried out softly in dismay while de Gabin merely stared at Alura in confusion. "What do you mean?" he asked gruffly. "You're not going anywhere."

"Oh, but I am!"

With that, Alura turned and ran toward the door of the great hall.

Behind her, Katharine called, "Alura, no!" while her father thundered, "Come back here!" Alura ignored them both, caught at the latch of the massive wooden door, and heaved it open.

She dashed out of the great hall toward the towering double doors that led from the keep to the inner bailey. She heard her father's footsteps behind her, but at his age he could not hope to match her speed. She paid no attention to the commands he roared after her. Servants gaped at her as she sped past them, but she ignored them, too.

Her mind was numb with horror. She had known, ever since she was old enough to understand such things, that her father's main concern in life was the accumulation of wealth and power. She had known as well that even though he loved her, he would not hesitate to make use of her in that quest. The marriage he had arranged with Morvyn Warrick was proof enough of that. Morvyn was not a monster, not like his infamous younger brother had been, but he was not the sort of man Alura would have chosen to wed, either.

But never had she dreamed that her father would stoop so low as to gossip about her virtue—or lack of the same—to the ruler of England! He had even suggested that she lie with a man—any man—and give birth to a child simply to strengthen his claim to Stavebrook!

No one stopped her as she ran out of the keep and into the rain. Though it was only late afternoon, the low, thick clouds

made it almost as dark as night. The rain was cold and hard
and felt like scores of tiny daggers piercing her as she stumbled toward the outer wall. Bits of ice intermixed with the rain
pelted her. She gasped and hesitated, looking back over her
shoulder.

Her father stood in the doorway of the keep, glowering after
her.

She might catch her death in a downpour such as this,
thought Alura as she ran on, but if that was what fate willed,
it was fine with her. Better that than become what her father
wanted.

Perhaps she ought to visit the barracks of the men-at-arms,
she thought wildly as she stumbled forward again. She could
lie down and spread her legs for all of them, one after the
other. Surely one of them would plant a seed in her that would
take hold, and that was what her father wanted. He didn't care
who swole her belly, only that he could point to the child and
say, *There! There is the heir to Stavebrook!*

She was only halfway across the bailey when she tripped
and went to her knees in the mud. Once she had fallen, she
found she lacked the strength to get up. She threw her head
back and let the rain stream over her, plastering her headdress
to her hair and her gown to her body. She shook with sobs,
but the tears that welled from her eyes were indistinguishable
from the raindrops that covered her face.

It was the sound she became aware of first, the splashing
thud of a horse's hooves as it walked slowly toward her. Alura
opened her eyes and blinked, trying to clear away the tears
and rain in which they were awash. She saw the massive shape
looming up in the gloom and realized it was a man on
horseback. One of her father's soldiers, no doubt, come to see
what was wrong. The man reined his mount to a halt and sat
there for a breath, studying her in the dim light.

Alura heard her father call for her. Strength flooded back
into her. She came to her feet and ripped the sodden headdress
off, freeing her hair. Looking back to see her father watching,
Alura stepped toward the man on horseback. Fate had sent this
man to her at this particular moment in time, and no matter
who he might be, she would make use of him. She could not

see his face in the shadows as he swung down from his saddle, but that mattered naught.

"Take me, sir knight," she said loudly as he turned toward her. "Use me as you will."

And with that, she threw herself into his arms, lifted her face to his, and kissed him with all the passion she could muster.

Connor had witnessed many a strange sight in his travels, but none quite so startling as the scene that had greeted him as he and Jeremy rode through the gates of Brynclair.

The guards had been reluctant to admit them at first, but once Connor had told them who he was, they had grudgingly lowered the drawbridge and raised the portcullis. They were wise enough to know that their lord would want to speak with this particular visitor. One of the guards had walked alongside Connor's horse to announce him, but now the man stood by gaping at the fiery-haired young woman who was soaked to the skin.

Connor's eyes swept from her head to her toe, from the crown of red hair to the dainty feet shod in slippers that were covered with mud at the moment. The woman's gown had several large splotches of mud on it as well, most notably around the knees where she had fallen, but the steady rain was washing that mud away. Her long, full gown was richly embroidered and was pulled in tightly to her body with a golden girdle. The dark-green gown was so wet that it clung to every inch of her form, outlining clearly the small but well-formed breasts. It must have been the chill of the rain that had hardened her nipples. They stood out clearly against the soaked fabric of the gown. He noted that as objectively as he noted all the other facets of her beauty. She might as well have been nude, and though he felt a stirring in his groin, he ignored it. Judging from her garments, if not her demeanor, she was a lady, and he had no desire to couple with her.

He wondered who she was.

Something had clearly disturbed her greatly. She was staring up at Connor, her eyes as green as the gown. Though he did not want anything to distract him from the errand that had brought him here, he felt that he had to do something, had to respond in some way to this strange woman. Perhaps she was mad.

He dismounted and stepped forward, intending to ask her name.

Before he could speak, she made her bold, totally unexpected demand, and suddenly she was in his arms, her body pressed tightly against him. He wore mail and a thick surcoat, but he seemed to feel the heat coming from her through the heavy garments, even though he knew that was impossible. His left arm went around her, the gesture as much a matter of instinct as anything else.

Then her arms went around his neck, pulling his head down to hers. Her lips sought his, and he could think of nothing else but the softness, the heat, and the sweet taste of her mouth.

Dear God, but he was strong! Even with but one of his arms around her, she could barely breathe. Though she had spoken in anger and kissed him to spite her father, who she knew was watching from the door of the keep, she found herself responding to the contact in a completely unexpected manner. She had thought that her heart was beating quickly before, but now it broke into a gallop and felt as if it might tear itself out of her chest at any moment. The keep seemed to spin madly about her, but she sensed that she would be safe as long as she was snugly in the grip of this stranger. She no longer felt the cold and the damp. The heat from this man's lips had banished all other sensations. Kissing him was like plunging into the heart of the sun.

He took his lips away from hers, and she whimpered faintly with the loss. As she looked up at him, she realized he was not one of her father's soldiers. She had never seen him before. . . .

No, wait, there was something vaguely familiar about him, as if she had glimpsed something about him that she should know well. She saw, too, the glow of recognition in his widening eyes.

"Good Lord," he said hoarsely. "You are the lady Alura."

"Do . . . do I know you, milord?" she managed to gasp.

From the start, his body had been taut, as if he was trying to control a reaction that threatened to overwhelm him. Now he stiffened even more, and instead of keeping his arm around her, he put his hand on her waist and moved her back a pace.

"Alura!" Herve de Gabin shouted from the doorway of the keep. "Who is that?"

She echoed the question, looking up at the stranger and whispering, "Who are you?"

His eyes blazed down at her from beneath the hooded cloak he wore over his helm. "Connor Warrick," he said. "Lord Ridglea."

Alura fell back another step, alarms clamoring inside her head. "C-Connor," she gasped out.

"And you are Alura," he went on, his voice now a merciless grating. "You were naught but a girl when I left."

"Connor," she repeated, stunned by the fact that she had been kissing this man only heartbeats earlier. "Why . . . how . . . we were told—"

"That I was dead?" he snapped. "Killed in the Holy Land by the Saracens? So I was, or as good as."

Footsteps splashed through the mud behind her. "God blast it!" her father said, angry at the way she had acted earlier, even more furious that he had been forced to come out into the rain. Alura was backing up without even knowing it, and she suddenly bumped into de Gabin's broad chest. His hand fell heavily on her shoulder.

"You, sir!" de Gabin said. "Who are you, and why have you come to my home?"

Connor Warrick's hand went to his sword, and he said flatly, "I am the master of Stavebrook, and by all rights, de Gabin, I should be here to kill you."

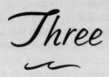

Three

Foolish. No, more than foolish, thought Connor. What he was doing was insane. Here he was, a near-cripple, with naught but a squire of four and ten years to fight at his side, and he was challenging a warlord such as Herve de Gabin in the middle of de Gabin's own bailey. True, de Gabin was old, but in his time he had been a fierce warrior, and he still commanded a goodly number of soldiers who knew their business.

Definitely mad.

And yet Connor's anger was such that he could do nothing less. He had been nursing that rage ever since leaving Stavebrook earlier in the day after his long conversation with Mossgrave, his late brother's seneschal. De Gabin meant to steal Stavebrook, and Connor would kill the old man before he would allow him to get his greedy hands on the estate.

De Gabin stared at Connor, his mouth opening and closing like that of a fish. His eyes were bulging a bit like a fish's eyes, too. When he finally recovered the ability to speak, his voice shook slightly with incredulity.

"You cannot be Connor Warrick!" de Gabin declared. "He was killed in the Crusades—"

"I am alive," Connor said flatly. "Do you doubt the evidence of your own eyes?"

The answer was slow in coming, and when it did, the word had a hollow sound to it. "No."

Connor knew that he had changed a great deal since leaving for the Holy Land two years earlier. He was thinner, and his face had been pared down by the elements and the life he had led until it was all hard planes and angles. But he was still undeniably Connor Warrick.

Connor Warrick, Lord Ridglea. The title sounded strange to him even now, despite the fact that he had had a sennight to grow accustomed to it. That much time had passed since he had arrived in London and learned of his older brother's death. A sudden fever had carried Morvyn off, he had been told, and for two days he had debated with himself what to do with that knowledge. A part of him wanted to do nothing, to hold with his original plan and not go anywhere near Stavebrook. If necessary, he could take a new name and find a warlord who would be glad to receive the allegiance of an experienced soldier. He had never wanted anything to do with being the lord of an estate, which was the reason he was never bothered by the fact that he was the second son. Let Morvyn be Lord Ridglea, he had always thought. Connor had more exciting things to do.

But now his excitement was going to be limited by the injury he had received. His right arm was much better, as Jeremy had predicted it would be. Connor could grip a sword with his right hand now and could even wield it in a clumsy fashion, but he was far from the man he had once been. He could perhaps teach others how to fight, but his own days of battle were over.

With that in mind, and with his unexpected discovery that the ties of family meant more to him than he had believed they did, he had decided at least to ride to Stavebrook and pay the place one last visit before he moved on.

Then he had seen it, cold and forbidding in the rain, and to his great surprise, he had felt his heart begin to beat faster. This was his home, and even though he had expected never to come back here, he found that he was glad he had.

Until his conversation with the nervous old seneschal, Mossgrave. Then anger had replaced any other feelings that

might have begun to grow in Connor's breast, and he had
mounted up immediately and ridden here to Brynclair to confront Sir Herve de Gabin, the man who intended to steal Stavebrook from its rightful owner.

Him. Connor Warrick. The new Lord Ridglea.

Connor shook himself out of his momentary reverie and
said, "As you can see for yourself, I was not killed in Palestine. War is a confusing thing, Sir Herve. Mistakes are made.
False reports are carried from the battlefield."

De Gabin nodded. When someone spoke of war, he could
understand. He forced himself to say, "It is . . . good to see
you, lad."

The words were patently untrue. There was nothing good
about Connor's return, not where de Gabin was concerned,
and everyone standing here in this downpour knew it. The
dampness and the chill were making Connor's right shoulder
ache intolerably, so he nodded toward the keep and suggested,
"Perhaps we should continue our conversation inside."

"Of course," said de Gabin, his stunned expression clearing
slightly. "Where are my manners? Come inside, Warrick."
Alura still stood in front of him. He put his hands on her
shoulders and moved her aside, turning her at the same time
so that she faced him. "Go along, my dear, and tell your
mother that we have a guest."

Alura stared at her father, horrified. Clearly, he had not
heard what she had said to Connor Warrick, but he had seen
her kissing him. And now he wanted to bring Connor into the
keep as if nothing had happened.

Connor. Connor, who had seduced countless women, who
had fathered bastards without number, who had subjected his
lustful conquests to all manner of twisted desires . . .

Connor the killer.

Had her father completely lost his mind?

"Go on, girl," de Gabin said sharply when Alura did not
move. "We'll not insult a visitor to Brynclair." His glance
toward Connor added the silent words, *No matter how big a
monster he may be.*

Connor saw the look and ignored it. He was well aware of
the reputation that had stained him before his departure with

King Richard for the Holy Land. If people wished to believe those things about him—and he had some complicity in those beliefs, he had to admit—then so be it. He would use that unsavory reputation to his favor. No one wanted to cross a man known to be a ruthless killer.

As Alura finally turned and hurried toward the keep, Connor's eyes followed her for a moment. Objectively, he admired what he saw. The coltish, awkward girl Alura had been a few years earlier had grown into a lovely young woman. Even in a muddy gown, with her hair plastered to her head by the rain, Connor had been able to see her beauty. It had no affect on him, of course, but he still acknowledged the fact of it.

But when she turned her head and looked over her shoulder at him, something seemed to crackle between them, like traceries of lightning across the dark skies overhead. Connor forced himself to ignore the feeling, but he was glad when de Gabin moved between them and he no longer had to feel the power of those green eyes on him.

"Come along," de Gabin said, holding out a hand. "Your squire can tend your mounts, can he not?"

Connor nodded. Without taking his eyes off de Gabin, he said, "Jeremy, take the horses around to the stables."

"Come to the kitchen when you're through, boy," de Gabin added heartily. "I'm sure the cook can find something for you to take the chill off this miserable day."

De Gabin seemed to have shaken off the amazement he had felt earlier when he recognized Connor. Being able to play the host had helped him regain his composure. He stood back, then fell in beside Connor as the two men splashed through the bailey toward the keep.

"Nothing more miserable than winter in England, is there?" commented de Gabin.

" 'Tis spring," Connor said. "Things will soon change."

De Gabin cleared his throat. "Yes, well, I suppose you're right."

Things were indeed going to change, thought Connor, and chief among them would be de Gabin's perfidious plans. . . .

•   •   •

Katharine was waiting just inside the door of the keep. "Dear Lord," she cried as she caught hold of Alura's shoulders, "you're soaked, child! I know you were upset, but whatever possessed you to run out into that storm?"

She had run out into more than a rainstorm, Alura thought. She had run into a storm of emotions as well: anger at her father, surprise as the sight of the stranger in the bailey, spite that had propelled her into the arms of that stranger . . . and then an explosion of heat and passion as she had kissed him.

Followed by fear when she discovered who he was.

When Alura did not answer her mother's question, Katharine looked past her into the bailey and asked, "Who in heaven's name is that with your father?"

"Not in heaven's name," Alura said softly. "Never in heaven's name. That is Connor Warrick, come back from the Crusades, Mother."

Katharine lifted her hands to her mouth in shock. "No! It cannot be."

"It is," Alura said grimly. "Now that I know who he is, I recognize him myself. The resemblance to Morvyn is not strong, but 'tis there."

Katharine shook her head, surprised and not a little frightened by what her daughter had just told her. She looked past Alura and whispered, "Dear God, your father is bringing that . . . that demon into our home."

"Aye," Alura said with a nod. "He has bid Connor welcome."

Long ago, Connor Warrick *had* been welcome in this keep, Katharine thought. But that was before word had spread through the countryside of the evil doings that went on at Stavebrook.

Katharine shook off her shock and applied her thoughts to the matter at hand. Women had to be practical, she knew, since men so seldom were. She said to her daughter, "Go to your bedchamber and get out of those wet clothes and cover your hair. Then stay there until you are summoned."

"I'm coming back down—" began Alura.

"You will not," Katharine said firmly. "Not with that man here. No young woman is safe around him. You know that."

"He holds no charms for me," Alura said, but the quickening of her heart and the flush that warmed her face belied that bold declaration. "I'll not fall prey to him."

"I was not worried about him charming you. Connor Warrick is known as a man who takes what he wants."

"He'll not take me," Alura said boldly.

Though she had implored him to do that very thing only a few moments earlier, she reminded herself. If she had known then that she was speaking to such a man . . . dear God, how close had she come to sheer disaster?

"Go," Katharine commanded, and Alura went, but not without a last glance over her shoulder. Her father and Connor Warrick were close to the keep now. Even if age had not shrunk Herve de Gabin, even if he had been as strong and straight and vital as in his youth, Connor would have nearly dwarfed him. Such an aura of raw power came from the knight that it seemed to Alura the very drops of rain themselves should have been unable to touch him.

Yet touch him they did, and so had she. Her hand went to her lips. Already they felt slightly bruised from the kiss she had shared with Connor.

Trying to put the memory of that searing moment out of her mind, she hurried up the curving staircase.

To look at de Gabin now, Connor thought, it was difficult to tell that only a few moments earlier, the two men had stood tensely in the bailey, the threat of impending violence a palpable thing in the air between them.

Now de Gabin seemed quite at ease as he handed Connor a cup of mead. "To your health, lad," he said.

Connor lifted the cup and drank, his iron control preventing his face from revealing the pain in his shoulder as he raised his arm. He tried to move as naturally as possible, so that de Gabin would not suspect he had been injured. If the conversation deteriorated and this meeting came down to swords, Connor didn't want to give the old warrior any unnecessary advantage.

"And to yours, Sir Herve," Connor said.

"Oh, I'll drink to that." De Gabin did so, then licked his lips as he lowered the cup.

The two men stood in the great hall near the fireplace, letting the heat from the blaze dry their wet clothes. Katharine hovered not far away, the anxious expression on her face making it clear that she expected trouble to break out at any moment.

Connor was determined not to allow that to happen. True, he had felt a burst of rage when he first confronted de Gabin, but now that anger had receded. Still, his voice was taut as he said, "I spoke at length to Mossgrave earlier today when I arrived at Stavebrook."

De Gabin cleared his throat. "I would not put too much stock in what that old man has to say. He misunderstands things—"

"On the contrary," Connor cut in, "he seemed quite clear on the matter. He told me that you have sent a petition to Prince John asking that title to Stavebrook be granted to you."

"I am certain I was not the only one to do so," blustered de Gabin. "Stavebrook is a fine estate. Other barons will be seeking to add it to their holdings, since it was assumed that your brother died without an heir."

"But according to Mossgrave, you assert in your petition that your claim is the strongest because your daughter was betrothed to my brother at the time of his death."

De Gabin nodded solemnly. "That is the truth. Had Morvyn lived, his family and mine would have been joined. Since that was his wish, and since the dowry had already been paid, it seems only fair to me that Lackland make it so."

Connor drained the rest of his mead, again hiding the pain as he did so, and said, "Mossgrave also told me that your daughter is with child by my brother."

De Gabin's face was dark with anger, and Connor imagined most of it was directed at the old seneschal. Mossgrave had spoken entirely too freely, but then, he had been utterly shocked to find out that Connor was still alive.

Before de Gabin could reply, his wife spoke up. "That scurrilous charge is untrue, Sir Connor. My daughter Alura is a maiden, pure and chaste."

Alura had certainly not seemed to match that description earlier when she had thrown herself into his arms and kissed him with such passion, Connor thought.

"My dear," de Gabin said quickly, " 'tis fine to defend our daughter, but under the circumstances we must hew strictly to the truth of the matter—"

"I have spoken the truth," declared Katharine, "and none dare say otherwise."

Connor glanced down to hide the fleeting smile of admiration that passed across his face. Katharine reminded him of a lioness defending her cubs. She moved between the two men and looked boldly at Connor. "Stavebrook is yours, milord," she said. "My husband shall withdraw his petition."

"Wait just a moment!" exclaimed de Gabin. "We don't know that the lad even *wants* the estate. Perhaps an arrangement could be made. . . ."

Connor set the empty cup on the mantel above the fireplace. "I do not wish to sell Stavebrook," he said.

"But . . . but you can't *live* there!" de Gabin sputtered.

"And why not?"

"No one has forgotten the death of that poor lass," de Gabin said with a scowl.

Connor stiffened, his expression hardening into a mask. "In civilian life, as in war, false reports are sometimes made," he said.

"You claim that the charge is false?" de Gabin challenged.

"I claim nothing save Stavebrook, which is rightfully mine. When I came here, I had given no thought to actually staying, but now I believe that I will."

Anger and disappointment warred on de Gabin's face, manifesting themselves in a cunning frown. "It would be unwise," he said. "I tell this to you as an old friend of your family who would see no more disgrace heaped on the name Warrick."

Connor shrugged his broad shoulders. "I will take my chances." His voice hardened again, and the warning was clear as he added, "And anyone who seeks to heap disgrace on my family name does so at his own risk."

De Gabin cleared his throat and glanced at his wife, who had a worried expression on her face. Katharine would not like it if there was swordplay here in the great hall. De Gabin changed the subject by saying, "Tell us, then, about the Crusades. How fares our good king Richard?"

"When I sailed from the Holy Land, he was attempting to bring about an agreement with Saladin that would put an end to the fighting and once more make it possible for pilgrims to visit the holy shrines."

De Gabin was aghast. "Richard is bargaining with that . . . that heretic?"

"They call *us* infidels," Connor said with a slight smile, "and many of Saladin's men feel equally distressed that the war may soon be over. It's possible that even as we speak, Richard may be on his way back to England."

De Gabin's frown deepened, and Connor could almost see the wheels of the old warrior's brain turning. If Richard assumed his rightful place on the throne, that would put an end to his brother John's ambitious connivances. John would no longer have the power to grant title to a garderobe, let alone an entire estate.

Which meant that if de Gabin still entertained any notion of getting his hands on Stavebrook—as impossible as that was going to be—he would have to act quickly.

"See here, Warrick," said de Gabin after a moment. "I'll not deny that I sent a petition to Prince John asking that I be granted title to your estate. At the time, I believed that you were dead, and I make no apologies for what I have done."

"I'll grant you that," Connor said. "But nothing else."

The comment slowed de Gabin only momentarily. "I was acting in the best interests of my daughter and her unborn child," he went on.

Connor inclined his head toward Lady Katharine, who was standing nearby and biting her lip angrily. "According to your good wife, there is no child, Warrick or otherwise, growing in your daughter's belly."

"God's eyes, but you speak bluntly, lad!"

"This is a time for blunt talk." Connor allowed his left hand to stray to the butt of his sword and rest lightly on it. "And blunt action."

De Gabin held up a hand, palm outward. "No need for that.

Besides, if you attack me, you'll never leave this keep alive. Surely you know that. My men will cut you down if you try."

"I faced great odds in Palestine and never worried about living or dying, only doing what I must."

"Well, there's no need for violence here." De Gabin had regained all his self-confidence. He reminded Connor of a strutting peacock as he paced back and forth in front of the fire. "There's no need for violence because I realize what must be done."

"You must withdraw the petition you sent to Lackland," said Connor.

"Done," de Gabin agreed without hesitation, taking Connor by surprise, as well as Katharine, to judge by her expression. "I shall send a rider to London at first light in the morning advising the prince to disregard my claim. Will that satisfy your honor?"

For a moment, Connor made no reply. He had the unmistakable feeling that no matter what he said, he would be stepping into some sort of trap devised by the canny old knight. Finally, he said, "That would be satisfactory."

"Excellent! I wish no trouble between neighbors."

"Nor do I," Connor said.

"I'm very glad to hear that, lad. Because you see, you have a debt of honor to pay, as well."

"I?"

"Certainly. Your brother, before his untimely death, was betrothed to my daughter with the dowry having already been paid. And although the matter is in some dispute, there are at least rumors to the fact that he got her with child."

"Herve . . . ," Katharine said warningly.

"What are you getting at, de Gabin?" snapped Connor. "Would you have me answer for something my brother might, or might not, have done?"

"That is exactly what I mean. To protect Alura's good name, and to fulfill the bargain made by your brother, your honor as a knight of the realm demands that you, Connor, be wed to my daughter."

Four

"No!"

The cry came from the staircase, where Alura shrank back against the rough stone of the curving wall. She saw Connor's head snap around in surprise, and their eyes locked once more. She tried to force down the fear she felt at the power of his gaze and appear defiant instead. From the way his eyes blazed as though he had been challenged, she thought she had succeeded.

She had changed out of the soaked gown and dried her hair as best she could, though the thick mass of red curls resisted her efforts. Then she had rebraided it and wrapped a fresh wimple around it, tucking the white linen into the neckline of the fresh gown of a somber color. She knew she looked much more respectable than she had the last time Connor had seen her.

But if that was the case, why did she feel as if she stood naked before him? His gaze raked over her, and he was no doubt remembering the way she had looked in the bailey, her gown so sodden that it revealed every slender curve of her body. Alura felt her face warming with a heat that had nothing to do with the flames leaping and dancing in the fireplace.

"Alura!" her father thundered. "Return to your bedchamber."

She steeled herself and started down the stairs once more. It was one thing to allow her stubborn nature to make her defy her mother's orders to remain upstairs; it was quite another to fly in the face of her father's daunting anger. But she went anyway.

"This discussion concerns me, Father," she said as she reached the bottom of the staircase. "Do you not think I should be party to it?"

"I do not," de Gabin said. "I arranged your betrothal to Lord Ridglea . . . to the *other* Lord Ridglea . . . without consulting you, and I can handle this as well."

For the first time since Alura had returned to the great hall, Connor spoke. "It would seem that the lady has no wish to become my bride, Sir Herve."

"Pay no attention to her," rumbled de Gabin with a dismissive sweep of his hand in Alura's direction. "Like all women, she has no idea what she really wishes."

"I know that I will not be wed to this . . . this man, Father, no matter what his title or what estate he holds."

Katharine came closer and said, "Please, Alura, return to your chamber. You should not be here. . . ."

Alura turned toward her, disappointment etched in her face and voice as she said, "Then you believe, too, that I have no voice in my own life, Mother?"

"I believe that God will lead us all to the proper path—"

Alura turned away. "God serves those who hold the reins of power," she said bitterly. "At least, that is what they would have us believe, and as long as we do, it is true."

De Gabin was flabbergasted. "My own daughter, a blasphemer and a heretic, as well as a . . . a . . ."

"Harlot?" Alura rounded sharply on him. "I've not forgotten what you asked of me earlier, Father. Did you tell Sir Connor"—the name came from her with difficulty—"what you wanted me to do?"

De Gabin glowered at her. "That is a matter between family members, Alura. . . ."

She spun to face Connor, who was as grim-faced as ever

as he watched the angry exchange. But deep in his eyes, Alura thought she detected a sparkle of amusement. That did nothing to lessen her own anger.

"You should know, Sir Connor, that my father suggested I allow one of his men at arms to couple with me so that I would be with child. He thought it would strengthen his claim to Stavebrook if I could produce an heir to the estate, spurious or not."

His name came more easily from her lips this time, but still she felt uneasy as she spoke it. For the past several years, to speak of Connor Warrick had been much the same as speaking of the devil. And during those same years, mothers who worried as their daughters came of age were known to advise them that they should take care to guard their emotions, lest they fall prey to a man such as Connor, who would seduce them, ruin them, subject them to unknowable degradations, and then—if they were lucky—abandon them.

But even knowing all that, as she looked at Connor now, Alura saw only a man who might have been handsome once, before hard times had stripped away any veneer he had possessed. True, she feared him, because she had heard the same stories as everyone else and because he had such an air of raw, barely contained power about him. But there was no charm about him. He was blunt, strong—even fierce. He could kill her, but he could never break her heart, because she would never give it to him for safekeeping.

He turned slowly to look at her father. "Is what your daughter says true, Sir Herve?" He spoke softly, but the scorn was clearly evident in his voice.

"She misunderstood," blustered de Gabin. "I would never . . . would never ask such a thing of any woman, let alone my own daughter. . . ."

The old man was lying, thought Connor. He remembered the fury that had been on Alura's face when he first saw her in the bailey, remembered as well her bold words and the way she had thrown herself into his awkward embrace and kissed him. That kiss had been motivated by emotion, but it was anger and not passion that had prompted it. He must have

ridden into Brynclair right after the argument between Alura
and her father had broken out.

A part of Connor was outraged that any man would stoop
so low as to do what de Gabin had done. The man was willing
to sully the reputation of his own flesh and blood, and over
what? Some land and a castle. Fine land and a sturdy castle,
to be sure, but still . . .

"It matters not what you asked of her," Connor said into
the silence that had fallen. "You can cease your scheming,
Sir Herve. You'll not get your hands on Stavebrook through
this bit of matchmaking, though it might have worked with
my brother, had he lived. I've no intention of taking the Lady
Alura or any other woman to be my wife."

Alura felt a surge of relief, mixed with some other, unde-
finable emotion.

"And since you have already pledged to withdraw your
petition to the prince, our business is done," Connor went on.
"I'll take my leave."

Alura thought her father looked stricken. Only a short time
earlier, he had been brimming with confidence, but since then
his carefully laid plans had been shattered, and each of his
attempts to rebuild them had been rebuffed. He had been
checkmated at every turn, first by Alura and then by Connor.

De Gabin grasped at one final straw. " 'Tis too late to ride
back to Stavebrook tonight," he said, "especially in such a
storm. Stay the night, lad, and return to your home in the
morning."

Connor's lips curved slightly in a humorless smile. "And
what will you do if I stay?" he asked. "Send your daughter
to my bedchamber to seduce me in hopes that a real heir will
be planted in her belly?"

De Gabin's face was already ruddy in the light from the
fire. It darkened even more as he reached for his sword. "By
God, sir," he roared, "you've insulted me once too often—"

"You insult yourself, Sir Herve." Connor's words were as
cold and as sharp as a finely honed blade, and they cut through
de Gabin's outrage just as easily. "Given everything I've
heard here this evening, what else am I to make of your offer?

'Tis clear that little matters to you except your vaulting ambition to own Stavebrook.''

De Gabin's fingers were still wrapped around the handle of his sword, but he had not withdrawn the blade from the scabbard. ''I made the offer out of hospitality, nothing more,'' he said, his voice shaking. ''You can accept in the same spirit, sir, or you can draw your sword and defend yourself.''

Alura stood on one side of the two men facing each other, Katharine on the other. Both women looked as if they wanted to intercede, but neither of them moved. De Gabin was a scoundrel, but Connor was not totally without honor. He had no wish to kill the man in front of his wife and daughter.

Besides, in his current condition there was no guarantee that Connor could even dispose of such an elderly knight, to say nothing of the men-at-arms who would come running to avenge their master if de Gabin was slain. . . .

Connor inclined his head. ''I accept your offer of hospitality,'' he said.

De Gabin tried not to look relieved and failed miserably. ''Very well,'' he said haughtily. ''I shall have a servant show you to your chamber.''

''And send my squire up as well,'' said Connor.

''The lad can sleep in the stable.''

''Certainly, but I would speak to him first.''

With a shrug, de Gabin nodded. ''Of course.'' He turned and bellowed for a servant.

Katharine came over to Alura and took her hand. ''Come with me,'' she said quietly as she started toward the staircase. '' 'Tis over, thank God.''

But was it? Alura asked herself as she looked back. Connor stood there before the fire, tall and straight, his form silhouetted by the flames so that she could not see his face as her mother led her up the staircase. But she felt his eyes following her.

Had he truly expected that she would come to his bedchamber in the night and offer herself to him? Had that, indeed, been what her father had had in mind when he asked Connor to stay? Alura did not want to believe that, but after everything that had happened, she was no longer sure just what her father might be capable of.

One thing was certain, however. She would *not* go to Connor's chamber. If that was what he thought was going to happen, if that was what he would wait for, then he would be waiting for a long, long time.

Forever, in fact, she vowed.

Connor looked up as a tentative knock sounded on the heavy door of the guestchamber. Was Alura here already? he asked himself, then discarded the very thought. After their first encounter in the bailey, Alura had made it plain through her words, actions, and expressions that she wanted naught to do with him. And that was just fine with Connor, since he had no need of any added complications in his life right now.

But if that was the case, why could he not rid himself of the lingering image of her green eyes?

"Who is it?" he growled as the knock sounded again.

"Jeremy, milord," came the voice of the squire. "Sir Herve's seneschal said you wished to see me."

Connor stalked over to the door and swung it open. "Come in, lad," he said, his voice less harsh now. As he closed the door behind Jeremy, who was carrying a small bundle, he went on, "We shall be staying the night here at Brynclair. Sir Herve suggested that you sleep in the stable, but I would prefer that you stay here in the keep, right outside my door."

A fierce look came over the young man's face. "You fear treachery, milord?"

Connor shook his head. "I doubt that Sir Herve would stoop to assassination to get what he wants. Still, it seldom pays to tempt an already greedy man." Gesturing at the bundle in Jeremy's hand, Connor added, "What do you have there?"

Jeremy opened the bag and took out the small chest containing the gems and jewelry Connor had brought from the Holy Land. "I did not want to leave this in the stable, milord," he said. "I know not what sort of men Sir Herve's servants might be, but I thought it wise not to trust them overmuch."

"Wise indeed," agreed Connor with a nod. He reached out

and took the chest as Jeremy extended it toward him. "We shall keep this safe with us."

"No one will disturb you, or your possessions, tonight, milord. I vow that."

Connor clapped a hand on Jeremy's shoulder. "Good lad. Here, take some blankets and pillows with you to make your bed in the corridor." He nodded toward the opulent bed that filled half the chamber.

"But these are your quarters. . . ."

"After the past two years, too soft and comfortable a bed will make it difficult for me to sleep. You could take half the blankets and all the pillows, and still this would be a more luxurious bed than the sands of Palestine made."

" 'Tis true," Jeremy admitted with a grin. He began gathering up some of the bedding. His grin widened as he said, "Perhaps one of the castle's maids will pass by in the night and decide she wishes to stop and curl up with me for a bit."

That was a rather far-fetched possibility, thought Connor, but he didn't want to dash the lad's hopes. "In that case, I'm sure you will accommodate her like the young gentleman you are," he said.

Still smiling broadly, Jeremy left the chamber with his borrowed bedding. Connor closed the door, then carried the chest of jewelry over to a small table and set it down. He started to turn away, then paused and worked the concealed latch on the chest's lid instead. He lifted the lid and peered inside. Candlelight gleamed and sparkled on the gold and gems.

Jeremy had said that the contents of this chest would make him a rich man upon their return to England, but Connor knew that was not the case. The jewelry had considerable value, of course, but it was far short of the fortune Jeremy made it out to be. However, now that Connor owned Stavebrook as well, he supposed he could be considered wealthy.

Riches held no great appeal to him, not in and of themselves. The only good thing about wealth was what a man could do with it.

He might as well admit it, he told himself. He had no earthly idea how to go about being a rich man. The only possessions he had ever cared about were his sword and shield and battle-ax; his armor and his horse. The trappings of war.

Connor reached into the chest and brought out the ring and slave bracelet Jeremy had been polishing on board the ship sennights earlier. They were pretty baubles, no doubt valuable, but Connor had no idea what they were worth. His eyes narrowed as he stared at the fire opals, which seemed to wink at him in the candlelight. Surprisingly, he felt like touching them. The impulse to stroke his fingers over the gems was strong in him.

Instead, he grimaced and tossed the bracelet and ring back into the chest. That was what greed did to a man, he supposed. It was one thing to stroke the tender flesh of a woman, quite another to fondle a cold, unliving thing that had value only because poor, deluded fools thought it did.

Connor was determined that he would never give in to the allure of either.

But that bracelet, he thought suddenly as the image flashed into his mind, would look lovely indeed on the slender wrist of Lady Alura.

What a horrible day this had been, Alura thought as she stood at the window of her bedchamber and peered out at the night, brushing her long, thick hair as she did so. The rain and sleet had stopped, and in fact, the clouds were parting to allow stray beams of moonlight and starlight through their oppressive mantle. The sight should have cheered her, she thought. The passing of the storm could have been taken as the end of winter and a harbinger of spring.

But the faint breeze that blew through the window still chilled her, and so did the knowledge that not far away, in another hall of the keep, a monster slumbered.

Alura could not remember when she had first heard of Connor Warrick. It seemed that she had known of him forever. By the time she was seven years old and he was four and ten, he had acquired a reputation as something of a scoundrel where the ladies were concerned, though Alura had been even older before she understood what the whispering was about. At that time, Connor had not been badly thought of. Men guffawed and ladies hid their smiles discreetly when they talked of his romantic exploits.

It was only later, after the death of the old Lord Ridglea and Morvyn's assumption of the title and holdings, that Connor's reputation had begun to grow darker. There were tales of young women gotten with child, only to have Connor deny responsibility. It was said that he had begun to treat his conquests roughly, as well. Now the ladies frowned and the men glowered when they spoke of Connor Warrick and his rakehell behavior.

No one spoke too loudly or too bluntly against him, however, because even as he had become known for his ruthless dealings with women, he was also developing a reputation as a fierce fighter. He was never defeated in any of the tournaments he entered and seldom even unhorsed. None of the men who condemned him wished to have him challenge them, so they made their complaints and judgments behind his back.

Then, some two and a half years earlier, had come the affair of Elspeth Lyle, a young woman of good family who had been raped by Connor Warrick when she would not succumb voluntarily to his rough charms. Alura had known Elspeth slightly, had known her to be a virtuous young woman. After Connor had ruined her, Elspeth had gone to Stavebrook to plead with him in hopes that he would not abandon her as he had done all the others like her. When pleas had not worked, she had demanded instead.

And then she had fallen from the tower room where she had confronted Connor, her life—and the life of the babe growing within her—dashed out on the unforgiving stones of the courtyard below.

The fact of rape could have been overlooked as something that had happened in the heat of the moment, an excuse that the neighboring lords would have seized on readily and their ladies would have tolerated. But murder was not so easily condoned, and no one believed that Elspeth Lyle had fallen accidentally from the tower. Connor had lost his justly feared temper and had either pushed or thrown her. That assumption was accepted throughout the countryside.

Still, no formal charges were ever brought forth, and it was said that Morvyn Warrick, Lord Ridglea, had paid Elspeth's family to get them to allow the matter to pass. Connor was Morvyn's brother, after all, and although Morvyn had a sterling reputation himself, no one expected him to stand by and see his own flesh and blood condemned of such a horrible crime without doing everything in his power to prevent it.

And everyone involved had been thankful when, less than a year later, Connor had left England, journeying to the Holy Land with Richard to liberate Jerusalem and the other holy shrines from Saladin and the heretics who held them. The news that Connor had been killed in battle was even more welcome. A form of rough justice had been accomplished, or so everyone had thought.

But the reports of Connor's death had been false, and now he was back. Even worse, he was now Lord Ridglea, following the death of his brother, and he would have the wealth and power to resume the wicked ways that had made him widely regarded as some sort of raging beast.

That was the man into whose arms Alura had flung herself, the man she had kissed, the man whose embrace and whose hot, hungry lips had sparked such a fire within her. She shuddered, then put her hairbrush aside and said aloud, " 'Tis impossible. I could not have felt such things. I must have imagined them.''

But she knew she had not. Connor had indeed made her feel like a woman in the arms of her lover. At least, given her lack of firsthand knowledge, Alura imagined that it was so.

She must stay here in her chamber until he was gone from Brynclair, she told herself warningly. She could not risk the power of his gaze falling upon her again, to say nothing of his touch.

With that decision ringing in her mind, she flung herself on her bed to wait in vain for sleep to claim her.

Five

The sound of horses' hooves woke Alura from the deep sleep that had finally overtaken her far into the night. She forced herself to lift her head from the pillows and look around her chamber. Sunlight streamed warmly in through the window. She pushed herself out of bed and stumbled to the opening wrapping the bedding around her naked form. When she looked down, she saw two riders moving through the bailey, unhurriedly leaving the keep. One of the riders was a young man, little more than a boy.

Beside him was the lean yet broad-shouldered unmistakable figure of Connor Warrick.

Alura's breath caught in her throat. Connor was leaving Brynclair. *Good,* she told herself. *We do not need such as him here.*

But she had not expected him to leave quite this early.

Then she realized a moment later that the hour was not early. The sun was already well up over the horizon. She had slept much later than she usually did, no doubt due to the exhaustion, both physical and mental, that the events of the previous evening had caused.

Her slumber, in fact, had done little to relieve her weariness, and she reached up to rest her hands on the sides of the window hewn into the thick stone wall of the keep.

As Alura did so, Connor abruptly reined in for some reason in the bailey below, and as he did so he turned in his saddle to peer upward at her.

Connor's breath caught in his throat. The morning sun was shining full on the window where Alura stood. She was visible to him from the waist up. If he had been closer, he might have been able to see her breasts through the gap in the bedding wrapped loosely around her, he thought, but even at this distance, he could witness an even more spectacular sight: her hair, unbound and falling in thick waves of flame around her shoulders.

Alura clasped the bedding tighter around her form and stepped back sharply, away from the window, and Connor felt an undeniable sense of loss as she moved out of his sight.

Whatever had possessed Connor to stop so suddenly and turn to look back up at the keep? Alura asked herself. Her heart was pounding wildly, the way it had done every time he gazed at her with that same peculiar intensity.

She stayed back, well away from the window, until she heard the soft clopping of hoofbeats once more. Only then did she venture close enough to peer out again, and she saw to her relief that Connor and his young squire were moving through the gates beneath the raised portcullis. Their horses' hooves thudded on the drawbridge, then the sound of their leave-taking began to fade away.

Alura closed her eyes. This whole ugly episode was over now. With any luck, her father would give up his impossible dream of owning Stavebrook, and none of them would ever have to see Connor Warrick again.

The word that a new Lord Ridglea had come to Stavebrook spread quickly through the countryside, but if everyone expected Connor to return to the scandalous ways that had earned him such an unsavory reputation, they were sorely disappointed. He retreated to the great, grim keep of his ancestral home, and there he stayed. Few even of his own people saw him as the sennights passed; the seneschal, old Mossgrave, handled all the details of the running of the estate.

The last gasps of winter had died away, and spring lay lightly on the land. It was inevitable that someone would decide to hold a tournament to take advantage of the pleasant weather. Sir Oswald Duparc was the first one to do so, and invitations to the tournament and the ball that would follow it were carried by Duparc's servants to all the lords and ladies of the district.

Including Lord Ridglea of Stavebrook. It would have been bad form to exclude him.

Connor stood in the great hall of his keep and looked down at the scroll in his hand. He could read fairly well, so he was able to understand the words that had been ornately lettered on the scroll by Duparc's scribe. With a grimace, Connor rolled the parchment back into its usual shape and threw it down on a nearby table. The last thing he wanted to do was subject himself to the furtive stares and whispered gossip of the people who had made his life so miserable in the months before he had left for Palestine with Richard.

And yet there was a good chance that Alura would be there. . . .

Connor pushed that thought out of his mind and asked, "What do you think, Jeremy? Should we attend?"

Jeremy was standing nearby, and he didn't bother trying to conceal the eagerness in his voice as he asked in return, "Would you participate in the tournament, Sir Connor?"

Connor's scowl deepened. "Are you that anxious to see me killed, lad?"

"Milord! It shames me that you can ask such a thing—"

Connor waved a hand to forestall the young man's words of protest. "I know you would never wish that," he said, "but such might well be the result of any competition at arms in which I was entered."

"Your arm is as strong as it ever was, milord, and moves as freely as it ever did. Surely you have seen that for yourself."

Connor hesitated. It was true that since returning to Stavebrook, he had worked long and hard to regain the strength in his crippled right arm. In truth, perhaps physically it was no longer crippled. He could swing a sword or a battle-ax from

dawn to midday, could cut and slash and parry until sweat
soaked his tunic and dripped from his face, had in fact done
just that many times. He had practiced with Jeremy, the sound
of steel ringing against steel filling the keep. If he had been
attacked by some clumsy bandit, no doubt he could have defended himself quite adequately with either hand, for he had
continued to practice with his left as well as his right.

But to face another knight in battle, even the mock battle
of a tournament, was just asking for trouble. Asking for death,
that was what it was, thought Connor, because men died in
tournaments when they were less than fully prepared.

"No," Connor said with a shake of his head. "We shall
not attend the ball, and there will be no tournament for me. I
wish only to stay here and live my life in peace."

"Never seeing anyone save myself and Mossgrave and a
few servants, you mean," Jeremy said boldly. "You say you
wish to live your life in peace, milord, but what you mean is
that you wish to shut yourself away from life."

Connor stared at him in surprise. For a moment, he was
tempted to cuff the boy for such defiance. Perhaps a few blows
to Jeremy's head would knock some sense into it.

But Connor could never do that, and both of them knew it.
Though neither of them ever spoke of the debt that was between them, it was never forgotten.

"Your tongue is too bold for a squire," Connor growled.
"Perhaps the time has come for you to leave me."

Jeremy paled. "You cannot mean that, milord. My place is
with you—"

"Aye," Connor said with a sigh. "Truly, I would not have
you leave. But I have made my decision, and I will abide by
it. I expect no less from you."

Jeremy bowed. "As you will, my lord."

Connor flicked his hand at the scroll. "Send word to Sir
Oswald that I regret I will be unable to attend."

"Aye." Jeremy left the room.

Connor drew his sword, hearing the old familiar sound of
steel rasping against scabbard. He held the blade up, turning
it slightly so that the light from the window reflected off the
polished steel. He slashed the sword to the side, brought it

across his body in a backhand stroke, spun and lifted and chopped.

Yes, the muscles had healed, but he had lost something besides blood in Palestine. He had lost the will to fight.

And what sort of knight could he be without that?

"At last," Sir Herve said as he tossed the scroll onto the table in the great hall of Brynclair. "I had begun to think that no one was going to take advantage of this beautiful weather and hold a tournament."

Alura and Katharine looked at him. "Who is the invitation from, Herve?" asked Katharine.

"Sir Oswald Duparc, Baron de Lancie. We shall travel to his estate for the tournament and ball in one fortnight."

Alura felt a small twinge of excitement. She had never cared overmuch for tournaments or balls, but after the sennights that had passed, she would be grateful for the opportunity to get out and see people again. She had kept herself shut up in the castle ever since that horrible incident with Connor Warrick. It had been her own choice to keep to herself, but still, the solitude was growing wearisome.

A worrying thought suddenly occurred to her. Would there be talk about her at the tournament? Her father had withdrawn his petition to Prince John, as he had promised Connor he would do, but the damage might have already been done. Had the rumor that she was with child by the late Lord Ridglea already made its rounds through the countryside?

Alura stood up and lightly ran the palm of her hand over her flat stomach. If indeed there was talk about her, the sight of her in a gown fitted with her gold girdle ought to put any gossip to rest. She was definitely not with child, and anyone with eyes could see that.

Sir Herve was lighting his pipe with a twig from the fire-place when his wife asked him, "Will everyone be there for the tournament?"

"I expect so," replied de Gabin. "I know that Sir Oswald has done extensive renovations on his castle, and he will want everyone in the district to see and admire the place for themselves. And that wife of his!" De Gabin snorted. "Nothing but the most elaborate, well-attended ball would do for her.''

''Then 'tis likely Connor Warrick will be there,'' Katharine said softly.

Alura stiffened at her mother's words. She had not even considered that possibility. Connor! Surely not. Surely, with the reputation he had, he would not attend.

Yet his reputation as a breaker of hearts and an abuser of women had never stopped him from participating in tournaments before he had left with Richard on the Third Crusade. He had fought frequently in them and had always done well.

But that was before the affair with Elspeth Lyle, Alura recalled. After the poor girl's tragic death, little had been seen of Connor Warrick. He'd had few friends to begin with, and after that he had been shunned by those few, as well as by all the other landholders in the district.

So it was unlikely that he would be in attendance at Sir Oswald's tournament and ball, but just to make certain of that, Alura asked Sir Herve, ''Would you send a message to the baron, Father, and inquire as to whether or not Lord Ridglea will be there?''

De Gabin frowned darkly. '' 'Twould be bad form to do such a thing, lass, an insult to Sir Oswald's hospitality.'' He pulled on his short beard as he thought. ''But perhaps I can discover in some other manner what Warrick's plans are. I shall speak to the seneschal and have him get in touch with Mossgrave. Servants sometimes know more than their masters.''

Alura gave him a hug and said, ''Thank you, Father. I would like to attend the tournament and ball, but I have no wish ever to lay eyes on Connor Warrick again.''

''I cannot say that I blame you,'' de Gabin replied with a scowl. ''The lad is insufferable.''

Her father felt that way because Connor had thwarted his plans to take over Stavebrook, Alura knew. But she agreed with him anyway, for reasons of her own.

Though Connor's grim but composed demeanor gave little hint of the beast beneath, she knew it was there. Like everyone else, she had heard all the stories, and she believed them.

But in unguarded moments, the memory of what she had

experienced in Connor's arms came flooding back to her, causing heat to grow strong within her and pool in places where it had absolutely no right to be. It was a reaction of the body only, but it was still disturbing. Even though she had not known who he was when she threw herself into his embrace, she still should have felt nothing but revulsion at his touch.

She would not take a chance on being around him again. Not as long as her body was so eager to betray her. . . .

Jeremy was so upset that he was practically foaming at the mouth like a mad dog as he came running into the great hall in the keep of Stavebrook. "Sir Connor! Sir Connor!" he shouted.

It was evening. Connor had said his prayers and was eating alone as usual. He lowered the cup of mead from which he had just taken a draught and frowned at the excited squire. "What is it, Jeremy? Is the castle under attack?"

"Not the castle, but you yourself are, milord," Jeremy panted.

"What do you mean? *I* am under attack?" Connor smiled and added dryly, "I was not aware of it."

"Not your person, but your good name. That is what is being sullied, Sir Connor."

"Then we have nothing to worry about, because I have no good name to sully," Connor said with a short bark of laughter. "I've not had such a thing for years now."

Jeremy had caught his breath. He drew himself up stiffly and said, "No one has ever insulted your courage before, milord."

Connor pushed the bowl of half-eaten food aside. His appetite was usually none too good, and it deserted him easily, just as it had now. "What do you mean?" he asked. "What have you heard, lad?"

"One of the serfs returned a short while ago from Baron de Lancie's castle," Jeremy explained. "He went there to trade a hog for a cart full of figs. While he was there he heard the servants talking about your refusal to attend the baron's tournament."

Connor waved a hand dismissively. "I care little for what some yammering serfs might say about me."

" 'Twas not just the serfs, milord. They were but repeating what their master had said. According to the baron, you have lost your taste for combat and therefore refused to attend the tournament."

Well, that charge was true enough, Connor thought as he drew a deep breath. Yet he did not want to say as much to Jeremy. The lad would be devastated to learn that his lord and master no longer wished to test his strength and skill against other men. Jeremy had always assumed that once Connor's injured arm healed, he would resume the same sort of life he had led before the battle in the Holy Land that had left him wounded almost to death.

Connor had expected, had even hoped for, the same thing at first. It was only as the months passed, during the voyage back to England and since his return to Stavebrook, that he had come to understand fully what he had really lost.

"What would you have me do?" he asked quietly.

"Attend the tournament. Knock Sir Oswald on his bloody arse!"

Connor gave a bleak laugh. "Sir Oswald is a fine warrior. 'Tis more likely he would knock me on my arse, and perhaps break my neck in the process."

"Never," said Jeremy with a determined shake of his head. "You have a stable full of fine chargers, Sir Connor. Once you were mounted on one of them, with a lance in your hand again, all the old skills would come back to you. I know they would."

" 'Tis my life you would be wagering, lad, not your own," Connor pointed out.

He saw pain and anger flare in Jeremy's eyes and knew he had hurt the squire. But Jeremy had to understand. . . .

"Then I will challenge Sir Oswald myself," Jeremy said.

"What?" Connor came to his feet, eyes widening in surprise. "Are you mad?"

"Aye. But if you will not defend your own honor, milord, then it falls to me to do so."

Connor was careful not to laugh scornfully at the bold gesture Jeremy was making. Inflicting such a blow to the lad's already outraged pride would be the worst thing he could do. Instead, Connor said, "Sir Oswald would not joust with you, Jeremy. You know that."

"He would if I called him an ill-bred lout. I know many insults, milord, and I would use them all if need be."

He meant it, Connor realized. It was doubtful that the baron would allow himself to be drawn into a joust with a mere squire, no matter what insults Jeremy purveyed. But it was possible, indeed highly likely, that Baron de Lancie would have his servants give the young man a thrashing to repay him for his impudence. Jeremy might be badly injured by such a beating. He might even be hurt so grievously that he could never accomplish his dream of becoming a knight.

And Connor had made a promise to a dying man that he would do everything in his power to see that Jeremy reached his dream.

"You put me in a bad position, lad," growled Connor. He suspected that Jeremy was well aware of what he had done. "You are my squire, and as such, I am responsible for you— and your actions. You have never shamed me, and I would not have you begin now."

"Then pick up the gauntlet Sir Oswald has thrown down before you, milord," Jeremy pleaded. "You know he meant for his words to reach your ears. Otherwise he never would have said them."

Jeremy was probably right, thought Connor. He and de Lancie had never been friends, though Connor would have stopped short of calling the baron an outright enemy. Still, there was no love lost between them, and de Lancie was probably enjoying the current situation immensely.

Connor took a deep breath and let it out in a long, weary sigh. "All right," he said. "I will attend the tournament, though I cannot promise that I will face Sir Oswald himself. That decision will rest with fate."

"And the ball afterward?" Jeremy asked.

Connor nodded. "And the ball afterward."

That, at least, was an easy promise to make, since there was a very good chance he would not live to see the end of the tournament.

Six

The day of the tournament dawned bright and clear, but to Alura, it might as well have been overcast and damp, so low were her spirits. For the past fortnight, her emotions had been in a turmoil. At first she had been glad when rumors reached Brynclair that Connor Warrick would not participate in the tournament. But then she had felt an undeniable sense of disappointment as well. That reaction had been roughly wrenched around a few days later when word arrived that Lord Ridglea had changed his mind and would attend the day-long celebration after all. At that news, Alura had known both fear and excitement, apprehension and anticipation. A part of her wanted to see Connor again.

But an even larger part was afraid of what she would feel when she did.

Sir Herve bustled about the castle, overseeing the preparations for the journey, which would take most of the morning. He was excited and looking forward to the tournament. At his age, he no longer took part in the jousting, but he would observe with great relish. Katharine seemed filled with anticipation as well. This would be the first opportunity she had had to see her friends among the other ladies of the district since the tomb mass of Morvyn Warrick, and that had hardly been a joyous occasion. The servants and men-at-arms who would accompany the family on the trip were excited, too. Today's festivities were more than welcome as a respite from the drudgery of the long winter just past.

It seemed to Alura that she was the only one not looking forward to this day, and that was because her wariness of Connor's reputation had finally won out over her physical reaction to his presence.

She considered pleading ill health and asking her father for permission to remain at Brynclair, but she knew it would do no good. He would insist that she come along anyway and would override any objections her mother might make. But there would be a large crowd at Welwynd, Baron de Lancie's estate, and Alura thought that if she tried, she would be able to avoid getting too close to Connor.

The party set out on horseback, Sir Herve leading the way, as was usual. At least he gave the appearance of leading, though there were outriders a good distance in front of him. Guards surrounded the family on the other three sides, and bringing up the rear were servants pulling two-wheeled carts containing the things that would be needed for an overnight stay at Welwynd. The ball following the tournament would last far into the night, and none of the guests would return to their homes until the morrow.

"I think I shall give a tournament," Sir Herve mused as he rode along. " 'Tis been too long since the halls of Brynclair have rung with the sounds of guests."

"As you wish," said Katharine. "Remember, though, a great deal of work is involved."

"Not for me."

That was true, thought Alura. It would fall to her and her mother to take care of all the preparations. And they would have to invite Connor. . . .

No, that would never do, she decided. She would have to persuade her mother to talk Sir Herve out of the idea. It was bad enough that they must see Connor again at Welwynd. To have him once more at Brynclair was unthinkable.

•　•　•

Connor shifted his shoulders so that the heavy hauberk of chain mail settled more securely about his torso. When the hauberk was in place, Jeremy lifted the dark-blue surcoat that went over it and held it so that Connor could slide his arms through the proper openings. Connor shook his head, and his long, dark hair brushed his shoulders.

"I had forgotten how blasted hot and uncomfortable this garb is," he said.

"You'll be thankful for it later on, once the tournament has begun," Jeremy reminded him.

Connor gave the squire a baleful glare. He was thankful for nothing on this day.

He had brought no servants, only Jeremy, and they had carried what they needed on their horses. Connor had ridden his favorite charger, a magnificent golden sorrel, while Jeremy's mount was a mouse-colored dun with a darker stripe down its back. They had arrived at Welwynd, Sir Oswald's estate, in midmorning, and Jeremy had quickly pitched the dark-blue tent where Connor was now preparing for the tournament. There would be no midday meal for those knights who would take part in the jousting. No one wanted to face his opponent with a full belly. Hunger gave a man a sharper edge.

But all that meant to Connor was that he would die with an empty stomach.

How many times had he gone into battle in his life? he asked himself. Too many to count. He had fought in many tournaments when he was younger, and then in the Holy Land, fighting at Richard's side, he had faced death on numerous occasions. Never, though, had he gone into combat with such an air of doom hanging over him.

Jeremy picked up Connor's helmet, which had a long streamer of dark-blue fabric attached to its round, flat crown. Connor shook his head and said, "Not yet." He turned and stalked over to the tent's entrance flap, thrusting it back and stepping out into the sunlight.

A scene of color and gaiety met his eyes, belying the darkness within him. The tournament would take place in a large meadow at the foot of the hill surmounted by Castle Welwynd. The meadow was broad, open, and gloriously green with the new grass of spring. All along its edges, tents and pavilions in every hue of the rainbow had been set up. Red, green, blue, and yellow pennants flapped and fluttered in the warm breeze. Lords and ladies in equally gaudy adornment stood under the pavilions. When the tournament got underway, the ladies would all gather together under one pavilion known as the bower of beauty, while the lords would congregate on the other side of the field in a pavilion of their own. Other knights were emerging from their tents, just as Connor had done, some already wearing their helmets, others bareheaded so that the ladies could see how handsome they were. Connor grunted and reached for his helmet, taking it from Jeremy. He had no wish to impress any female with his appearance.

But as he settled the helmet over his head and then peered through the eye slits, he found himself looking for a particular lady. A lady with red hair and green eyes. . . .

"I don't see her, milord."

"Stop that!" Connor turned sharply toward Jeremy. "Are you some sort of sorcerer, lad? How do you know my thoughts before I know them myself?"

"I could tell you were looking for someone, milord," Jeremy replied with a grin. "And I knew that were I in your place, I would be searching for the Lady Alura, too. She is the most beautiful lady these poor eyes have e'er beheld."

So it wasn't just him, thought Connor. Alura really was beautiful. And since that was the case, doubtless she would be receiving more than her share of attention from the other lords and knights in attendance. If he just looked for a group of men clustered about a woman, surely he could find Alura that way. . . .

But she was not here, he determined after several moments of scanning the perimeter of the meadow with his keen eyes. He spotted Alura's parents, Sir Herve and the Lady Katharine, standing under one of the pavilions, but there was no sign of Alura herself.

Connor hoped she was not ill, and then another thought crossed his mind. What if the rumors started by that old villain Sir Herve had some basis in fact? What if Alura was indeed with child and ashamed to make an appearance here at the tournament?

Connor's hands clenched into fists in their metal gauntlets. The thought of Alura in his late brother's arms, the very idea of her lying under Morvyn while he rutted with her, made anger blaze inside Connor with a heat as brilliant as that of the sun overhead.

What was it about Alura de Gabin that made him feel this way? He had known other women before, appreciated their beauty, enjoyed their company in his bed. But never had he fully succumbed to their charms. Why should he care now if Alura had lain with his brother? Why did it matter to him if Morvyn had gotten her with child?

At any rate, he told himself, there had to be some other explanation for her absence. He knew Alura hardly at all, but during their brief meeting, he had seen the intelligence in her eyes, as well as the strong will. She would not have allowed herself to be taken by Morvyn until the wedding ceremony had been performed.

But what if she'd had no choice? Connor wondered as the pendulum of his emotions swung back the other way yet again. What if Morvyn had raped her?

If that was the case, then Morvyn was a lucky man indeed that he was in his tomb and beyond the reach of Connor's anger.

Connor finally succeeded in pushing all these thoughts out of his head. He could not allow himself to become distracted if he was to have any hope of surviving this tournament. What might be had to be forgotten in favor of what was. And the reality of the situation was that he was in no way ready to pit his strength and skill against that of another knight.

He had no choice. Things had proceeded too far. There would be no turning back now.

As trumpets began to blow, Connor swung toward the golden sorrel, which wore trappings and a harness of dark blue that matched his master's surcoat. As Connor grasped the harness and lifted himself into the saddle, his scabbarded sword slapped against his left leg. Jeremy hurried up, awkwardly carrying Connor's heavy shield and the long, unwieldy lance. "Milord," he panted with the effort.

Connor reached down and took the shield from Jeremy, slipping his left forearm through the pair of leather straps on the back of it. The shield was made of hardwood overlaid with a thin sheet of azure-painted steel. Emblazoned on its plain field was a silver crescent, the sign of the second son. Connor had carried that shield from one end of Palestine to the other, and it had borne many nicks and dents when he returned to England. Jeremy had spent long hours repairing and repainting it until it appeared as if it were new. Despite his pessimism, the shield felt good on Connor's arm, as if it belonged there.

Jeremy came around on the other side of the golden charger and lifted the lance, struggling to keep it balanced. Connor wrapped the fingers of his right hand around the lance's handle and took it from the squire. A muscle in Connor's shoulder twinged painfully as his arm took the weight of the weapon. The sensation lasted only an instant, however. Connor raised the point of the lance, testing its balance. He had practiced for many hours in the days before the tournament, galloping up and down one of the open fields near Stavebrook, and once he was satisfied that he would not be dragged out of the saddle by the very weight of the lance, he had recruited Jeremy to play his opponent. Their practice had been rough, and more than once, one of them had gone tumbling to the ground. But Connor's injured arm and shoulder had stood up well to the punishment. At first the muscles ached at night, so much so that he ground his teeth together as Jeremy tried to massage the soreness out of them. That had all passed, and by now, Connor felt fairly confident that he could give a good account of himself.

That knowledge, however, did nothing to alleviate the sense of foreboding that had crept strongly over him as the tournament approached. Today, his mood was the blackest that it had been.

Perhaps 'twould be best if he met his end this day, he told himself as he urged the charger forward. Death would at least put an end to his status as an outsider in his own homeland.

The grave welcomed everyone, no matter what their reputation might be.

The ladies were moving now into the bower of beauty, and the knights who would participate in the tournament rode slowly toward the pavilion with its red-and-white-striped canopy. Each of the combatants would salute the ladies, and some would be given tokens by their wives or sweethearts to carry into combat, usually a small scarf.

Connor knew that he would be receiving no tokens today. He had no sweetheart here. These ladies all knew him as the Beast of Stavebrook, and they knew what had happened to Elspeth Lyle.

At least, they thought they knew what had happened. Poor Elspeth. Connor felt a sharp pang at the memory of her.

He had no wish to dwell on the past. Nothing that had happened could be changed. Not ever. One wrongful death had begat another, and there was no way to take them back. . . .

More trumpets blared as the knights began their procession past the bower of beauty. Connor thought about remaining where he was in the middle of the field and not taking part in the spectacle, but he had no wish to insult Sir Oswald or Lady Maryoth, Sir Oswald's wife. He edged the charger forward and joined the line of knights. Besides, this would give him one last chance to look for Alura. She might have joined the other ladies in the pavilion without him noticing.

If he really was to die today, he could do much worse than to have the lady Alura's lovely face as one of the last sights his eyes beheld on this earth.

But she was not there, he saw as he rode slowly past the pavilion with the other knights. He saw instead the way the ladies dropped their gazes toward the ground so they would not have to look at him. His spine stiffened. If they wished to pretend he did not exist, then so be it. They were as nothing to him in their frippery and finery.

He turned the charger and heeled it into a trot that carried him back to the center of the field. The other knights joined him in due course, and then Sir Oswald Duparc rode out to face them. "The pairings have been drawn," he announced in a loud voice that carried across the field. "The first match will be Sir Connor of Ridglea against Sir Phillip of Staunton."

Connor drew a sharp breath. He had not expected that he would fight in the first joust. But that was fine, he told himself. Get it over with quickly. Sir Phillip was a well-respected warrior, if not the sort who would have given Connor much of a challenge on Connor's best day. . . .

But this was far from his best day.

Connor walked his horse forward a few steps. Several men away down the line of knights, Sir Phillip did the same. The two of them turned their chargers so that they were facing each other, exchanged curt nods, then wheeled their mounts and galloped toward opposite ends of the field. The other knights scattered to take up positions of their own so that they could watch the match.

Connor reached the boundary of the tournament field and turned his horse again. Sir Phillip had done the same. Now the two knights faced each other again, with the length of the field between them this time. Connor glanced toward the ladies' pavilion. Lady Maryoth sat there in the front row, and in her hand was a long, red scarf. It would be her privilege to raise the scarf, then lower it in the signal for the tournament to begin.

Connor took a deep breath and steadied the lance. He held his right arm tightly against his body to brace the weapon. The butt of the handle extended behind him.

Lady Maryoth raised the red scarf.

A cheer welled up from the throngs assembled around the field.

The scarf dropped.

Alura heard the roar from dozens of throats and stopped in her tracks where she had been hurrying with a hobbling gait toward the field. She was too late. The tournament had already started.

But she had no way of knowing whether Connor was taking part in the first match. She started again toward the nearest pavilion, limping heavily on her right foot.

When she and her parents had arrived at Welwynd earlier,

she had still been searching for some way to avoid having to attend the tournament itself. But she knew her father would not accept just any excuse. She could not plead illness when she had no symptoms to speak of.

Then fate had intervened, and while one of the servants had been carrying a small chest into the keep, it had slipped from his hands and dropped onto Alura's right foot. The pain that made her cry out was real enough; she had no need to pretend. And anyone with eyes could have seen the swelling on her foot when her slipper was taken off.

But only Alura knew the injury was not as serious as it appeared. True, she had been unable at first to put any weight on the foot without wincing and gasping in pain, but that had passed within an hour or so. She had spent that hour resting in the bedchamber she had been given for her family's stay here at Welwynd, having been carried there in a chair by a pair of burly retainers.

That time had given Alura more than just a chance to ease her injured foot. It had provided her with an opportunity to think, as well, and she had spent it thinking about Connor Warrick. That was not her choice. He had barged into her mind, a vision of his rugged, brooding features insinuating itself into her thoughts until she could see nothing else.

She realized, finally, that she was worried about him. There was no reason to be concerned, she told herself sternly. She recalled how, before he had left England for the Crusade, he had emerged victorious from every tournament in which he'd fought. She remembered as well the strength in his arm, the lean muscularity of his body, when he had embraced her there in the bailey of Brynclair. Surely he would defeat any opponent who might come against him today.

But then a thought that had never before occurred to her made her sit up sharply on the bed where she was resting. On that day long sennights ago, that rainy day when she had run out of the keep and into his embrace, he had used only his *left* arm to encircle her. It might have been her imagination, but she thought he had winced slightly as he did so, as if in pain.

What did that mean? Why did it have to mean anything?

she asked herself in turn. It could have been simply a whim on Connor's part. If she was looking for evidence that he was no longer at the height of his prowess, that momentary embrace was flimsy testimony indeed.

But what if there was some truth to the thought? Word that Connor had been killed in the fighting in the Holy Land had reached England. Perhaps the report had become garbled in its long passage. Perhaps the news should have been that he had been seriously wounded, almost to the point of death. If that was the case, then it was possible he was unable to use his right arm. Such a supposition required a stretch of the imagination, true, but . . .

She would have to see for herself.

She had swung her legs out of bed, tested her injured foot against the stones of the floor, and winced slightly as pain darted through it. The pain no longer shot all the way up her leg, however, so she thought she could manage to walk. Quickly, she had slipped into a mantle and donned her wimple, then she left the castle and started toward the huge field where the tournament was being held. Several of Sir Oswald's servants saw her leaving, but none of them attempted to stop her.

The walk was longer than she had thought, and her foot and ankle were throbbing by the time she heard the cheer from the crowd that signaled the beginning of the tournament. Instantly, she ignored the pain and hurried ahead.

The nearest pavilion was full of lords talking loudly, exchanging wagers and ribald comments as they watched the contest unfolding on the field. They fell silent in surprise as the slender figure of a lovely young woman pushed among them. Sir Herve, who was in the front rank of the lords, saw his daughter and exclaimed, "God's eyes, Alura, what are you doing here? The ladies' pavilion is across the field."

"I cannot go that far, Father," she told him, breathless from the pain in her foot and the exertion of hurrying here.

Sir Herve looked down at her foot. "I thought you were hurt."

"I am. But I have to see the tournament." Alura knew she was flying in the face of all the protests she had made about being dragged here to Welwynd, but there was nothing she could do about it. Logical or not, she felt that she had to be here. She peered past her father's bulky shape as a knight on a magnificent golden charger flashed past the pavilion at a full gallop. "Is that—"

Before Alura could finish her question, Sir Herve put an arm around her and drew her gently away from the other lords. They stood together at the edge of the shade cast by the pavilion's canopy. " 'Tis Ridglea," he said curtly, "matched against Sir Phillip of Staunton."

Alura's breath seemed to freeze in her throat, but at the same time her heart was beating so fiercely that she feared it would tear its way out of her body. She watched, eyes wide, as the two knights on horseback came together.

For an instant, just before the clash, it seemed that the tip of Connor's lance dipped slightly, as if he could no longer hold it straight. That tiny disadvantage made the steel tip of the lance glance harmlessly off Sir Phillip's shield with a ringing crash of metal against metal. At the same time Sir Phillip's lance struck a solid blow against Connor's shield. Connor rocked back, and for a horrible instant Alura thought he was going to be unhorsed.

But then the knights were past each other and Connor was still in the saddle. Alura thought he seemed shaken, but that had to be her imagination. With that helmet over his head, solid save for the eye slits, there was no way she could even begin to guess what he was feeling.

"I thought you didn't want to watch this tournament," Sir Herve growled as he kept his arm about her to support her and take some of the weight off her injured foot.

Alura didn't answer him, but kept her eyes fixed on the action before her.

Connor's arm and shoulder ached almost intolerably as he swung the golden sorrel around and prepared for the second charge against Sir Phillip. His strength had deserted him at the last moment in the first charge and almost proved to be his ruin. He knew how close he had come to being unhorsed, and judging by the shouts of approval from the pavilions as Sir Phillip rode by, so did everyone else in attendance.

With his muscles trembling, Connor raised the lance once more until it was straight. He glanced toward his tent and saw Jeremy standing there, hands clenched in anxiety, face pale with worry. Jeremy was starting to realize now that Connor had known all along what he was talking about. He was not ready for a tournament. Likely, he never would be. The next blow from Sir Phillip's lance would surely knock him from the horse, and more than one knight had been killed by a broken neck from such a tumble. Connor could see that happening in his mind's eye.

For a moment he thought about casting his lance on the ground and conceding the match to Phillip. Such a demonstration of cowardice was almost unheard of, but surely the lords and ladies who had come here today could not think worse of him than they already did.

But the same perverse pride that had led him into so much trouble in his life asserted itself again. Perhaps he had not lived honorably, at least in the minds of those assembled here, but by God, he could die honorably!

With a hoarse shout, he urged the charger forward into a gallop, leaning over the flowing golden mane as he brought the lance to bear on Sir Phillip's shield.

Then, as he raced past one of the pavilions, he saw from the corner of one of the helmet's eye slits a young woman standing next to an older man. She turned sharply and buried her face against the chest of the elderly knight, as if she could not bear to watch; but Connor had seen enough.

Alura!

He was past her and could not look back, not with Sir Phillip bearing down on him, but he knew she was there. That knowledge filled him, and for some reason his right arm stiffened with newfound strength and tipped the lance up as it started to sag. Sir Phillip was almost upon him. Connor twisted slightly in the saddle so that his shield covered more of his body.

They came together with the same roar from the crowd and crash of lance against shield that had marked their first clash. The impact that came through the lance shivered all the way up Connor's arm, and in that split second, he knew he had struck a good blow, and had struck it first.

Then the steel tip of Sir Phillip's lance slammed into Connor's shield. Again he felt himself knocked backward, and this time he could not maintain his grip on the charger with his legs. Suddenly, there was nothing underneath him save empty air.

'Tis over! Pray God Alura keeps her face turned away, so she does not have to witness my death!

That thought flashed through Connor's head with amazing rapidity, and then he hit the ground. The impact knocked all the air from his body, and a menacing blackness tinged with red streaks swam before his eyes.

But it receded, leaving him still conscious, and he realized as he lay there gasping for breath that he was not dead. The knowledge that he still lived was astonishing. He got one gauntleted hand on the ground and pushed himself upright.

Sir Phillip lay a short distance away, also unhorsed.

Connor bit back a groan. The collision with the ground had numbed him at first, but now the pain was starting to seep back into his body. He wanted nothing more than to sink back onto the grass and lie there.

But the match was not over. Since both knights had been knocked from their saddles, they had to continue the combat on foot. Connor looked around for his shield as Sir Phillip began to stir.

Going into this match, Connor had had no thought of winning. He had been convinced, in fact, that he would not live through it. Now he sensed that victory was in his grasp if only he could get to his feet. Somehow, that had become important to him.

It was seeing Alura that had done it, he realized. He had not wanted her to see him die, even though he expected such an outcome.

Now he did not want her to see him defeated.

He saw his shield lying on the turf, out of reach. By the time he could get to it, Sir Phillip would be upon him, because Staunton was already wavering to his feet, clearly shaken by the fall just as Connor was. Connor braced himself with his left hand and pushed himself up, staggering upright. He tried to reach for his sword.

His right arm would not work.

He heard the rasp of a blade being withdrawn from a scabbard. Sir Phillip was coming for him, sword upraised. The opposing knight's stride was unsteady, but it would suffice to bring him within range. The blow would be aimed at his helmet, Connor knew, intended to knock him down and claim the victory.

Connor ducked as the sword swept at him. That was all he could do. He lunged forward, crashing into Sir Phillip. He reached across his body with his left arm and grasped his right hand with his left, lacing the fingers together. He brought them up, letting the left arm do the work, and as Sir Phillip staggered back, Connor brought his clubbed, gauntleted hands down against the front of the helmet. The blow knocked Sir Phillip backward. He sprawled on the ground, and Connor almost fell atop him.

Connor managed to stay upright, however, and he brought his left foot down on Sir Phillip's right wrist, pinning the knight's sword arm to the ground. Sir Phillip yelled in pain. Connor stooped and used his left hand to pluck the sword from his opponent's hand. He brought the tip of the blade to a point just underneath the bottom of Sir Phillip's helmet, in the narrow gap between helm and hauberk.

"Do . . . do you yield?" rasped Connor.

If Sir Phillip refused to yield, Connor would be within his rights to lean his weight on the sword and plunge it through the knight's throat. He would not do it, though. He knew that as well as he knew his own name.

He had killed his last man. No matter what Sir Phillip said, Connor would not take his life.

"I . . . I yield," Sir Phillip said.

Connor lifted the sword away from his throat and tossed it aside. No roar of appreciation came from the crowd, even though it was clear he was the victor. In fact, a strange silence had fallen.

Or perhaps they were cheering, and Connor could not hear them for the blood rushing through his head like a great river, pounding louder and louder until the noise of the torrent seemed to fill the entire world. . . .

He turned away from Sir Phillip, took two steps, and plunged forward onto his face, dropping into a welcoming darkness that swallowed him whole.

Seven

Alura had not meant to turn away as Connor rode past. It was his fierceness, she thought, that made her flinch, though why she would have expected anything less from a man with his reputation, she could not have said. But as Connor and Sir Phillip came together, she had turned her head again, so that she could look over her shoulder and see the awful collision.

A cry of dismay was jolted from her as she saw Connor fall. He lay so still on the ground that for a terrible moment, she had thought he was dead. Then he had begun to move around, and so had Sir Phillip. *Stay down!* she had cried out silently to Connor. *Let this be over!*

But of course he had gotten up, and he had dodged Sir Phillip's sword stroke and knocked him down. Connor had won! Alura knew that as he turned aside and stepped away from Sir Phillip's recumbent figure.

Then Connor fell again, and Alura cried out once more and would have run to his side had not her father's hands clamped down firmly on her shoulders.

"Let his squire tend to him," Sir Herve said sternly. "The field of battle is no place for a woman."

"This is not a battle," Alura protested. " 'Tis only a tournament!"

"That you believe so, daughter, only shows how little you really know."

Alura seethed with frustration as she watched Jeremy run forward onto the field from the dark-blue tent where he had been watching the joust. The squire knelt next to Connor and began tugging off his helmet. A short distance away, Sir Phillip rolled over, pushed himself onto his hands and knees, then staggered upright to stumble off toward his charger.

Connor was alive. He began to move around slightly as Jeremy lifted his head into his lap. Relief flooded through Alura at the sight.

Silence hung over the field. There had been no cheers when Connor had triumphed. And rightly so, Alura told herself. Even in victory, he was not a man who deserved to be acclaimed. Not after everything he had done. It was perfectly all right for her to be glad that he was not dead; that was nothing more than simple human compassion. She warned herself not to read any more into it than that.

Yet she had to acknowledge, at least to herself, the pain she had felt when she thought he had been killed.

Sir Herve was tugging gently at her. "Come along, my dear," he told her. "I shall take you to the ladies' pavilion and give you into the charge of your mother."

"I'm fine, Father—" she began.

"You should be back in the keep and off that injured foot of yours." He frowned. "You had no business coming out here in the first place."

"I did not want to attend this tournament in the first place," she reminded him rather acerbically.

He ignored both her words and her tone of voice, saying again, "Come along."

Alura allowed him to lead her out of the pavilion. It was a long walk to the bower of beauty, and with each step her foot throbbed more. She could not stop herself from wincing and catching her breath at the pain.

Sir Herve stopped. He bent, put one arm behind her knees, and lifted her, carrying her in his arms as if she were a babe. "Father!" exclaimed Alura. "You'll hurt yourself."

"Nonsense," he said, his voice taut with the strain of lifting her. "I carried you all over Brynclair when you were a child, and you are still my child. I'll not have you suffering if I can do aught to prevent it."

That was the tenderest sentiment he had expressed to her in a long time, and Alura put her arms around his neck and hugged him. At moments like this, she could almost forget how crass and mercenary he was most of the time.

Almost.

Katharine saw them coming and hurried out of the ladies' pavilion to meet them. "Dear Lord!" she said. "What is the poor girl doing here? I thought she was resting in the keep."

"She decided she wanted to see the tournament after all." Sir Herve was frowning as he spoke, and Alura decided that she did not care for the look in his eyes. He was perhaps making more out of her actions than he should have.

He carried her into the pavilion and sat her down on one of the benches. As he straightened, breathing heavily, Alura saw how red his face was from the exertion of carrying her over here. Katharine frowned anxiously as she put a hand on her husband's arm. "Are you all right, Herve?" she asked.

"Fine, never better," he replied heartily, if a little breathlessly. He waved a hand at Alura. "See if you can talk some sense into the girl and convince her she must rest that foot. In the meantime, I'll fetch a horse to carry her back to the keep."

"No, Father," Alura said. "Now that I am here, I want to watch the rest of the tournament." The worst was over, she thought. Connor had already fought his match.

Sir Herve shook his head and muttered something. Alura heard, ". . . must puzzle the Almighty, Himself."

She paid no more attention to her father, looking back across the field instead of toward where Connor had fallen. He was on his feet now, she saw. Jeremy had gone to fetch the golden charger, and he led it by the reins back over to where Connor waited. Connor did not try to mount; instead he simply hung on to the horse's harness for support and walked slowly off the field, back to the azure tent. He thrust the entrance flap aside and disappeared into the tent.

Alura hoped he was all right, even though she told herself

that it did not really matter to her one way or the other. Sir Connor Warrick was nothing to her.

If she told herself that often enough, she might even come to believe it.

"Alura . . . ?"

"Nay, milord. 'Tis me—Jeremy."

Even now, as he sank wearily onto the three-legged stool inside the tent, Connor felt shame at the way that redheaded damsel's name had been the first word on his lips as he regained consciousness. She had made it clear that she despised him, yet she was the first person he had thought of as awareness seeped back into his brain.

Connor sat with his mail-clad legs spread, hands dangling between his thighs. His shoulders slumped, and his head hung low. He was exhausted, and every bone and muscle in his body ached miserably. The worst pain was in his right shoulder. A horrible fear gripped him: today's joust might have undone all the hard work of strengthening his right arm and shoulder.

Jeremy hurried into the tent, carrying Connor's helmet. He placed it carefully on the ground. "I saw to the charger," he told Connor, "just as you asked me to do. Now, milord, I can help you."

"I need no help," snapped Connor.

"Please, milord, allow me to perform my duties as your squire."

Connor sighed and lifted his left hand, motioned tiredly for Jeremy to get on with it. Truth to tell, he *did* need help. As bad a shape as he was in, he doubted if he could get out of the chain mail by himself.

Jeremy removed his master's boots, then the surcoat and hauberk, leaving Connor clad from the waist up in only a sweat-soaked tunic. Connor stood shakily and allowed Jeremy to take the chain mail off his legs, then gratefully sank back onto the stool. He wished he could lean back, close his eyes, and go to sleep.

That would come later. Now, he had to get dressed again and put in an appearance at the remainder of the tournament.

Enough tongues were no doubt already wagging; he would not give the lords and ladies a fresh excuse to gossip by not showing up for the other matches.

After resting a few more moments, he stood and stripped off his tunic, hose, and braies. Jeremy brought fresh clothing, while Connor washed himself with a wet cloth. As Connor dressed, he tried not to look at the ugly scars on his shoulder and upper arm. Anyone seeing those reminders of the horrible wounds would have likely thought that the flesh would never knit together again enough to make the arm useful.

And it might have been better, Connor thought, if that Saracen battle-ax had completely sheared his arm off. He might have bled to death—as he nearly had anyway—or at the very least, if he had returned to England with only one arm, no one would have expected him to take part in a tournament. He would have been left alone to sit in the keep at Stavebrook and brood.

"Here you are, milord," said Jeremy, assisting Connor with the braies, hose, and tunic of dark blue, followed by a silver surcoat and cloak. Connor ran his fingers through the tangle of his dark hair. Leather slippers completed the outfit, and he was ready to face the lords and ladies.

Well, not ready, perhaps, but lacking in any excuse not to do so.

"I'll stay here and wait for Sir Phillip's squire to bring the spoils," Jeremy said.

Connor nodded. He had no need of Staunton's charger and the armor and weapons that had been used in the joust, but tradition demanded that as victor he collect those winnings. He stepped out of the tent and walked toward the pavilion, hoping that he did not appear as shaken as he felt.

Another joust was about to begin. Connor glanced at the field and recognized the colors of two of the district's knights as they rode toward opposite ends of the field. There had been a time when he would have watched the ensuing matches carefully, searching for any weakness in the combatants so that he could take advantage of it later, when it might be his turn to face one of them. But he would fight no more on this day, even though as the victor of his match he could have proceeded in the quest to become the ultimate champion of this tournament. He would plead injury from his combat with Sir Phillip, and there would be no disgrace in withdrawing from further competition. Everyone here had seen how hard he'd hit the ground.

Sir Oswald Duparc stood in the first rank of the lords beneath the pavilion's canopy. He looked over coldly as Connor approached. The other men drew back, both to allow Connor room and to ensure that none of them was forced to stand too close to a man they all despised.

"Sir Connor," Duparc said curtly. "Well fought."

The compliment was a matter of rote. Like the rest of the knights here, Sir Oswald would have much preferred that Sir Phillip had emerged as victor in the first contest.

"I must withdraw from the tournament," Connor said, not bothering with any sort of insincere pleasantries. "My shoulder was injured in the fall when I was unhorsed."

Duparc nodded. "It was a hard fall. Very well. But you will stay for the ball, I hope?"

Connor hesitated. It would be much easier simply to ride back to Stavebrook with Jeremy. With luck, they could reach the keep not long after nightfall . . . if they started almost immediately.

But before Connor could say anything, he heard one of the men behind him mutter, " 'Tis a wonder Richard ever won a battle with men such as that fighting at his side."

Connor stiffened. It was all he could do not to turn and glare at whomever among the knights had spoken. He would not dignify such an insult by doing so, however.

"Please convey my regrets to the Lady Maryoth—" he began.

"No one regrets your leave-taking, least of all the ladies." Those harsh words came from another man, and this time Connor had no choice but to turn. He could not ignore such a direct challenge.

"I am a knight of the realm, the same as all of you," he said sharply. "And at least I went to the Holy Land to fight at Richard's side, rather than staying here at home as you did."

He saw more than one man reach for a sword as his words lashed at them. The confrontation had drawn the attention of the ladies in the opposite pavilion, and Lady Maryoth had not yet signaled for the next joust to begin. The two knights waited on their chargers at opposite ends of the field.

One of the lords moved smoothly between his fellows and Connor. "There's no need for such hostility," he said. "We have all proven our prowess in the past." Sir Herve de Gabin turned toward Connor. "You should weigh your words more carefully in the future, young man. Someone might accidentally misunderstand them."

"No one misunderstood me," Connor shot back.

From behind him, Sir Oswald said, "I think perhaps 'twould be best if you did leave Welwynd now, Ridglea. I shall convey your regrets to the Lady Maryoth."

Connor turned, gave him a curt nod, and stalked away. He did not look back, but he could feel the eyes of the knights following him. Their disdain burned him like a brand.

Jeremy met him at the entrance of the tent. "What do we do now, milord?" he asked.

"We leave this place," Connor told him. "As soon as possible."

From across the field, Alura spotted Connor talking to the knights in the other pavilion, and she leaned forward on the bench where she sat, wishing that she could hear what was being said. Lady Maryoth and the other ladies were watching, too, and Alura sensed the tension in the bower of beauty. In the past, bad blood had caused more than one battle to break out among the spectators at such tournaments.

And in this case, the bad blood ran deep. No one in this district had any liking for Connor.

But then Connor stalked away, and a sense of relief filled the bower of beauty. Lady Maryoth raised the red scarf to begin the second joust.

Alura pushed herself to her feet as the scarf fell and the two knights on horseback thundered toward each other, accompanied by cheers of encouragement from the pavilions and tents.

Katharine caught hold of Alura's hand. "Where are you

going?'' she asked. ''You are supposed to refrain from walking on that injured foot.''

''I'm fine,'' Alura lied. ''It feels much better now.''

''Do you wish to go back to the keep? I'll have a horse brought for you.''

On the field of battle, lances met shields, and more cheers welled up.

Alura shook her head. ''Stay here and enjoy the tournament, Mother. I'm perfectly capable of returning to the keep on my own.''

''I'll not hear of it,'' said Katharine as she came to her feet. ''Your father would be angry if he heard that I allowed you to wander about Welwynd unsupervised, especially since you're hurt.''

Alura felt an upsurge of frustration. She wasn't sure what she planned to do—she was acting on instinct, not intellect, she realized—but she knew that she did not want her mother to be part of it.

Still, there was nothing else she could do. ''Very well, Mother,'' she said. ''Have one of the servants fetch a horse.''

Katharine bustled out of the pavilion, and Alura sank back down on the bench. Truth to tell, her foot still ached badly, and she was afraid that walking on it would be quite painful. She turned her eyes toward the field and saw that the two knights were still locked in combat. They were afoot now, so obviously both men had been knocked from their horses. One man fought with a mace, the other with a sword. Weapons crashed against shields as the onlookers shouted in appreciation.

Alura looked past the field to the azure tent where Connor had disappeared. She saw him emerge from it now, followed by his squire.

Connor was moving slowly, and Alura could tell that he was in pain. He mounted the golden sorrel with the squire's assistance. Then Jeremy scrambled into the saddle of the mouse-colored horse and took the reins of the charger that had formerly belonged to Sir Phillip. He led it, falling in behind Connor as the knight turned his horse away from the field.

They were leaving, Alura realized. Connor was going back to Stavebrook.

Good riddance, she told herself. A man such as him did not belong among civilized people.

She found herself on her feet, moving slowly but steadily out from under the pavilion, going in the opposite direction from her mother who had left in search of a servant and a horse. No one tried to stop her. Each step sent a fresh twinge of pain through her foot and leg, but Alura kept moving, although if asked, she could not have said why she was doing this.

She knew *what* she was doing, however.

She had a few things to say to Sir Connor Warrick.

Eight

Blast it, what was the lass up to *now*? Sir Herve de Gabin asked himself as he watched his daughter limp away from the pavilion on the other side of the field. She was moving fairly quickly, considering her injury. Sir Herve's eyes searched the bower of beauty for some sign of his wife, but he did not see her. Where had Katharine gone?

More important, where was Alura going?

Sir Herve thought he saw the answer.

"God's eyes," he breathed. Alura was moving to intercept Connor Warrick as he rode away from the field.

Frowning darkly, de Gabin muttered excuses to his companions and strode away from the pavilion, skirting the edge of the field where the two current combatants were still flailing away at one another.

Movement in the corner of his eye caught Connor's attention. He drew back on the golden sorrel's reins and brought the charger to a halt. A slender young woman was coming toward him, and though her wimple concealed her hair, he knew it to be a fiery, breathtaking red. When loose, it would fall like waves of flame around her shoulders and down her back.

The thought made his heart pound harder in his chest.

"Milord . . . ?" Jeremy said tentatively.

"Wait here," growled Connor. "I shall be back in a moment."

He urged his mount into motion again and rode toward Alura.

She was limping, he saw with concern. Something had happened to her, and that was probably why she had not been at the tournament earlier. As Connor drew closer, he saw that her face was set in tight, masklike lines. Still, though she tried to conceal it, he could see the pain reflected in her features every time she took a step. He felt a burst of sympathy for her. He knew all too well what it was like to have to keep moving when the body cried out to stop.

Alura saw him coming and gratefully slowed her pace even more. She glanced back at the pavilions and knew that many of the lords and ladies under the shade of the canopies would be watching this encounter between her and Connor. They might consider it even more entertaining than the battle that was still in progress on the field. But she didn't care. Her sense of honor would not allow her to let Connor leave Welwynd until she had apologized to him for her father's abominable behavior. She had to be certain, too, that Connor did not believe the accusations Sir Herve had made about her.

Connor brought his horse to a stop again when he was a short distance from her. He did not dismount, and Alura thought that was rather rude of him. He was forcing her to look up at him if she wanted to speak to him face-to-face. He loomed before her like some monster out of a myth, but he was no figure of the imagination. He was real, flesh and blood and everything that went with it.

"Lady Alura," he said with a brusque nod.

"Sir Connor." Alura cast about desperately for something else to say and to her dismay found nothing. This was starting out badly, much worse than she had feared. He would think her a simpleton. But why should she worry what he thought about her?

Reasonable or not, she did worry. She realized that it was important to her what Connor thought of her. After the debacle of their meeting there in the rain and sleet in the bailey of

Brynclair, she wanted him to know that she was not a complete, utter fool.

She lifted her chin and said, "I am surprised you came to this tournament."

"As am I," he said dryly. "When I hit the ground after being unhorsed by Sir Phillip, I wished that I had not come." He leaned forward in his saddle. "But I am not the only one who is injured. I saw you limping rather badly. Are you all right?"

Alura's shoulders rose and fell in a shrug. "A servant dropped a small chest on my foot. 'Tis painful, but I will be fine."

"You should be resting," said Connor.

"So my father and mother have told me." Alura glanced over her shoulder, her instincts warning her, and saw that her father was hurrying toward them. She turned her attention back to Connor and hurried on, "What will you do now, Sir Connor? Return to Stavebrook?"

"I am not overly welcome here—nor anywhere else. Sir Oswald and the other lords have made that plain enough even for a blind man to see."

"Then you'll not be staying for the ball?"

"I've no wish to dance," he said.

Alura felt a surprising rush of disappointment. With her father approaching rapidly, she gave in to the impulse that gripped her and rushed on, "I cannot dance with this injured foot. Perhaps if you stayed, the two of us could talk while the others danced."

Judging from the look on Connor's face, he was as astonished by the suggestion as she was by the fact that she had made it. "You . . . wish me to stay?" he asked.

Again she shrugged. "It matters little to me. I just thought that, since we both seem to be wounded . . ." She allowed her voice to trail off, letting him draw whatever conclusion he might from her words.

But his expression hardened, and he said, "Your injury will heal, milady. I fear that mine runs deeper."

And with that, he turned his horse and heeled it into a trot that carried him back toward Jeremy.

Alura stared after him, unable to believe that she had been dismissed so curtly. Anger washed over her, anger at Connor, and at herself as well, for allowing herself to give in to such a foolish idea. She had been right all along: Connor Warrick had no place among civilized people.

At the same time, she felt a keen sense of disappointment. If she had attended the ball with Connor, tongues would have wagged so hard that the breeze from them would have flapped the pennants hanging from the towers of Welwynd's keep.

"Did he insult you?"

The question came from behind Alura. She turned and saw her father standing there, red-faced again, but this time not from exertion. He had his hand on the hilt of his sword as he stared at Connor's retreating back.

Alura shook her head. "No more than the fact that such as he is an insult to anyone of honor."

Sir Herve took his hand away from his sword and asked, "Whatever possessed you to come over here and talk to him, girl?"

Alura could only shake her head once more. "I don't know, Father. I truly do not know."

Connor was asking himself a variation of the same question. Why had he ridden over to Alura and stopped to talk to her? All it had gotten him was another moment of pain and bewilderment and the torment of looking into those green, green eyes. Given the chance, he could make those eyes shine with happiness and contentment.

He stiffened in the saddle, shocked that such a thought had come to him. Even in the wildest flights of fancy—which he was not given to in the first place—he should not have been able to conjure up such a thought. True, Alura had been a bit more friendly this time, and she had put herself through some added pain just to speak with him, but still . . . she knew his history, or what she and everyone else *thought* was his history. She had made it plain, too, in their earlier meetings, what she thought of him.

Not counting their encounter in the bailey at Brynclair, of course, when she hadn't yet realized who he was and had wound up in his embrace, her mouth locked with his, her body pressed tightly to him. . . .

"Sir Connor?" Jeremy edged his horse ahead until he was riding alongside his master. "Did you say something, milord?"

Connor realized that reliving the moment when he'd kissed Alura had caused him to voice a low growl of desire from deep in his throat. He shook his head and told Jeremy, " 'Twas nothing."

"Oh. I would have sworn I heard—"

" 'Twas nothing, I said." As soon as Connor gave voice to the sharp words, he regretted them, but it was too late to draw them back.

Regrets were insidious, he was discovering. He had been rather abrupt with Alura when he'd taken his leave of her, and he was beginning to feel sorry about that, too. He had no idea how badly her foot was hurt, but he had been able to tell from the way she'd looked as she'd limped toward him that she'd been in pain with each step. Yet she had come on, determined to speak with him. She had even suggested that he attend the ball so that they could talk more.

And what had he done? Snapped at her, turned his horse around, and ridden away. Given her a good view of the golden sorrel's hindquarters.

That wasn't the only horse's arse she had been looking at, he thought.

Connor pulled back on the reins and started to turn the charger. "Milord?" said Jeremy, surprised. "What are you doing?"

"We're going back to Welwynd," Connor said. "I've decided to attend the ball after all."

Jeremy just sighed and followed. These days, it was a waste of time trying to figure out what Sir Connor might do next. 'Twas clear that Sir Connor himself had no idea. . . .

Katharine had been upset, of course. She had come back to the pavilion with a horse and a pair of servants to assist her in getting her daughter back to the keep, only to discover that Alura was gone. Then she had seen both her daughter and her husband, walking slowly back toward the pavilion, Herve supporting Alura with an arm around her. Katharine had murmured, "Dear Lord, what has happened now?"

She did not have to wait until the other two members of her family had rejoined her to find out the reason. Lady Maryoth turned toward her with a smile that was more of a smirk and said, "Alura seems rather taken with Lord Ridglea."

Katharine's eyes widened in shock. "What?"

"They were just speaking together. They seemed quite . . . intimate . . . until Sir Herve joined them, and then for a moment I thought there might be swordplay."

Several of the other ladies smiled and even laughed quietly behind their hands. Katharine felt herself flushing in shame. Had Alura really dishonored herself by leaving the pavilion to speak with Connor Warrick? Katharine had believed that her daughter was in too much pain from her injured foot to do such a thing. And even had Alura been healthy, Katharine would not have thought that she would have any interest in conversing with such a wicked man.

Of course, Katharine had to admit to herself that Connor didn't really *look* wicked since he had returned to England from the Crusade. Weary of the world and all the pain in it, definitely. And bitter, yes, even that. But wicked? No.

Katharine swept up to Alura and Sir Herve as they reached the bower of beauty. "You frightened me severely, Alura," she said sternly. "I thought you would wait here for me."

"I'm sorry, Mother," said Alura. "There was something I had to do."

"What? Speak with Connor Warrick?"

Alura sighed. She should have known that her mother would be angry with her when she found out what had happened. And it had not taken long at all for Katharine to discover what Alura had done. No doubt Lady Maryoth and the other ladies had been eager to share what they had seen.

"There, there, Katharine," murmured Alura's father, surprising her. " 'Twas only a moment of simple conversation. Our daughter was merely being polite to Sir Connor."

"He does not deserve politeness."

Alura looked back and forth between her parents. The swiftness with which they had exchanged roles shocked her. Always before, it had been her mother defending her against her father when he began to rail at her about some wrong she had perpetrated, real or imagined. Now, Sir Herve's seeming tolerance surprised her, as did the depth of Katharine's anger. No doubt being embarrassed in front of all the other ladies had something to do with it.

"Come along, now," said Sir Herve, tugging gently on Alura's shoulders. "Let's get you back to the keep, shall we?"

"What about the rest of the tournament?" Alura asked. "Do you not desire to watch it, Father?"

He waved a hand. "A group of knights pretending to do battle with each other? Nay. I have seen such sorry spectacles many times before." He inclined his head. "Begging your pardon, Lady Maryoth. I meant no offense to you or your husband."

Lady Maryoth just sniffed. Whether Sir Herve had meant offense or not, she had grasped it with both hands.

Alura and Katharine were both astounded by Sir Herve's behavior now. He loved tournaments, enjoyed nothing more than watching the fierce combat. Now he was turning his back on it willingly.

He had something devious in mind, Alura thought. But what?

By evening, Alura's foot felt quite a bit better. She had spent the afternoon lying in bed with the injured member propped up on a pillow. Her mother had kept her company for a time, until Alura had pleaded weariness and a desire to sleep. Then Katharine had pulled the curtains in the bedchamber and quietly left.

Alura did not sleep, however. Her mind was much too busy to allow her to relax sufficiently for that. Instead she spent the time reliving those moments when she had stood before Sir Connor. Bit by bit, she conjured up his image in her mind's eye until she knew she had an accurate representation of him.

And she knew, as well, how much pain he had been in. She hadn't really thought about it at the time; she had been too filled with her own pain and confusion and not a little fear. But the agony had been there in his eyes, nonetheless, and in the strained lines of his face. The punishment he had taken during the joust must have been considerable. Falling off a horse like that would be painful to any man, let alone one who had only recently recovered from an earlier injury. Now that she thought about it, she recalled that he had used his right arm only sparingly after being unhorsed, though he had been holding the lance in that hand earlier. Something *was* wrong with his right arm, she told herself. It had been hurt, and he had reinjured it during the tournament. That confirmed her earlier suspicions about why he had embraced her with only his left arm in the bailey of Brynclair.

Thoughts of that moment made her heart beat faster. She seemed unable to catch her breath for a short time. There had been nothing rough, nothing harsh about either his embrace or his kiss. In fact, his lips had been hesitant at first and had become demanding only after the burst of desire that had passed between them like lightning leaping from the clouds. Now that she pondered the matter, it seemed odd that a man with such a reputation for being a scoundrel could possess such gentleness.

But perhaps that was how he began to bend young women to his will, Alura thought as she rolled onto her other side. Perhaps he made them believe that he could be kind and tender, before he showed his true colors later on.

She sighed and told herself to stop thinking of such things. She had no wish to solve the enigma that was Connor Warrick. He had been rude to her, after all, and he had gone back to Stavebrook. Let him stay there.

Katharine returned to Alura's chamber in the early evening and found her daughter brushing her hair by candlelight. Alura braided the long red strands and wrapped them around her head, then reached for her wimple as she said, "Have you come to help me downstairs, Mother?"

"You still wish to attend the ball?" asked Katharine.

"Of course. Who emerged victorious in the tournament?"

"Sir Ambrose of Snowden."

Alura nodded. She knew Sir Ambrose slightly; he was a handsome young knight who had made it known in the past that he considered her comely. Unfortunately, he sparked absolutely no interest in return from Alura. She was glad that her foot was still slightly swollen. If it had not been for that excuse, she would have no doubt had to dance with Sir Ambrose several times during the evening.

"Are you ready to go downstairs?" Katharine asked.

Alura finished tucking the ends of her wimple into her gown. She stood up. "I am."

"And your foot?"

"Much better. Still, I'll not be dancing tonight."

Katharine linked her arm with Alura's, and together they left the chamber and went down a stonewalled corridor to the narrow set to stairs that curved around the inside wall of the keep and led to the great hall of Welwynd. This castle was built along the same lines as Brynclair, and Alura almost felt as if she was home as she and Katharine started down the stairs, Alura on the inside staying close to the wall and resting one hand on it for added support.

The sounds of music and talk and laughter welled up from the great hall. The hall was full of lords and ladies dancing and flirting. The long table of polished hardwood in the center of the hall was stacked with platters heaped so high with food that Alura almost expected it to sag in the middle. The benches were packed, as well, as some of the lords indulged their appetites with roast fowl, ham hocks, thick slices of beef, and pots of savory stew swimming with wild onions and carrots. Mead was flowing swiftly, too, from barrels into cups.

A small group of musicians stood at the far end of the hall and tried valiantly to produce notes from their lutes and lyres loud enough to compete with the chatter and laughter of the guests. Several couples moved in rough harmony with the music.

The hall was decorated with elaborate tapestries hanging on the walls and colorful pennants dangling from poles. Fresh rushes had been laid, which gave off scents of lavender and sage. This was a celebration of many things, not the least of which was the return of spring, so it was only appropriate that there was such a profusion of color and the scents of spring. It represented the wildflowers that would soon be sprouting in the fields.

"Are you hungry?" asked Katharine as she and Alura began to make their way through the crowd of guests.

Alura glanced at the table, which was crowded with grunting and smacking lords who practically lunged for more food as soon as they finished the morsels they were chewing. Her father was among them, she noticed, his fingers and chin coated with grease. She shook her head. "I want to sit and listen to the music," she said.

"There is a bench here by the wall. . . ."

Katharine led Alura over to a bench carved of marble that sat underneath one of the tapestries. The walk down the stairs had made Alura's foot begin to ache a bit more, so she was grateful for the opportunity to sit down and take the weight off it. She took a deep breath, letting it out in a sigh.

"Would you like anything?" asked Katharine. "A cup of mead, perhaps?"

Before Alura could answer, her father appeared at her mother's shoulder. "There you are," Sir Herve said, lifting his arm to wipe away the grease on his face with the sleeve of his tunic. "I thought I saw you. Dance with me, woman."

Katharine frowned at him. "I am attending to Alura's needs—"

"But I have none at this moment, Mother," said Alura. "I think you and Father should dance." She smiled, knowing that her mother truly enjoyed being swept around the floor in Sir Herve's arms.

"Are you sure?"

"Quite certain, Mother," Alura said.

Katharine shrugged a little and smiled at Sir Herve. "In that case, milord, I suppose I am yours to command."

"You always were," Sir Herve growled rather high-handedly, but Katharine was still smiling as he took her in his arms and turned her toward the area where the other couples were dancing.

Alura leaned back slightly. She would have rested her head against the wall, had she not known how hard the stone was. She watched her mother and father and told herself that she should be glad for their happiness. True, things did not always go smoothly between husband and wife, but most of the time they seemed to be quite content that they were wed.

A shadow moved in front of her, blocking the light from the torches that blazed in sconces along the walls of the hall, and a voice that she knew all too well despite having heard it only a few times said, "I have heard certain things spoken of as being as beautiful as a picture. Now I know the truth of it."

Alura's breath caught in her throat as she looked up at the last man she had expected to see here tonight.

Sir Connor Warrick.

Nine

Alura was sitting beneath a tapestry that showed a broad sweep of landscape with woods in the foreground, rolling grassy hills in the middle distance, and a hill surmounted by a castle in the background. A group of pilgrims, pious and holy, moved along a path through the woods, and peering out from behind the trunks of trees were forest nymphs. Connor was no expert on art, but the tapestry was lovely, no doubt about it.

But not half as lovely as Alura herself. Her beauty took his breath away, and to be able to stand here and drink in her loveliness made all the awkwardness worthwhile.

And awkward it had certainly been when he and Jeremy had reappeared at Welwynd. At first, the guards at the gate had been unwilling to admit them and reluctant to fetch Sir Oswald. But Connor had insisted, and eventually one of the men-at-arms had gone to the keep to bring the master back.

Duparc had stared long and hard at Connor through the lowered portcullis, then demanded, ''What are you doing here, Ridglea?''

''I was invited to the ball,'' Connor said.

''You departed earlier today, after the first match of the tournament.''

"I am well aware of that. Does that mean the invitation is withdrawn?"

Sir Oswald had glared at Connor for a long moment, then sighed heavily. "Sometimes having a code of honor is damned inconvenient," he muttered. He flapped a hand at the men-at-arms. "Raise the portcullis and admit Lord Ridglea."

Jeremy had tended to the horses, leading them off to the stables while Sir Oswald and Connor had walked into the keep. There had been a momentary silence as the two knights entered the great hall; even the musicians had stopped playing. The lords at the banquet table paused, legs of mutton halfway to their open mouths. Everyone had stared in surprise at the tall, broad-shouldered figure in silver and azure beside Sir Oswald. Then the lord of the keep had gestured curtly at the musicians, and once again they began to pluck out their tune. Gradually, the dancing and the laughter and the gluttony had resumed. Left to his own devices, Connor had found a small alcove where he'd stood and searched the crowd with his eyes, looking for the Lady Alura. When he saw no sign of her, he'd felt keenly disappointed. There was no one else here he really wanted to see or speak with, and judging from the way all the guests were doggedly ignoring him now, they felt the same way about him.

Then he spotted her coming down the stairs with her mother, and his heart began to thud in his chest almost as heavily as if he had been about to go into battle.

His right arm and shoulder still ached like the devil, but at least he was able to use that arm again. Some of the strength that had been jarred out of it by the fall had seeped back into muscle and bone during the afternoon, bringing with it relief that he had not permanently crippled himself by participating in the tournament.

And as he walked across the room toward Alura, he no longer felt any pain at all. Any awareness of it had been driven out of his mind by the sight of her.

When he spoke, he had no real idea what he was going to say, and he expected the words, whatever they might be, to come out haltingly. Instead, the mere sight of her gave him renewed confidence, and when she looked up at him, he suddenly felt taller and stronger than he ever had before.

She put a quick end to that. Her voice was cold as she said, "Sir Connor."

It took every ounce of self-control she possessed, but Alura was determined not to allow him to see how she felt at this moment. He was a dangerous man, and if he sensed any weakness in her, any weakness at all, he would swoop in for the kill like a hunting falcon. There was something of the look of a falcon about him, at that: the hard, predatory lines of his face; the potential for violence, barely leashed and ready to explode; the sheer, compelling strength. It was an apt comparison, thought Alura, and one she could not allow herself to forget.

"I did not . . . thank you . . . for your kind words earlier today," he said. "You were the only one who bid me farewell."

"You fought well," Alura said. "I thought that you deserved some recognition of that fact."

It was not only his prowess in the field that had led her to intercept him as he rode away, she knew. But his courage *had* touched her. She had always admired bravery in any person, even one as unsavory as Connor Warrick.

"Perhaps I would have fought even better had you bestowed upon me some token to carry into combat," he said.

Somehow, Alura kept her voice cool as she murmured, "That would have implied a closeness between us that does not exist, Sir Connor."

"We were quite close . . . that day in the rain."

With a sharply indrawn breath, Alura stiffened. Connor felt a surge of panic. He had gone too far by reminding her of the day they had kissed. The memory of that incredibly sensuous moment when the rain had streamed down around them and her body had been pressed so closely to his that he could feel every soft curve shattered the last of his control, and his mind exploded with the knowledge of what he wanted to do with her, what he had wanted to do ever since the moment he had first laid eyes on her. . . .

Alura was recalling that same instant in time, frozen indelibly in her mind, complete with all the details that might have been woven by a master craftsman into a tapestry such as the one that hung just above her head. Heat flowed through her like a slow river with a current too strong to be denied. Though she might rage against it, though it went against everything she had ever believed about herself, the fact was plain.

She wanted Connor Warrick.

And he wanted her, too. She saw that in his eyes. Dear Lord, he wanted her, too.

"—with child by the monster's brother, you know."

Alura's head snapped around, her attention drawn by the barely overheard words. She could not tell which of the ladies nearby had uttered them; there were several who were smirking and tittering behind their hands, and Alura knew that all of them had been talking about her. Not only that, but they had been repeating the sordid rumor started by her father—damn his eyes!—about her relationship with Morvyn. She was sure her father had meant no lasting harm by his actions; he had wanted Prince John to grant him title to Stavebrook, and his thinking, dominated as usual by greed, had not gone beyond that point. But harm had been done, and people were still talking despite the fact that Alura was obviously not with child.

"—must have scoured the brat," another woman whispered loudly enough for Alura to hear. Worse, Connor heard, too. Alura could tell that when she glanced at him and saw the anger on his face.

"—replace one Lord Ridglea with another—"

"—couples with anyone who strikes her fancy—"

Connor's face had grown harder and harder until it resembled that of a statue chiseled out of stone. Alura felt her own face burning hot with shame. Had she possessed two good legs at that moment, she would have leaped to her feet and dashed out of the room. As it was, though, trying to hobble away would only draw more attention to her. All she could do was sit here and endure this humiliation. Connor was not so unfortunate. He could turn and walk away whenever he chose.

Instead, he held out his hand toward her.

"Milady, would you honor me with a dance?"

Alura could not believe what she was hearing. "I . . . I cannot," she finally managed to say. "My foot . . ."

"I will make it simple for you," said Connor. "Take my hand."

"I . . . cannot . . ."

"Take my hand." The command was spoken softly, but his voice rang with power despite the quietness of it. Then, as Alura looked up at him, his stonelike features softened as well, and a smile appeared on his face. "The music is too lovely to be wasted, too lovely to be ruined by the twittering of magpies."

His voice rose slightly on the last words, and Alura heard some of the nearby ladies who had been gossiping about them sniff in disdain. That as much as anything won her over to Connor's side, but she still had difficulty bringing herself to take the hand he extended toward her. She sensed most of the eyes in the room watching her.

"I give you my word, milady, I will never harm you in any way."

The softly spoken pledge was more than Alura could resist. She reached up and allowed his fingers to close around hers.

He lifted her as if she weighed nothing. The fingers of his right hand twined with those of her left. His left arm went around her waist, capturing her, urging her toward him. She went willingly. His arm was unbelievably strong, and so much of her weight rested against it that she was able to move her feet and legs without causing too much pain to her injured foot. In fact, as he swept her around, her feet barely brushed the floor.

The other couples got out of their way as they danced. Connor was grateful for that. He did not know how long he could manage to hold Alura like this, so that she could move without hurting herself. If he could have, though, he would have held her forever. The feel of her body pressed against his was more intoxicating than the strongest mead, more exciting than a hard-fought joust, more compelling than a real battle. In the Holy Land, he had discovered what many men who had been in battle knew: life was made all the sweeter by the closeness of death. But the feelings cascading through him now were even stronger.

Alura caught a glimpse of her parents as Connor swirled her around. They were watching with the same astonishment as the other guests at the ball, but Katharine was horrified by what she saw, too. As well she should have been at the sight of her daughter, her only child, clutched tightly in the arms of the Beast of Stavebrook.

Sir Herve had a somewhat different expression on his face, Alura realized. He looked somehow . . . satisfied.

Her own reaction should have been one of horror, she told herself. She had willingly given herself into the embrace of a man known for his evil. Her virtue, her very life, might well be in danger simply from being this close to Connor Warrick.

Yet she felt no danger at all. Instead she felt overwhelmingly safe, as if no harm could ever come to her as long as Connor held her. Everyone else could think whatever they wanted to about him. She no longer cared.

The music stopped as the musicians reached the end of the tune. Alura experienced a moment of disappointment as Connor came to a halt, too. She had wanted the dance to go on all night. He still held her tightly enough, however, so that she did not have to rest much weight on her foot.

"There will be much talk about this night," he said softly.

She shook her head. "I don't care. I would not barter it for all the gold in the world."

Someone cleared his throat behind her. Alura turned her head and saw her father standing there. Connor released her, so that she could turn to face Sir Herve. She rested her injured foot gingerly against the stone floor.

"It seems to me," said Sir Herve, "that there is an announcement that needs to be made."

A wave of dizziness struck Alura. She was unsure what her father was talking about, but she was certain he was up to no good. She had seen that calculating look in his eyes too many times before not to recognize it now.

"Father . . ." she said warningly.

Connor held himself tensely. If Alura's father was going to challenge him, he would have to find some way to mollify the old man. He had no desire to kill Sir Herve—and no guarantee that he could even do such a thing. *He* might be the one who wound up with a length of finely honed steel in his guts.

Battle was the last thing Sir Herve had on his mind, as Alura and Connor both discovered in the next moment. Katharine appeared at her husband's side and plucked urgently at his sleeve, but he shook her off and ignored her. In a loud voice, with the attention of everyone else in the room resting solidly upon him, he said, "The house of de Gabin and the house of Warrick were to unite, but fate's cruel hand intervened when Morvyn Warrick, Lord Ridglea, was taken from this world. Now fate has touched us more lightly and brought us another Warrick, another Lord Ridglea, another noble knight to be wed to my daughter, the fair Lady Alura."

"No!" Alura gasped, and that gasp was echoed from dozens of throats around the great hall. Of gossip along those same lines, there had been aplenty, but few if any of the gossipers had expected such a thing ever to come to pass.

Tautly, Connor said, "I have not spoken of marriage to the lady, nor to you, Sir Herve, nor to anyone."

Sir Herve shrugged. "I have eyes that can see despite their age, my boy. I know when a man and a maid have decided that they are meant for each other."

In a low, urgent voice, Katharine said, "Herve, you are mad. . . ."

"I know what I know," de Gabin practically thundered.

And Alura knew what she knew. Her father had seen his chance to make another play for Stavebrook. He had been unsuccessful in his first attempt to marry her into the Warrick family, so he was trying again.

But this was not Morvyn to whom her father was trying to give her in matrimony. It was Connor Warrick, known far and wide to be . . . to be . . .

What? A seducer of young women, a breaker of hearts, a killer? Alura looked at him and saw none of those things.

But then, Connor's previous victims had probably been convinced that the stories about him were untrue, too.

"Sir Herve, I am not interested in a bride. . . ." Connor said, and despite Alura's own roiling emotions, she felt a flash of disappointment.

"Your brother was betrothed to my daughter, and the dowry was paid," Sir Herve rumbled, an ominous note creeping into his voice. "You now hold the title of Lord Ridglea, and it is your duty to honor all the obligations into which the previous lord entered."

"I have no such duty," said Connor.

"If your brother had a debt of money, you would pay it, would you not?" de Gabin asked shrewdly.

"I . . . of course."

"Of course," repeated Sir Herve. "Your honor would demand your payment. Well, Sir Connor, this is a debt that must be discharged as well!" He pointed a finger at Alura. "A debt to this young woman!"

"But Father," Alura cried out, "I have no wish to be married to this . . . this man!"

The words were like a sword thrust in Connor's belly. No, the target was slightly higher, he decided. It was aimed at his heart, rather.

Despite his own protests to Sir Herve's absurd suggestion, it pained Connor to see how Alura reacted. He could see all the old fears and suspicions come flooding back into her at the very idea of being wed to him. Though he knew it should not have been important to him, he had thought that she was coming to trust him, at least a little. He had hoped as much, anyway.

Now he saw that there was no possibility of her trusting him.

Struggling to keep what he was feeling out of his voice, he said, "If I wished to be wed to your daughter, Sir Herve, 'twould not be because of any sense of obligation or duty, nor because of anything my late brother did—or did not do. 'Twould be because *I* wished for such a match to take place."

"And do you not find my daughter fair to look upon?" Sir Herve shot back. "Do you find her ugly?"

"Herve!" hissed Katharine. "Cease this spectacle immediately! Everyone is looking. . . ."

Why are you doing this? Alura wanted to scream at her father.

But she already knew the answer to that question. He was doing it because he wanted to bring Stavebrook under his influence. The same thing he had wanted when he'd arranged her marriage to Morvyn.

Only Morvyn had reacted quite differently to the proposed match. He had been very enthusiastic. In fact, his enthusiasms brought a slight shudder to Alura as she recalled them. . . .

That had not been the only difference, either. It was possible that Sir Herve could have dominated Morvyn Warrick and gotten his way whenever there were decisions to be made.

That would never happen with Connor. Surely her father could see that. Surely he could see that even if the marriage he was proposing took place, he would still fail in his ultimate goal.

He was blinded by greed and ambition and saw nothing of the sort, Alura realized as she looked at her father. He saw what he perceived as an opportunity, and he was seizing it for all he was worth.

"I made a mistake coming back here," Connor said. "I see that now. I should have returned to Stavebrook and been content that no further damage had been done."

"So you have no interest in marrying my daughter?" demanded Sir Herve.

"None at all," Connor answered without hesitation and began to turn away.

Only he and God knew how much it cost him to make that statement.

As he turned from Alura, the voices began again; the smug, almost gleeful whispers. He wished he could shut them out, but he could not.

"—bedding with so many men not even the Beast will stoop to marrying her!"

"Aye, and if she is with child, think how the poor babe will suffer without a father, all because of Alura's looseness and wickedness."

The comments were enough to make Connor hesitate for a heartbeat. If he had heard them, then likely Alura had, too. He dared not look over his shoulder at her, he warned himself, lest he see her stricken look and feel his heart melt, despite the harsh things she had said about him.

Then Connor heard the smug tones of Sir Oswald Duparc's voice as the knight said, "You should have expected nothing more from him, Sir Herve. Has he not always run away from every responsibility in his life? Was he not such a disappointment to poor Morvyn?"

Connor froze. Alura could tell from looking at the stiff lines of his back that Sir Oswald's vicious words had struck home. Slowly, Connor turned back to face her and her parents and the rest of the crowd.

When she saw what was in his eyes, she wanted to scream *No!* But her mouth refused to work, and all she could do was stare at him in horror.

"Do you accuse me of cowardice, Sir Oswald?" asked Connor, his voice little more than a whisper.

"No," Duparc answered without hesitation. "You have courage. But you are without honor. You always have been. I regret that I ever invited you to set foot inside my walls."

"Then I'll not sully the hallowed ground of this keep for much longer," Connor said with biting sarcasm. "I shall stay long enough only to conclude my business with Sir Herve."

"You have no business with me, Sir Connor." De Gabin glared at him. "Not unless you have changed your mind about honoring the commitment made by your late brother."

"That is exactly what I am prepared to do." Connor glanced at Alura's stricken face, which had been drained of all color, and rushed on while the madness was still upon him. "Sir Herve, I wish the hand of your daughter, the Lady Alura, in marriage. Will you grant me this boon?"

Ten

"If an arrangement agreeable to all parties can be reached, I grant you the boon you request, Lord Ridglea," Sir Herve said.

The room swam dizzily before Alura's eyes. The words her father had spoken were exactly what she expected to hear, but the impact of them still struck her like a terrible blow. He had just promised her in marriage to a man who was known to be worse than a scoundrel. Though Alura had been unable to control her own body's reaction to Connor, her mind had not been deceived by the passion she felt pooling in her belly. She knew what kind of man Connor Warrick was. Everyone there at Welwynd knew.

It would have been so easy, at that moment, to close her eyes and give in to the swoon that was threatening to overcome her.

Alura chose not to. She stiffened her muscles and forced herself to say, "Have I no voice in this matter?"

None at all. That was what her father would say if he replied to her with the truth. But instead, he said smoothly, "I have acted in what I believe are your best interests, lass, and I'll not have my decision questioned. You would have been happy with the previous Lord Ridglea. Now you will be happy with this one.''

Alura doubted the truth of both of those statements. But her happiness had never been her father's compelling interest. She cast about for words to say that might change his mind, but found none.

Her mother did not have that problem. Katharine said to her husband, ''You would turn our daughter over to a . . . a murderer?''

Sir Herve glanced around, no doubt seeing the disapproval on the faces of many in the great hall. He cleared his throat loudly and waved a hand in dismissal of his wife's strident question. ''Those old stories are just that,'' he said. ''Stories. I do not believe they have any basis in fact. Do they, Sir Connor?'' He stared directly at Connor as he voiced the question.

For a long moment, Connor made no reply. Then he said, ''I have never yet told anyone what to believe about me. I'll not start now.'' He glanced around and saw that Jeremy had crept into the great hall. The squire stood at the edge of the crowd, gaping openmouthed in awe at everything that had transpired. Over his shoulder was slung a pouch on a leather strap, and Connor knew what was in that pouch.

He raised his left hand and crooked a finger at Jeremy, then turned back to Alura, Sir Herve, and Lady Katharine. ''We will meet later to settle on the arrangements,'' he said, ''but for the time being, it seems that a gift is needed to seal this bargain. Jeremy . . .''

The squire was at his side, having squirmed and pushed his way through the crowd. ''Here, milord.''

Connor extended his hands, wincing a little at the pain in his right shoulder. ''The chest.''

Jeremy reached into the pouch and brought out the small wooden chest. It would have been safer, perhaps, to leave it and its contents at Stavebrook, but after everything that had happened while he was gone, Connor did not fully trust his seneschal Mossgrave. Jeremy placed the chest in Connor's hands.

Connor smiled at Alura. ''I vow I'll not drop this on your

foot, milady,'' he said. He used his thumbs to open the lid of the chest, then held it carefully in his left hand while he reached inside with his right. He brought out the most beautiful piece of jewelry, the slave bracelet with its attached ring, both of them decorated with magnificent fire opals. Gasps of admiration came from the onlookers.

Efficient as always, Jeremy whisked the chest away from Connor, closed it, and put it back in the pouch. That left Connor free to step up to Alura with the bracelet in his hand. He reached down, took her right hand in his left, and lifted it.

She was numb. She wanted to snatch her hand away from him, wanted to turn and run despite her injured foot. But she could do nothing except stand there and watch as Connor slipped the ring onto her finger, then followed it by sliding the bracelet over her wrist. The fire opals gleamed brilliantly in the torchlight.

''There,'' Connor said. ''A symbol of our troth. The ring is slave to the bracelet as I am slave to you, milady.''

Words. They were nothing but empty words meant to impress the crowd, Alura told herself. She knew they were false.

But deep within her, she wished with all her heart that they were true.

He bent toward her, and there were gasps from the ladies in the crowd as they realized what he was about to do. Alura knew, too, and she was torn between competing desires. Her mind screamed out a warning to pull away from him, to run for her life, while her body was equally insistent that she stay. Her body won.

Connor kissed her.

His lips brushed hers in a contact that was gentle, polite, almost formal. If he had drawn back fairly quickly, that was where it would have ended. But his mouth lingered on hers, and in a handful of heartbeats, the warmth had become heat. Connor put his hand on Alura's trembling shoulder, and it was all he could do not to slide it on around her and pull her against him. With everyone in the great hall watching, however, he did not want to embarrass her any more than she already must be.

Once again, Sir Herve cleared his throat, and Connor

stepped back. Alura tried to catch her breath. Her heart was pounding so hard it seemed that any second it might burst out of her body. Never had she experienced such a mixture of emotions. She was almost whimpering with need, but at the same time she was ashamed and horrified at her reaction to Connor's kiss. Had she totally lost all reason? A kiss meant nothing in the face of all the evidence of Connor's terrible past.

Connor glanced around the room. He saw anger on the faces of the lords, outrage on the faces of their ladies. He cursed Sir Herve for ever putting him in this position.

Well, actually, he *had* wanted to kiss Alura again. He had desired that ever since their first meeting, even though he was loathe to admit it even to himself. But to propose marriage had never entered his mind. That had been Sir Herve's idea.

None of it would have happened, mused Connor, had he not ridden back to Welwynd after departing earlier in the day. *That* had been his mistake. Perhaps, in the back of his mind, he had hoped that people would accept him, would begin to forget all the stories from the past. . . .

But that would never happen, he saw now. He would always be the Beast of Stavebrook, even if he was married to a well-thought-of young woman such as Alura. People would feel sorry for *her*, trapped in a marriage to a monster, but they still would not give him the benefit of the doubt.

To hell with them, Connor decided. To hell with them all.

He turned his back on the crowd and spoke to Alura and her parents. "I will visit Brynclair in a sennight," he said. "The arrangements will be made then, if everyone still wishes this match to take place."

"Nothing will change in a sennight," said de Gabin. "I can assure you of that."

"We shall see." Connor motioned to Jeremy and turned away. He would have shouldered through the crowd on his way out had it proved necessary, but a path cleared for him.

Alura watched him go and felt hollow inside. A sennight. An entire sennight without seeing him. That was good, she told herself. The time would give reason and logic a chance to reassert themselves, so that she was thinking with her head instead of her body. And it would give her a chance to persuade her father that a marriage between her and Connor would be a terrible mistake. If he insisted that she go through with it, he would be putting her life in jeopardy. Connor had killed one lover already. Why not two?

Lover. The word seared through her brain, leaving an indelible imprint behind. If she and Connor were married, they would be lovers. He would take her to his bed. . . .

Don't think of that, she chided herself. Think only of the sort of man he is, not the way he makes you feel when he touches you, when he kisses you. Think of the past, not the future.

Would that she could.

A sennight. Alura lifted her right hand and looked at the slave bracelet and the ring. The fingertips of her left hand brushed lightly over the thick golden bracelet. A sennight without seeing Connor, a sennight to think of some way out of this dilemma. That was the true gift.

"Surprised I was when you called for me, milord. But I think you did the right thing. The Lady Alura, she's one of the most beautiful women I've ever seen. She'll brighten up the halls of Stavebrook, that's certain."

"What made you slip into the great hall of Welwynd, anyway?" Connor asked idly.

Jeremy shook his head. "I don't rightly know, milord. I was sitting out in the kitchen with the servants, hanging on to the chest, not letting it out of my sight, you know, when I heard the strangest thing. It seemed to be a voice calling to me, summoning me to the hall. Did *you* call me, milord?"

Connor shook his head curtly and let his thoughts drift away. He had been listening to Jeremy's prattling for leagues now as they rode back to Stavebrook. Darkness had fallen, but Connor pushed on anyway. He was being foolish and he knew it, but the idea of spending the night at Welwynd was simply too much for him to bear. The walls of the keep had begun to close in on him, and he'd had no choice but to get out, taking Jeremy with him.

Besides, if he had read Alura's eyes correctly, she wanted

some distance between him and her, along with the time he had specified. The separation would be good for them.

He half-hoped that during the coming sennight Alura would be able to persuade her father to abandon his plans for the marriage. To have the match called off after it had been announced in front of all the lords and ladies of the district would be something of a scandal, but the gossip that would result would be mild compared to some of the things that had been said of him in the past.

Of course, Alura was not accustomed to being talked about in such a manner, and Connor felt sorry that she would have to bear the whispers behind her back. However, if the marriage did take place, Alura would still be the subject of much talk. Since that situation was the same either way, it would no doubt be better for her not to be married to him at all.

God, he wished he had never tendered the proposal. He had been goaded into it by Duparc's assault on his pride. Connor bit back a groan. When would he learn that honor and duty were traps, nothing but snares set to catch a man who was cursed by having a conscience?

"Milord."

Connor had paid little heed to anything Jeremy had said since they'd left Welwynd. His mind had been full of the debacle that had somehow come about despite his best intentions. But now, even though the squire's voice was quiet, there was an edge to it that caught Connor's attention.

"What is it?" he asked, slowing his horse and turning to look at Jeremy. The young man was only a vague shape in the darkness beside him. The route they followed ran through thick woods, so the moonlight and starlight that filtered through the branches of the trees did little to illuminate the road.

"I heard something, milord," Jeremy whispered. "A rustling in the brush. . . ."

"A night-roaming animal, no doubt," said Connor.

"Perhaps, but—"

Jeremy's voice was cut off by a sudden fluttering sound, followed immediately by an ugly thud. Jeremy cried out.

Connor knew what had made that fluttering: an arrow, flying out of the shadows under the trees.

They were under attack.

"I will talk to your father," Katharine promised grimly, "but I fear that little good will come of it, Alura. Once his mind is made up, all the arguing in the world will seldom change it."

Alura gave her mother a glum nod. "I know. But we must try to make him see reason. I simply cannot marry Connor Warrick."

She was sitting up in the bed in her chamber, pillows propped behind her, and one underneath her injured foot as well. Katharine had fussed around, arranging things so that Alura would be comfortable, and though an abundance of attention had always bothered Alura, she had allowed her mother to go ahead and fuss over her. Right now, Katharine needed to stay busy, so that her mind would not have a chance to dwell constantly on the horrible thing that had come about this evening.

"Are you quite comfortable?" Katharine asked as she stood at the head of the bed.

"Quite," replied Alura. "You have done plenty, Mother. Now you should go and get some rest yourself."

Katharine sighed. "I fear I'll not sleep this night. My mind is still too shocked by what your father has done. I know he has had his heart set on controlling Stavebrook for a long time, but to barter away his only child . . ."

"He was prepared to do it before," Alura pointed out.

"To Morvyn, not to that awful brother of his!"

Alura practically had to bite her tongue to prevent herself from telling her mother some of the things she had discovered about Morvyn Warrick. Everyone had thought him to be so good and noble, but perhaps that was only because they compared him to his brother. Connor's name carried such dark stains that anyone would look better beside him.

"Ah, well," Katharine went on, "perhaps we shall yet be able to make your father see the light of reason. I shall try, anyway."

" 'Tis all you can do."

Katharine nodded and went out, leaving a single candle burning in a small stand beside the bed.

Alura turned toward it, intending to blow out the flame and try to sleep, even though she feared that would be a futile pursuit, tonight of all nights. How could she sleep when she faced life as the bride of one of the most evil men England had ever produced?

Before she could blow out the candle, she noticed its glow reflecting from the golden surface of the slave bracelet, which lay on a small table where she had tossed it after coming into the room. She had not been able to take it off quickly enough to suit her, knowing that it came from Connor.

And yet . . . it did gleam with a lovely light, she thought. The rich luster of the old gold was perfectly offset by the more brilliant sparkle of the fire opals. And the bracelet and the ring had fit her perfectly, as if they had been made especially for her. She had noticed that much in the short time she had worn them.

If the wedding was called off, she would have to give them back to Connor. She could not think of keeping such a gift under those circumstances, no matter whether he urged her to or not. Not that he would have any reason to ask her to keep them, she reminded herself.

Alura sighed and bent once more toward the candle. She resolved to ignore the bracelet and the ring. They were nothing but reminders of a man she should despise and the terrible predicament into which she had been placed through no fault of her own. She pursed her lips to blow out the flame.

She stopped as someone whispered her name.

No, she thought after a heartbeat had passed. It was not a voice she had heard. 'Twas only the wind, she told herself, murmuring outside the keep of Welwynd. She was alone in the chamber. Once again she prepared to blow out the candle.

And once again, her gaze strayed to the bracelet and the ring.

Alura . . .

Her heart began to thud. It was almost as if the pieces of jewelry were calling to her. But that was mad, and she knew it. She was imagining things. The day had been long and pain-

ful and difficult, and she was even more tired than she had
believed. Perhaps she had already dozed off and was merely
dreaming.

She heard it again.

Enough was enough. Angrily, Alura threw back the bed-
covers and swung her feet to the floor. She would not have to
stand up to reach the bracelet and the ring. All she needed to
do was sit up and lean toward them, extending her arm past
the stand where the candle still burned fitfully.

And what would it prove if she did pick up the jewelry?
she suddenly asked herself. Only that she was doubting her
own sanity. If anyone knew that she thought a bracelet and a
ring were calling out to her, speaking to her in a human voice,
she would no doubt be taken immediately to a nunnery and
locked away for the rest of her days. With an angry sigh, she
pulled her feet back onto the bed.

The bracelet and the ring fell off the table and clattered to
the floor.

Alura gasped as her hand flew to her mouth. No one had
been near the table, and nothing had shaken it so as to dislodge
the bracelet and the ring. Truly, she *was* losing her mind.

But without thinking about her injured foot, she stood up
quickly and bent to retrieve the jewelry, intending to place it
back on the table. Instead, she paused, holding the two golden
circlets in her hand and staring down at them. As she did so,
the banked fires within the two opals seemed to grow and
swirl. Alura said softly, "Oh," and brought a fingertip close
to the gems. She stroked the fire opals, first the one on the
ring, then the one on the bracelet.

A terrific thunderclap shook the room, and a flash so bright
it hurt the eyes blinded Alura for a moment. She dropped the
bracelet and the ring and staggered back. When her legs hit
the bed, she sat down hard on it. She was unaware of what
had happened. Her eyesight was coming back to her, and all
of her attention was centered on the incredible thing that was
transpiring right before her eyes.

Thick tendrils of white smoke were rising from both of the
gems, as if the fire opals were truly on fire. The smoke twisted
and coiled about on itself, forming columns that were similar,

if not exactly identical. Alura had forgotten to breathe. Her heart hammered wildly in fear and awe as the two columns of smoke began to take on vaguely human forms.

She had no way of knowing how much time was passing. It was as if nothing else existed in the universe save this room.

Gradually, the figures became more defined as the smoke thickened even more. Colors and shapes formed and took on definite human outlines. A man and a woman, Alura realized with the small part of her stunned brain that was still functioning reasonably well. A man and a woman were appearing to her out of the smoke that had come pouring from the two fire opals.

But they were a man and a woman unlike any Alura had ever seen before in her life.

The man was short and thick-bodied, with broad, muscular shoulders and a prominent belly beneath a leather vest and a shirt made of some sort of shiny green material. He wore pants that bloused out around tree-trunk-like legs, and his feet were shod in slippers that curled up at the toes. His broad face was tanned to the shade of well-cured leather, and a fierce black beard jutted out from his chin. His eyes were dark pits. A scarf made of the same material as his shirt was wrapped around his head. Rings sparkled on his thick, blunt fingers.

The woman was every bit as amazing-looking. She wore red instead of green, and her vest was short and fastened in the front, since she wore no shirt underneath it. The blousy pants she wore were thinner, so that Alura could see her muscular legs through them. Instead of the scarflike headdress sported by the man, a round cap with a tassel on top of it was perched on the thick mass of dark, luxuriant curls that fell around her shoulders and down her back. She wore golden bracelets around both wrists and both ankles, and a golden chain was looped around her throat. She gave Alura a warm smile as the last of the smoke faded away, leaving both the woman and her companion standing before her, apparently as solid as the walls of the keep.

"Well," said the man, who had come from the fire opal on the bracelet, "what took you so long? You were waiting for an engraved invitation before you rubbed the jewels, perhaps?''

Alura moaned and fell backward on the bed, gratefully retreating into the blackness that welcomed her.

Better that than madness.

Eleven

Only she was not allowed that escape, no matter how much she desired it. Mere seconds had passed before someone was kneeling on the bed beside her, gripping her shoulders and shaking her.

"You have to wake up, Alura," a woman's voice said urgently. "Connor is in danger."

Alura groaned as she fought her way back to consciousness. She heard Connor's name, and a moment later the rest of the woman's words penetrated Alura's brain. Her eyes flew open, and she gasped, "Danger?"

"We can help him," the man said from where he stood beside the bed. "But you have to command it of us."

Alura stared from one to the other of them and back again. "Who . . . what . . . are you . . . demons?"

The man waved a hand. "Demons, no. No demons here." He took a deep breath, swelling his chest proudly. "We're djinn."

"Djinn . . ." Alura repeated the unfamiliar word, stumbling over it. "I . . . I do not know . . . I have never heard of . . . where did you come from?"

"I can tell you all about it," the man began.

"Pay no heed to Zahir," the woman interrupted. "He will

talk until your ears fall off, simply for the pleasure of listening to his own voice. Now there is a more important task to be done. Connor needs our help.''

"But . . . Connor left the keep. He is many leagues away by now," Alura mumbled, still in somewhat of a daze.

"Leagues are as nothing to us," said the man—Zahir, that was what the woman had called him. "Why, I remember once when we had to go from Baghdad to Damascus in the twinkling of an eye—"

"Trust us," the woman said, interrupting again. "Connor's life is in danger, but we can help him. You must command us to do so."

"All right." Alura did not waste any time wondering how they knew anything about Connor. Obviously they were connected to him in some way, since they had come from the slave bracelet and ring he had brought back from the Holy Land.

The Holy Land! She had thought the names of the places mentioned by Zahir were familiar somehow. She had heard of Baghdad and Damascus when the knights spoke of the Crusades. Freeing Jerusalem from the grip of the Saracens had been the first goal of the Crusaders, of course, but the battle to do so had encompassed other places as well. . . .

She was wasting time in such speculation, and for some unknowable reason, she believed what the woman had said about time being short. "Go," Alura said abruptly. "Help Connor."

"You won't be sorry," Zahir told her. "Come along, Radiya."

"Come along yourself," the woman said with a sniff of disdain. "I'll be there first."

"You forget yourself, woman." Zahir's dignity was wounded. "I taught you everything you know about being a djinni. . . ."

His voice faded away, and their bodies did the same. Before Alura's astounded eyes, the two djinn turned back into smoke, but instead of being drawn into the fire opals once more, they shot toward the wall of the keep in streamers of gray. . . .

Only to disappear *through* the stone.

Once again, Alura felt as if she was about to pass out. She clutched the bedding tightly, fisting her hands in it. She closed her eyes for a moment and took several deep breaths.

Then she raised a hand and slapped herself on the cheek, not lightly. The blow stung. She was convinced that this was all a dream, and she was determined to wake herself from it.

But when she looked down, the bracelet and the ring still lay on the floor where she had dropped them when she staggered back from the thunderclap and the blinding flash.

It couldn't have happened. It simply couldn't have. If the thunderclap had been real, someone would have heard it and come to investigate why such a sound had come from her chamber. People . . . spirits . . . even those so-called djinn could not live in gems. It was impossible.

And if what she had seen and heard tonight was simply the fevered ravings of a mind descended into madness, then Connor was safe.

She prayed it was so.

Bandits! That thought flashed through Connor's mind even as he reached for Jeremy to catch the lad in case he toppled from the saddle.

"I'm all right, milord!" Jeremy said. "The arrow did not strike me!"

Perhaps that shaft had missed, but now more were flying toward them from the shadows. Connor felt an all-too-familiar disturbance in the air next to his ear and knew that an arrow had almost struck him. He reached out and slapped Jeremy's horse on the rump, calling to the squire, "Ride, boy, ride! Leave Sir Phillip's horse behind!"

Perhaps the fine charger Connor had won by defeating Sir Phillip would distract the thieves and satisfy them. But even as Connor leaned forward over the golden sorrel's neck and urged the magnificent animal into a gallop, he knew that was unlikely. The bandits would be after that chest of treasure he had brought back with him from the Holy Land. Someone at Welwynd, probably one of the servants, had gotten word to a band of confederates that Connor and Jeremy would be on their way back to Stavebrook tonight. The bandits had acted quickly to set up their ambush.

But if he and Jeremy could escape the volley of arrows, they stood a good chance of getting away, Connor knew. Few horses in all of England could match the pace of the golden charger, and Jeremy's mount, for all its less impressive appearance, was also a fine animal with plenty of speed. Connor heard the drumming of its hooves right behind him as he rode.

Of course, dashing along at a dead gallop through this darkness carried its own dangers. One of them could crash into a tree or be swept off by a low-hanging limb. Or one of the horses could trip and fall.

No sooner had that dire thought passed through Connor's brain than he heard Jeremy's horse break stride. Jeremy shouted to the horse and hauled up desperately on the reins, but as Connor looked over his shoulder, he saw Jeremy go down, horse and squire tumbling to the path in a welter of dimly seen arms and legs.

Connor pulled his own mount to a sliding stop and dropped from its back almost before the golden sorrel had halted. His injured arm, still sore and aching only moments earlier, was forgotten now. Connor managed to draw his sword as he dashed to Jeremy's side.

He realized he could see better now, but that wasn't a blessing. The garish glow of torches penetrated the woods. The bandits were pursuing them and lighting the way with blazing brands. As Connor glanced back the way they had come, he spotted three or four torches converging on the path.

He reached down with his left hand and closed it around Jeremy's arm, lifting the young man with a grunt of effort. "Are you hurt?" Connor asked.

"N-no, milord," gasped Jeremy. "Just the . . . breath knocked out of me."

"You're certain?"

"Yes, milord." Jeremy looked around and saw what Connor had already noticed. Jeremy's horse was back on its feet, limping slightly as it moved nervously around on the path but apparently none the worse for its spill. Both Jeremy and the horse had been miraculously lucky not to have been seriously hurt.

But that was the bad thing about miracles, thought Connor. They used up a man's supply of good luck all too quickly.

"Hurry, milord," Jeremy urged him. "We must mount up and hie ourselves away from here—"

"No time for that now, lad." Connor nodded grimly toward the torches, which showed clearly that the bandits had almost overtaken them. One of the burning brands, in fact, had drawn even with them and was less than half a bowshot off the path. The others were almost as close. No doubt other bandits had arrows nocked at this very moment, just waiting for a signal from their leader before loosing the shafts.

"Sir Connor . . ."

Connor heard regret in the squire's voice, but no fear. "Draw your sword, lad," he said softly. "Perhaps we can lure the rats from their holes and at least give a good accounting of ourselves."

He raised his voice and shouted into the woods, "Show yourselves, if you dare!"

A voice came back from the darkness. "We dare, sir knight," it said mockingly. "We would dare much indeed to make ours that chest your squire is carrying."

Connor and Jeremy both glanced at the pouch where the chest rested. They saw to their surprise that an arrow was embedded in the pouch. Most of the shaft was broken off, no doubt in the tumble Jeremy had taken when his horse fell. Only the fact that the arrow had struck the chest had prevented it from piercing Jeremy's side.

Connor laughed harshly. "I'll not give up my goods to the likes of you," he said, taunting the unseen bandits.

"You'll have no choice in the matter, sir knight. We shall take them from your dead bodies."

Connor lifted his sword and challenged, "Come out and fight, damn you!"

"I think not. Lads, ready your bows."

Connor felt his heart sinking. 'Twas not dying he minded so much, he thought; 'twas dying with his sword unbloodied and his enemies unscathed. His muscles tensed in anticipation of steel-tipped arrows driving into his body.

The sky opened, and lightning leaped and crashed all through the wood.

Connor stumbled back, lifting an arm to shield his eyes from the terrible blinding glare as sheets of white fire ripped through the trees on both sides of the path. Beside him, Jeremy cried out in shock and fear. Screams came from the woods as trees toppled and flames leaped high. A man clad in the rough green garb of a woodsman came running onto the path, his face twisted with sheer terror. He carried a sword in his hand, and as he saw Connor and Jeremy, he shouted curses and lunged at them, lifting the blade high. "Demons!" he screeched. "Ye've called down demons on us!"

Connor shoved Jeremy out of harm's way and brought up his own sword to block the crazed bandit's stroke. The impact as blade met blade shivered up Connor's arm, but he felt no pain. There was no time for it now. This was life and death.

The bandit was too frightened to fight effectively. Connor parried skillfully, then thrust with his own blade. It sank into the bandit's chest, causing the man's eyes to bulge in pain. The bandit fell as Connor pulled his sword free.

The clash of steel behind him made him whirl around. Another of the bandits who had survived the cataclysm was crossing swords with Jeremy. The squire, though white-faced with fear, fought valiantly. Connor wrapped both hands around the handle of his sword and chopped at the back of the bandit's neck. The blade sunk deep beneath the man's helm. He fell forward, his head practically shorn from his shoulders. Jeremy scrambled to get out of the way of the falling corpse.

"Your back to my back!" Connor shouted as he looked around for the next enemy. He felt Jeremy's back pressed against his as they defended each other.

But there was no one to defend against now. No more of the bandits came out of the trees. They were either dead, struck down by the incredible force of nature that had erupted without warning, or they had fled.

Connor was breathing hard, and now that the excitement of battle was dying in his veins, his shoulder began to ache again.

He straightened from his fighting crouch and looked into the woods. Small fires burned here and there, started by the lightning.

"Did . . . did you ever see anything like it, milord?" Jeremy asked in a trembling voice. "I never did," he went on without waiting for an answer. "The sky was clear, I swear 'twas, Sir Connor. Lightning cannot strike out of a clear sky, can it?"

"Evidently it can," said Connor as he slid his sword back into its scabbard. He looked around and saw that both horses were some distance down the path. They had bolted when the heavens had exploded, but they were well-trained and had come to a halt when the cataclysm had ended.

" 'Twas magic," whispered Jeremy. "That was no natural lightning."

Connor took a deep breath. He had heard stories of odd things while he was in the Holy Land, but that had never made him believe in magic.

"I care not what brought the lightning," he said, "only that it delivered us from certain death—"

"Milord! Look!"

Connor looked where the squire was pointing. The fires that had been burning in the woods were dying out. The flames grew smaller and smaller until they eventually disappeared, as if they had snuffed themselves out.

Connor swallowed and said, "Fires go out. 'Tis a natural occurrence."

"Not when they have such an abundance of fuel." Jeremy sniffed loudly. "And smell the air, milord. Do you smell aught of burned wood?"

Connor took a deep breath, and truth to tell, he smelled nothing other than the scent of rich earth and horse droppings from the path. It was impossible to tell from any sensory indication that the woods had been ablaze in half a dozen places only moments earlier.

"Magic," Jeremy repeated, his voice filled with awe.

Connor would argue that with him later. Right now, he was interested only in putting this section of the wood behind them. "Come," he said. "We must catch those horses."

And yet, as he strode along the path with a still-shivering

Jeremy beside him, he could not help but glance behind and wonder what lurked back there in the darkness of the wood.

Alura had almost convinced herself that the entire experience had been a flight of fancy when the two djinn reappeared, coming through the wall once more as streamers of smoke that swirled and coalesced into the forms she had seen before.

"Connor . . . ?" Alura asked.

The woman smiled at her. "He and his young companion are safe, but 'twas a near thing. Now, you should know who we are. I am Radiya, and this is my husband Zahir. We are the djinn of the bracelet and the ring."

Alura nodded. What else could she do?

"Sir Connor brought us with him from what you call the Holy Land," Radiya went on. "We have been watching and waiting for such a long time to be free of the gems once more."

"You are from . . . Palestine?" asked Alura. She tried not to think about the strangeness of this conversation.

"Not originally," Zahir said. "Originally we're from the glorious kingdom of Azlon, but we have had many masters in our time as djinn. We were carried to Palestine by a merchant in a caravan. He bought the bracelet and the ring from a thief who stole them from a sultan, who had traded fifty virgins to a sorcerer for them, and the sorcerer got the bracelet and the ring from an ancient tomb deep in the desert guarded by a demon—"

"I warned you, did I not?" said Radiya. "He loves nothing more than the sound of his own voice. To him, it is as sweet as the tinkling of temple bells in the evening."

Alura closed her eyes and pressed the balls of her hands to her forehead. After a moment, when she was able to look at the two djinn again, she said, "You . . . you live in the bracelet and the ring?"

"Of course," Zahir said. "Where else? Some djinn like lamps, but I never cared for them myself. People pour oil in there, and let me tell you, it's terrible trying to get lamp oil out of carpets. Not to mention when they try to light the things—"

"Enough," snapped Radiya. Clearly, she was accustomed to breaking into Zahir's ramblings. She turned back to Alura and went on, "Our history is not important. All you need know is that we are magic spirits, and we are bound to your will now that you have summoned us from the fire opals. We must fulfill your every wish, and our magic is very powerful." Her voice became more solemn. "Therefore, you must be very careful when you speak. Do not wish for anything that you do not really want."

Alura nodded in understanding. Perhaps it was a dream after all, she thought. Perhaps she had only dreamed that she slapped herself, which was why it had failed to awaken her. That made as much sense as believing that these two so-called magic spirits could live inside gems and could be summoned to fulfill the wishes of whoever had summoned them.

" 'Tis time to wake up now," Alura said, barely aware that she had spoken the words aloud.

Radiya smiled and said gently, "You *are* awake. I know this must seem like a dream to you, but it is not. It is real, Alura."

"But . . . but you speak our language! How can that be possible if you are from this . . . this Azlon? I have never heard of it."

"We're djinn," Zahir said, as if that explained everything.

"As I said, our powers are considerable," Radiya said. "We can observe what is happening in the outside world while we are in our gems, and we learned your tongue from watching Connor and Jeremy ever since they set sail from Palestine bound for England. It was not difficult."

"Then you know about Connor."

"We know . . . what we know," Radiya said, and Alura could tell that she was being deliberately vague.

"He has asked for my hand in marriage, and my father will see to it that the match comes about." Alura frowned. "Perhaps I should wish that Sir Connor Warrick would disappear."

Both Zahir and Radiya looked stricken. "You . . . you don't really want to do that, do you?" asked Zahir. "We could do it, of course, but—"

"It would be a mistake," Radiya finished for him.

"Besides," Zahir added, "marriage is a wonderful thing! Everyone should be married. It's the best thing since fire, and I should know—"

"Pay no heed to his prattling, Alura. You really do not wish for Connor to disappear, do you?"

Alura took a deep breath and sighed. "No, I suppose not. What I really wish is that my father was a reasonable man."

Zahir and Radiya exchanged a quick look. "Miracles we can perform right away," said Zahir, "but some things take a little longer."

"Our magic has more effect on the physical realm," Radiya said. "It's much more difficult to change a human mind."

Zahir nodded. "Stubborn as boulders, you humans are."

Alura could take no more. She had seen things tonight that human eyes were not meant to see, had witnessed things that had stunned her brain and brought her to the brink of oblivion. Now, suddenly, she was tired. "You have to do what I ask of you?" she said.

Both djinn nodded. "We are bound to follow your will," Radiya said.

"All right. I want both of you to go back where you came from and let me sleep. I . . . I cannot think about any of this again tonight."

Zahir crossed his arms over his chest and nodded. "Your wish is our—"

"Come along," Radiya told him. "There's no need to say that every time."

Already, her form was turning back into smoke. Alura sat on the edge of the bed and watched as Zahir also became transparent and wispy. When both djinn had transformed once more into smoke, they were sucked back into the fire opals, vanishing in the blink of an eye.

Alura reached down and picked up the bracelet and the ring. She looked at the pieces of jewelry for a long moment. There was movement in each of the gems, she saw. Deep within them, something swirled and eddied, reminding her of the smoke that had given birth to the two strange creatures who had visited her. For a heartbeat, Alura poised her fingertip over the gem on the bracelet, then withdrew it. She didn't want to test her sanity again so soon.

Instead she placed the bracelet and the ring on the table, and this time she succeeded in blowing out the candle.

But as darkness fell over the chamber, the two fire opals glowed briefly with a light of their own, reminding Alura of eyes watching her from the shadows.

Exhausted though she was, it was a long time before sleep claimed her.

The darkness outside the circle of firelight was so thick that it was almost a living thing. The roughly garbed men who hunkered around the small blaze cast furtive glances at the shadows, glances filled with fear and bordering on panic. All save one man, whose scowl was dark with anger.

"Magic," he muttered. "Satan's teeth, but I hate magic!"

"Near got us all killed," growled one of the other men. "We lost Merton and Farrar, as 'twas."

"Aye, Dermot," said another man. "A high price to pay for naught."

Dermot, the man who hated magic, swung around toward the two who had complained. His expression was even darker now. His hand went to the short sword sheathed at his waist. "Think you to challenge me and my leadership of this band?" he demanded. His eyes glittered with rage in the firelight.

The two who had spoken shook their heads quickly and looked down into the dancing flames. Neither of them wanted to meet the baleful gaze of their leader.

Dermot uncoiled from his sitting position, coming to his feet in one lithe motion. He turned his back to the fire and stared instead into the surrounding darkness. He had not been looking directly into the flames; he was too wise in the ways of the wood for that. Fire stole a man's sight, and the few heartbeats that were required for it to return might mean the difference between life and death.

Slightly over medium height, Dermot was a compelling figure with piercing eyes and a shock of dark hair. He had a closely trimmed beard, and his jaw was slightly prominent on both sides of his face. His woodsman's garb bulged with muscles in his arms, shoulders, and legs. A sheathed sword hung from the broad belt around his waist, and a quiver of arrows rode on his back. His longbow, curved with a deadly grace, was near at hand. He had lived in these woods and led this band of cutthroats and thieves for nearly a year, and in that time, he had never failed. Not once.

Defeat was a bitter, galling taste in his mouth.

Somewhere out there in the darkness was a force, he thought, a force unlike any he had ever before encountered. He did not fear swords or arrows; he would match his men and their weapons against anything short of an army.

But white fire that crackled and struck like lightning out of nowhere could not be warded off with a wooden shield. It could not be pierced with an arrow or cut with a sword. There was no defense against the thing that had attacked them tonight and saved that damned nobleman and his squire.

It had seemed like such an easy task. One of the serving girls at Welwynd, a wench named Nessa who enjoyed a visit from Dermot from time to time, had passed word to the band that a visiting knight who had come to the keep for a tournament was carrying a small wooden chest full of gems and jewelry and other treasures from the Holy Land. This evening, unexpectedly, the signal had come that the knight was already leaving Welwynd, accompanied only by his squire. The chest full of treasures was ripe for plucking.

Dermot and his men had tracked the knight and the squire for several leagues before moving ahead and setting up their ambush. It should have worked, too. Only bad luck—and poor aim—had allowed the two intended victims to escape the first volley. Then, Dermot had known some bad moments when it looked as if they would escape on their fine horses.

Fate had once again intervened, this time on the side of Dermot and his bandits. The squire's horse had taken a tumble, and then, for some unfathomable reason, the knight had stopped to aid the boy, rather than simply abandoning him as any intelligent man would have.

The reason wasn't totally unfathomable, Dermot reminded himself as he brooded over the events of the night. The squire was carrying the treasure chest. That would have been enough by itself to make the knight turn back.

But Dermot had seen something else in the knight's fierce gaze. Courage, honor, loyalty to the squire, the look of a man whose blood grew hot at the prospect of battle. Dermot shared that last quality. He would have liked nothing better than to stride out of the woods and answer the knight's challenge, settling things man against man, steel against steel.

Of course, that would not have been the prudent, profitable thing to do, so Dermot hadn't done it. He had been about to give the signal for his men to fire another volley of arrows . . .

. . . when the sky had opened up and loosed all the forces of hell upon them.

Not since Dermot had been a child, cowering under the beatings given him by his master, had he known such terror. When the lightning struck and trees toppled and burst into a terrible flame that somehow consumed without giving off heat, he had thrown himself on the ground and cowered there until it was all over. He could still taste dirt in his mouth, could still hear the awful crackling of the lightning and the howling of the wind and the screams of his men. His jaws ached from the force with which he had clamped them shut to keep from shrieking. Only he knew how afraid he had been.

And he hated that feeling.

The only way to end fear was to conquer the cause of it. That was a hard lesson Dermot had learned years earlier, when he had finally tired of the beatings from the knight he was bound to serve. The arrogant warrior had certainly never expected the whipped, cowering boy to strike back. Surprise had been on Dermot's side.

Surprise, and the strength given to him by his rage, had allowed him to thrust a sword completely through the unsuspecting knight's body. All these years later, Dermot still felt a rush of satisfaction whenever he thought of the look of pain and shock that had bloomed in the knight's eyes just before he had died.

So his course was clear. The mystical force that had brought fear back to him tonight had to be conquered, and to do that, he would have to possess it.

"I know not where or what you are," he murmured as he stared out at the night and its portents, "but you will be mine. This I swear . . . no matter who has to die."

Twelve

Alura awoke from an exhausted sleep the next morning in the chamber she had been given at Welwynd. Despite her slumber, she was still weary, and at first the events of the night before seemed naught but a dream, and a strange, fevered, impossible one, at that. Then her gaze fell on the bracelet and the ring, still lying on the table where she had left them the night before, and her breath froze in her throat.

Had it all been real? Were such things even possible? Alura reached out and picked up the bracelet and the ring, feeling the weight of the heavy gold in her hand. She held them close to her face and squinted, narrowing her eyes as she tried to peer into the glowing depths of the matching fire opals.

Something—or someone—seemed to be looking back at her.

Alura gasped and thrust the jewelry away from her. She was sorely tempted to rub the gems and see what happened, but not here, not while she was at Welwynd. For some reason, she wanted to be back home at Brynclair before she experimented with the gems again.

She arose and dressed, wincing occasionally from the pain in her still-sore foot, then started to pack away the bracelet and the ring with her other belongings for the journey back to

Brynclair. She recalled then that Connor had given them to her as a gift to mark their betrothal. A sense of mischief arose within her, a desire to set the tongues of the ladies still at Welwynd to wagging again. She slipped the ring onto her finger, then thrust her wrist through the bracelet. Once more she was struck by how well the jewelry fit her. The gold felt warm against her skin, almost as if it were alive.

Alura did her best to banish that thought as she went downstairs to the great hall. Her mother and father were waiting for her, and her father looked pleased when he saw she was wearing the bracelet and the ring. He probably took it as a sign that she had come to accept what had happened.

"Good morning, daughter," de Gabin said heartily. "I trust you slept well."

"I slept," said Alura as she sat down at the table next to her mother. Servants were bringing out platters of meat and bread and jugs of ale and mead. The long table was crowded with the guests who had remained overnight at Welwynd, and as Alura glanced along its length, she saw that that was everyone except Connor. Sir Oswald was sprawled in the great chair at the head of the table, his chin propped on his hand, a drowsy expression on his face. He winced every time there was a loud noise, as did most of the other men. Clearly, they had downed too many flagons of mead the night before. Sir Herve was one of the few who seemed unaffected, but Alura knew that his capacity for strong drink had reached near-legendary status in the area.

"Eat, eat," muttered Sir Oswald as he waved his free hand at the food. He himself seemed not to have much of an appetite.

Alura, on the other hand, found herself to be quite hungry. As she took bites from a piece of bread that was still warm from the oven, her father gestured at the jewelry on her left hand and said, "I see that you are wearing Sir Connor's gift."

That quieted some of the talk around the table. Mention of Connor's name usually did, thought Alura. She glanced at the bracelet and the ring and said, "It would be impolite not to wear such a gift, would it not?"

"Then the fact that Sir Connor is to be your husband is satisfactory to you?"

Katharine de Gabin shot a glare at her husband, as if trying to warn him that he was assuming too much, and too quickly, at that. Alura merely said, "The arrangements have not yet been made."

"They will be," said de Gabin.

"We shall see."

He frowned. "You are a headstrong young woman. Sometimes I wonder if you are my daughter at all."

"Herve!" Katharine's eyes widened in anger and shock.

"A changeling, that is what I meant," de Gabin said hurriedly. "I assure you, dear wife, I meant no stain on your honor. I meant merely that sometimes I wonder if imps from the pit exchanged our sweet little babe for a . . . a demon child."

Katharine sniffed. "That is little better than what you originally said." She turned to her daughter. "I apologize for your father, Alura."

She shook her head and said, "No matter."

They would all believe her to be a demon child indeed, she thought, if she rubbed those two fire opals and summoned up the djinn. . . .

After everyone had eaten, preparations got underway for the guests to depart from Welwynd. Some lived within a day's ride, but others would be almost a sennight on the road before they reached home.

That thought went through Alura's mind as she stepped out into the hubbub of the castle's bailey, and it reminded her that Connor would be visiting Brynclair in a mere sennight to make final the arrangements for the marriage. She had only seven days to come up with some acceptable reason for not marrying him.

Perhaps she should summon the djinn and wish all her problems away, she mused. Better yet, she could wish herself away from the problems and into an impregnable castle of her own, with a high tower where she could retreat and no one could ever bother her again.

But such a life would be terribly lonely, she told herself.

As annoying and venal as her father could be, she would not wish to spend the rest of her life without ever seeing the old knight again. And Alura would certainly miss her mother so desperately that she would not be able to stand the loss.

Besides, who was to say that the djinn would actually appear if she rubbed the gems once more?

By midmorning, the party was on its way back to Brynclair, and they arrived there while the sun was still fairly high in the sky that afternoon. Alura pleaded fatigue from the journey—which was not, in itself, a falsehood, since she was quite tired—and went upstairs to her bedchamber to rest.

When the door of the room was firmly shut behind her, she sat on the edge of her bed and held her left hand out in front of her hesitating. Was what she was about to do somehow blasphemous? She remembered warnings from the priests about evil spirits.

The late afternoon light that came in through the window gleamed on the gold and gems. Alura took a deep breath and moved her right hand to the bracelet and the ring, spreading her fingers slightly so that she could rub both of the fire opals at the same time. When she had done so, she gave a little gasp and jerked her hand back, expecting the same deafening thunderclap and blinding flash that had followed her summoning of the djinn at Welwynd. She half-expected her arm to be burned, since she was actually wearing the jewelry this time instead of holding it.

Instead, she felt only a slight tingling on her skin. It was not an unpleasant sensation. Then she gasped again as coils of thick gray smoke spiraled up from the gems.

The pillars of smoke separated from the bracelet and the ring and formed themselves into human shapes, just as they had done before. Alura watched, openmouthed with awe, as Zahir and Radiya became solid. It was beyond her comprehension how smoke could turn into something real and substantial, but she could not doubt the evidence of her eyes. Powerful sorcery was at work here.

Zahir looked around the room for a moment and then nodded. "So this is your home," he said. "It's nice. Nothing like our castle back in Azlon, mind you, but perfectly acceptable.''

''Our castle back in Azlon has been rubble-strewn on the bottom of the sea for thousands of years,'' Radiya pointed out. ''I much prefer this.'' She smiled at Alura. ''How are you today, dear?''

''I . . . I'm fine,'' replied Alura. ''You . . . you are real.''

''Of course we are,'' said Radiya with a smile. ''Do you doubt the evidence of your own eyes?''

''After the past few days, I doubt my own sanity half the time.'' Alura reached out. ''Can . . . can I touch you?''

She gasped as Radiya took her hand. ''You see, we are as real as we can possibly be.''

Zahir patted her shoulder in an avuncular fashion. ''Now you have to believe in us.''

Alura swallowed. ''Not yet. Show me some magic.''

''Surely our very appearance from the gems—'' began Radiya.

Alura shook her head and said, ''No. I want to see something really magical. I command it.''

Radiya and Zahir exchanged a glance, and then Zahir said, ''Well, if you insist. Take our hands.''

With her heart pounding, Alura clasped hands with both of the djinn. They led her over to the window of her bedchamber. ''Are you ready?'' asked Radiya.

Alura managed to nod shakily as she wondered what the djinn had in mind. ''I am ready,'' she said, sounding more courageous than she really felt.

''Hold tight,'' cautioned Zahir.

Then, with no more warning than that, they flew out the window, taking Alura with them.

She screamed as the ground was suddenly flashing past, far beneath her. Flanked by the djinn, each of them holding tightly to one of her hands, she flew above Brynclair and the surrounding grounds at dizzying heights and speeds.

''God save us!'' Alura gasped.

''You really need a magic carpet to fly properly,'' Zahir shouted over the roar of the wind that filled Alura's ears, ''but we can manage just fine on our own when we have to.''

Now that the initial shock was fading and Alura began to

feel that the djinn would not allow her to fall, she found herself growing interested in what she was experiencing. As they swooped back and forth over the estate, she peered down and saw her father's serfs moving around. They reminded her of insects scurrying at her feet.

"Why don't they look up?" she called after a moment. "Don't they see us?"

"We have cast a pall of invisibility over the three of us," explained Radiya. "None can see or hear us unless we wish it."

This was amazing, thought Alura, and still more than a bit terrifying, as well. But she had to admit it was certainly an impressive piece of magic, and that was what she had asked for.

"Take me back," she called. "I've had enough!"

"You're sure?" asked Zahir.

"I'm sure! Take me back!"

They banked into a turn that carried them back toward the castle at blinding speed. As the thick stone walls loomed up in front of them, Alura squeezed her eyes shut in fear. She kept her tight grip on the hands of the djinn. Suddenly, she felt the floor under her feet again, solid and steady. She opened her eyes, saw that she was back in her own chamber, and looked to each side. Radiya and Zahir stood there, beaming with pride.

Alura's eyes rolled up in her head, and she pitched forward onto her bed.

She came to a few moments later, blinking her eyes open to find Radiya and Zahir staring down at her anxiously. Radiya was rubbing her wrists. "You are all right, mistress?" asked Zahir.

Alura sat up. She gave a little shake of her head, trying to clear away the cobwebs of passing out. There was no doubt about it now, she thought. She could not have imagined what had just happened. The djinn were indeed real, and she would have to accept that.

"I am fine," she said. "I believe you now."

"Wonderful," said Radiya. "Do you want to know how Connor is today?"

"Why should I?"

Zahir said, "You're betrothed to the lad. Surely you feel some affection and concern for him."

"Not necessarily," said Alura. "Besides, how can you tell anything about him when you're here and I assume he is at Stavebrook?" That was a foolish question to ask, she realized as soon as she had said it, considering how they had just demonstrated their powers to her.

"Our ability to see into the human realm is not without limits, but it *is* far-reaching," Radiya explained patiently. "We are especially able to observe the lives of those who are closely bound to our master."

"Or in this case, our mistress," added Zahir.

"I am bound to Connor Warrick only by ill fortune," said Alura. "And I believe he would agree. I do not think he wants to marry me any more than I want to be wed to him."

Radiya looked solemnly at her—or at least, as solemnly as anyone could look while wearing such a gaudy, outrageous costume. "And yet you *are* betrothed to him."

"He was forced into making that proposal," said Alura. "Sir Oswald Duparc goaded him into it, along with my father."

"Do you really believe that a man such as Sir Connor Warrick can be forced to do anything he does not wish to?" Radiya asked softly.

Alura hesitated, unsure of the answer to that question. From what she knew of Connor, he had always gone his own way, little caring what anyone might say to or about him. He did as he pleased and took what he wanted. That, more than anything else, defined the Connor Warrick she knew.

Yet the Crusades could have changed him, she thought. Perhaps the ordeal he had gone through in the Holy Land made him more likely to care about what others thought . . . although to be honest, Alura had seen no evidence of such a change in him.

Nor had she seen the vile, unfeeling brute that he was supposed to be, either. It was all quite vexing, trying to reconcile what was said of a man with what he was really like.

"Whether Sir Connor wants to marry me or not, I do not

want to marry him," Alura said. " 'Tis as simple as that, and I must find a way to make both my father and Connor accept that decision."

Radiya shook her head in amazement. "Things must have changed a great deal in the world since we last walked it as humans, if a female can now bear sole responsibility for deciding what path she will walk."

Alura frowned, wondering if the djinni was making light of her.

Zahir said, "You mean the king does not decide who weds, and who does not?"

"Well . . . to a certain extent the king wields such power . . ."

"And the priests of your religion?" asked Radiya. "Do they not also have a great deal of influence?"

" 'Tis true that a priest must bless every marriage."

"So, let me be sure I understand," said Zahir. "If your father wants you to marry Sir Connor, and the king approves, and the priests give their blessing . . . you can still say no?"

Alura took a deep breath. In truth, she could not refuse to marry Connor if he and her father concluded their arrangements successfully and Prince John approved of the marriage. But she hated to admit that, even to herself.

"I could wish that the two of you would make a pox fall on Stavebrook and all its inhabitants," she said in a surly voice.

Zahir shook his head rapidly. "Oh, no, you don't want to do that! Poxes are dreadful, filthy things. Better an earthquake or a nice clean bolt of lightning—"

Radiya stepped between him and Alura. "We do not like to destroy things," she said. "We are bound to your will, of course, but would it not be much better to see if a suitable compromise could be reached?"

"Compromise?" repeated Alura. "What sort of compromise?"

"Get to know the boy," suggested Zahir around Radiya's shoulder. "See if perhaps he might make a good husband for you after all."

"He is the Beast of Stavebrook!" Alura could not stop the exclamation from leaping out of her mouth.

"He is called one thing," said Radiya. "Might he not really be something else entirely?"

Similar thoughts had gone through Alura's head only moments earlier, and now, hearing them spoken to her, she knew that there could be some truth to them. Connor was not nearly as bestial as she had always been led to believe. He had even been kind to her at times. She had seen the look in his eyes when he asked her to dance at Sir Oswald's ball. He had done it because he knew how much the malicious words of the ladies had hurt her. When she closed her eyes and cast her mind back to that moment, she seemed to feel the hard warmth of his body once again. She remembered how his arm had supported her and how safe she had felt in his embrace.

If only the evening had ended there. If only her father had not made his totally uncalled-for declaration. If only Sir Oswald had not goaded Connor....

"If only," thought Alura, were two terrible words indeed.

The djinn were right. She looked up at them and said cautiously, "I will give him a chance. But I make no promises."

Zahir and Radiya both beamed. "I do not think you will be disappointed," said Radiya.

Alura came to her feet. "But now, there is another question."

"What's that?" asked Zahir.

"What in God's name am I to do with the two of *you*?"

It was amazing to Connor how drab and lifeless the halls of the keep at Stavebrook seemed now. Not that the place had ever been overly gaudy and ringing with laughter, even when he was a child. Connor's mother had died when he was quite young, and his father had never remarried. The only feminine touch the keep had known had been that of the servants.

But now, as Connor frequently found himself stalking back and forth on the rushes in the great hall, images of long red hair that was like silken fire filled his mind. Memories of a slender, graceful shape haunted him. And there were times he could have sworn that he still tasted Alura's lips.

Once she was here, he would have to brighten the place up, he thought. He would set the weavers to the task of making tapestries for the walls that would rival her brilliant beauty. His mother's silver and crystal, long since packed away and replaced by sturdier, more efficient wooden bowls and utensils, would be brought out and displayed once more on the sideboards. He would even hang brightly colored silk pennants from the ramparts and battlements of the keep, he decided. All of this to welcome his new bride. There was only one problem with his plans.

He had no wish to marry. A wife was perhaps the last thing he had wanted when he returned to England from the Crusades.

It was a devilish problem, brought on by pride, poor timing, and plain bad luck. And the most vexing thing about it was that he could not hack his way out of this dilemma with a sword or a battle-ax. Connor knew that Alura desired this marriage as little as he did, yet how could he call it off without making it appear that he was rejecting her?

He was sitting in his chair in the great hall, brooding over that very question, when Jeremy came in. Connor noticed the scrap of multicolored fur draped over the lad's shoulder and said, "Good Lord, what is that?"

The scrap of fur lifted its head and turned it to look at Connor with wide green eyes. " 'Tis a cat, milord," said Jeremy as he lifted a hand to stroke the creature perched on his shoulder.

"I can see that. The animal should be in the granary, keeping out the vermin." Connor had no great liking for cats, but as long as they did their job, he could put up with them. He had never believed, as some of the priests did, that the creatures were frequently possessed by demons.

"Mossgrave says she's too old and cannot catch mice anymore," replied Jeremy. "I thought, with your permission, milord, that I might take her as a pet."

Connor frowned. He had never had a pet when he was young, but he supposed he could understand why Jeremy might want one. He shrugged and said, "It matters naught to me, so long as the beast does not drink up all the cream from the kitchen. And keep her away from the hounds, lest she claw their noses.''

"Thank you, milord." Jeremy scratched the cat's ears, causing it to paw at his shoulder in contentment. "I think I shall call her Matilda."

"Call her Beelzebub, for all I care," muttered Connor.

"Were the men-at-arms able to find the trail of those bandits?" Jeremy asked, changing the subject.

Upon arriving safely at Stavebrook two nights past, Connor had alerted his men-at-arms to the attack in the woods, and a group of them, captained by a knight named Berenger, had set out at first light the next morning in an attempt to track down the brigands. They had returned this very afternoon, unfortunately having been unsuccessful in their quest.

Connor shook his head in response to Jeremy's question. "They slipped away like foxes," he said, "all save the two we killed. Sir Berenger and the other knights recognized neither of them. Woodland louts, interested only in what they could steal, no doubt."

"Sir Connor, we have not spoken of what else happened that night."

Connor's hands tightened on the arms of his chair. "You mean the lightning storm?"

"I mean the magic, milord," said Jeremy, his voice little more than a whisper.

"I saw no magic," snapped Connor. "I saw only a . . . a freak of nature."

"But the night was clear, milord. Surely, lightning cannot strike out of a clear sky, can it, Sir Connor?"

Connor was not sure of that. Each time he met Alura's eyes, he felt as if the very air itself was crackling with a mysterious power about to be unleashed. . . .

"I know not," he said in answer to Jeremy's question. "I know only that I have never seen anything I would call magic."

Jeremy shifted the cat on his shoulder and looked down at the rushes. "Very well, milord. We shall speak no more of it."

"Good." Connor came up out of his chair, uncoiling in a

lithe motion. All this thinking was bad for a man, he decided. He felt the need to be out and about, doing something instead of sitting. His right arm was still sore and stiff from the fall he had suffered during the tournament, but it was hardly an incapacitating injury. He could ride with no pain at all. Perhaps it was time that he inspected the fields and assured himself that the spring planting had been carried out as it should have been. There was a great deal to running an estate of this size, a great many things that had never been his concern while Morvyn was still alive. And though Mossgrave, while clearly not trustworthy in certain matters, had always been competent when it came to managing Stavebrook, Connor found himself unwilling to leave things completely to the seneschal.

He would run Stavebrook, by God! The place was his, and the workers would simply have to grow accustomed to having him around, looking over their shoulders as they went about their tasks.

Connor stalked toward the entrance to the great hall, and Jeremy called after him, "Do you require my services, milord?"

"Not now," replied Connor. He thought that despite Jeremy's promise, the lad was entirely likely to bring up those strange happenings in the woods once more, and Connor definitely did not want to think about that.

Nor about the Lady Alura, and his impending marriage to her. . . .

Three days gone, thought Alura. Three out of seven. Three closer to the day Sir Connor Warrick would return to Brynclair and make the final arrangements for his marriage to her.

A part of her mind still wanted to believe that it would never happen, that somehow fate would intervene and that she would not be forced to wed the so-called Beast of Stavebrook.

But even if that came to pass, unlikely though it might be, would she always wonder what she had missed by not being Connor's bride?

And then there was the matter of the djinn. . . .

So far they had been quite cooperative, returning to their homes in the gems whenever Alura commanded it. Of course, they had no choice, she reminded herself. They had to obey her; it was in their very nature. But Zahir was growing restive. He wanted leave to go out and explore the surrounding countryside at leisure.

"It's so much different here than where we come from," he explained in Alura's chamber when she had summoned them that evening. "So green everywhere. Azlon was a paradise, of course, with trees and gardens and mountains and the deep blue sea surrounding everything, but since we've been djinn, most of the places we've visited have been desert. So much sand everywhere, and it's so hot you think you're melting. I remember once when we were in Egypt, and our master's slaves were building this pyramid and thousands of them would die from the heat—"

"Enough of your prattle," Radiya cut in. "Can you not see that the poor girl is worried?"

"Worried?" Zahir looked bewildered. "About what?"

"I am betrothed to Sir Connor, remember?" said Alura with a sigh. "And I do not wish to marry."

"You said you would give him a chance," Zahir reminded her.

"We had many opportunities to observe him during the voyage from what you call the Holy Land," said Radiya. "He is a man of honor, Lady Alura, though what he regards as honorable is not always the same as everyone else."

"I sensed that about him. He has his own code." Alura sat down on the edge of the bed, putting out of her head the thought that she was carrying on a conversation with a pair of magical spirits. She had come to regard them as visitors from a foreign land. Powerful visitors.

"And you liked it when he kissed you, too, I'll wager," Zahir said with a broad grin.

Alura felt herself growing warm with embarrassment again. She made no reply, leaving it up to Radiya to say, "Oh, go back in your bracelet, Zahir. *I* will speak with the Lady Alura."

Zahir bristled. "You want me to go back in the bracelet, do you?"

"Yes, I do."

"All right, that's just what I'll do." He glanced at Alura. "If my mistress so commands, of course."

Alura nodded, suddenly anxious to speak with Radiya alone. Zahir might still be able to hear what was being said, but at least she would not have to face him.

Zahir was already turning smoky. He finished his transformation, and his wispy form disappeared into the fire opal on the bracelet as if it had been sucked into the gem. Radiya sat on the bed beside Alura and said to her in a conspiratorial tone, "So tell me, how does it make you feel when Connor is around?"

"Very . . . odd," Alura said. "Frightened at times. After all, he is known to be a ruthless man, and he murdered one of his lovers."

"You know this to be true?"

"Everyone says—"

Radiya stopped Alura's reply by shaking her head. "Do *you* know it to be true, beyond a doubt?"

Alura thought for a moment, then drew a deep breath and said, "No. Poor Elspeth died of a fall from one of the towers at Stavebrook, but that is all I know of a certainty."

"What else does Connor make you feel?" prodded Radiya.

Alura frowned. "I was grateful when he danced with me at Welwynd. And he made me feel . . . safe somehow . . . when his arm was around me."

Radiya leaned closer. "And when he kissed you?"

This was decidedly bizarre, thought Alura. She was sitting here and gossiping with Radiya as if the other woman were a maiden aunt instead of a centuries-old djinni. She had never even heard of djinn until a few days earlier, and now she had seemingly accepted her two strange visitors as a part of her life. Perhaps that ease of acceptance was part of the magical spell cast over the bracelet and the ring.

Alura took another deep breath and said, "When Connor kissed me, it was like nothing I have ever experienced before."

"You were betrothed to Connor's brother. Surely you kissed him at some time?"

" 'Twas not the same," Alura said emphatically. "Morvyn's touch never excited me, especially after he—''

She stopped short, not wanting to return, even in her mind, to the day that had changed everything between her and Morvyn Warrick.

"Connor is different," Alura went on quickly. "His kiss stirs me, Radiya. It . . . it may be sinful to admit to such feelings, but I have felt them nonetheless. I wanted him to continue kissing me, and to touch me . . . I wanted to touch him." Alura's hand went to her mouth. "Oh! This is shameful."

"Not at all," said Radiya. "There is no shame in what a man and a woman in love do together."

"In love?" Alura laughed shakily. "That cannot be. He is Connor Warrick, the—''

"I know, the Beast of Stavebrook. One thing you must remember, Alura: the past is gone. And as Zahir would say, we should know. Look you to the present, and the future. Everything else is naught but shadows in the mist."

And from the bracelet, Alura seemed to hear Zahir rumbling in agreement.

Thirteen

⌒

The sennight had passed more quickly than either Alura or Connor would have dreamed that it could, and so Connor came again to Brynclair, on a day when spring rains swept the countryside. There was something about Connor and rain, thought Alura as she stood in the window of her chamber and watched as down below Connor and his squire Jeremy entered the inner bailey on horseback, followed by a group of Connor's men-at-arms from Stavebrook.

The rain today was much different than the time before, however. Today's showers were much gentler, as the rain fell almost softly from the heavens. It was warm, with no bits of ice mixed in with it now to sting the cheeks. Connor dismounted and turned his horse over to Jeremy, then pushed back the hood of his surcoat so that his dark hair hung down to his shoulders and drops of rain pattered on his hard-planed face. He paused there only a moment, then strode on into the castle, out of Alura's line of sight.

She took a deep breath and looked down at the bracelet on her wrist and the ring on her finger. The djinn were safely ensconced in their gems, but she seemed to hear their voices anyway, encouraging her to go down and greet Connor. Drawing strength somehow from the sensation, she left her chamber and started down the winding staircase that led to the great hall of Brynclair.

Her father had been waiting for Connor, of course, guards having brought the news that Lord Ridglea was approaching the castle. They were both in the great hall, Sir Herve's hand resting companionably on Connor's left shoulder. Connor did not look particularly pleased with the older knight's familiarity, thought Alura as she caught sight of them. She had a moment to study Connor's face before he realized she was descending the stairs and lifted his head to gaze up at her. In that moment, she saw that his expression was set as hard as ever, but she saw not even a hint of actual cruelty in his face.

Then he was looking up at her, his eyes meeting hers, and she stopped short on the stairs for a heartbeat, as if she had encountered a wall.

Good Lord, but her beauty could take a man's breath away, thought Connor as he openly stared at Alura. She wore a dark-green gown with a flowing brown cloak fastened in front by a simple gold pin. Around her small waist she wore the plain gold girdle that she favored. He wished her fiery hair was loose, instead of being covered by the plain white wimple.

He might not want a wife, but if he had, he could have done much worse than Alura de Gabin, he told himself. She was lovely, she was intelligent, and she had amply demonstrated that she was not afraid to speak her mind. To some men, that last quality would have been an obstacle to any possible marriage, but Connor had never had any use for meek women who were hesitant to voice an opinion for fear that it might offend some man.

None of that really mattered. He was here today to tell de Gabin that he was not going to marry the lady Alura. And scandal be hanged.

De Gabin followed Connor's gaze and saw Alura coming down the stairs. He took no note of her slight hesitation when Connor first looked at her. Instead he held a hand out to her and said, "Come, lass, and greet your husband-to-be."

Again Alura paused, but then she came on doggedly. She recalled her promise to Radiya and Zahir. She would get to know Connor better and give him a chance to win her over.

If such a goal was, in fact, what he had in mind. Looking at him now, at his impassive face and unreadable eyes, she had to wonder if he still intended to wed her. With no djinn to influence him, perhaps he had decided to call off the marriage after all.

In a way that would be a relief, since it would take the decision out of her hands, but at the same time, a surprising pang of loss shot through her as she considered the possibility.

Her father took hold of her hand and said heartily, "And here is the bride-to-be now." Before Alura could stop him, he had grasped Connor's arm with his other hand and brought Connor's hand to hers. Their fingers clasped, the gesture as much a matter of instinct as anything else.

Connor had never liked being touched, and his impulse was to jerk his arm away even before de Gabin could place Alura's hand in his. Once their fingers had folded over each other, however, Connor knew he could not pull away sharply without giving offense. He stood there somewhat awkwardly, holding Alura's hand. He watched as her face began to flush.

Truth to tell, the touch of her hand *was* quite pleasant. Her fingers were soft, but not weak. Her skin was warm and smooth and seemed to invite further exploration. He suddenly wondered what it would feel like to trail his fingertips over the inside of her wrist.

Alura saw something flicker in his eyes, and for an instant, just an instant, his face relaxed. The mask that his iron will kept raised most of the time was gone. In that moment she felt the strength of his fingers as they closed over hers, and she found herself wishing that she could feel that powerful touch roaming elsewhere. Perhaps up the length of her arm to her shoulder and neck. She could imagine him cupping his hand behind her head and drawing her toward him. . . .

De Gabin chuckled, breaking into whatever it was that had sprung up between them. "Well, she doesn't look as if she wants to sink a poniard into your chest, my boy. I suppose that is progress."

Alura slid her fingers out of Connor's grasp and turned angrily to her father. Before she could say anything, however, de Gabin had once more placed a hand on Connor's shoulder and steered him toward the table. "Come and sit down," said de Gabin. "I'll have one of the servants bring us a tankard of mead. We have much to discuss." Over his shoulder, he added to Alura, "Your mother is in the bakery. Please join her."

Alura almost balked. She knew what her father wanted: her out of the room while he and Connor discussed the marriage. It was not right for them to decide her future while she was not even present.

But of course, it was entirely legal according to the laws of God and man. Alura managed to nod. She left the great hall, glancing back as her father and Connor sat down at the long table. Then she turned a corner in the corridor, and that was the last she saw of them.

The air in the bakery was stiflingly hot. Katharine stood near the door of the small, square building just outside the keep, fanning her face. Clouds of steam billowed from the open door. The rain had stopped. Katharine looked at her daughter as Alura walked up. She said, "Sir Connor is here, is he not?"

Alura nodded. "Father practically chased me out of the great hall at sword's point."

"Oh, I'm certain he was not quite that abrupt."

"Almost," said Alura.

"How did Sir Connor look?"

Very handsome, Alura wanted to say, but she knew that was not what her mother meant. She shook her head and said, "I could not tell if he intends to go forward with the marriage or not."

"If he casts you aside now, there will be much talk."

"If he and I are wed, there will be much talk," said Alura. "Which is better—or worse?"

Katharine sighed. "Truly, I cannot say." She looked shrewdly at her daughter. "What do *you* want?"

"Does it matter?" said Alura, a hint of bitterness in her voice.

Her mother touched her on the arm. "In your heart, it matters."

But in neither her heart nor her head, thought Alura, could she truly answer the question of what she really wanted.

De Gabin drank deeply from the cup of mead, then cleared his throat and said, "As you know, a dowry was paid to your late brother."

Trust the man to begin with the money, thought Connor. "The coins remain in Stavebrook's coffers, untouched," he said. " 'Twould be a simple matter to return them."

De Gabin held up a hand. "No, no, that was not what I meant, Sir Connor. Are you satisfied with the amount, or will an additional sum be required?"

Connor did not answer right away. Instead he took a moment to study de Gabin, and what he saw in the old knight's eyes surprised him. De Gabin was truly worried about what Connor's answer might be concerning the dowry. Connor knew that de Gabin was notorious for his penury; 'twas said of the man that he threw farthings around as if they were giant boulders. But as de Gabin's eyes flicked away under Connor's scrutiny, Connor wondered if there was more to the question of the dowry than simple greed.

Perhaps de Gabin wanted the amount already paid to be sufficient because he had no more coin to spare.

Looking around Brynclair, one would never guess that the estate might be facing financial difficulties. But at the same time, the opulent furnishings had been here for many years. They were no indication of de Gabin's current status.

Connor put those thoughts aside. They were nothing more than idle speculation, and the matter was not really relevant. He said, "No further payment will be required."

The relief that flashed through de Gabin's eyes was unmistakable. He was right, Connor thought: de Gabin must be skating along on the very edge of poverty, keeping up appearances here at Brynclair but little more than that. And it was entirely possible that Lady Katharine and Alura knew nothing of the situation.

"Very well, then," said de Gabin, bluff and hearty once more. "All that's left to do is read the banns and petition the king for permission for the marriage to take place. I cannot imagine that Lackland would wish to stand in the way."

Connor shook his head. "No, Lackland's grip on the throne

is tenuous enough so that he would not want to risk offending either of us.''

De Gabin poured more mead from the tankard into his cup. ''Richard will come back one day, and then things will be different in England. Mark my words, Sir Connor.''

''I have no doubt you are right, Sir Herve. I served with Lion-heart in the Holy Land, remember?''

''Of course, of course.'' De Gabin downed a healthy swallow of mead. ''Now, we should determine when the wedding will take place.''

''It will not.''

For an instant, Connor thought de Gabin was going to spit out the mouthful of mead he had just taken. Instead, he managed to swallow, and his cup thumped against the table as he set it down hard. ''What do you mean, the wedding will not take place?'' he demanded.

''Just that,'' Connor said coolly. ''I have decided to withdraw my proposal. The dowry you paid to my late brother will be returned, and you will be free to seek a more suitable match for your daughter.''

''But . . . but she is betrothed to you!'' sputtered de Gabin.

Connor shook his head. ''I cannot marry her.''

''God's teeth, man! Why not?''

Like lightning striking, an idea flashed into Connor's mind. He spoke quickly, before he could consider all the implications of what he was about to say and perhaps decide not to. ''I cannot be a true husband to any woman,'' he said. ''My . . . injuries . . . in the Crusade preclude that.''

De Gabin crossed himself and muttered a prayer. Connor could tell that he was horrified by the very prospect of being unmanned. ''I thought 'twas only your shoulder,'' said de Gabin.

''The injury to my shoulder brought me nigh unto death,'' said Connor. ''The other has ofttimes left me wishing that I *had* died.''

''I can but imagine.'' A shudder ran through de Gabin. He placed his hands flat on the table and took a deep breath. ''This puts an entirely different face on things.''

Connor drank deeply from his cup of mead. He had suc-

ceeded in putting a stop to any talk of marriage, and in such
a way that the Lady Alura would bear none of the disgrace of
the broken betrothal. Of course, it would soon be bruited about
the entire countryside that he was no longer able to function
as a true man, but he supposed he could live with that. He
had no plans to bring any woman to his bed anytime soon,
anyway.

"You have my complete sympathy, lad," said de Gabin.
"And this will certainly make the business of an heir more
difficult. But not impossible, eh?"

"What?" Connor asked in surprise. "I told you, Sir Herve,
I cannot act as a husband to your daughter."

"You know that, and I know that, and so, in the fullness
of time, will she, I suppose. But we are reasonable men, and
there are other ways a woman can be got with child besides
the marriage bed. Perhaps that squire of yours. He appears
young and strong, and he is of an age when, ah, standing in
for his lord and master might be quite an appealing prospect."

Anger flared up inside Connor, anger so strong that he did
not fully know what he was doing. He stood up and stepped
back, and his hand went to his sword. "You devious old bastard!" he exclaimed as his blade rattled out of its sheath. "You
would do anything to gain control over Stavebrook, even turn
your own daughter into a whore!" Connor whipped the sword
around so that its point rested lightly on de Gabin's wattled
old throat.

If there was any fear in de Gabin, it did not appear in his
eyes. "Do you have any better suggestion?" he asked calmly.
"Since you yourself cannot produce an heir—"

"I can produce an heir!" Connor said hotly.

Then he saw the faint smile tugging at de Gabin's lips and
knew he had been tricked.

"So, the injury you received in the Holy Land was perhaps
not *quite* as bad as you previously indicated?"

Connor's lips drew back from his teeth in a grimace. He
took a step backward, which pulled the blade away from Sir
Herve's throat. With a snarled curse, Connor rammed the
sword back in its sheath.

Then he became aware of the rapid patter of running footsteps, and a man shouted, "There he is!" In little more than the blink of an eye, half a dozen of de Gabin's men-at-arms had surrounded Connor, and he was ringed by the steel of their drawn swords.

De Gabin had not moved from where he sat at the table. With a mocking laugh, he waved his hand and said, "Put away your weapons, lads. Sir Connor has sheathed his blade, and I'm sure he regrets his outburst."

One of the servants must have run to fetch the guards, thought Connor. He looked at the men around him and said defiantly, "My only regret is that I did not run my blade through your throat when I had the chance."

De Gabin shook his head. "That is no way to speak to your betrothed's sire." To the guards, he added sharply, "Put away your weapons and leave us."

One of the men protested, "But, Sir Herve, this man has threatened you—"

"I said leave us."

The men-at-arms obeyed, though somewhat reluctantly.

When they were alone again, Sir Herve leaned back on the bench and said, "Now then. You were saying that you cannot act as a true husband and cannot produce an heir."

Connor's teeth grated together. "I am unimpaired in that respect," he said tautly.

"Then you lied to me."

"To spare your daughter from the shame of being cast aside even before the marriage took place."

For a moment, de Gabin did not say anything. Then, "I cannot fault you for wishing to spare my daughter pain. But you must understand, Sir Connor, you have proposed marriage before witnesses. We have agreed on the terms. Now the marriage *must* take place. Nothing can stand in its way."

Before Connor could speak, he heard more rapid footsteps. They were lighter this time, so he knew the men-at-arms had not returned. Instead, he heard a distinctly feminine gasp behind him and turned to see Alura coming to a stop just inside the entrance to the great hall. Her mother was behind her, coming at a slower pace but looking just as frightened as Alura.

"One of the servants said the two of you were . . . were in here killing each other," said Alura.

"Nonsense!" boomed her father. "There was a slight disagreement, eh, Ridglea? But 'tis all settled now." He came to his feet. "Save for the question of when the marriage will take place. I suggest a fortnight from now. What say you, Sir Connor?"

Alura realized she was holding her breath as Connor slowly turned his head to look at her. She saw anger in his eyes, a vestige from the argument with her father, but it was fading. He said, "I suggest we ask the lady Alura."

She swallowed hard and thought of her pledge to the djinn. She thought as well of all the contradictory but intriguing feelings that being around Connor Warrick aroused in her.

And so she said, in a voice stronger and more confident than she really felt, "A fortnight will be fine."

Fourteen

It was an hour before dawn when the young woman slipped out through the postern gate at Welwynd. One of the guards was dozing, and the other had been willing to turn a blind eye to her leave-taking as soon as she had dropped to her knees in front of him and quickly pleasured him. "Whate'er ye're goin' to do for the lad ye're slippin' out to meet, ye can do the same for me," he had said, and Nessa had obliged without hesitation.

Dermot was waiting for her.

Here at the back of the castle, the moat was spanned only by a slender tree trunk. Nessa traversed it carefully in the darkness, feeling her way with slipper-shod feet. She knew that underneath the water, there were sharp, jagged rocks on the bottom of the moat. A fall could easily prove fatal.

She was willing to run that risk for the outlaw.

Reaching the other side of the log, she stepped off into thick grass made wet by dew. Within a few strides, her slippers and the hem of her gown were soaked. Nessa ignored the discomfort and continued on. She knew the path by heart, even in the clinging darkness.

She was in thick woods several bowshots from the castle when a hand came out of the shadows and gripped her arm.

Despite the fact that she was expecting to be met, she gasped in surprise.

"Shhh." A finger pressed her lips. "Be quiet, little one." Then the finger went away and was replaced by Dermot's mouth, hungrily plundering hers.

Nessa surged against him as his arms went around her. His kiss was hard and cruel and selfish, but she didn't care. There was nothing tender about their joining. It was sheer, animalistic coupling, almost a battle.

And that was all either of them wanted.

When it was over, Dermot asked, "Did anyone see you leave the castle?"

"Nay," she lied. "The guards are old and blind and sleepy."

"Then mayhap I and my men should just take Welwynd for ourselves."

Nessa lifted herself on one elbow and laughed. "You are a group of forest brigands, not an army."

Dermot's hand streaked to her throat and closed on it, forcing her back down onto the ground. He rolled atop her and kept his tight grip on her throat as he hissed, "We take what we want, and no one will stop us. Do you understand?"

Unable to force a sound past the brutal vise of his grip, Nessa managed to nod. Dermot felt the response and abruptly let go of her. He leaned down, brushed his lips across her bruised throat as she drew in a deep, ragged breath. "I . . . I'm sorry, Dermot," she said.

He sat up and seemed to have forgotten about the brief moment of violence. "Have you heard any more about Connor Warrick?" he asked.

Nessa sat up beside him. She lifted her hand to her throat and touched it briefly, then said, "His marriage to Lady Alura de Gabin will take place in less than a fortnight. The banns have been read, and Lackland has been petitioned for his approval of the marriage. I heard Sir Oswald speaking to Lady Maryoth about it last night. Sir Oswald thinks that someone should kill Lord Ridglea so that Lady Alura will be spared from having to marry him."

"With the magicks at Warrick's command, anyone who

tries to murder him will likely have a difficult time of it," said Dermot. He came smoothly to his feet and adjusted his clothing, then held a hand down to Nessa. "I have a task for you," he said as he helped her to her feet.

"What sort of task?" asked Nessa. She knew from experience to be wary of this man. If not for the hungry fires he kindled within her, she would have had nothing to do with him. As it was, though, she felt as if she had no choice save to do his bidding, otherwise he would abandon her.

"I want you to leave Welwynd."

"Leave Welwynd!" Nessa could not stop the exclamation from escaping her lips. "But I have always lived there."

In the shadows, she could not see Dermot's face, but from his voice she could imagine the mocking grin he wore. "Then a change will most certainly be welcome."

"But where would I go? What would I do? And why should I leave?"

He reached out and took her chin in his hand. "I shall answer the most important question first," he said as his fingers tightened. "You leave because I tell you to. You go to Stavebrook, and once there you secure a place among the servants."

Nessa had difficulty speaking because of the grip he had on her. "You . . . you want me to serve L-Lord Ridglea?"

"Nay. You serve *me*. Your task is to discover what sort of magic Warrick used to save his life when we waylaid him in the woods. When you find out what it is, and how he commands it, you will come to me and tell me all his secrets. Do you understand?"

Once more Nessa nodded. Dermot released her and stepped back. "Go now," he told her.

"Now? But . . . but my things are at Welwynd."

"Are any of them worth your life?"

Nessa had to admit that they were not.

"If anyone notices that you are gone, 'tis likely they shall think you ran away with a man. You will not be missed overmuch, or for long."

Again, he was right, thought Nessa. She had no family left, and she would not miss her uncomfortable, insect-infested bed in the servants' quarters. Besides, if she was successful in her quest to discover Connor Warrick's sorcerous secrets, then Dermot would be able to command the magic, too, and he would surely become a rich, powerful man.

Nessa could share in that wealth and power. Surely he would be grateful to her for her help. Perhaps someday Dermot would be able to seize a barony of his own, and she would be Lady Nessa, instead of just Nessa the servant, Nessa the slut.

Seized by ambition, Nessa nodded and said, "Yes, I will go to Stavebrook now."

In the east, the sky was gray with the approach of dawn.

What had she done? What *had* she done? When yesterday had dawned, Alura had been determined to do everything in her power to have the wedding called off. From the look on Connor's face, the same thought might have occurred to him. And yet both of them had gone along with her father's suggestion that the wedding take place in a fortnight.

At least Connor had drawn his sword, thought Alura. His discussion with her father had almost turned violent. But in the end, Sir Herve had gotten his way.

Alura and Radiya were sitting in Alura's bedchamber. She had summoned the djinn earlier and had given Zahir permission to look around the estate, with the understanding that he would not reveal his existence to anyone else.

"Worry not about that," he had assured her. "If we want anyone except the master or mistress who summoned us to be able to see us, we have to will it to happen. I just won't manifest physically."

Alura had agreed to that, and Zahir had turned into a pillar of smoke, then dispersed so that he was no longer visible as he drifted out the window of Alura's chamber. That had left Alura alone to talk to Radiya, who was rapidly becoming something like the older sister Alura had never had.

Very much older, thought Alura. According to the djinn, they had been in those fire opals for thousands of years. Alura had never heard of the island kingdom of Azlon until she had accidentally summoned the djinn, nor had she seen it on any maps, no matter how ancient.

Now, to distract herself, Alura said to Radiya, "You cannot . . . touch each other?"

Radiya shook her head in response to the question. "Not while we are inside the gems," she said. "Zahir and I can see each other, though the gems make it appear as if a wall of red glass is between us. We can converse, too, but that is all."

"How lonely it must be for you. For both of you."

"It could be worse. Believe me, we came close to utter destruction, so we are grateful for having life, no matter what sort it is. And there have been times, when we were both materialized, that we have been able to . . . well, you shall know all about that soon enough, when you are wed to Sir Connor."

Alura felt her face growing warm. She had thought a great deal about the feelings that Connor roused in her, and her curiosity about them was overwhelming. And, she reminded herself, she now possessed the power to satisfy any sort of curiosity. . . .

"I want a castle," she said.

Radiya frowned. "A castle," she repeated. "But you have this fine chamber here at Brynclair—"

"No," Alura said firmly. "I want my own castle, the most beautiful castle in all of England. And I want Connor to be there, too."

"Mistress, this is not a wise path for you to travel," cautioned Radiya. " 'Tis dangerous to tamper with the fabric of reality."

"Now," insisted Alura. "A castle of my own, where no one can disturb us. And Connor must be there."

"Mistress . . ." Radiya practically wailed.

"I command it!"

As soon as the words were out of her mouth, thunder roared and lightning flashed, just as it had the night she first summoned the djinn. Alura felt a jolt, as if the floor had leaped beneath her feet, and she could not help but gasp in momentary fear.

Then, abruptly, she realized that she was no longer in her bedchamber at Brynclair. Instead, she sat on a gleaming golden throne in a great hall with an arching roof. A long, gleaming table stood before her. The most magnificent fire-place she had ever seen was to her right, and in front of it lay a huge wolfhound. The walls were hung with tapestries and banners, and the air had a fresh, evergreen scent to it. Luxury abounded.

And at the far end of the table stood Connor, wearing a dark-blue tunic and silver hose. His sword was buckled around his waist. He wore a faintly puzzled frown on his face, but when he looked along the length of the beautiful table and saw Alura, his expression cleared. "Ah, I understand now," he said. " 'Tis a dream."

"Aye," said Alura, the word threatening to choke her. "A dream, that is all, and when you awaken you will remember naught of it."

He came around the end of the table and strode toward her. "Then 'tis not real," he said.

"How could it be?" murmured Alura. She came to her feet and went to meet him.

He lifted his arms, and she thought he was going to embrace her. Instead, he placed his hands on her shoulders and looked down into her eyes. " 'Tis said that a man's dreams but reflect his innermost desires," he said huskily. "Do you believe that?"

Alura nodded. "A man's desires," she said, "or a woman's."

He pulled her toward him, and she went willingly. His mouth came down on hers, his lips and tongue gently plun-dering. Her arms went around him, and her body molded to his.

Suddenly, Alura stiffened as conflicting urges raced through her. This was the Beast of Stavebrook in whose arms she was being held. Rogue, despoiler of young women . . . murderer. She wanted to pull away from him, to run for her very life.

Yet there was nothing beastlike in the way he held her. Just the opposite, in fact. He was tender and gentle, careful not to hurt her, but still insistent in his wantings.

He had called this a dream, and perhaps it was. So she pressed herself more tightly to him, took her mouth from his, and sensuously whispered the words she had spoken to him in the rain and sleet and mud of Brynclair's bailey.

"What do you dream of, sir knight?"

His lips descended on hers again, and she felt herself being borne backwards. Her eyes had closed when he kissed her, but as a feeling of disorientation washed over her, she opened them and saw that they were no longer in the great hall of her fantasy castle. Now they were in a bedchamber, but not her bedchamber at Brynclair, nor any other she had ever seen. It was as luxuriously appointed as the great hall, with a huge bed covered by thick down comforters and overhung by a silken canopy with fine lace along its edges. She and Connor stood on the rush mat beside the bed, locked in each other's embrace.

Connor opened his eyes, too, and his head jerked in reaction as he took note of their surroundings. Then he shrugged and smiled slightly. " 'Tis only a dream," he said, "so I suppose we can be anywhere we choose."

"As long as we are together."

"Aye." He looked at her. "I did not wish to marry you, you know."

"Nor I you," she said sharply, a momentary surge of irritation overcoming the passion she felt. "But I made a pledge. . . ."

"To me?"

To the djinn, she thought, but she could not explain that to him. Instead she shook her head and said, "It matters not. We are here, milord, and bold though it may be—"

"You want me," he said with a mocking smile.

"And you want me. You cannot deny it."

A solemn expression replaced the mockery on his face. "Nay, I would not deny it," he said quietly. "I want you, Alura." He drew her closer again and brushed his lips across hers in a heated, tantalizing caress.

I can end this any time I choose, Alura told herself. *All I need do is command Radiya to make everything as it was before.*

But she did not want to end it. She wanted to continue, to discover for herself what was the truth about Connor Warrick:

the scandalous stories she had heard about him, or the things
her own instincts told her.

She slipped her hand behind his neck and held him as she
deepened the kiss.

His hand came up and cupped her breast through her gown.
She groaned as his touch made her nipple harden. He caught
it between thumb and forefinger, and his playful teasing of the
erect bud only made her want him more.

She reached boldly under his tunic searching for the ties to
his braies. Her fingers tugged on the ties, loosening the braies
so she could reach his manhood. His hips surged forward as
she explored him. He found the clasp of her girdle and unfastened it so that it fell around her feet. Then he untied the string
that was knotted at her throat, loosening her gown.

"Wait," whispered Alura. She reached up and pulled the
wimple off her head so that she could toss it aside. Though she
hated to move the fingers that were curled around his shaft—
and he hated it, too, judging by the look of loss on his face—he
helped her unplait her braids and then he raked his fingers
through her hair so that it fell loosely down her back, like waves
of fire.

"You are the most beautiful creature on the face of the earth
. . . or whatever strange dream world this is," breathed Connor.

She smiled and said, "Undress me, milord. Make me thine
and only thine."

With an expression of taut anticipation on his face, Connor
did exactly what she asked. He slid the gown and shift from
her body so that she stood gloriously nude before him. Alura
thought she would feel ashamed to be like this, but she felt
no shame at all, only a sense of overwhelming rightness. This
was meant to be.

He pulled his tunic over his head, revealing the broad, muscular, lightly furred chest. Alura saw as well the long, white,
jagged scar on his shoulder and arm. Her suspicions had been
correct. He had been badly wounded in the Holy Land, and
that accounted for the slight hesitation he displayed when using his right arm. Perhaps it still pained him. She felt a flash
of pity but almost immediately put it aside. Connor Warrick

was not the sort of man to want pity from anyone.

For that reason, she stopped herself when her instinct told her to reach up and touch the scar. She could not bring herself to pretend it did not exist, however. She looked at it, then back into Connor's eyes. He could read the truth there. She was not repulsed by his injury, but neither was she going to fawn over him because of it.

She sat down on the edge of the bed. He kicked off his leather slippers and came closer to her, and she reached out to him. She pulled down the garments, freeing his manhood, and as she did so, she was extremely aware of how close it was to her. She wondered what he would do if she leaned over and planted a kiss on the tip of it.

The boldness, the sheer decadence of that thought, surprised her, so much so that she drew back involuntarily, afraid that God might strike her dead on the spot for the impurity of her thoughts. When that did not happen, she glanced up at Connor and saw a frown of concern on his face. To reassure him, she lay back on the bed and opened her arms to him. "Come," she whispered.

He came to her, just as she bid him to do. His arms went around her, and his weight atop her was a wonderful pressure. Her legs parted and her knees lifted as one of his hands slid down her flank. His fingers stole under her left leg to prod and caress the tender muscles at the back of her thigh. Alura opened herself even wider as the heat that had been building within her began to seek a way out. She longed to feel his touch at her core.

Instead, maddeningly, he transferred his massaging caress to the back of her other leg. Alura whimpered from both pleasure and frustration.

Then, finally, Connor's fingertips brushed over the finespun triangle of red hair and parted it so that he could caress the folds of feminine flesh. Alura gasped as he boldly penetrated her, and he covered her open mouth with his own as he delved even deeper. Their tongues danced delicately around each other.

Like the warmth of the rising sun, a feeling of intimacy washed over Alura. At this moment, she knew it mattered not

what had been said of Connor Warrick's past. She trusted him
and was willing to give herself completely to him. She had
never been closer to anyone in her life, and she was overcome
with eagerness to share both body and soul totally with him.
This was right. It had to be.

A moment later he moved over her and began to fill her.
His entrance was easy, so aroused was she, yet he proceeded
slowly, and she soon knew why. Her maidenhead stopped him,
and he hesitated until she looked up at him and breathed,
"Yes."

He surged forward, so that the pain was sharp but short.
The discomfort passed quickly, to be replaced by a glorious,
glowing fervor. Alura found her hips moving in time with his,
so that she was meeting his thrusts and giving as well as receiving. Her arms were around him, holding him tightly to
her. Their mouths were open so that they shared each other's
breath. They were so close that they were almost one instead
of two, and then as Connor crested the peak of his passion
Alura, too, slid over the top of her climax and began the long,
shuddering plunge to ecstasy. It seemed to take an eternity. . . .

And then she fell, not to earth, but back into her bedchamber at Brynclair.

Connor sat bolt upright at the table in the great hall of Stavebrook. He had been going over the estate's accounts, and the
sheets of parchment covered with the scribblings of the monks
were still scattered on the table in front of him. But he was
breathing hard, as if he had just run a league.

Or made love to a beautiful woman. A woman with hair as
red as the setting sun and skin as soft as the kiss of dew on a
newly bloomed flower.

He hauled a deep, ragged breath into his lungs. He had not
had such a dream in many years. Jeremy would surely say that
it meant he had been too long without a woman.

Connor had no idea what it meant. But if dreams did indeed
have the power to foretell the future, as some people claimed
they did, then perhaps being married to Alura de Gabin would
be a good thing after all. A very good thing.

· · ·

Alura swallowed hard. She looked down at herself. She was dressed as she had been before. The beautiful gown she had worn in her fantasy was gone. The castle, the luxurious bed-chamber . . . Connor . . . it had all been a dream, concocted by Radiya to show her what it would be like.

But if that was true, then why did she feel so different?

"Are you all right?"

Alura looked up at Radiya, eyes widening in shock. "It . . . it was *real*!" she said. "Connor and I . . . we really . . ."

"That is what you commanded," Radiya said coolly.

"But . . . but I thought 'twould be different."

"And how do you feel about Connor now?"

Alura took a deep breath, trying to force her stunned brain to function. "He is a good man," she said finally. "I know that. What the truth of his past is, I cannot be sure, but I know now that he is a good man." Her eyes widened even more. "Does he know? Does he remember?"

Radiya shook her head, and relief flooded through Alura. "You said nothing of whether or not he should remember," said the djinni, "so I used my own judgment. I thought it best he regard the whole episode as nothing more than . . . a pleasant dream."

Alura nodded. "Aye," she said hollowly. "A pleasant dream."

She had to put this out of her mind for the moment. A portentous thing had happened, but she could not think about it now. To change the subject, she said to Radiya, "Won't you tell me about Azlon, and about how the two of you came to be imprisoned in the bracelet and the ring?"

Radiya hesitated before asking, "Is this another command? Because 'tis a long, sad story, and I think 'twould make you unhappy to hear it."

Alura considered whether to change the request into a command, so that Radiya would have to answer. From the sound of the djinni's voice, Alura suspected that telling the story would make Radiya unhappy, and Alura did not want that. So she said, "Tell me the good things about Azlon."

That brought a smile to Radiya's face. "Oh, there were many," she said. "Our palace gardens were the finest in the known world. There were tall trees, and flowering shrubs, and vines that embraced everything like the arms of a lover. The palace itself was beautiful, made of green stone quarried from the slopes of Mount Calabus.''

"Green stone?" Alura repeated in wonder.

"Aye," said Radiya with a nod. "And ships would put into the harbor, so that one could stand in the tower of the palace and look out at the water and see sails of all shapes and sizes and colors, moving about the harbor like butterflies."

"It does sound beautiful."

"It was," said Radiya. "And there were fields full of crops, and forests where roamed the famous black stags of Azlon, and everywhere the people were happy and lived their lives with joy and loved their king and queen, who loved them in return."

Alura could not help but wonder how much of that part of the story was true. Radiya was remembering a time when she and Zahir had been absolute rulers of everything in their world. Being one of their subjects would have been an entirely different sort of life. As for whether or not the people of Azlon had loved the two of them, well, people in England swore allegiance to King Richard, but Alura knew of no one who actually professed to feel any real affection for him.

Still, perhaps Radiya was right about how things had been in Azlon. For the djinni's sake, Alura hoped she was.

"Ah, Azlon, timeless Azlon," Radiya said with a sigh. "Would that we could have returned there someday." She shook her head. "But, 'tis not to be." With a bittersweet smile, she looked at Alura and went on, "But you and Connor can make us very happy by becoming man and wife."

That brought the conversation right back around to where it had been before, thought Alura. However, there was something a little different in Radiya's voice now. Alura thought it was a hint of neediness, perhaps even of desperation. "Why should it matter to you," she asked, "if Connor and I are wed?"

"Why . . . why, you are our mistress! Your happiness is our happiness. That is how things are."

"Then there is no other reason why it is so important to you that Connor and I are wed?"

"Of course not. What other reason could there be?"

Alura was wondering that very thing. She put the question aside for the moment, since it was clear that Radiya did not want to give her a true answer. Perhaps at another time, Alura could discover if there was another reason for the matchmaking efforts of the two djinn.

She stood up and went to the window to look out at a glorious spring day. It was hard to imagine that so much had changed since she had arisen that morning. She wondered what Connor was doing at this very moment, and without thinking, she sighed and said, "I wish I could see him right now."

Radiya stepped up behind her and with a laugh, said, "That, too, can be arranged, mistress."

Before Alura knew what was happening, Radiya had reached out with one bare, elegant arm and made a gesture. With a sound akin to the fingers of a minstrel plucking languidly at the strings of a lyre, the air in the window before Alura began to shimmer and blur. She gasped and muttered a prayer as the image in front of her eyes changed. Suddenly, it was as if she no longer stood at the window in her chamber, looking out at Brynclair. Now, her view was as if she stood outside the keep at Stavebrook, peering *in* through a window that opened into the great hall of the castle. No such window existed, but that fact proved no hindrance to the djinni's magic.

Connor was in the hall, and Alura felt a twinge of guilt at the sight of him, knowing what they had done together a short time earlier, even if Connor had remembered it as a dream. And now she was spying on him, with the assistance of Radiya, and he surely had no idea he was being observed. Alura knew she ought to be ashamed of herself—for more reasons than one—and knew as well that she should command Radiya to put an end to this sorcerous seeing.

And yet she said nothing, and watched. . . .

●   ●   ●

Connor frowned and glanced over his shoulder. Nothing was there, of course. He was still alone in the great hall, having put away the parchments with which he had been occupying himself before he'd dozed off into that odd but rapturous dream. He shook his head and reached for the sword sheathed at his hip. Steel rasped as he drew the weapon. He inspected the edge of the blade and found it sufficiently keen. Then he laid the sword on the table and grasped the hem of his tunic, lifting it up and peeling the garment over his head and off his body. It was warm in the great hall, and Connor intended to work up a sweat.

He took the sword in his right hand again. Its weight pulled against muscles that were still slightly sore. Other than that night in the forest, following the tournament, Connor had drawn his sword only once, and that was to threaten Sir Herve de Gabin. On both occasions, Connor's actions had been a matter of instinct. He had been too overcome by emotions to be truly aware of his body and what it was feeling. Now, the time had come to gauge fully the extent of the damage the fall from his charger had done to his injured arm and shoulder.

Slowly, Connor turned, holding the sword level and bringing it around in a slashing motion. He stopped, tipped the blade up, and twirled it over his head before launching into a backhand stroke. This move was a bit faster, and when the blade suddenly thrust out in front of Connor like a striking snake, it moved faster still. Soon, as the sword went through the intricate steps of its deadly dance, it became a blur of polished steel. Connor leaped, spun, twisted, thrust. He was partner to the blade. Beads of sweat sprang out on his forehead, and a fine sheen of moisture stood on his back and chest.

He swung a final blinding backhand and let the weight of the sword carry it behind him. He reached back with his left hand, and the weapon's leather-wrapped haft passed smoothly from hand to hand behind Connor's back. Now gripped firmly in his left hand, the sword was truly like a living thing as it whipped around in front of him once more and thrust out as Connor crouched slightly.

He froze there for a moment, his breath coming a little faster than normal, his pulse racing in his head. Then slowly he straightened, spun the sword in his left hand, and slid it back into its sheath. He picked up his tunic and mopped his face with it.

His right arm hurt like blazes, yet it still answered his commands. His shoulder had moved freely when he passed the sword from hand to hand behind his back. He took a couple of deep breaths and realized that the ache in his muscles was already beginning to subside. Relief washed through him. He was satisfied that no permanent damage had been done to him during the tournament.

Now, if he could just shake this devilish feeling that he was being watched. . . .

"Milord."

Jeremy's voice broke into Connor's thoughts. He turned and saw the squire coming into the great hall. As usual, whenever Jeremy was inside the castle these days, that infernal cat was draped over the lad's shoulder. Connor wondered if Jeremy intended on carrying the creature into battle with him, should it still be living when he came of age to attain his knighthood.

"You've been practicing, milord," said Jeremy, a slight chiding tone in his voice. "I would have been glad to help you—"

"This was something I needed to do alone," said Connor.

"And did it go as you wished?"

Connor nodded curtly. "It did."

"Good. Mossgrave wishes to speak with you, milord."

"Very well," said Connor as he pulled his tunic on again.

The seneschal came into the room a few moments later with a young woman beside him. She was perhaps twenty years old, with dark brown hair, and was attractive in a coarse way. From her plain garb, it was apparent she was a servant, though Connor did not recognize her as one of Stavebrook's people.

"Milord, this is Nessa," said Mossgrave, tugging on his sparse white whiskers as he spoke. "She wishes to live and work here."

Connor frowned. "Where is your home, woman, your people?"

The woman called Nessa curtsied and kept her eyes downcast nervously. "I have none, milord. Neither home, nor people. My family is all dead."

"Not of the plague, I hope?" said Mossgrave sharply, sidling away from her.

Quickly, Nessa shook her head. "Oh, no! My father was a man-at-arms and was killed in battle many years ago, and my mother recently died from the weight of her years. She and I were vassals of Lord Ipswich, whose barony is east of here."

Connor grunted and said, "I know of Ipswich. His estate is over a sennight's journey from here. Did you walk all that way?"

"Aye, milord," replied Nessa, bobbing her head.

"You found no place that would allow you to work for your keep closer to your former home?"

"Well . . . I stopped at a castle called Welwynd. The lord of the place, a very kindly man called Sir Oswald, would have taken me in, but his wife would not hear of it. I . . . I fear Lady Maryoth cared not for the way her husband looked at me."

"Here now," snapped Mossgrave as he drew back a hand and threatened to cuff her. "Have a care how ye talk about your betters, woman."

Connor gestured for Mossgrave to step back. "You shall have no such problem here," he told Nessa. He turned to the seneschal. "Mossgrave, put her to work."

"Aye, milord." Mossgrave jerked his thumb toward the entrance and said, "Go on with ye." As Nessa turned and started out of the room, he slapped her smartly on the rump.

"Mossgrave, wait a moment," Connor said.

Nessa went on out of the room, as Mossgrave looked anxiously at Connor. "Aye, milord?" Clearly, he thought Connor was going to reprimand him about that swat on the woman's backside.

Connor was willing to let that pass, but he was curious about something else. "Mossgrave, you are in charge of the servants and vassals at Stavebrook. Why did you bring this woman here to me, for my approval, before you took her in?"

"Well, milord, ye've been very . . . interested . . . in all the doin's of the estate since ye came back." Mossgrave sniffed.

"I thought ye might like to pass judgment on the servants, as well."

"I see," said Connor. Mossgrave had his nose out of joint because Connor had been closely overseeing the operation of the estate lately. So he had chosen to bring something as trivial as this to the lord's attention, and no doubt would do so again, just to make a point.

That was fine with Connor. He smiled so that Mossgrave would know his efforts to be irritating had come to naught. "Very well," Connor said. "Go on about your work."

Mossgrave nodded, turned, and scuttled out of the great hall. When he was gone, Jeremy said, "That old man ought to be whipped for his insolence to a noble knight such as yourself, Sir Connor."

"Whipping is more trouble than he's worth," Connor said offhandedly.

"But that Nessa, now, she was a choice morsel."

Connor glanced at Jeremy, saw the look of lust on the lad's face, and tried all he could not to laugh. "She's a bit long in the tooth for you, isn't she? She must have been half a dozen years older, at least."

"An experienced woman, that's just what I need, milord. To teach me all the tricks of lovemaking, I mean."

Connor shook his head. "There is no trick to lovemaking, Jeremy. All it requires is that you be with someone you love."

Jeremy frowned. "But, milord, surely you have not been in love with all the women you've bedded?"

"Simply bedding a woman is different. That is nothing more than lust, a pleasant diversion for the moment but soon forgotten. Love is, I assure you, much different." He frowned a little, as unbidden thoughts tickled fleetingly at the back of his mind for an instant, then vanished.

Jeremy reached up to stroke the cat on his shoulder. "You mean what you have with the Lady Alura," he said.

Connor thought about that. He certainly felt pangs of desire for Alura. That was odd, since he had believed that his appetite for such things had died in the burning heat of the Holy Land, when the rest of him had come so close to death. But what he felt was undeniable. Did it run even deeper?

"We shall see, Jeremy," he said softly. "We shall surely see."

"But, milord, surely you have not been in love with all the women you've bedded?"

"No more!" exclaimed Alura, covering her eyes with her hands and wishing she could cover her ears as well so that she could not hear Connor's answer to the question. "I command you, show me no more!"

The hastily spoken command came in time. With a flick of Radiya's fingers, the mystical window into the great hall of Stavebrook disappeared. Alura turned away from the real window in her chamber, still shaken by what she had seen and heard.

At first, though she had felt guilty about spying on him, she had to admit she had enjoyed watching Connor practice with the sword. There had been something undeniably thrilling about the sight of him bared to the waist as he and the sword went through their dance. Alura's breath had come faster as she watched the smooth, rippling play of his muscles underneath his skin, remembering how that skin had felt against hers. Even when he turned so that she could see the ugly white scar that began on the top of his right shoulder and disappeared underneath his arm, she still thought he was truly a beautiful man. Not classically handsome, no, he was too hard-visaged for that; but beautiful just the same.

Then, when he was finished, Jeremy had come in, and Alura had seen Connor's face soften just slightly. The mask he so often wore had slipped enough for Alura to tell that he loved Jeremy as if the boy was his own son.

The visit of Mossgrave and the serving woman had meant little to Alura. She had simply watched Connor and paid little attention to what was being said.

But then she had heard Jeremy's question—or was it a statement?—about all the women Connor had bedded, and suddenly Alura had been desperate for the vision to end. Now she flung herself down on her bed.

The straw-filled mattress shifted slightly as Radiya sat beside her. "Why are you so upset, mistress?" asked the djinni.

"Surely it comes as no surprise to you that Sir Connor has known other women before you?"

"Of . . . of course he has. He is a man, after all."

"Exactly. And men do these things. Why, even my own Zahir always had a harem full of concubines. It was his right as king." A note of pride entered Radiya's voice as she went on, "However, none of them could ever satisfy him so well as I. And none of them sat on the throne of Azlon beside him, either."

Alura rolled over and sat up. "Then it is not important?"

"What is important is what passes between the two of you. Nothing else." Radiya smiled and said with some satisfaction, "Besides, all of Zahir's concubines have been dead for thousands of years now. He has been completely faithful to me ever since we became djinn."

"Perhaps I should have waited and heard Connor's answer."

Radiya patted Alura's hand. "Sometimes 'tis best not to know quite *everything*."

Smoke suddenly began to swirl in the air in front of them. "Not know everything about what?" asked Zahir as he materialized.

"None of your affair," said Radiya. "Did you enjoy your excursion?"

"This is a wonderful place," Zahir said excitedly. "I could stay here for a few hundred years. But what do you mean, none of my affair? I'm a djinni. Everything about the mistress is my affair." He leaned closer to Alura and frowned. "Say, have you been crying?"

"Just a little," said Alura, summoning up a smile. "But 'tis nothing to worry about, Zahir. I was just being foolish."

"Ohhhh." He nodded sagely. "I should have known. 'Tis a womanly thing to do, being foolish, I mean."

"Zahir . . ." Radiya said threateningly.

Alura put out a hand. "Allow me." With her other hand, she expertly threw a pillow from the bed. It smacked across Zahir's face, leaving him looking shocked and exasperated.

"Look not so surprised," Radiya advised him. "You had it coming."

Fifteen

There was much to do before the wedding could take place. Lady Katharine had all of Brynclair's seamstresses hard at work designing and sewing the gowns she and Alura would wear. Likewise the cooks were planning for the wedding feast. Katharine was unsure how many guests would attend, since the groom was almost universally disliked in the district, but Sir Herve insisted that they prepare for a large crowd.

"Connor Warrick may be a scoundrel, but he controls one of the finest estates in this part of England," de Gabin said as he and his wife and daughter discussed the situation. "No one will wish to give offense to him, nor to me."

"Besides," added Alura, "if they do not attend the wedding, what will all the ladies gossip about for the next half of the year?"

"Alura!" Katharine chided. "You speak as if gossip is the most important thing to them."

"Well? Is it not?"

Katharine could not deny that, and Sir Herve threw his head back and laughed at the look of frustration on his wife's face.

The days passed in a whirl for Alura. It seemed she had barely looked up when more than a sennight had passed. Now, in less than seven days' time, she would be wed to Connor Warrick.

She confronted her father in his solar and said, "I would like for you to send a messenger to Stavebrook."

De Gabin looked up in surprise and worry. "You do not wish to call off the wedding, do you?"

She shook her head. "The wedding will go on as planned," she said. "But I want Sir Connor to come here to Brynclair and speak with me." An inspiration came to her. "Better still, I wish to go to Stavebrook myself for a visit."

Her father stared at her, dumbfounded. "I have never heard of such a thing," he said after a moment, when he had regained the faculty of speech.

Alura shrugged and looked down at the bracelet and ring on her left hand. 'Twould be easier, she thought, if her father was more like the djinn and had to obey her every command.

"It is what I wish to do," she said simply. "And besides, we visited Morvyn at Stavebrook. I would do the same with his brother."

She would do things with Connor that she would never have done with Morvyn, in fact, but she kept that thought to herself.

Sir Herve sighed. "Have you spoken to your mother concerning this?"

"No. 'Tis my idea, and mine alone."

"And you are determined to go through with it?"

"Aye, Father. After all, in less than a sennight, I will be mistress of Stavebrook, will I not?"

A shrewd look appeared in de Gabin's eyes as he nodded slowly. " 'Tis true. And you no doubt wish to see exactly what you will be gaining." He slapped a palm on the table. "A daughter who takes after me! Very well, girl, I shall send a rider to Stavebrook with the message that you shall visit on the morrow."

Alura nodded. If he wanted to believe that her motives in visiting Connor were purely mercenary, then so be it—as long as it achieved her end, which was to gain more knowledge of Connor Warrick himself. Her father might see the marriage as a union of two estates, but Alura knew it was something else. She was marrying the *man,* nothing more, nothing less.

• • •

Connor stared down at the scrap of parchment in his hand and stood silently for a long moment. Mossgrave, who had just delivered the message, cleared his throat and said in his reedy voice, "It says that the lady Alura will be coming to Stavebrook on the morrow."

"I can read what it says," snapped Connor. "Damn your eyes, Mossgrave, what does this mean?"

Jeremy was seated on a three-legged stool in front of the fireplace, which was cold at this time of year. He reached down with his left hand and petted Matilda, who was rubbing back and forth against his ankles and flicking them with her bushy tail. With his right hand, Jeremy was rubbing the ears of an old hound. "It means the lady is coming to visit you, Sir Connor," he said.

Connor swung toward him, clearly irritated, though he controlled it better with Jeremy than he did with the seneschal. "Why would she do such a thing?" he asked. "In less than a sennight she will be the mistress of this keep, of this entire estate. Why come now?"

"Perhaps that is why, Sir Connor."

Understanding dawned in Connor's eyes. He nodded slowly and said, "She wishes not to barter for a pig in a poke." Suddenly, he laughed. "That would make me the pig."

Jeremy could not remember the last time he had heard Sir Connor laugh so. It was a good sound. "I doubt that the lady regards you as swinish, milord."

"I care little if she does, but I'll not have her thinking that I dwell in a pigsty." Connor turned toward the seneschal and spoke sharply once more. "Mossgrave, I want this place cleaned from top to bottom. All the dust swept away, fresh rushes for the floor, all the silver and crystal shining. See to it."

"Aye, milord. And all this is to be accomplished by the morrow, I take it?"

"You take it correctly," Connor told him.

"And shall I send a message back to Brynclair bidding the lady Alura to visit and be welcome?"

"Aye," said Connor. "Welcome she shall be."

Mossgrave nodded and hurried away to see to the task. He seized the arm of the first servant he encountered, who happened to be the young woman called Nessa. "The entire keep must be cleaned by the morrow," he told her.

Nessa raised her eyebrows in surprise. "Why?"

"Because I say so, slut," snapped Mossgrave. "And because Lady Alura of Brynclair is coming to visit."

"The master's betrothed?"

Mossgrave nodded. "Aye. Naturally, he wants to make a favorable impression on her. Gather all the servants and send them to me, and I shall parcel out the tasks."

"Sir Connor asks a great deal. To clean an entire keep overnight . . . 'tis a chore that would almost seem to require magic."

"Well, there be no magic around here, only the need for hard work." Mossgrave snorted. "What do ye think, lass, that Sir Connor can simply snap his fingers and command the keep to clean itself?"

"He is a powerful man," said Nessa.

"No one is that powerful. Now, get on with you!" He whacked her hard on the rump, as he was wont to do at the slightest excuse.

Nessa did not complain about the swat. She simply hurried away to be about the task he had given her. Mossgrave watched her go and thought again what an odd bit of baggage she was. Though she had only been at Stavebrook for a few days, she had somehow wormed her way into working in the keep itself, though Mossgrave had intended at first to put her to work in the fields. It was that backside of hers, he decided. It was particularly fine, firm and well-rounded and a great pleasure to watch as well as to slap. But it was still strange how she always seemed to be nearby wherever Sir Connor was. Perhaps she intended to seduce the master, thought Mossgrave. If that was the case, she would soon see what a futile effort that was. The only woman in whom Sir Connor had shown any interest since his return from the Holy Land was that redheaded wench from Brynclair.

But if Nessa really wanted to seduce someone, she could

do worse than the seneschal of the estate, aye, she could indeed, thought Mossgrave.

The next day dawned bright and clear, and Alura was grateful for that. No showers today. It would be good for traveling.

She felt the excitement of what was to come. Wanting to share it, she reached down to the bracelet and ring and lightly stroked the fire opals. The by-now familiar ritual of the smoke emerging from the gems and coalescing into a pair of human forms took place, and as Radiya and Zahir materialized, Alura said, "Good morning to you both."

"You look happy," said Radiya. "This is the day you go to visit Connor, is it not?"

"Aye," Alura replied with a nod.

Zahir folded his muscular arms across his broad chest. "And we, of course, shall observe."

"Of course," said Alura. "But not interfere."

Zahir arched his bushy eyebrows. "Interfere? Us?"

"This day is for you and Connor," said Radiya. "If you wish, we do not even have to watch."

"You can do that?" Alura asked in surprise. "Not know what is transpiring in the world outside the gems, I mean?"

"Certainly," said Radiya, ignoring the vehement shaking of Zahir's head. " 'Tis simple. All you have to do is command it."

That was a relief to Alura. She had already begun to worry about what the djinn would see and hear on the night of her wedding to Connor. The private moments between husband and wife should indeed be private, she thought, and doubtless Radiya had already seen too much when she'd executed that dream.

Clearly, Zahir did not like the fact that Alura now knew she could limit their powers of observation. Alura supposed she could understand that. Trapped as they were by whatever force had transformed them into djinn, they had to live their lives for the most part through others. Still, Alura was glad to know she and Connor could have some time unobserved.

That thought raised another question in her mind: after the wedding, what was she going to tell him, if anything, about the djinn? If she simply told him, without demonstrating how to summon them, he would surely believe her to be mad.

This was something else she would have to discuss with Radiya. For the moment, however, Alura had other things with which to concern herself, primarily the visit she was about to make to Stavebrook.

"Watch all you wish today," she said as she held out her left arm. "Now, 'tis time for me to go."

This command did not even have to be voiced. The djinn knew what she wanted. They transformed once more into smoke, and the twin pillars were drawn back into the fire opals. Alura smiled warmly at the gems, knowing Radiya and Zahir could see her, then went down to the great hall to greet her mother and father.

Both Sir Herve and Lady Katharine would be accompanying her to Stavebrook, of course. It would be entirely improper for Alura to visit the estate of her future husband without her parents along. Sir Herve was clearly looking forward to it, rubbing his hands together impatiently, wanting to be leaving. Katharine looked excited about the prospect, as well. She kissed Alura on the cheek and asked, "Are you ready to depart?"

Alura nodded.

"As soon as we have broken our fast," said Sir Herve. Anxious to be on the way or not, he was not going to miss a meal.

Alura ate only sparingly. The hunting dogs lying under the table got most of her food. She was not particularly hungry. Her mind was too much in a whirl for that. She had no idea what this day was going to bring, nor even what she *hoped* it would bring. But she sensed that it would be important.

Their mounts were waiting for them when they stepped out into the inner bailey a short time later. Sir Herve rode his usual horse, a magnificent black destrier, while Alura and Katharine were mounted on a pair of chestnut palfreys. Surrounded by men-at-arms, the group moved out of the castle.

There had been rumors of bandits haunting the woods recently, so Alura felt a slight nervousness as the party rode toward Stavebrook. That sensation compounded the anxiety she was already experiencing over this visit to Connor's estate. She glanced down at the bracelet and ring. The djinn would never allow any harm to come to her, she thought. If they were attacked by bandits, Zahir and Radiya would protect her and her family. But that would mean revealing the existence of the spirits to the rest of the world, and for some reason Alura was loath to do that. More of the ensorcelment that had resulted in the creation of the djinn in the first place, she supposed. The magic spell helped the wearer of the enchanted jewelry to accept the existence of the djinn, and also prompted the wearer to keep that secret if at all possible.

The good weather held, and the travelers encountered no trouble on the way to Stavebrook. The party arrived at Lord Ridglea's estate late in the morning. Alura had visited before, when she was betrothed to Morvyn Warrick, but then she had paid little attention to the details of the estate itself. Now, she saw that the fields were well cared for and that the workers seemed to be well treated. The village that had grown up around Stavebrook was somewhat smaller than the one at Brynclair, but it was relatively clean. Alura recalled the filthy hovels that had made up the village the last time she was here. Clearly, Connor kept a firmer hand on his people than Morvyn ever had. No doubt that was a good thing. A firm hand was usually also a fair hand.

The drawbridge was lowered and the portcullis raised at the gates of Stavebrook. That was not due to any lack of preparedness on the part of Connor and his men-at-arms, noted Alura. She saw the watchmen in the guard tower that rose above the gates and knew that the arrival of the visitors had been announced well in advance. Connor was waiting.

Waiting for her.

The thought sent strange tingles through her body. She leaned forward slightly in her saddle as the hooves of the horses clattered on the planks of the drawbridge. She found that she was eager to see him again.

They rode through the barbican, then the main gate, then the short passage underneath the gatehouse, emerging into the outer bailey. A tall, lean figure clad in dark blue hose and a tunic under a hauberk of chain mail strode through the gate leading into the inner bailey. He paused there and let the visitors come to him.

"I bid you welcome to Stavebrook," Connor called as they rode up to him. While his greeting was not overly hearty, at least it sounded sincere.

Sir Herve dismounted first, then turned to his wife to assist her. Connor took a step toward Alura's palfrey, then stopped short, as if uncertain whether he should help her to dismount or not. Alura waited to see what he would do. After a span of a couple of heartbeats, he came forward and held a hand up to her. "Milady," he said.

Alura took his hand without hesitation, sensing the rightness of it as his fingers closed around hers. She felt the strength of his grip as he helped her down from the saddle, and once again she experienced a sensation of safety. He would never allow her to come to any harm if he could prevent it, she realized. The djinn were not her only protectors.

Connor turned toward de Gabin and clasped wrists with him. "'Tis good to see you again, Sir Herve," Connor told the older knight, though in truth he would have preferred it had Alura visited him alone. That was, of course, utterly impossible.

It was good to see *her* again, no matter what the circumstances. She had looked magnificent, riding through the gate like that, the morning sun glinting off the golden girdle that encircled her small waist. She wore the bracelet and ring he had given her, as well, but other than that and the girdle, she was unadorned by jewelry.

Even though he was playing the host today, he was wearing his sword, Alura noticed. That was the sort of man Connor Warrick was. His blade would never be far from his hand. His reputation as a warrior was well-deserved, and Alura knew now what a valiant heart he possessed. Otherwise, he never would have been able to recover from the horrible injury he had received in the Holy Land. She had twice seen the scar for herself, thanks to Radiya, and she knew enough about wounds to realize how grievous it had truly been. Yet to look at him now, one would never guess what he had endured.

He had won his battle at the tournament against Sir Phillip

on sheer determination alone, Alura told herself. Her admiration for him grew that much more.

He led the visitors through the inner bailey and thus to the doors of the keep itself. They stood wide open. The seneschal, Mossgrave, waited there, and so did Jeremy, Connor's squire. They stepped aside, smiling, as Connor ushered his guests into the keep.

The meal that had been laid out on the long table was something short of a feast, but it was still formidable. Putting it together, especially on such short notice, must have strained the larders of Stavebrook. But Connor, ever gracious, said quietly, "Please, sit down and eat with me."

Servants bustled around as the visitors were seated. Tankards of ale and mead were brought, as were even more platters of ham and potatoes and bread. Alura noticed one of the serving women who looked vaguely familiar, but she could not recall where she had seen the woman before.

Again, she could not help but note the contrast between the welcome she and her family received this time and the way it had been when she visited Morvyn. Though on the surface Morvyn had been every bit as gracious as Connor, Alura had sensed then that he looked down on them, that there was a definite undercurrent of arrogance in his words and expressions. Later, of course, she had discovered that to be true. Morvyn Warrick had been arrogance personified.

She forced her thoughts away from those memories. It would serve no good to bring them up now. Morvyn was dead, thank the Lord, and Alura had never been forced to endure the indignities he had had in mind for her. Now she was betrothed to Connor, and though *he* was the supposed Beast of Stavebrook, Alura had discovered the truth. No matter what he had done in the past, Connor was no beast of any kind. Even if everything that had been said of him before he went away to the Crusade was true, he was a changed man now.

But could a murderer ever truly change?

Alura pushed that thought away as well. When the time came, she would have the truth from his own lips, and that would be soon enough. It was enough for now to know that her life was not at risk, thanks to the mystical protectors she carried with her in the fire opals. After traveling with Connor for months, even though unbeknownst to him, Zahir and Radiya doubtless knew him much better than she did.

She had already begun to remedy that, Alura told herself as she remembered what had passed between them, even though Connor, if he still remembered it, thought it but a dream.

The food was simple fare, but well-prepared. Alura enjoyed the meal, but not to the same extent that her father did. Sir Herve ate with gusto, piling his trencher high more than once. Alura's mother did well to preserve even a small portion for herself.

Connor, on the other hand, who shared his trencher with Alura, was courtesy personified. He made certain that she had the best slices of ham, the most succulent morsels, the warmest pieces of bread. Her cup of mead never ran dry.

She was a beautiful woman, even while she was eating, thought Connor, and that was not an easy thing to accomplish. They spoke of things that were not truly inconsequential—the weather, politics, war—but at the moment they seemed so. The only thing that really mattered to Connor and Alura both was that they were together, and the initial awkwardness soon eased, so that they were chatting together like old friends.

Based on Connor's reputation, Alura would have thought him a brooding, humorless sort who cared for nothing except lust and warfare. Instead, she found him to be well-informed and at times even dryly humorous, as when he commented, "Land is not the only thing our good king is lacking. Graciousness and honor are qualities he could do with more of."

" 'Tis bordering on treason to say so," commented Alura, "though I might well agree with you if I were not a mere female."

"Milady, you could never be a mere anything," murmured Connor.

Where were the words coming from? he wondered. Morvyn had always been the glib one in the family; it was a talent Morvyn had developed at an early age, no doubt out of self-defense. Yet Connor found it astoundingly easy to talk to Alura.

The meal was almost over, and both of them were loath to

see it end, when it came to a sudden, unexpected conclusion.
A man appeared at the door of the great hall and called in an
agitated voice, "Sir Connor!"

Mossgrave moved to intercept the man, putting up a hand
and saying irritably, "Here now, ye can't come bursting in
here to bother his lordship. Go on about yer business, ye
bas—"

"But 'tis my son," interrupted the man. "He's been hurt!"

Connor rose to his feet and motioned to the seneschal. "Let
him pass."

The man hurried over to the table. He was clutching a cap
in his hands as he bowed nervously to Connor. His garb made
it plain he was one of the men who worked in the fields of
Stavebrook. "Beggin' your lordship's pardon," he babbled,
keeping his eyes downcast, "but my lad's been hurt, and I
thought perhaps your healer could do something for him."

"What happened?" asked Connor.

The man swallowed. "Bert—that's my boy—he was usin'
a scythe, an' it slipped and cut his foot. Cut it mighty bad."

"And for that you bother Sir Connor?" said Mossgrave,
sounding aggrieved.

Connor held up a hand. "No, 'tis all right. Where is the
boy?"

"Outside in the bailey, milord. I brung him meself."

Mossgrave sniffed. "Ye ought to be out tending to yer
work."

Connor ignored the seneschal and said, "Take me to him."

Alura came to her feet as Connor strode out of the great
hall, accompanied by Mossgrave and the worried father. She
had started after them when her father said sharply, "Alura,
this is none of our affair. How Sir Connor treats his people is
not our concern."

Alura looked over her shoulder at him. "How quickly you
forget, Father, that it will soon be *my* concern, after Sir Connor
and I are wed." Then she hurried after the men.

She found Connor outside the keep, bending over a boy
perhaps ten years old. The lad had a bloody rag wrapped
tightly around his left foot. Connor bent, put his arms around
the boy, and straightened, lifting the boy effortlessly. "Go tell

Father Iain that he has work to do," Connor said to Moss-grave.

"But, milord—"

"Now."

Mossgrave hurried off, muttering under his breath, and Connor turned toward the boy's father. "Father Iain is more than a priest; he is one of the best healers in England," Connor told the man. "I have seen him work wonders with his herbs and poultices. Would that he had been with me in Palestine last year when that Saracen battle-ax nearly sheered my arm off."

Alura caught her breath. This was the first time she had heard exactly what had happened to Connor, and the words conjured up such a gruesome image that she felt sickened.

Connor heard her gasp and cast a startled glance at her over his shoulder. He had not known that Alura had followed them from the keep. He had certainly not intended that she should see this. Women should be protected from witnessing such things as severe injuries.

Yet, as he reminded himself, only moments earlier he had told her that she would never be a mere woman, at least not in his mind.

He could talk about this with Alura later, if she so wished. For now, the important thing was to get Bert to Father Iain's hut, so that the priest could care for him. He crossed the bailey with long strides.

Alura noted how gently Connor cradled the young boy with each step he took. That he would extend such a combination of strength and tenderness toward the child of a serf was not totally unexpected. It was the mark of a strong man that he could be gentle toward those weaker than him, she thought, and Connor Warrick was nothing if not a strong man. It boded well for how he would treat their own children.

Alura gasped again as she realized what she was thinking. She had leaped ahead in her mind past the wedding to the time she and Connor would have children of their own. Sons, no doubt, though Alura wanted daughters, too. And he would be gentle with those children, and laugh with them, and carry them about the castle on his shoulders, and . . .

And she had no idea how she knew these things to be true, but she was utterly convinced of them anyway. She glanced down at the bracelet and the ring. Were the djinn trying to tell her something? Were the gems glowing a bit brighter than usual? It was hard to tell in the sunlight. Should she summon them to help the child, or wait for the healer?

Alura heard footsteps approaching her and looked up to see Connor striding toward her. "The boy?" she asked.

"Badly cut, as his father said. But he is in the hands of Father Iain now, and they are capable hands indeed." Connor glanced past her at the entrance to the keep. "Your father and mother are still inside?"

Alura nodded. "They thought I should not come out here while you were tending to the boy. At least, my father said it was not our concern."

"But you reminded him quickly enough that it soon would be, I'll wager."

Alura couldn't help but smile. "Yes, and in those words, too."

"We think alike at times."

"But not alike at others."

"Can you tell me what I am thinking now?"

The question took Alura by surprise. She shook her head and said, "No."

Connor held out his hand, reminding her of the night of the ball at Welwynd. "Come riding with me. I would show you Stavebrook, since it will soon be your home."

Alura hesitated. "Alone, you mean?"

"You will trust me, Alura," said Connor, again not knowing exactly where the words came from. "Now or later, but you *will* trust me."

She took a deep breath. "I trust you," she said. "Now."

And again, just like on the night of the ball, she took his hand.

Sixteen

Alura could hardly believe she was doing such a thing. Without even going back into the keep to let her parents know what was happening, she prepared to accompany Connor. He called out to a servant and had the man fetch their horses, and a few moments later a pair of grooms returned with Alura's chestnut palfrey and the glorious golden sorrel that Connor had ridden in the tournament at Welwynd.

"Allow me to assist you, milady," he said.

Finally Alura glanced at the entrance to the keep. "My parents . . ."

"One of my men will tell them that you are inspecting the grounds of the estate with me." He shifted his grip to her waist and boosted her easily into the saddle. Then he strode over to his sorrel and swung up easily onto its back.

He looked magnificent on horseback, poised there as if ready to go into battle. Yet there was nothing posed about his appearance; that was simply the way Connor Warrick was. He looked over at her and smiled as he took up the reins. "Ready?" he asked.

Alura hesitated only a heartbeat before nodding. "Ready."

Side by side, they cantered their mounts out of the castle, emerging into the village. "You ride well," Connor told her, and Alura felt a surge of pride at the compliment from him.

"My father taught me to ride when I was quite young," she said, "as well as how to swing a wooden sword and carry a wooden shield."

"A man with no sons will sometimes do such things. Have you kept up with your swordplay?"

"Alas, no. My mother thought it unladylike, and eventually she won that argument."

Connor laughed, and Alura liked the sound of it. "Again, not an uncommon occurrence," he said.

As they rode through the village, Alura took note of the way the people reacted to Connor's presence. They were quite respectful, the men doffing their caps, the women looking down humbly at the ground. Alura sensed that there was no fear in their actions, however, as there might have been on some estates. The people of Stavebrook were simply giving Connor his due as their lord and master. There were no furtive glances, no hate-filled stares directed at his back after they passed.

As they left the village behind and began riding through the fields, Alura asked, "Is it safe for us to be out here like this? There have been rumors of bandits in the area."

"More than rumors," replied Connor.

She wondered if he would say anything about the attempt on his life the night he and Jeremy left Welwynd, the night she had helped save them by summoning the two djinn and sending them to his aid. He would know nothing of her part in the adventure, since the djinn had not revealed their presence to him.

Instead he continued, "I have sent men to search for them, but so far the brigands have eluded pursuit. However, you need not worry while you are with me on the estate."

"I was not really worried," said Alura, and that much was certainly true. Between Connor's sword and her magical protectors, neither of them had any cause to worry about being attacked.

"I have outriders patrolling the borders of Stavebrook at all times," he said. "There are no bandits in my forests now."

"That seems a great deal of trouble, and expense."

"I would have my people safe," he said simply.

What Alura saw as they rode through the countryside confirmed her earlier estimation: Stavebrook was prosperous, well-managed, and a fine property indeed. No wonder her father had always coveted some measure of control over it. Adjacent to Brynclair as it was in places, if the two estates were ever fully merged, they would constitute perhaps the largest, most profitable barony in all of western England.

And that could happen quite readily, she realized. If she married Connor and had children by him, their firstborn son would ultimately inherit both estates.

They reached a stretch of thick woods, and Connor asked, "Do you hunt?"

"I can use a bow," Alura told him honestly, "but I prefer not to."

He nodded. "Then you shall never have to. But I will teach our sons to hunt in these woods, when they are old enough."

"Our sons . . . how casually you speak of them."

Connor reined in, and Alura did likewise. He looked over at her and said firmly, "If we marry, we will have sons."

"And daughters." Clearly, he had given some thought to children, but so had she.

He nodded without hesitation. "And daughters," he said. "Beautiful, like their mother."

"And our sons will be"—she started to say "handsome," but finished instead—"strong, like their father."

"Aye." He leaned forward in the saddle, resting his hands on the pommel, as he looked out across the forests and fields of Stavebrook.

After a moment, Alura said, "Milord . . . ?"

"Connor."

"Connor," she agreed, then continued, "does it strike you as odd that less than a fortnight ago, we had no intention of marrying, were in fact stubbornly set against it, and now we are talking about our future children?"

He shrugged. "Things change. People change."

"So quickly?"

His head turned and he looked over at her, his eyes intent

on her face. " 'Twas not quickly at all,'' he said, his voice little more than a whisper. " 'Twas slow.''

"S-slow?'' Alura had trouble finding her own voice.

"Ever since that moment in the rain, in the bailey at Bryn-clair, I have known that you and I were fated to be together, Alura. At least, a part of me has known. It took a long time for the rest of me to realize it.''

She heard her own heart beating and felt the languid warmth of the sun seeping into her as she looked at him. His face was still powerful and hard-edged, but there was nothing grim about him now. Serious, aye, almost solemn, in fact. Yet there was a twinkle of joy lurking in his eyes at the same time. A heat stronger than that of the sun began to gather itself inside her.

"If I . . . recall correctly . . . I told you on that day to take me . . . and do with me as you would,'' she whispered. She was actually speaking the words for the third time, but he could not know that.

His voice was a low, rough purr. "That is exactly what I intend to do.''

Something inside her shattered, and at that moment she once again gave her heart completely to Connor Warrick. Twice before, he had held out his hand to her. Now she extended hers to him, and he took it, their fingers twining together tightly as they sat side by side on their horses.

The sudden rumble of thunder made both of them flinch.

"By all that's holy,'' muttered Connor as he twisted in the saddle to look back over his shoulder. Alura did the same, and she saw thick, dark clouds scudding toward them through the sky.

"Where did that storm come from?'' she asked. "The sky was clear only moments ago!''

"Storms can blow up quickly,'' he said. "We'd best get back to the castle before it catches us in the open. Would you like me to lead your horse?''

"I can keep up with you,'' she said. A wind sprang up and plucked at her cloak.

"Very well. Come on.''

They heeled their mounts into motion. The sorrel and the

chestnut both galloped smoothly over the ground, but no matter how fast they ran, the storm clouds seemed to move faster. Abruptly, Connor pulled his horse to a halt. "We cannot reach the castle before the storm," he said.

Alura feared he was right. "What will we do?"

"Follow me. I know another place where we can find shelter."

He wheeled the sorrel and rode quickly into the woods. Alura followed with trepidation. The branches were lashing back and forth wildly in the gale, almost as if they were alive and reaching for her.

Connor seemed to know every twist and turn of the path he took through the forest. No doubt he did, thought Alura. Growing up at Stavebrook as he had, he probably knew every bit of the estate. He had likely played in these very woods as a boy.

The path suddenly dipped down next to a stream. Connor followed it for a short distance, with Alura right behind him, until they came to a high bank that had been undercut at some time in the past by the stream. The brook had changed its course since then, however, leaving a broad, grassy stretch of ground that was partially overhung by the bank.

The sun had been completely obscured by the clouds now, leaving the area underneath the bank thick with shadow. Connor nodded toward it and said over the howling of the wind, " 'Tis not much shelter, but better than naught."

Alura nodded in agreement. Connor dismounted and helped her down from the chestnut, then took the reins of both horses and led them under the bank. With his other hand he clasped Alura's hand.

So far no rain had fallen, but surely it was only a matter of time. No storm could threaten so without producing a downpour.

Alura's eyes adjusted somewhat to the dimness, and she saw that the cavelike area underneath the bank was floored with hard-packed dirt. The grass ended at the edge of the area shaded by the overhang. The air under here smelled of rich, damp earth.

A few roots protruded from the bank, part of the trees that

grew up above. Connor tied the reins of the horses to a particularly sturdy root, then took Alura's hand once more and led her over to a smooth, level spot. He unfastened his cloak from around his neck and spread it on the ground. "Your seat, milady," he said, sweeping his hand around in a gesture of mock grandiosity that made her laugh.

" 'Tis a veritable throne," said Alura in the same spirit. Holding his hand, she sank down gracefully onto the cloak.

Connor sat cross-legged beside her. Together, they peered out at the trees on the opposite side of the stream. The branches were being whipped about by the powerful wind. After a moment, Alura said, "When the storm reaches Stavebrook, my parents will be quite worried about me."

"Surely they know I will keep you safe."

"Safe from the storm, perhaps." Alura turned her head and looked at him.

"Lady Alura . . ."

"Just Alura," she whispered as she leaned toward him.

She knew she was being overly bold once more, but she could not stop herself. The storm had interrupted the feelings that had sprung up inside her, but it had not banished them. Her heart was still galloping along faster than any racing charger, and the coolness of the air had done nothing to diminish the heat that was coursing through her.

Connor lifted his hand and stroked the fingertips along the smoothness of her cheek. "Alura," he murmured. He wanted her in ways he had thought lost to him forever. He had known when he had brought her from the castle that it was improper for the two of them to be alone together. Now, thoughts that were even more improper were tormenting him. His senses were awash in the glory of her. Her beauty filled his eyes, and her scent was like the sweetest flowers in the finest garden in all of England. The warmth of her skin sent a jolt from his fingertips all through him. He wanted to pull her closer and experience more and more of her, to taste her and drown in her. . . .

Their lips met as he leaned toward her.

If the mere touch of his fingers had been enough to make her mad with desire, the hot, hungry pressure of his mouth against hers was sufficient to shake the very foundations of the world. Or perhaps that was just the peals of thunder that suddenly rolled out of the storm clouds shaking her so strongly, Alura thought fleetingly.

No, it was not the thunder at all. 'Twas Connor's kiss, and Connor's kiss alone, that was doing this to her.

She surrendered to it, sliding her arms around his neck and pulling him closer as she opened herself to him. His tongue gently insinuated itself into her mouth, probing and seeking with a series of darting movements she met eagerly with her own tongue. The boldness that a sennight ago she never would have guessed she possessed came over her, and she did some plundering of her own, exploring his mouth. The sensation was exquisite.

Alura became aware that Connor's hands, which at first had gripped her waist, were now beginning to roam. His right one brushed the underside of her left breast, and the mere touch alone was enough to make her moan deep in her throat. Instantly, he drew back, a look of alarm on his face.

"Milady," he said hastily, "forgive me. I meant no offense."

She grasped his wrist and brought his hand fully onto her breast. Connor hesitated, then closed his fingers gently. Alura felt her nipple hardening so that it prodded against his palm as he tenderly cupped the mound of flesh.

She threw back her head and closed her eyes as he caressed her. His lips found her throat, and the tip of his tongue drew a line of fire across her skin. The heat generated by his touch rippled through her and then drew together in her most secret of places until she felt as if the blaze growing there would totally consume her.

Connor slipped her gown off her left shoulder so that he could kiss her there. As his lips grazed hotly on her skin, it was the most natural thing in the world to lower the gown even more, so that her breast was bared. The aureole around her nipple was small and only a slightly darker pink than the rest of her skin. The nipple itself was a tiny, erect bud that seemed to call out to him. He answered the call and fastened his lips over it, sucking delicately. Alura cried out and arched her back.

He was tender beyond belief. All the times Alura had felt that she was safe with him, that he would never hurt her, were now borne out. He could have possessed her, could have leaned her back on the cloak and taken her, and she could have done nothing to stop him. A part of her, in fact, wanted him to do that very thing. Sir Connor Warrick was not known for being kind and considerate, especially where women were concerned.

Yet that was exactly what he was at this moment. What was passing between them was a sharing, not a taking. Alura's gown was around her waist now, along with the shift she wore beneath it. Both of her breasts were bared. Connor moved from one to the other, molding and caressing them with his fingers, all the while using his lips and tongue to coax her higher and higher up the slope of passion. She rested both hands on his head, trailing her fingers through the thick, dark hair.

Finally, when Alura thought she would go mad from wanting him, he lifted his head and said quietly, "These things should wait for our wedding night."

The wind howled even louder, but the overhang protected them from it. Alura looked down into his eyes and said, "I have given my heart to you this day, Connor. I would give you my body, too." *Again.*

He lifted a hand to her hair and stroked the red strands. "In less than a sennight, we will be wed. . . ."

"So what does it truly matter?" Alura finished for him. "I want to make love to you, Connor."

"To the Beast of Stavebrook?"

Alura stiffened. Why did he have to say that? She had put his past reputation completely out of her thoughts. It had nothing to do with the man he was now, nothing to do with the Connor Warrick she had come to know and love.

"You are no beast of any kind," she said, searching his hard-planed face.

"No?" He moved away from her suddenly, not going far, but far enough so that she felt a pang of loss go through her.

"Do you know what people will say when we return to Stavebrook after being alone in the storm this afternoon? They will say that I brought you out here and ravished you." He gestured toward her, sitting there nude to the waist with her breasts heaving from a combination of passion and anger. "Looking at you now, none could doubt that they would be right."

"You did *not* ravish me!" she exclaimed. "Nothing has been done here today that I did not wish to be done."

"Your father would be justified in trying to kill me to avenge his daughter's lost honor. No priest has yet spoken words of joining to us."

"You have seen how little Father cares for my honor. I tell you, it does not matter!"

"But it does," Connor said, his voice practically a whisper again. "I have made truth out of every rumor ever spoken about me."

Inside, he was cursing himself bitterly for the streak of black contrariness that had prompted him to bring up the past. It was clear that Alura no longer cared what had been said about him. At first, his reputation had frightened her, but that was before she had seen what he was really like.

Still, could she forget everything that had stained him? Was that truly possible? No one had ever been able to before. What made Alura de Gabin so different? She might say she did not care, or did not believe, but deep down the knowledge of all the misdeeds that had ever been laid at his feet would still be there.

He turned away from her and muttered, "I never should have brought you from the castle."

She pulled her garments back up around her shoulders and said, "Connor, I understand none of this. I thought . . . I thought that since we will soon be married . . . you *do* still wish to go through with the wedding?"

"I will marry you," he said. "And our marriage will be consummated, of that you may have no doubt. But beyond that, I will never force you into my bed. I will certainly never attack you, as I have today."

But you did not! she wanted to cry out to him. If anything, she had been the aggressor. In her heart, she had known that if she left the castle with him alone, they might find themselves in a position such as this. True, she had even been somewhat nervous about just such a thing. But being nervous about it, and not wanting it to take place, were two entirely different things.

Connor came to his feet. He looked out at the trees across the stream and said, "The wind is not blowing as hard now. Perhaps the storm will pass."

The violence of the wind was indeed subsiding, and the peals of thunder had diminished to a distant rumbling. Alura realized, to her surprise, that the grass just beyond the overhang was dry. No rain had fallen.

"That was . . . an odd storm," she said.

"Very odd." Connor turned toward her at last and extended a hand to help her to her feet. "We must return to the castle as quickly as possible."

It was over, Alura told herself. There would be no lovemaking today. The moment, as charged with power as it had been, had passed, and nothing had really changed.

That was not quite true, she realized as she took Connor's hand yet again. She had seen for herself how deeply it must hurt him to be known as the Beast of Stavebrook. The pain within him must be strong indeed for it to have interrupted what was transpiring between them. Suspicions that had been filtering through her brain were stronger now, and she almost spoke them aloud.

But before she could, he turned abruptly away from her and strode over to the horses. He jerked the reins loose from the root to which they were tied and led the mounts over to her. He helped her into the saddle, then swung up onto his charger. They rode out from underneath the bank and saw blue sky overhead. The black clouds had vanished.

"So very strange," said Connor.

Indeed, thought Alura. What had happened here today was *very* strange.

"You miserable, thrice-damned, donkey-brained excuse for a djinni! You did *what*?"

Zahir folded his arms across his chest and managed to look properly indignant as he glowered through the red barrier that separated him from Radiya. She was in her gem and he in his, and at the moment he was glad of that, though he would not have admitted as much to save his life, such as it was.

"It was romantic," he declared. "What could be more romantic than getting caught in a storm together?" He raised his eyebrows. "Remember that night at our villa on the slopes of Mount Calabus, when we watched the sea gods and the sky gods doing battle? Oh, how the lightning flashed, and oh, how the wind blew and the waves pounded, and what did you do? You know very well what you did. I never saw you so passionate!"

"That was different," insisted Radiya. "We were already married."

"So will they be, in only a few days' time."

"And we already knew we loved each other! Those two are just discovering that."

Zahir spread his hands and shrugged. "So I gave them a little nudge."

Radiya rolled her eyes, shook her head, and turned so that she would not have to look at her husband. " 'Tis my fault," she muttered to herself. "I should have known better than to close myself off from them so they could have their privacy."

"Alura said we didn't have to do that today," Zahir pointed out. "So I didn't."

Radiya swung back toward him. "But you knew I was going to! And you went ahead on your own with that storm anyway."

Again Zahir shrugged. "It seemed to be the right thing to do at the time. You know I want the two of them happily married as much as you do, my love."

"Do not seek to turn aside my wrath with endearments," Radiya warned him.

"I would never do that," Zahir said solemnly. "I just thought, after our night together on Mount Calabus—"

"And stop reminding me of that! It was different, I tell you."

Zahir threw himself down on the cushions that were piled

thickly on the floor of his fire-opal abode. "Well, it does not really matter. It's not as if they called off the wedding or anything. They're still going to get married. The important thing is that we'll be one couple closer to our freedom."

"Only if Alura and Connor are *happily* wed. If they are unhappy together, we are no better off than we were before."

Zahir gestured toward the outside world. "They're happy, they're happy! See for yourself."

"That is exactly what I intend to do," said Radiya, fixing her husband with an ominous stare.

"I do not understand it," Connor said, shaking his head as he looked up at the sky above them. "It is as if no storm ever occurred."

Alura thought the same thing. No rain had fallen, no damage had been done by the winds, and the sky was every bit as clear now as it had been before the sudden tempest. It was almost as if the storm had not been real at all, but rather some-thing . . . magical.

She glanced at the bracelet and ring on her left hand and wondered. As soon as she was back in the privacy of her bedchamber at Brynclair, she would have to have a talk with a certain pair of djinn. . . .

Seventeen

⌒

Jeremy lifted the heavy battle-ax, his muscles straining under its weight. It seemed so effortless when Sir Connor hefted the ax, thought Jeremy, but that was an illusion. A great deal of strength and practice was required to be able to wield one of these weapons effectively.

The time would come when he could do that, Jeremy told himself. The day was coming when he, too, would be a knight of the realm. Sir Connor had made that promise to Jeremy's father on that day that now seemed so long ago, the day the crusaders had waited inside the castle known as Al Sajihd, which they had liberated from the Saracens. Now Saladin and his hordes were on their way back to Al Sajihd, however, determined to cleanse it of the men they regarded as infidels. The crusaders had been just as determined to hold it, but they were, at times, practical men, so they had sent the women and the younger squires out of the castle in the predawn gloom, sent them back to the oasis where Richard Lion-heart's forces were camped. . . .

With a shake of his head, Jeremy put the battle-ax aside. He liked it not when thoughts of that bloody, terrible day invaded his mind. Richard had moved to reinforce Al Sajihd, but the crusaders had gotten there too late—

"Jeremy?"

He turned with a start at the sound of the woman's voice. He had thought that no one had seen him enter this small, stone-walled garden, tucked onto the side of the keep at Stavebrook. It was where he came when he wanted to practice alone with the weaponry of his chosen profession.

The servant called Nessa stood there, just inside the narrow iron gate that was covered with ivy. She shut it behind her and smiled at Jeremy. "What are you doing here?" she asked.

That was none of her business. She certainly had no authority over him, and he was on the verge of saying as much when he found his eyes drawn to the way her ample breasts thrust out against the fabric of her dress. Instead of speaking, he ran his tongue over suddenly dry lips.

Nessa smiled and came toward him. She gestured toward the battle-ax he had lain across a small stone pedestal and asked, "Is that yours?"

"Nay, 'tis Sir Connor's," answered Jeremy without hesitation. He would have liked to impress Nessa by claiming the weapon as his own, but he figured she would know better. He did not want her to catch him in a lie.

"But you can use it, can you not?"

"Of course," he said instantly. "Sir Connor is training me to be a knight."

"He seems a mighty warrior."

"Aye, he is. He fought bravely in the Holy Land for the forces of Christendom."

Nessa came closer, and Jeremy could see the way her nipples stood out against the dress she wore. His lips were still dry, no matter how much he licked them, and his mouth was parched now, too. His breath seemed to catch in his throat. He had to swallow hard.

Though she was several years older than him, Nessa was only slightly taller. Jeremy could almost look her straight in the eye. That is, he could have had his own eyes not kept straying down to her chest. Nessa's smile broadened, and Jeremy knew she was aware of where he was looking. His boldness did not seem to annoy her, however. On the contrary, she seemed to take pleasure in the attention.

"Sir Connor is a very powerful man," Nessa said, and her voice was lower now, more throaty.

Jeremy had to swallow again before he could speak. "Aye, he is one of . . . one of the mightiest knights in all England."

Nessa reached out and put a hand on Jeremy's arm. "I wager you will be, too," she said, "once you have learned all of Sir Connor's secrets."

"S-secrets?"

She leaned closer to him and whispered, " 'Tis said that he has some sort of mystical powers."

"What?" exclaimed Jeremy, hating the way his voice went up a little. "Mystical powers? I've ne'er heard anything so . . . so ridiculous."

Nessa nodded solemnly. "I have been told that he was taught how to perform magic by some wizard while he was in the Holy Land."

"Of course not. I was with him the entire time . . . well, almost the entire time. I was not there for the siege of Al Sajihd . . . but I know that we encountered no wizard."

"Then what is the explanation for the powers that Sir Connor possesses?"

Suddenly, Jeremy realized that she might be talking about that night when he and Sir Connor had battled the bandits on the way back from Welwynd. But how would she even know about that? As Sir Connor had requested, Jeremy had said nothing about what had happened in the woods.

Or had he? It was well-known that he and Sir Connor had encountered bandits; Sir Connor had sent out Sir Berenger and some of the other men-at-arms to search for the thieves. Jeremy wracked his brain, trying to remember if he had mentioned any of the mysterious happenings before Sir Connor had asked him not to. It was possible, he decided. That night was something of a blur in his memory.

Obviously, he *had* let it slip, because now the servants were gossiping about Sir Connor being some sort of wizard or magician. Jeremy knew he had to put a stop to those rumors. If they got back to Sir Connor, the knight would immediately know who was to blame for them.

"Sir Connor possesses no magic powers or mystical abilities of any sort," Jeremy said emphatically. "I know not where you got such a foolish notion, but it is false."

Nessa was even closer now, and her nearness made Jeremy's heart pound wildly. She was so close, in fact, that the tips of her breasts brushed against his chest. "You can tell me," she said quietly. "I promise you, 'twill go no further."

"But I cannot—"

She did not allow him to finish. She put her hands on his shoulders and said, "Someday, when you are a knight, no doubt Sir Connor will pass along all his secrets to you."

"I tell you, Sir Connor has no secret—"

Again she interrupted him, this time by pressing her mouth hard to his. Jeremy's eyes opened so wide he felt as if they were going to leap right out of his head. Instinctively, his arms went around Nessa. She leaned against him, her body molding easily to his.

Panic surged through him, running a race with lust. He had long dreamed of the moment when he would find himself with a warm, willing female in his arms. Despite his habit of intimating otherwise, he had never even kissed a woman, let alone done anything more passionate with one. Now that it was actually happening, he was afraid that he would do the wrong thing—or that he might wake up from this dream, for surely that was what it was.

It was no dream, he realized as Nessa broke the kiss and whispered, "Tell me Sir Connor's secrets."

Jeremy felt as if a bucket of icy rain had just been poured down his back. Though he gloried in the way Nessa's breasts were pillowed against his chest, he managed to get his hands on her shoulders and gently but firmly put some space between them. In a voice made hoarse by both desire and anger, he said, "Sir Connor's secrets are his own, if he has any, which I very much doubt. He is a good man, and there is nothing magical about that."

Nessa looked at him intently for a moment, and he saw the interest in her eyes die away. She twisted out of his grip and turned away toward the garden gate.

"But if you wish," Jeremy called after her, desperation creeping into his voice, "we can kiss again."

"I think not," Nessa flung over her shoulder. "You are naught but a child, and I do not kiss children."

The words struck Jeremy like a mailed fist in the belly. His own hands balled into fists, then slowly relaxed as he watched Nessa leave the garden, clanging the gate behind her.

He hoped Nessa would forget about the gossip she had heard. He hoped all the servants would cease spreading rumors about Sir Connor. Perhaps he ought to say something to Mossgrave, thought Jeremy, so that the seneschal could have a talk with the servants.

He decided against that. Taking the matter to Mossgrave would just risk spreading the gossip even more, since 'twas well known that the old man could not keep his mouth shut.

No, Jeremy decided, he would keep his own counsel about this and hope the whole thing died of its own accord. With the wedding to Lady Alura coming up in less than a sennight, Sir Connor certainly had more important things to worry about right now.

"Well, you two have certainly been gone long enough," Sir Herve grumbled grumpily as Alura and Connor walked back into the great hall of Stavebrook. He was seated at the table, his legs stretched out in front of him.

Katharine got to her feet. "Alura, are you all right?" she asked.

"Of course, Mother," replied Alura. "I was with Connor. Why would I not be all right?"

Sir Herve grunted loudly. His meaning was clear. Alura glanced over at Connor and saw him flush slightly. Her father could be quite tactless at times.

To change the subject, she said, "Did you hear thunder a short time ago?"

"Thunder?" repeated Sir Herve. "There was no thunder. The sky is clear. 'Tis a beautiful day."

Alura and Connor exchanged a glance. "It must have been . . . something else we heard," said Connor.

"No matter." Sir Herve got to his feet. "Are you going to offer us the hospitality of your castle for the night, since you have kept my daughter out riding most of the afternoon?"

"Of course," Connor answered instantly. "You are all welcome to stay. In fact, I insist upon it. 'Twould not be safe for you to start back to Brynclair this late, not with the brigands that sometimes haunt the roads. You will stay until the morrow."

"Very good," said de Gabin with a nod.

Alura was not sure if she liked the idea of spending the night at Stavebrook. She had been looking forward to sleeping in her own bed, and besides, being under the same roof with Connor might prove to be an uncomfortable temptation. She would not give in to that temptation, she told herself; the moment when she would have had come and gone that afternoon, in the cavelike hollow under the bank of the stream. She was confident that she could now control her desires until she and Connor were properly wed. But given her choice, she would have preferred not to stay here at Stavebrook tonight.

Connor glanced around. One of the servants had followed them into the hall, the woman called Nessa. He said to her, "Take Lady Katharine and Lady Alura upstairs so that they may select sleeping chambers for themselves."

Nessa bobbed her head. "Yes, milord."

Katharine took Alura's arm, and together they followed the servant up the curving stairs. Alura thought she noticed a time or two when Nessa cast a look back at them that was decidedly hostile. She was certain it was not her imagination, either. For some reason, the woman did not like them.

Well, it mattered little whether Nessa liked them, Alura decided. Once she was the mistress of this house, if Nessa was unable to show her the proper respect, she would see that the woman worked elsewhere. That would probably be better for all concerned.

Nessa led them down a corridor and into a small chamber. "Will this do for the lady Alura?" she asked in a surly voice.

The bed was freshly made, and there were clean rushes on the floor that gave off a light scent of mint. Alura nodded and said, "This will be quite acceptable."

Nessa turned to Katharine. "Milady, the chamber shared by you and Sir Herve will be directly across the corridor."

"Good," said Katharine, with a meaningful look at Alura.

Clearly, she intended to make sure there were no nighttime visits to her daughter's chamber by the lord of the castle.

Alura felt her face growing warm. Did everyone at Stavebrook think that she and Connor had coupled this afternoon? That might explain why Nessa evidently did not like her. The woman could be jealous. She might be attracted to Connor herself.

"You may leave us now," Katharine said to Nessa, and Alura was glad her mother was dismissing the servant. Alura wished that her mother would leave the small chamber, too, so that she could summon Zahir and Radiya to check on the injured child and find out what, if anything, the djinn had had to do with that mysterious storm.

As soon as Nessa was gone, Katharine cooperated, by expressing a wish to lie down for a time. The journey from Brynclair had made her weary, she said, and there had been no chance to rest since their arrival at Stavebrook. She hugged and kissed Alura and said, "Soon, this will be your home."

"Yes," said Alura, her voice sounding slightly hollow even to her own ears. "Soon."

When Katharine had withdrawn from the room, Alura made sure the heavy wooden door was securely shut, then stroked the twin fire opals in the settings of the bracelet and the ring. Thick smoke billowed from the gems, twisting and writhing and growing even thicker until it took on the familiar shapes of the two djinn. As soon as she had materialized, Radiya said, "Mistress, I am so sorry about what happened today—"

"*You* summoned that storm!" said Alura reproachfully.

"Not I," said Radiya, shooting an angry glance at Zahir. He folded his arms across his chest and tried to look dignified as he pretended that he had not even heard her veiled accusation.

"Zahir, I want you to go check on the child that was injured today and then come back and tell me if you caused that storm. I command you," said Alura.

Zahir winced, then left and returned in a wisp of smoke. "The child will be fine. As for the storm, it seemed like a good idea at the time," he began. "Some wind, a few claps of thunder, maybe a little rain—not enough to get you too

wet, mind you, just a shower—and off you go to some place
secluded to watch the storm and, ah, be together.'' Clearly,
Radiya had told him nothing of what had transpired between
Connor and Alura while he was out exploring Brynclair.

"That would have been highly improper," said Alura, col-
oring as she thought about her time in her dream castle.

"Oh, not really," said Zahir. "After all, you're going to be
married soon, and you love each other—"

"You *do* love each other, do you not?" Radiya interrupted
to ask.

Alura was not sure how to answer. "I am coming to love
Connor," she finally said. "And I believed that he was coming
to love me. Now I am not so certain."

Radiya looked stricken. "Why not? What did he say, or do,
to make you think so?"

"Were you not watching?" snapped Alura. True, she had
not commanded the djinn to cease their observation today, but
she still felt spied upon.

"I was not, not all the time," said Radiya. "Not in time to
prevent Zahir from acting so rashly."

"Rashly?" he yelped. "You call that rashly? I was just
trying to make things a little more romantic! I thought every-
body would be happy."

Slowly, Alura said, "Connor has been hurt . . . badly."

"You mean that Saracen battle-ax—" began Zahir.

Alura stopped him by shaking her head. "I mean the reputation he carries as the Beast of Stavebrook. He may not be
able to feel love, truly, because he fears he does not deserve
to be loved in return."

Zahir sighed. "Thousands of years go by, and you females
are still the same. You all *think* too much!"

"Ignore this old fool," said Radiya. "You and Connor can
make each other happy, mistress. I know this as well as I know
anything in the cosmos. You must not give up."

Alura's chin lifted defiantly. "I do not intend to give up,"
she said. "But it may take time—"

"That's something you do not have an abundance of," said
Zahir. "The wedding will be here before you know it."

Alura nodded. She was all too aware of the nearness of the

wedding. As much to herself as to the djinn, she mused, "There is something I can do that may help."

"Then you should do it," Radiya said without hesitation.

"But it could make things worse."

"All of life is a risk," said Zahir. "Look at us. Do you think we were ever afraid to take a chance?"

"And look where—and what—we are now," snapped Radiya. As Zahir shrugged, Radiya turned back to Alura and went on, "What is this thing you speak of?"

Alura took a deep breath. "I can tell Connor the truth about his brother Morvyn . . . and about myself."

Connor shrugged out of his tunic and flung it angrily in the corner of his bedchamber. He'd planned to dress in fresh clothing for dinner, but instead he strode over to the window and threw the shutter wide so that he could look out over Stavebrook.

Whatever had possessed him to be so bold with Alura this afternoon? he asked himself. He should have known better. She was the daughter of a baron and not to be trifled with. He certainly had no business kissing her and baring her breasts as he had.

But he knew that in the back of his mind, he had planned to do exactly that when he led her to the hollow underneath the bank of the stream. That, and more. The memories of his dream had burned within him for days now, and he had to extinguish that fire.

Then the moment had indeed come, and he had asked her the question that had ruined everything. He had reminded her of his past, and she had recoiled.

He could not blame her. Knowing all the things that had been said about him, he knew that any woman would have to be a fool not to feel some trepidation at the thought of being made love to by him. Lady Alura de Gabin was many things, but a fool was not one of them.

He'd had to be sure, though. Had to be certain that she really wanted him, that she had no other reason for what she was doing.

He had his answer now. She would submit to him once they

were married because the law required it, but always she would know that she was lying with the Beast of Stavebrook.

A sudden noise behind him broke into his reverie. Connor turned, his hand going to his hip where his sword usually hung. The weapon was not there now, however. He had unbuckled the sheath and tossed it on the bed when he'd come into the chamber. It was careless of him. Two quick steps would bring him within reach of the sword, but in the time required for those steps, a proficient enemy could have run him through.

But there was no need to worry about that, he saw. The person standing hesitantly in the doorway was only one of the servants. "What is it, Nessa?" asked Connor.

"I thought you'd like to know, milord, that your guests are in their chambers."

"Where did you put them?"

"In the west wing, milord."

Connor grunted. His own bedchamber was on the second floor of the tower that rose in the center of the keep. Two more stories above him was the room where Elspeth Lyle had met her tragic end. Connor had not set foot in that room since that day, and he wondered why he thought about it now.

As he struggled with the black mood that gripped him, he managed not to scowl as he nodded to Nessa and said, "That will be all."

She came a step farther into the room. "Is there naught else I can do for you, milord?"

Connor shook his head and started to turn away, but Nessa came on into the room anyway. "If there is ever anything you need, milord, anything at all," she said. "I am so grateful to you for allowing me to stay here—"

Connor waved a hand in dismissal. "Just do your work, that is all I require."

"But I can do . . . so much more."

The husky edge in her voice finally made him look more closely at her, and he saw the boldness in her eyes. He became aware that he was stripped to the waist. Her gaze was fastened on his broad, muscular chest, lightly furred with dark hair, and on his powerful shoulders and arms. She looked at the long scar on his right shoulder and said, "You were badly hurt."

"Aye. A Saracen battle-ax near cleaved my arm off."

"How in God's name did you ever recover from such a wound, milord?"

Connor wanted her to leave, but he thought he might get rid of her more quickly if he indulged her curiosity and told her what had happened to him in the Holy Land. Some of it, anyway, he reminded himself. Some of the atrocities he had witnessed were so terrible that he would take them to the grave with him. He would never tell anyone, not his squire, not his wife, and certainly not this servant girl.

"I was blessed to have the attentions of an excellent healer. A Frankish priest, he was, and he knew much about poultices and herbs. Almost as much as our healer here at Stavebrook, Father Iain. If you ever have need of him, do not hesitate to seek his services."

"I will, milord," said Nessa. "Then there was nothing . . . unusual about the way your wound was healed?"

"Unusual?" repeated Connor with a frown. "There was nothing unusual save that the wound did not kill me, when many men succumbed to lesser injuries. But that was God's providence, for which I am thankful."

Though he had not been sure at first if he was thankful or not, when it had appeared that he would spend the rest of his life as a cripple.

Nessa persisted, coming closer to him, so close that he could feel the warmth of her breath against his bare chest. "I am told it was more than that that saved you, milord. There has been talk of . . . magic. This Frankish priest, he was not a sorcerer of some sort?"

"Father Alistair? A sorcerer?" Connor did not know whether to laugh at such a suggestion or be angry about it. "If you had ever known the man, you would not ask such a question, Nessa," he said sternly. "He was a deeply religious man."

"But the Holy Land is a mysterious place, I have heard. Perhaps you encountered someone else there with powers beyond the scope of what we know."

"Someone has filled your head with wild tales, girl. The

only thing mysterious about Palestine is why so many have died fighting over it, all these many years.'' Connor stepped back. He was growing uncomfortably aware of how close Nessa had come to him. Whether she was motivated by gratitude or ambition, clearly she wanted him to know that he could take her any time he wished.

She grew even more bold, reaching out to rest the warm palm of her hand against his chest. "Milord . . ." she said softly.

"Go now," he said between gritted teeth.

"I wish only to please you."

"You may please me by going on about your tasks," Connor told her. "This room is no place for you."

"But milord—"

Connor grasped her wrist, restraining his strength so that he would not hurt her. There was enough power in his grip, though, to show her that he meant what he said.

"Do not come here again unless I summon you," he ordered. Nessa had gone pale when he took hold of her wrist, and now she nodded her understanding.

Connor released her, and she backed away quickly. He saw fear in her eyes. She was remembering Elspeth Lyle and what had happened to her, remembering that he was called the Beast of Stavebrook. "I . . . I meant no offense, milord," she said.

"Just go," said Connor, his voice barely above a whisper.

He turned away, grateful when he heard the door close behind Nessa. Perhaps it had been a mistake to allow her to come here to Stavebrook, he thought. But he doubted if she would be so bold around him again. Surely she had learned her lesson this day.

Alura had, that was certain, Connor told himself, and the black mood that had never really gone away descended upon him once more.

Eighteen

"Milord, I must speak with you."

Connor paused on the second-floor landing and turned instantly at the sound of the voice behind him. He saw Alura coming toward him along the corridor. She looked beautiful and gracious in a gown and a flowing cloak. Her red hair was covered with a wimple, giving her a somewhat more demure appearance than when it was unbound and flowing around her shoulders.

How did he know that? he thought with a sudden frown. Ah, yes, the dream.

"Milord," she said again, but Connor stopped her.

"You agreed to call me Connor," he said, "at least when we are alone."

She had come close enough to him that he could smell the faint scent of roses about her. She said, " 'Tis because we are alone that I would speak with you now—"

"There you are, Alura," came her mother's voice. Both Alura and Connor turned to see Sir Herve and Lady Katharine coming along the corridor toward them. Katharine went on, "I knocked on the door of your chamber, but I suppose you must have already left."

Alura felt her heart sink. She had several things to say to

Connor, things that required privacy. They were matters she could not discuss in front of her parents.

For his part, Connor felt a surge of relief. He had decided that he could not allow himself to be alone with Alura again until after the wedding. It was clear she shared the passion he felt for her, but at the same time, she still feared him, even if only slightly.

Once they were man and wife, he could tell her the truth.

"Come downstairs," he said to Sir Herve and Lady Katharine, mustering up a heartiness he did not really feel. "I am certain the cooks have prepared an excellent meal."

"One can but hope," said Sir Herve. Arm in arm with his wife, he started down the staircase.

Connor took Alura's arm and followed. She leaned close to him and hissed, "Connor, I must speak with you alone."

"Later," he said.

Much later, he thought. In fact, after the wedding had taken place.

The two couples descended the staircase, Alura seething with frustration as she allowed Connor to lead her to the table in the great hall. As Connor had predicted, the cooks had provided a fine meal for them: roast boar, lentils, and still-steaming loaves of bread. The mead and ale flowed freely, and Sir Herve's mood visibly improved.

Connor was glad to see that Nessa was nowhere in sight. He planned to speak to Mossgrave and have the seneschal see to it that Nessa no longer worked inside the keep. Connor had no doubt he would be able to withstand the temptation of having her around; Alura was the only woman who had succeeded, even temporarily, in piercing the barrier he had erected around himself. But he had no wish to remind himself of the encounter with Nessa, either.

Alura's frustration grew more intense as the evening progressed. She had hoped that her father and mother would return to their chamber when the meal was over, but instead Connor and Sir Herve wound up standing in front of the fireplace with cups of ale in their hands as they talked about the Crusades.

"Things will be different when Richard returns from Outremer," Sir Herve declared. "John believes himself to be the true king, as if his brother had never held the throne."

"That is what Lackland would have everyone else believe," said Connor. "He knows better. And if he refuses to give up the throne when Richard comes back from the Holy Land, there will be civil war."

Sir Herve snorted in contempt. "A war that John will lose almost immediately. Few if any of the barons will support him over Lion-heart."

"Nor should they."

Sir Herve raised his cup and said, " 'Tis good that we are in agreement on this matter. I would hate to have to take up arms 'gainst my own son-in-law, should war come."

"I would not like that, either, Sir Herve."

The older man nodded in satisfaction and then drank deeply. Connor joined him. Sir Herve was a schemer and a blowhard, but at least he was a loyal supporter of the true king.

At the table, Katharine clasped Alura's hand and said, "We should leave them to their talk. Mayhap 'twill be late before they finish."

Alura suppressed a groan of disappointment. Her conversation with Connor would have to wait, it appeared. Grudgingly, she allowed her mother to lead her upstairs.

"Sleep well, dear," said Katharine as they paused in the corridor outside the bedchambers. She brushed a kiss across Alura's cheek. With a sigh, Alura went into her chamber and closed the door.

Downstairs, Connor sighed, too . . . with relief. He had survived this night's temptation.

Nessa had been looking for a way out of Stavebrook all evening. The guards here were not as careless, nor as lustful, as the ones at Welwynd. Even the sentries on duty at the postern gate were alert, and when she approached them with a jug of ale, thinking to distract them with it, they had glared at her and sent her away.

They probably feared the wrath of the Beast of Stavebrook, she thought. They did not want to face what might happen to them if they were caught being derelict in their duty.

Several people were camped in the outer bailey, including a group of itinerant monks. They had entered the castle shortly after dark, pulling their carts with them. Now they were sitting around and chanting some sort of prayer, and Nessa found the sound grating on her nerves as she crossed the bailey toward the outer wall. She had to find a way to leave the castle so that she could meet Dermot. If she failed, he would be angry with her, and she feared that as much as the guards feared angering Connor Warrick, but for very different reasons. Nessa could not bear the thought of Dermot withholding his passion from her.

She gasped and flinched as a robed and hooded figure suddenly loomed up close beside her. One of the monks, she realized. What did he want with her? Monks took vows of chastity, did they not?

"My child," murmured the hooded figure, "how fare you?"

"Dermot!" she exclaimed. "What in God's name—"

"Probably 'tis best not to ask that, considering my garb," he said quietly. "Follow me—just not too closely."

He made a vague sign with his hand, as if he was blessing her, then strode off toward an even more shadowy part of the bailey. Nessa made as if to go in another direction, then turned and followed as soon as she reached a thick enough patch of shadow.

A hand came out of the darkness and closed on her arm. She gasped again and felt a surge of anger. Dermot liked to do that. Did he not have such a grip on her heart, she would have enjoyed slipping a knife into him, she thought.

Instead she went eagerly into his arms. The sides of the cowl he was wearing brushed her face as she kissed him. After a moment, he pulled back and cupped her chin. "I'll wager you've never been ridden by a holy man, have you?" he asked mockingly.

"Not until tonight," she replied, though that was patently untrue.

She did not have to see his face to know that it wore a leer as he began groping at her clothes.

Later, they sat next to each other on the ground and Dermot

asked, "What have you found out about Warrick's mystical powers?"

"He has none," replied Nessa. "At least, none that I can discover."

"What?" snapped Dermot. " 'Tis impossible. The man summoned up demons to protect him and the squire, that night in the woods."

"I have asked everyone in the castle about Warrick's powers, and none of them has the least idea what I am talking about. The man is no wizard or warlock, Dermot."

"I told you to get close to Warrick himself, to work your own particular sort of magic."

"Aye, and I tried," said Nessa. "He sees naught but that redheaded witch."

"What about the squire? He was there that night, he must know something."

Nessa smiled slightly at the memory of the way young Jeremy had looked at her. "That one I had panting so hard he would have told me anything, had he known it. And I've allowed the seneschal to fondle my bottom so much there must be a permanent imprint of his hand there, all with no results. I am sorry, Dermot, but there is no magic to be found here."

He came to his feet, uncoiling like a cat. "Dammit!" he said. "I was so sure. . . . There was magic afoot that night, Nessa, I swear it!" He paced a few steps, then stopped short and suddenly turned back toward her. "What did you say about Warrick's betrothed?"

"I called her a redheaded witch," Nessa said with a scowl. She had no liking for Alura de Gabin.

"Perhaps you are more right than you know," Dermot said slowly.

Nessa lifted a hand to her mouth in surprise as she understood what he meant. "You think the woman is the one with the mystical power," she said.

" 'Tis said that those who possess magical abilities can sometimes see far distances. From Welwynd to the woods where we laid in wait for Warrick and the boy, perhaps." Dermot nodded, as much to himself as to Nessa. "Aye, that would explain it. Lady Alura must have sent those spirits to protect the man she plans to marry.''

"What are you going to do now?" asked Nessa. "Send me to work at Brynclair?"

Dermot's laugh was scornful. "Nay, I think not. 'Tis time I took this matter into my own hands.''

Nessa scrambled to her feet. "What do you plan?" she demanded. "That woman cannot be trusted—"

"I do not intend to trust her, little one," said Dermot. He laughed again. "Methinks you are jealous of the fair lady Alura.''

"Jealous?" said Nessa. "Jealous of that skinny, dough-faced, thin-blooded—"

"Do not worry, her charms will have no effect on me. But if I am to discover her secrets, I must be near her." Dermot lifted a hand and rubbed his angular jaw in thought. "Perhaps her father could use a new man-at-arms.''

"And what of me? Am I to stay here?"

"I still have need of someone to watch Warrick. Who knows, perhaps you will stumble over something useful after all." He stepped closer to her and pulled her into his arms. "Now, give me another kiss before I return to my saintly companions.''

"The other monks . . . they are the rest of the band?"

"Aye."

"You could take the castle," suggested Nessa.

Dermot shook his head. "The odds are too heavy, even with surprise on our side. We would all die, skewered by the arrows and pikes of Warrick's guards." He pressed his mouth hard against hers for a moment, then said, "But one day, all the power will be mine. That day will be but the beginning. . . .''

"The beginning of what?"

"A reckoning the likes of which England has ne'er before seen," said Dermot.

Frustrated by the fact that she had been unable to speak to Connor in private, Alura arose early the next morning hopeful of snatching a moment or two alone with him.

But not only were her father and mother already in the great hall when she descended the curving staircase, there was no sign of Connor, either.

"If you are wondering where that young man of yours has gone," said Sir Herve, "he and his squire left a short time ago for an inspection of the estate. Rather rude of him to desert his guests this way, if you ask me."

"Sir Connor's servants will take care of anything we need before we depart," said Katharine. "He made that quite clear."

Alura felt her heart sink. "Connor is not coming back before we leave for Brynclair?"

Sir Herve shook his head and said, "The errand on which he left will take most of the day, he claimed. If you ask me, he was simply tired of having to be gracious to us."

Katharine came to Alura's side and laid a hand on her arm. "Try not to be too disappointed," she said. "The wedding is only a few days away, and after that, you will see Connor every day."

Alura had hoped to clear up a few things between them before that day arrived. But there was nothing she could do about it now, she told herself.

Connor had not left the castle because he was tired of being their host, she thought. He had left because he did not want to see *her* again after what had happened the day before.

He had told her plainly that he did not intend to call off the wedding. That meant he was not so upset with her that he no longer wished to marry her. But her reaction to his comments about his reputation had indeed bothered him. Alura felt the frustration growing again inside her. She could probably put a stop to the uncertainties between them by asking him a few simple questions and answering those questions he would no doubt have for her. That conversation could not take place, however, except in private.

She sighed and said, "I am sure you are right, Mother," though in truth she was not sure at all.

After breakfast, servants supervised by Mossgrave packed up the belongings of the visitors and loaded them onto the horses. Alura saw her father talking quietly to the seneschal and wondered what they were discussing. She recalled how

Sir Herve had plotted with Mossgrave to seize control of Stavebrook when it appeared that Morvyn had died without leaving any heirs, and she hoped sincerely that the two men were not hatching more mischief between them.

The men-at-arms who had accompanied them from Bryn-clair were ready to travel, so the party was able to get under-way with a minimum of delay. For once, Alura wished things had moved more slowly. She had hoped that Connor would return to the castle before she and her parents left, though she knew that was unlikely. He might even be watching from a distance, making sure that they were gone before he came back.

The journey to Brynclair passed without incident. They arrived home shortly after midday. But no sooner had the party ridden through the gates into the outer bailey than the clashing of swords could be heard. Sir Herve reined in sharply and muttered, "God's eyes! What's that commotion?"

Alura brought her mount to a halt and looked toward the sound of the disturbance. She saw a man in a lightweight mail tunic over gray hose facing two other men in battle. Swords flashed in the sunlight as the combatants lunged back and forth. The lone man was especially nimble as he darted his blade from one side to the other to block the thrusts of his opponents, two of Sir Herve's men-at-arms who had been left at Brynclair. With a flick of his wrist and a sudden, unexpected twist, he disarmed one of his opponents, sending the man's sword spinning away through the air. Whirling to face the other man, he parried, feinted, and then sent a thrust of his own at the man's suddenly unprotected throat. Alura's eyes widened in horror. She thought she was about to see one of her father's men killed. But the point of the stranger's sword stopped a mere hand's breadth from the neck of his foe.

"Bravo!" called Sir Herve, who had watched the demonstration with admiring eyes. "Well done, lad! But who are you?"

The stranger stepped back, lowering his blade from the throat of his opponent. Sir Herve's man had gone slightly pale, but now he flushed with anger as the swordsman who had defeated him turned so casually away.

The man was several years older than Alura, perhaps three and twenty. He had a shock of dark hair and a handsome face. He sheathed his sword and then bowed respectfully to Sir Herve, Katharine, and Alura. When he straightened, he said, "I am called Dermot, milord. I make my way with my blade."

Sir Herve grunted. "A sell-sword, eh? What do you here at Brynclair?"

The man who had just been defeated by Dermot stepped up and said in surly tones, "This lout wagered he could defeat any two of your men-at-arms, milord. He claimed he was more proficient than us in the art of swordplay. 'Twas a challenge we could not allow to go unanswered."

"So you took up arms against him and allowed him to prove his claim," Sir Herve said scathingly.

"Merely a demonstration of my prowess, milord," said Dermot. "I am gratified that you were able to witness it, since 'tis you who hold my fate in your hands."

"I?" said Sir Herve with a frown.

"I grow tired of roaming the countryside," said Dermot. "I have not had a true home for many years. Since I am told that Brynclair is the fairest estate in this district, my hope is that you can use another man-at-arms."

"You wish to carry my standard?"

Dermot lowered his head respectfully. "If such be your wish, milord."

Sir Herve rubbed his bristly chin. " 'Tis true you seem to fight well with the sword," he said. "But can you handle a lance?"

"Unfortunately, I have neither horse nor shield, milord, else I would show you just how well I can wield a lance."

Sir Herve smiled slightly. "A horse and a shield can be arranged." He turned his head to bark orders at his knights. When some of them had gone to fetch the things that would be needed for Dermot to demonstrate his skill with a lance, Sir Herve said to Katharine and Alura, "You ladies can continue on to the keep."

Alura was curious as to how well the newcomer would fare in this test, but Katharine said, "Come, Alura," ending her hopes of remaining to watch the mock combat. The two of them, with their servants, rode on into the inner bailey.

As soon as she was inside, Alura went up the stairs to the second floor of the keep and entered her chamber. From the window, she could look down into the outer bailey and see the crowd that had gathered there, including most of her father's men-at-arms and many of the villagers. Alura saw wagers being exchanged as Sir Herve's knights readied the horses for the competition. Dermot was given a heavier coat of mail to wear, along with a helmet and a shield. A long, heavy lance was brought out and handed up to him after he had mounted one of the chargers. His opponent was helped up onto the other charger, and Alura recognized him as Sir Griffith, one of her father's best men with a lance. Dermot would have to be skillful indeed to defeat Sir Griffith.

While there was not as much room inside the outer bailey as there was on a tournament field, Sir Herve's men-at-arms were able to clear a large enough area for the jousting to take place. Sir Griffith and Dermot rode to opposite ends of the space and turned their horses to face each other. Sir Herve was still mounted on his charger and sat to one side with a gauntleted hand raised in the air. His hand suddenly slashed downward in the signal to begin.

This was the first time Alura had seen men do battle since the tournament at Welwynd. She remembered how she had felt as she watched Connor gallop toward Sir Phillip of Staunton. She experienced none of that fear now; she was fond of Sir Griffith as she was of most of her father's men, regarding them as uncles of a sort, and of course she knew the man called Dermot not at all. But she observed with keen interest anyway, and she could not help but flinch a little as the sound of lances striking shields shattered the peace of the warm spring air.

Neither man was unhorsed on the first pass, so they rode past each other, wheeled their mounts, and charged again. Again the crash of lances came to Alura's ears, and again both men stayed in the saddle. Shouts of encouragement and appreciation came from the crowd gathered in the bailey. The knights were supporting one of their own, of course. Dermot seemed to have no one cheering him on, but if that bothered him he gave no sign of it.

Again and yet again the two men charged at each other, and on the fourth strike, both lances broke. That brought a groan of disappointment from the crowd, since there would be no clear-cut victor. Normally, the combat might have continued with swords, but Sir Herve heeled his horse forward, riding out into the open space between the two men. "Enough!" he called in a voice loud enough for Alura to hear. He motioned for Dermot to approach him.

"Sell-sword or no, you have demonstrated your prowess sufficiently for me," Sir Herve said to the newcomer. "If you wish a place here, 'tis yours."

Dermot lowered his head and spoke, no doubt thanking Sir Herve for accepting him. The other knights looked on tensely as Sir Griffith rode over to join Sir Herve and Dermot. That tension evaporated as Sir Griffith raised the visor of his helmet and struck Dermot on the shoulder with a mailed fist. "Well fought, man!" he exclaimed.

Dermot grinned and nodded, accepting the compliment. The other men-at-arms surrounded his horse. One of them took the broken lance from him, while two others helped him dismount from the charger. The group started toward the keep, probably intent on sharing more than a few tankards of ale, thought Alura.

But before he left the outer bailey, the man called Dermot glanced up at the keep, and he must have seen Alura standing there, watching. Their eyes seemed to meet, even at this distance. Alura stepped back suddenly, shocked by her reaction to his gaze. He was still smiling, and there seemed to be nothing to fear in his face.

Alura had felt *something*, though, when Dermot had looked at her, and she cared little for the sensation that went through her. She almost reached for the fire opals, so that she could summon the djinn to protect her.

Then she stopped in mid-gesture, telling herself that she was being ridiculous. There was no need to fear Dermot. He was just a drifting fighter, the same sort of man who had come here to Brynclair before and found a home as one of her father's men-at-arms.

Besides, in less than a sennight, she would be wed to Connor and would then reside at Stavebrook. She would not even be here at Brynclair except to visit, so she might not ever see Dermot again.

She lowered her hand away from the gems, and the djinn remained where they were, in their fire-opal homes.

Nineteen

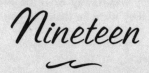

Plans proceeded apace for the wedding, and as the day itself approached, Alura found herself growing more nervous, as any bride would.

She was not just any bride, however. She was the betrothed of Connor Warrick, the Beast of Stavebrook, and she had that fact emphasized in a most unpleasant manner a couple of days before the wedding was to take place.

Guests had already begun to arrive at Brynclair. From all over the district they came, noblemen and their wives and children and servants and men-at-arms. Monks and minstrels, bards and barons, even a band of gypsies that set up their colorful tents outside the castle walls. Brynclair was crowded, with people coming and going all the time, and while Sir Herve's guards tried to keep track of everyone, it was next to impossible to do so. Had the situation been different, it was likely that Melusine Lyle never would have confronted Alura.

Alura rose early that morning, knowing that there was still much to do before the wedding could take place. She intended to spend the morning helping her mother to supervise the placement of the special wall hangings that the castle's weavers had been working on ever since the betrothal was announced. The hangings were ready now and would soon decorate the walls of the keep.

Before going downstairs, Alura summoned Radiya and Zahir from their homes in the bracelet and the ring. Radiya was quite excited about the impending wedding, but Zahir was rather grumpy this morning.

"Hmmph!" he said when Radiya commented on the preparations. "Foolishness, if you ask me. All these decorations, bah!"

Radiya turned on him with a scowl. "Foolishness?" she repeated. "What, would you have these two lovely young people united in a stable?"

"If the bond is true, it matters not where the joining takes place," said Zahir. He folded his arms across his chest and nodded curtly, as if to say that he would permit no further argument.

If that was his intent, he was to be disappointed, for Radiya said sharply, "Only an old fool would believe such a thing. A wedding is something that occurs only once in a woman's life, if she is fortunate."

"Some men might be more fortunate not to be wed at all," muttered Zahir.

"I heard that! Is that the way you feel, o prince of djinn? Prince of idiots would be a more apt description!"

Alura held her hands up to stop their habitual bickering. "Enough of this," she said. "With the wedding so close, I just wanted to know if the two of you foresaw any sort of ominous portents, or anything else I should know about."

"Now that you mention it . . ." began Zahir.

" 'Tis nothing," Radiya interrupted him hastily.

"What?" asked Alura.

Radiya grimaced. "Merely a slight . . . disturbance . . . in the ebb and flow of the cosmos. We can sense it, but there is no way of knowing what it means. But 'tis so small, most probably it means nothing at all."

"A plague of grasshoppers about to descend on the land, or something like that," added Zahir. "It doesn't have to have anything to do with you."

"I would think a plague of grasshoppers might affect me,

too," Alura said dryly. "But if you are certain I have no need to be concerned . . ."

Zahir thumped himself on the chest with a fist. "Not with us around," he declared. "We shall protect you from those grasshoppers."

"Or whatever else may come," said Radiya.

Alura smiled wistfully and said in a soft voice, "Can you protect my heart?"

Zahir looked pained. "Like we told you before, physical things are no problem—"

"But the way people feel about each other, that is much more difficult," finished Radiya. She touched Alura lightly on the shoulder. "Do not worry, Alura. Connor loves you, and you love him. That is enough."

Is it? Alura asked herself. She hoped the djinni was right, that love was enough to conquer all the obstacles placed in the way of happiness, but she could not be sure. Not yet.

At Alura's command, the djinn turned back into smoke and returned to their homes in the fire opals. She went downstairs and found her mother in the great hall, surrounded by servants.

"There you are, Alura," said Katharine. She held up one of the wall hangings. "Tell me, where do you think this should go?"

Alura stepped back to study the design on the hanging, then gestured toward one of the walls. "Perhaps over there?" she suggested.

"An excellent idea," agreed Katharine, and she gave the hanging to one of the servants. "You have an eye for color, my dear."

"A shame you have no sense of decency to go with it."

The harsh, unexpected words were delivered in a cold voice from behind Alura. She stiffened and then turned to see who had spoken. It was a woman's voice, but one unfamiliar to Alura.

The woman stood there, tall and haughty, regarding Alura with blue eyes that blazed brightly with hatred in a narrow face. She was older than Alura, perhaps thirty, and while she looked vaguely familiar, Alura could not recall her name.

"Lady Melusine," said Katharine, and as soon as Alura

heard the name, she knew who the woman was.

"You are her sister," Alura said in a choked voice. Despite the warmth of the morning, she suddenly felt cold all over.

"I have no sister," said Lady Melusine. "I did, until she was murdered by Connor Warrick."

Katharine stepped quickly around Alura, moving to position herself between her daughter and Lady Melusine. "You have no right to come here and spread vicious lies," she said in a low, angry voice.

Melusine Lyle folded her arms across her chest and gazed coolly at Katharine. " 'Twas my impression that all the noble families of the district were invited to this wedding," she said.

"True enough, but—"

"Even the family of the poor lass who met her death at the hands of that man."

Alura felt a surge of fury inside her. "You are wrong, Lady Melusine," she said around her mother. "I am certain of it."

"He has blinded you in some fashion to his true nature," accused Lady Melusine. "Just as he blinded my poor sister until he had got her with child."

Alura wanted to say that such a thing had never happened, but she could not. Not yet. The story of Elspeth Lyle's tragic death was so accepted in the district that she would be foolish to dispute it without proof.

And proof was something she did not have, no matter how much she had come to believe in Connor's innocence.

"He got her with child," Lady Melusine went on in a cruel voice, "and then when she dared to confront him with that fact, he lured her to the tower of his family's castle and threw her to her death!"

"I want you to leave," Katharine said through clenched teeth. "You are not welcome here, Lady Melusine."

A bleak smile curved the thin lips of the woman. "Shall I tell that to my father, so that he may challenge Sir Herve in order to avenge the insult to my family's honor?"

Alura took hold of her mother's arm. "Let her stay, Mother. Her lies mean nothing to me."

That was a lie in itself, but one that Alura could live with in order to keep this situation from growing worse. She would rather have Melusine around as a reminder of Connor's rumored villainy than to have her father challenged to do battle.

Was *this* what the djinn had sensed? she wondered. A slight disturbance, Radiya had called it. Well, Alura was determined that this disturbance would indeed be slight. She would allow it to be nothing else.

Katharine looked at her. "Are you certain?"

Alura nodded. "Her words are as naught to me."

"You should listen to someone's words, girl," Melusine snapped. "If you marry that man, you carry his shame. And if you are foolish enough to marry him, sooner or later *he will kill you, too.*"

"Enough," said Katharine as Alura stood there shaken by the confrontation. "You are welcome to stay and attend the wedding, Lady Melusine," she went on, though no one in the room believed the sincerity of what she was saying. "However, my daughter and I do not have to stand here and listen to your ravings. Come, Alura." She turned, took Alura's arm, and led her toward the stairs.

"Mark my words," Melusine called after them. "Death, girl! Death shall come for you at the hands of that man!"

Alura shuddered, and Katharine tightened the arm she had slid around her daughter's shoulders. "Pay that harridan no heed," she said quietly. "Melusine Lyle has been stewing in her own juices for years. There was a time she desired Connor for herself, you know."

Alura looked over at her mother in surprise. "I knew nothing of that."

"Aye, and when Connor chose Elspeth over her, Melusine never forgave him." Katharine shook her head. "The woman should have been in a convent long ago."

"Mother," Alura said as they reached the second floor, "you do not believe that Connor would ever . . . would ever harm me, do you?"

Katharine stopped and looked solemnly at Alura. "I'll not pretend that none of the stories about him have ever reached my ears. But I will say this, Alura . . . I have seen nothing in the man who returned from the Holy Land that would make me think he would ever hurt you. If I believed that to be a possibility, I would never allow you to marry him, no matter what your father or even the prince might say." She drew Alura into a hug. "I hope you will be happy. I believe you will be happy. But only time will truly tell."

And time had run out, thought Alura. Before she would have a chance to speak privately with Connor, she would be wed to him.

His wife . . . until death they did part.

The wedding itself would be a simple ceremony, but the festivities leading up to it, and the celebration that would follow it, were much more elaborate. The great hall of Brynclair would be crowded with guests, and nearly every one of them, thought Connor as he rode into the outer bailey, would likely despise him.

Jeremy rode at his side, and they were followed by a group of Connor's men-at-arms. The squire looked around eagerly and said, "Ne'er have I seen this many people in one place."

"What about Acre?" asked Connor.

"Well, that was a city. I meant, in one castle."

Connor nodded. If the crowd in the bailey was any indication, the wedding would be well-attended indeed.

Jeremy had tied a bag onto his saddle, and riding inside the bag with her head stuck out was the cat Matilda. Her whiskers twitched and her head moved almost constantly as she looked at everything around her. From time to time, Jeremy idly scratched her ears. Connor thought the lad was mad to have brought the cat along with him, but Jeremy would not hear of leaving her behind. Perhaps Connor's wry speculation that one day Jeremy would carry the cat into battle with him was not that far wrong, he thought.

"Did you see those gypsies outside the walls, milord?" Jeremy asked. " 'Tis said that some of their women can foretell the future simply by gazing into a man's palm."

"The only future they wish to foretell is whether or not a man has a coin in his palm," said Connor. He fixed Jeremy with a firm look. "I do not want you skulking about that gypsy camp. You might well wind up with a broken head or a knife 'twixt your ribs and all your belongings gone."

"I'll stay away from them, Sir Connor," promised Jeremy. But he twisted a little in his saddle to look back through the gate at the brightly colored tents, and Connor knew that he was going to need to keep a close eye on the lad while they were here—as if he did not have enough other things on his mind.

Sir Herve met them at the gate into the inner bailey. "Welcome, Sir Connor," he said heartily. "We are most pleased to have you and your party here at Brynclair."

Connor had brought only a small group with him, consisting of Jeremy, a dozen men-at-arms, and half as many servants. He gestured for them to dismount. Some of de Gabin's stablemen came forward to care for the horses. With Jeremy at his side, Connor walked into the inner bailey with Sir Herve, while Brynclair's men-at-arms greeted their fellows from Stavebrook. Several good-natured, ribald comments concerning the consummation of the marriage were called back and forth.

Connor tried to ignore what was being said, and so did Sir Herve. As they walked toward the keep, Connor asked, "How is the lady Alura?"

"She fares well," said de Gabin. "She awaits you inside." He squinted over at Jeremy. "What's that you have, boy?"

Jeremy lifted the sack he had untied from his saddle when he dismounted. " 'Tis a cat, Sir Herve."

"I can see that. Why are you carrying it about?"

"She likes it, sire," Jeremy answered simply.

Sir Herve grunted and shook his head. It was clear that he thought Jeremy's behavior bordered on the insane. But he was not going to say as much, not on this day, of all days. He would not risk an insult even to the squire of the man who was to marry his daughter this day.

There was much laughter and gaiety among the visitors to Brynclair, but as Connor, Jeremy, and Sir Herve strode through the crowd, silence fell around them. Noise still came from the outer bailey and the village that surrounded the castle, but here in the inner bailey was an ominous quiet. Sir Herve glared around at his guests, as if trying to will them back into a good mood, but to no avail.

Connor knew all too well what had caused the reaction.

Here amongst the nobles, he was well and truly hated. As his eyes scanned the hostile crowd, he saw one face in particular staring at him. Melusine Lyle was watching him with such loathing that he knew she wished heaven would strike him dead.

He intended to live, if only to spite the likes of her, and he did not allow his forthright stride to falter as he walked toward the keep. Beside him, Jeremy looked a bit embarrassed and uncomfortable, and Sir Herve was fuming.

Connor smiled tightly. Let them all think what they wished. *He* knew the truth.

And so, soon enough, would Alura. Connor had come to that decision, difficult though it had been. As his wife, she would deserve no less.

At a nod from de Gabin, servants swung open the great double doors at the entrance to the keep. The two knights and the squire walked inside, their footsteps echoing against the high ceiling of the great hall. The hall itself had been sumptuously decorated since Connor's last visit. Wall hangings and pennants threw bright colors at the eye, the rushes on the floor were clean and fresh-smelling, and four large, high-backed, ornately carved chairs had been moved into the room and placed in a position of honor. Sir Herve and Lady Katharine would occupy two of those chairs at the wedding feast, Connor knew.

The other two were for him and Alura.

She was already in the great hall, and Connor found himself vaguely disappointed when he saw her coming toward him. She looked as beautiful as ever, of course, and the smile that lit her face seemed genuine. It was just that she was so lovely descending the staircase. He had hoped to see that sight again.

But instead she came to him with her hands outstretched, and he took them, feeling the connection that leaped between them like a spark struck with flint and steel. Alura said softly, "Milord."

"Milady," whispered Connor. He wanted to pull her into his arms and press his lips to hers, but such wanton behavior would hardly be proper such a short time before the wedding.

Jeremy cleared his throat and stepped up boldly, surprising

Connor. "Milady," he said to Alura, "I have brought you a present on this, the day of your wedding to my lord Sir Connor."

With a frown, Connor asked, "What do you, Jeremy?"

Alura smiled at the young man, ignoring Connor's disapproval for the moment. "What is it?" she asked.

Jeremy thrust out the sack he held in his hands. "This, milady." Matilda's head was still protruding from the opening in the sack.

"Oh, my," said Alura.

"Her name is Matilda. 'Tis a cat," said Jeremy proudly.

"We can all see that," snapped Connor. "What in the name of the holy relics made you think such a creature is a proper wedding gift?"

Jeremy looked stricken, and Alura said quickly, "I think 'tis a lovely gift." She reached out to take Matilda from the sack and cradled the cat in her arms. Matilda began to purr. Alura looked up in delight and said, " 'Tis the sweetest cat I have ever seen. Thank you, Jeremy."

That brought a smile back to Jeremy's face. Connor took a deep breath. He had to be careful of his temper. Enough bad things had already been said about him without him having to prove that any of them were true. He clapped a hand on Jeremy's shoulder and said, "Obviously I erred. 'Tis a fine gift you have presented to my betrothed, Jeremy, and I thank you as well."

Sir Herve grumbled, "I never heard of anyone giving a cat as a wedding gift. A fine hog fit for butchering, mayhap, or a dependable milch cow, but a cat—"

"A cat is an excellent gift," Alura said as she scratched Matilda's ears. She asked Jeremy, "Are you certain you do not mind giving her up?"

"From the time I began caring for her, milady, I always intended to give her to you," he said. He broke into a grin. "Besides, when you come to live at Stavebrook, she will come with you."

"Aye, she will," agreed Alura. She turned and handed the cat to one of her maids. "Here, take Matilda up to my chamber."

A group of musicians stood nearby, and at a gesture from Sir Herve, they began to play. He took Katharine's hand and swung her into a dance, and the guests slowly began to follow suit. Connor reached out to Alura, and she slipped her fingers into his hand.

"You won't have to lift me up this time," she told him as she came into his arms. "My foot is completely healed."

"I did not mind," he said. " 'Twas one of the best dances I ever shared."

They swept into the steps of the dance, and as he held her close, Connor wondered if he could manage to say the things he needed to say to her. With the musicians playing, no one would be able to overhear . . .

No, he decided. Not here, not now. Though he would have liked to clear up all the questions and problems before the wedding itself, this was simply not the time. It would have to wait.

But this near the ceremony, what harm could be caused by one more small delay?

Dermot leaned against the wall of the inner bailey and watched as the servants who had come from Stavebrook blended in with the large crowd. One of them, a woman, glanced in his direction and momentarily pulled back the hood of the cloak she wore. He gave her a slight nod of acknowledgment, almost unnoticeable if one was not looking for it. He had hoped that Nessa would somehow manage to be one of the party that had come to Brynclair for the wedding. Probably, from what she had told him of the seneschal, a twitch of her rump had been all that was required to get the old lecher to agree to whatever she wanted.

Pushing himself out of his casual pose, Dermot strolled across the bailey toward the keep. As a newcomer, it would be more difficult for him to get inside without being noticed, but he was confident. He had to penetrate the keep, otherwise he could not carry out his plan.

He came up beside Nessa and as he pretended to look elsewhere said quietly, "Go to the lady's chamber before the wedding and wait there for me. If the lady arrives ere I do, keep her there.''

"But—"

"Do as I say," hissed Dermot.

Nessa nodded and moved away. Dermot walked around the keep toward the postern gate, nodding to the acquaintances he had made among Sir Herve's men-at-arms during the few days he had been here at Brynclair. He had already spied a rear door leading into the keep, and that was his true destination.

His plan was a bold one, but as far as he could see, it was the only one that might still win him the prize he sought: the mystical power that had nearly destroyed his band of outlaws on the night they had ambushed Warrick in the woods. Dermot wanted that power so that he could wield it himself; but even more important, he wanted to control it so that he would no longer have reason to fear it.

And fear, though he would not have wanted to admit it even to himself, was an even stronger motivation for him than greed and ambition.

The lady Alura was the key, he had decided. He was still not convinced that Connor Warrick possessed no magical abilities, but the wizard had to be either Warrick or Alura. In either case, having Alura in his power would give him the advantage he needed. If she was the witch, he could torture her secrets from her, and if 'twas really Warrick who was the magician, surely he would give up his secrets to save the life of the woman he planned to marry. That was why Dermot had decided to abduct Alura.

Dangerous it most definitely was. But his men were right outside the castle, posing as gypsies this time, and when they provided the proper disturbance this afternoon, shortly before the wedding, he and Nessa would take Alura out the rear door of the keep and through the postern gate where fast horses would be ready and waiting. His men would flee at the same time, then rendezvous later with them in the forest, and once they had retreated into their leafy sanctuary, Dermot was confident no one would be able to discover them unless he wished it.

And before this day was over, he vowed, *he* would wield the power that had launched him on this desperate adventure.

Twenty

Alura closed the door of her bedchamber behind her, leaned against it, and took a deep breath. After all the festivities of the afternoon, she was already tired. But now the time for the wedding itself was close at hand, and she needed a few moments alone to prepare herself for it. As soon as she was ready, she would step across the corridor to her mother's chamber, where she would be dressed for the ceremony by Katharine and several of the maids.

Matilda had been curled up in a ball on the bed, but she got up and began to purr as she paced back and forth, demanding attention. With a smile, Alura went over and rubbed a hand along the cat's back. Matilda arched her spine and purred even louder.

"Jeremy was so sweet to give you to me," Alura told the cat. "Although 'tis clear he intends to continue caring for you once I've gone to live at Stavebrook. You can belong to both of us, how would that be?"

Matilda butted her head hard against Alura's outstretched palm. Clearly, that plan suited her just fine.

Alura continued stroking the cat for a few moments, then turned toward the side table where a basin of water and a cloth lay. She wanted to wash up before dressing for the wedding, so she took off the bracelet and ring and laid them on the table, then slipped her gown over her head. Clad only in a chemise, she dipped the cloth in the basin and began wiping it over her face and arms.

Suddenly, Matilda leaped from the bed to the table, upsetting the basin. "Matilda!" Alura cried in surprise. She was angry for an instant, then realized that the cat just wanted to be near her, wanted to continue receiving the attention she had been getting a few moments earlier. Alura shook her head in a mixture of exasperation and affection and reached down to scratch Matilda's ears.

A step behind her made her stiffen, and then she gasped as the cold edge of a blade was laid against her throat.

"Not a sound," a voice hissed in her ear. "And don't move, either."

For a moment, Alura stood completely still and silent, as she had been instructed. Her mind was whirling feverishly. Who could this intruder be? The voice belonged to a woman, and Alura thought immediately of Melusine Lyle. Would Melusine, crazed by her hatred of Connor, actually come here and threaten her?

Alura glanced down at the table before which she stood. Matilda still stood there, looking up at her with a puzzled expression. The cat could not figure out why Alura was not petting her.

Alura had no time for Matilda at the moment, however. She was searching desperately for the bracelet and the ring instead. If she could summon Radiya and Zahir, they would surely save her, and the jewelry had been there on the table only a moment earlier. . . .

Until Matilda had knocked the bracelet and the ring on the floor, where they now lay, mostly out of sight under the bed.

Alura felt breathless, but she could not draw a deep breath with that blade pressed against her throat. Inhaling and exhaling shallowly instead, she managed to say, "What do you want?"

"Hush, I said!" The knife pressed a little harder. To herself, the assailant muttered, "Damn his eyes, where is he?"

Who? wondered Alura. Who else was going to invade her

chamber? This woman must have been hiding in here when she came in, Alura decided, perhaps under the bed, perhaps in the wardrobe where Alura kept her garments.

"Melusine, is that you?" asked Alura. She felt a warm trickle on her neck and knew that the blade had pricked the skin. She was bleeding slightly.

"No more noise, or I swear I'll cut your throat!"

The threat did not sound genuine to Alura. Nor did the voice sound like Melusine Lyle's, she decided. Whoever this intruder was, she had a reason to be here other than simple vengeance. And Alura did not think the woman would kill her, despite the threats.

She opened her mouth to risk a scream, but before she could make a sound, she heard the door of her chamber open. This would be her mother or her father, thought Alura, and they would soon put an end to this horrible assault.

"Good work, Nessa," said a man's voice.

"Nessa!" gasped Alura.

Then there was a heavy footstep right behind her, and something slammed into the side of her head. She pitched forward, stunned, and fell into welcoming darkness.

"She's bleeding!" Dermot said sharply. "She had better not be hurt badly. . . ."

"She will be fine," said Nessa. " 'Tis only the smallest of scratches. You're the one who fetched her a clout on the head."

"Not hard enough to do any permanent damage."

"Well, neither will she be harmed by a small scar on her neck."

"Enough of this pointless argument." Dermot bent and slipped his arms around Alura's limp body. He lifted her and placed her on the bed, then rolled her up in the fur bedding. Hefting her again, he draped her over his shoulder. " 'Tis time to leave this place."

"A moment," said Nessa. The glow of precious metal and gems had caught her eye, and she knelt beside the bed to snatch up the bracelet and the ring she found there. A vindictive smile curved her lips. "Now these pretties shall be mine."

"Take them and have done with it," said Dermot. He grunted a little under Alura's weight. "Let us go. The corridor was clear when I slipped in here, but you'd best check again before we leave."

Nessa did as he told her. She dropped the jewelry in a pocket on her gown and went to the door of the bedchamber, easing it open so that she could peer out into the corridor. After a moment she turned and jerked her head at Dermot. "Come on."

They hurried out of the room, leaving the door slightly ajar behind them.

Connor sat at the long table in the great hall, surrounded by his men-at-arms, many of whom were beginning to show the effects of the numerous tankards of ale they had guzzled down. Connor himself had drunk quite a bit, but he was as sober as an archbishop. Seated beside Connor was Jeremy. The squire's head was pillowed on his arms, and from time to time he let out a moan. Connor grimaced as he looked at the lad. He had allowed Jeremy to drink too much, and now the unfortunate squire was paying for it.

Well, there was still a short time before the wedding to sober him up, thought Connor. He stood up and grasped Jeremy's collar. A walk around the bailey would do him a great deal of good, and if that did not suffice, dunking his head a few times in a bucket of water would probably finish the task.

"Come along, lad," said Connor as he hauled Jeremy to his feet.

Jeremy's moan became a full-fledged groan, but he managed to stay upright when Connor let go of him. "M-milord," said Jeremy. "Is th' . . . th' wedding over?"

"Not yet," Connor told him. " 'Tis not even started, in fact. Come with me. We're going to take a turn around the bailey."

Swaying a little, Jeremy wiped the back of his hand across his mouth and said, "Aye, milord."

From the head of the table, Sir Herve, who was also a bit drunk, called, "Not running out, are you, Warrick?"

Connor controlled his anger at the man's crudeness. He said, "Nay, I shall be back shortly."

"Good," said de Gabin. "Wouldn't want to miss your own wedding, now would you?"

Connor ignored that comment and headed for the entrance with Jeremy. They stepped out into the inner bailey and crossed it, Connor's strides sure and purposeful, Jeremy's gait much more hesitant and unsteady. The squire managed to keep up, however.

They went through the gate into the outer bailey, which was still quite crowded with everyone who had journeyed to Bryn-clair not so much for the wedding but for the celebration that accompanied it. Fewer people noticed Connor this time, so his presence did not have the chilling effect on the festivities that it had had earlier. In fact, few of the celebrants were even paying any attention to Connor and Jeremy, and that was just fine with Connor. Instead, the people were dancing and eating and laughing, thoroughly enjoying this break from a life that was ofttimes grim and monotonous.

Suddenly, a disturbance broke out around the main gate. Connor heard the commotion and glanced idly in that direction. He saw several of Sir Herve's men-at-arms running through the tunnel under the gatehouse that led to the barbican. The men had their swords drawn, and that was more than enough to tell Connor that something was wrong.

He started in that direction, Jeremy stumbling along beside him. Before they could reach the gate, Connor reached out and grasped the arm of a man-at-arms who was hurrying away from there. "What is the cause of that disturbance?" demanded Connor.

The fellow was one of Sir Herve's guards. He inclined his head toward the gate and said, " 'Tis those damned gypsies, milord! One of 'em accused Sir Stilwell of not payin' for havin' his fortune told, and the whole thing started a dreadful row. Sir Griffith sent me to fetch more men to bring things under control."

"Go on with you, then," Connor told him. The man hurried toward the keep.

"Are we going to join the fray, Sir Connor?" asked Jeremy.

Connor shook his head. Now that he knew what had caused the disturbance and knew that it had nothing to do with the wedding, he no longer had any interest in it. "Are you feeling any better?" he asked Jeremy.

The squire nodded, bravely but weakly. "Oh, yes, milord, much better." No sooner were the words out of his mouth than his eyes rolled up in his head and his knees unhinged. Connor caught hold of him and kept him from falling on his face.

" 'Tis the bucket of cold water for you, lad," muttered Connor, and he went in search of just that, dragging Jeremy along with him.

A short time later, Connor strode into the great hall once more. Jeremy followed at his heels, water dripping from his hair. The upper part of the lad's tunic was soaked, but he appeared to be sober again. "Milord," he said to Connor, "if ever I drink that much ale again, please, take your sword and strike my head off my shoulders. I think 'twould hurt less that way."

Connor laughed and paused so that he could slip an arm around Jeremy's shoulders. "Don't worry, lad," he said. " 'Tis like most things in life—the next time will be less painful."

Sir Herve was striding back and forth impatiently in front of the four tall chairs. As Connor approached, he swung around and demanded, "Have you seen my wife or daughter?"

"The lady Alura has gone to prepare for the wedding, as you well know," said Connor. "I will not see her again until then."

"Katharine should have been back down by now. 'Tis time to get started." Sir Herve waved a hand toward the windows. " 'Twill be sundown ere long, and the priest wishes you to be married before then."

"Aye, as do I," Connor agreed.

Before either man could say anything else, a strident cry of "Herve!" cut through the jollity in the room. Connor and de Gabin swung around sharply and saw Lady Katharine hurrying down the stairs from the second floor. Sir Herve strode forward to meet her, followed by Connor. The crowd parted easily before them.

Sir Herve caught hold of his wife's shoulders as she reached the bottom of the staircase. "God's eyes, woman!" he exclaimed. "What's wrong? You look positively distraught."

Katharine looked up at him. "Alura is gone."

"Gone!" roared de Gabin. "But where would she go?"

Katharine shook her head and said, "I know not. All I know is that her chamber is empty, and she is nowhere else on the upper floors of the keep. I searched them before coming to you, Herve, so that I would not worry you unnecessarily if Alura was . . . elsewhere."

Hiding from the impending wedding, that was what she meant, thought Connor, but he shoved the thought aside. There was no time to search for offense now, not when he should be searching for Alura instead. He said tautly, "Take me to her chamber."

"Sir Connor," began Katharine, " 'tis hardly proper—"

"Propriety be hanged," growled Sir Herve. "My daughter is missing. *I* shall go look for any sign of what might have happened to her."

"Are your eyes still as keen as they once were?" Connor asked.

Sir Herve hesitated. "Well . . ."

"We are wasting time." Connor stepped past Sir Herve and Katharine and started up the stairs.

One of Sir Herve's men half-drew his sword. "Milord, should we stop him?" he asked.

Sir Herve sighed and said, "Lord Ridglea is right. My eyes are not what they once were. But I shall accompany him." He started up the stairs after Connor, trailed by Katharine, Jeremy, and several of the men-at-arms.

Connor reached a chamber whose door was standing wide open and guessed that it belonged to Alura. He stepped inside, and his supposition was confirmed. He could still smell her scent, lingering in the air of this chamber. Like a bolt of lightning, an unfamiliar feeling went through him, and he knew that what he was experiencing was fear. What if something had happened to her? In the past few years he had experienced pain and grieving, bitterness and anger, but little fear, because a man who cared not whether he lived or died had little reason to be afraid.

Now he knew fear, however. Aye, he knew it all too well.

He stood just inside the doorway, eyes searching everywhere in the chamber. He saw the gown Alura had been wearing earlier, which was now lying on the bed. He saw an overturned basin and a crumpled cloth lying on the floor beside the bed. And he saw something else on the floor, something so small that he almost missed it.

Connor moved beside the bed in a few quick strides. He went down on one knee and reached out to touch a fingertip to the tiny dark splotch he had seen on the stone floor, between two rush mats. The splotch was almost dry, but it was still a little sticky. Some of it remained on Connor's finger when he lifted it, and he brought his finger to his mouth, touched his tongue lightly to it. He stiffened at the realization that he was right.

Blood. There was a drop of blood on the floor. Alura's blood.

He uncoiled from his crouching position, and a roar of rage welled up in his throat without him even being aware of it. His hands clenched into fists and his arms were flung wide. He threw his head back and howled in a blend of fury and agony. He could not lose Alura now. He could not.

Someone grasped his shoulder. Connor whirled, his hand going to his sword. He was half-insane with the desire to yank the blade free and slash at the first thing he saw.

But what he saw was the face of Sir Herve de Gabin. The knight was pale and looked much older than his years. "Alura," he said raggedly. "My daughter . . ."

With an effort that sent a shudder rolling through him, Connor controlled his emotions. " 'Tis a drop of blood on the floor," he said.

At the doorway, Katharine gasped and brought her hands to her mouth.

"But . . . but only a single drop?" asked Sir Herve.

Connor nodded.

"Then she must be all right. She has been abducted, and she probably struggled, and that is how the blood came to be on the floor. But 'tis only a drop, you said so yourself, Sir Connor.''

"Sir Herve is right, milord," ventured Jeremy.

Connor dragged in a deep breath and nodded again. His brain had resumed functioning now, and he knew they were right. A thought suddenly occurred to him, and he said, "Those gypsies—what happened to them?"

One of Sir Herve's men-at-arms said, "They fled a short while ago, Sir Connor, after causing that brawl."

"Damn them!"

"You think the gypsies took her?" asked Sir Herve.

"I believe they had a part in it, whether they really be gypsies or not," said Connor. "The attention of everyone outside was turned toward the struggle beyond the main gate."

"The postern gate!" exclaimed Sir Herve. He turned and led the charge out of the room.

But it was Connor who reached the postern gate first and found the guards leaning against the wall as if dozing. A hard shove to the shoulder sent first one man, then the other, toppling off their feet.

"Dead, the both of them," Connor announced as the others came hurrying up. "Stabbed in the side of the neck."

"Then whoever has Alura took her out of the castle by this means and left these men propped against the wall," said Sir Herve.

Connor nodded. "Aye, 'tis certain." He lifted his eyes to the forest in the distance. "And somewhere out there," he said bleakly, "they have her now."

The first thing Alura was aware of was the sickness in her belly. She rolled over and curled into a ball without thinking about what she was doing, and the movement sent shattering agonies cascading through her head. She lay utterly still save for her breathing and waited for the pain to subside.

"Ah, so the fine lady is awake, is she?"

A foot slammed into Alura's side. She whimpered and curled herself more tightly, despite the horrible pounding in her skull.

"Stop that," a man's voice ordered sharply. "I've told you, Nessa, she's not to be harmed until *I* say so."

Nessa, thought Alura. She was still with the treacherous maid and the man who had come into her room while Nessa was holding the knife at her throat. She realized through her pain and sickness that his voice was vaguely familiar, but she could not place it.

"She doesn't look like such a lady now, does she, Dermot? Lying there in nothing but a chemise, huddled on the ground like a trapped rabbit."

Those gloating tones belonged to Nessa. The words penetrated Alura's pain-fogged brain. Dermot, Nessa had said. So her father's new man-at-arms had abducted her along with Nessa. No doubt that had been the plan all along, the reason he had come to Brynclair in the first place.

Alura forced herself to open her eyes and look up at them. Her vision was blurry at first, but then it focused on her two captors. She said, "My father . . . will ransom me. . . ."

Dermot laughed harshly. The setting sun painted his face with a hellish glare as he said, "Your father could not ransom anything, milady." His words dripped with scorn. "Brynclair has not even enough coin to pay its men-at-arms their full due. You would know that, had your father not gone to such pains to protect you from what has really been happening. Why do you think he was so desperate to marry you off to Warrick? The old fool has nearly bankrupted his own estate, and now he wants to start on someone else's!"

Alura wanted to shake her head in disbelief, but she knew what Dermot said was true. She had had the same suspicions herself when she pondered her father's motives in seeking a union between her and Connor. "Then why did you . . . why did you abduct me?" she asked.

Dermot hunkered beside her. Alura realized now that she was lying underneath a tree. A root was prodding painfully into her back. Dermot said, "I want a ransom, all right. I want the secret of the magical power that is possessed either by you or by your betrothed. Tell me now and save yourself much pain and trouble, Lady Alura: Are you the sorceress, or does Warrick wield the power?"

Alura glanced at her left wrist and bit back a moan of despair. The bracelet and the ring were gone, and she remembered now that Matilda had knocked them off the table just before Nessa had come out of hiding and captured her. They were probably still lying on the floor of her chamber, partially under the bed, where they could do her no good.

"I . . . I know nothing of what you speak!" she said. "I have no magic powers, and neither does Connor."

There was no way she was going to turn over the secret of the djinn to these two scavengers. She would die first, she told herself.

And she might get the chance to find out if she could live up to that vow, she realized, because it was quite likely Dermot and Nessa would try to torture the truth out of her.

But back at Brynclair, someone must have discovered by now that she was missing. Connor would come after her, she told herself. He would find her and rescue her from these two. She would hold fast to that thought until he came for her.

Dermot straightened at the pounding of hoofbeats. "Here they come now," he said, and a moment later a large group of horsemen came galloping along the path. Alura twisted her head so that she could see them in the fading light and recognized the colorful clothing of the gypsies who had been camped just outside Brynclair. As soon as the men spoke, however, she realized they were not gypsies at all, but rather members of Dermot's band of outlaws.

"I see ye've got the girl, Dermot," one of them said with a huge grin.

"Aye. Did all go as planned?"

"We had the whole castle watchin' us whilst we scuffled with de Gabin's men," boasted the man. "If anybody saw you leave besides the guards on the postern gate, I'd be mighty surprised."

"And we don't have to worry about them," said Dermot. "They'll tell no tales."

Alura's heart sank. She understood what he meant. The guards had been killed. Two of her father's men had met their deaths, indirectly because of her.

Dermot gestured at Alura and said, "Throw her on a horse,

and let us get out of here. I want to be much deeper in the forest ere night falls."

"They won't be able to follow us, will they?" Nessa asked worriedly.

" 'Twould take a better woodsman than any I've ever known outside of our band," said Dermot. "Nay, they shall not find us unless we want to be found."

Two of the outlaws dismounted and came over to Alura. They grinned lecherously as they bent to grasp her arms and legs and lift her. She was deposited unceremoniously on the back of a horse, and one of the men swung up behind her. He put an arm around her waist and pressed her against him. "Ye'll not be gettin' away from me, milady," he said with a coarse laugh.

Alura burned with shame, all too aware that she wore only the thin linen chemise. But worse than the shame was the pain in her head and the sickness in her stomach, which she knew must come from having been struck unconscious by Dermot. Even worse still was the sudden knowledge that if Connor *did* come after her, as he was bound to do, he might well be killed by these vicious bandits if he tried to rescue her.

She could not allow that to happen. She had to find a way herself to get away from them.

A short distance away, Dermot mounted one of the horses, then held a hand down to Nessa. She reached up to grip his wrist with her left hand, and as she did so, the sleeve of her gown pulled back slightly and Alura saw something she had not noticed before.

Fire opals winked redly in the setting sun. Nessa was wearing the bracelet and the ring.

Twenty-one

~

Connor had ridden the golden sorrel to Brynclair, and he was glad of that fact now. The charger was the finest horse he owned. He sent Jeremy ahead to the stables, and by the time Connor got there, the charger was saddled and ready.

Unfortunately, so was the mouse-colored mount Jeremy favored.

"No," Connor said flatly when Jeremy led out both horses. "I am riding alone, Jeremy. You shall stay here."

"But, Sir Connor—" Ignoring the hand that Connor raised to forestall his protest, Jeremy forged ahead, "You may need my help, milord. I can handle a sword and you know it, because 'twas you who taught me."

"Aye, but you are still not coming with me." Connor snatched the sorrel's reins from the squire's hand and swung up into the saddle. "You can ride with Sir Herve and his men if you must, but not with me. I'll be traveling fast, and if I find the devils who abducted Lady Alura, I'll not have time to watch out for you."

He saw the hurt on Jeremy's face and regretted that he had been forced to speak so bluntly to the lad. But he had told the truth: there was more at stake here than a squire's offended feelings. Connor's happiness, his very life, depended on getting Alura back safely. Hard though it would have been to believe when he first returned to England, he knew now that he could not live without her.

Connor tightened the reins and swung the charger's head around. His heels dug into its flanks and sent it leaping ahead in a gallop. The gates of Brynclair were open, and he rode through them into the fading afternoon light, leaving behind a castle buzzing with activity as Sir Herve and his men-at-arms prepared to ride out in search of the missing Lady Alura.

They would follow as soon as possible, but Connor had been unwilling to wait even an extra heartbeat. He rode around to the postern gate and drew rein, bringing the sorrel to a halt so that he could study the ground outside the wall. There was a narrow path here, leading off into the forest, and Connor's eyes narrowed as he saw the footprints of two people. Alura and her captor, he thought. Either that, or there had been two of them, and one had been carrying Alura, in which case she had probably been knocked senseless first.

Connor opened and closed his right hand. It was aching, but with a different sort of pain than he had known in the past when he was recovering from his wound. Now his hand ached to close around the hilt of his sword so that he could drive the blade through the base villain who had dared to harm Alura.

He wheeled the horse and rode toward the forest, restraining the urge to kick the sorrel into a gallop again. The trail was faint, and he could not afford to lose it.

Connor glanced toward the sun, only a short distance above the horizon, and bit back a curse of despair. If he did not find Alura before night fell, it might be morning before he could pick up the trail again.

They would not harm her, he told himself. The only reason to abduct her was for ransom, and in order to collect that ransom, her captors had to keep her safe.

Connor held tightly to that thought as he rode into the forest.

So many twists and turns. Alura had no idea how the outlaws even knew where they were going, let alone how anyone could follow them. The group penetrated deeper and deeper into the vast woods, and as the towering trees grew thicker and more leafy, the evening light faded even more, until it seemed to Alura that they were riding in almost complete darkness.

The sickness in her stomach had eased, for which she was grateful, and even the pounding in her head had subsided somewhat. The man who was riding with her had fondled her a bit, causing her to burn with mortification and anger, but he had done her no real harm. The shallow scratch on her neck from Nessa's knife was still her only physical wound.

Dermot finally called a halt when they reached a large clearing. The trees grew so thickly above the clearing that they were like the ceiling of a house. The outlaws dismounted, and Alura was lifted down from the horse. Her wrists were quickly lashed together with rawhide strips, and she was deposited underneath one of the trees. "Ye'll stay there, if ye know what's good for ye," growled the man who had bound her.

Alura's back was propped against the rough bark of the tree trunk. She sat there and watched as one of the outlaws used flint and steel to get a small fire going. Its glow pushed back the gathering darkness and lit up most of the clearing. Dermot nodded in satisfaction. "As long as the wind blows as it does, we've no need to worry about it carrying the smoke to any pursuers."

He and Nessa came over to Alura. Nessa still wore a gloating smirk. She thrust out her left hand, proudly displaying the bracelet and ring. "They look better on me than they ever did on you, milady," she said with a sneer.

Alura looked at the fire opals being waved in front of her face. If only she could get her hand on them long enough to stroke the gems. For an instant, the wild thought that she could see Zahir and Radiya inside the fire opals, pleading with her to summon them, went through her head.

Her hands were bound in front of her, so she suddenly lunged toward Nessa, reaching for the gems. Nessa snatched her arm back out of reach and kicked Alura in the shoulder, knocking her back against the tree. "Oh, no, they're my pretties now!" crowed Nessa.

Dermot hunkered on his heels in front of Alura. "If I was you, milady, I would worry less about my jewelry and more about my life. Because your life will surely be forfeit unless you tell me what I want to know.''

Another idea occurred to Alura. ''I will tell you my secret,'' she said, ''if you will return my bracelet and ring to me.''

''They mean that much to you?'' asked Dermot with a frown.

''No!'' exclaimed Nessa. ''She can't have them!''

Alura did not want to make Dermot too suspicious. ''Connor gave them to me,'' she said simply.

''Ah. A present from the man you love. I understand now.''

So did Alura. She realized suddenly that the jewelry *did* mean more to her because it had come from Connor. The bracelet and the ring were precious to her not because of their material worth, or even because of the djinn who lived in them, but because Connor had given them to her as a symbol of his love for her.

And that meant more to her than anything else in the world.

''They're mine,'' Nessa said spitefully. ''You can't give them back to her, Dermot.''

He stood up and turned to her with a cold smile. ''I think you have forgotten that I can do anything I please, Nessa. And if returning these baubles to her will loosen her tongue—''

''I'll fight her for them!'' said Nessa.

Dermot's eyebrows arched in surprise. ''What?''

''Call it a tournament.'' Nessa looked at Alura with hatred etched on her face. ''If she wins, she claims the spoils—this bracelet and ring.''

''And if you win?'' prodded Dermot.

''Then I've shown her that she's not such a high-and-mighty lady after all. She's still your prisoner either way, Dermot.''

''You won't kill her?''

''Of course not,'' said Nessa, but Alura did not believe her for an instant. In the heat of combat, Nessa would indeed try to kill her. Alura was sure of it.

Alura's head was spinning with the possibilities of this ''tournament'' Nessa had proposed. No doubt Nessa was an experienced fighter; there were frequent battles among jealous servant women, as they bickered over men or belongings. And

Nessa's companions were notorious outlaws, which meant she was probably even more experienced in such things.

Alura didn't care. All she wanted was a chance to get her hands on the bracelet and the ring. At close quarters, that might be possible.

She lifted her chin defiantly and said, "I will fight her."

Dermot looked at her. "Are you certain?"

Alura curled her lip in calculated disdain. "I have no fear of the likes of her."

Nessa lunged at her, foot drawn back to deliver a kick, but Dermot caught hold of her arm and threw her backward. Nessa stumbled and sat down hard, her skirts billowing up around her legs. That brought shouts of laughter from the rest of the band, who had begun gathering around as the battle between the two women was discussed.

"Let 'em fight, Dermot," called one of the men. " 'Tis some entertainment we're needin', and that'll give it to us."

Dermot looked at Alura. "And afterward, you'll tell me what I want to know?" he asked.

"Aye." And if she got her hands on the bracelet and ring, thought Alura, she would go him one better.

She would *show* him the magic he so desired, though it might well be the last thing he ever saw on this earth.

There was not enough room in the clearing to stage a joust on horseback, so it was quickly decided that Alura and Nessa would fight with swords instead. Nessa smiled and said, "Good. I was always best with a blade."

"You'll not use real swords," said Dermot. "I don't trust you that far, Nessa. You shall use wooden swords, as the pages and squires do in their training."

Nessa frowned in disappointment. Clearly she had hoped to use steel so that she could more easily "accidentally" injure her opponent.

But even wooden swords could do a considerable amount of damage, Alura knew. She had seen squires limping around the castle, bruised and sore, for days after such a mock combat.

Wooden swords were fetched from the packs of the bandits.

"We use these ofttimes to practice ourselves," Dermot explained as he knelt in front of Alura and drew his poniard to cut the bonds around her wrists. "Men get caught up in the heat of battle, even when it is not real, and I cannot afford to have my men lopping each other's heads off for no good reason."

Alura climbed to her feet, trying not to let any of them see how shaky she still was. She reached out and closed both hands around the hilt of the wooden sword Dermot offered her. Nessa was already armed, and she was slashing the wooden blade back and forth wickedly.

The sword was heavier than Alura had expected it to be. *Just like a real sword,* she thought. Otherwise it would do one no good to practice with. She hefted it, swung it back and forth slowly, and thrust it in front of her a couple of times.

"I am ready," Nessa announced.

Alura was not sure if she was or not. She was trying to remember those long-ago lessons from her father. He had explained all about parrying and thrusting, how to move her feet, when to retreat and when to advance. Alura had enjoyed those training sessions, but now she wished she had paid more attention during them. She had never dreamed that one day her fate might well depend on her skill with a sword.

"You are certain you want to go through with this?" Dermot asked her again.

Alura looked at Nessa, waiting on the other side of the clearing for her. Nessa's lips were drawn back in an expression that was part smile, part hate-filled grimace.

And the firelight sparkled on the bracelet and ring she wore.

"I am ready," said Alura.

Dermot shrugged and backed away. He gestured for them to begin.

The band of outlaws formed an eager circle around the two women. Alura and Nessa slowly approached each other. Nessa's blade was up, its tip weaving about in front of her, but Alura held hers down, ready to move it wherever it was necessary.

Nessa struck first, springing forward and swinging the wooden sword up to bring it whistling down at Alura's head.

Alura darted aside and twisted her own sword, knowing that if the blades hit directly, her sword might shatter under the blow. Instead the two swords glanced off each other, and Nessa stumbled a bit from the wasted momentum of her charge. Alura swung a backhand that caused Nessa to duck away frantically in order to avoid it.

The men hooted in laughter, and Dermot called, "She'll not prove easy, Nessa. The lady has more skills than one might expect."

Nessa glared at Alura and attacked again, slashing right and left with the wooden sword. Alura used the tip of her blade to turn aside the blows, darting it back and forth as quickly as she could. She had to give ground as she did so, slowly backing away from Nessa. She felt the heat from the fire and knew that she was close to the flames.

Suddenly, she launched a thrust of her own. Nessa hurriedly blocked it, so that the blades slid against each other until the guard on each weapon caught against the other. That was exactly what Alura wanted. She drove her hands upward, lifting Nessa's weapon with her own. That brought Nessa face-to-face with her, only a hand's breadth away.

Alura let go of the sword with her right hand and grabbed the front of Nessa's gown instead. She pivoted as sharply as she could and heaved with all her strength. Nessa went stumbling past her, off balance, and fell into the fire, scattering ashes and sparks and burning brands around the clearing. Nessa howled in pain as the flames licked at her skin. She rolled desperately out of the fire.

Alura was there when Nessa came to a stop. One foot descended on the blade of Nessa's sword, pinning it to the ground. Alura lifted her sword, knowing that if she wished, she could bring it down in a blow that would crush Nessa's skull. All she wanted, though, was the bracelet and ring, so if Nessa was prepared to yield them . . .

Nessa hooked a leg behind Alura's ankle and yanked, pulling Alura's feet out from under her. Alura fell. She had been overconfident, and it had cost her the advantage. She managed to hang onto her sword as she crashed to the ground, then rolled away quickly to get some breathing room between her and Nessa.

Nessa scrambled to her feet at the same time as Alura did. Her face was smudged with ashes, and holes had been burned in her gown, revealing red, singed skin beneath the clothing. "I'll kill you for that!" panted Nessa. "I'll stave your head in!"

"Come ahead," taunted Alura. If she could keep her own wits about her while Nessa was too overcome with rage to think straight, she would have a better chance.

Nessa charged past the scattered campfire. Alura met the charge, and for a long moment it was all she could do to fend off the flurry of blows that Nessa struck at her. Again she was forced to give ground. Her arms were tiring. Each time she lifted the sword, her muscles felt slow and heavy. Suddenly, one of Nessa's thrusts got through Alura's guard, and the wooden sword slammed against Alura's left shoulder.

Her entire arm went numb, and the fingers of that hand slipped off the hilt of the sword. "Nessa, have a care!" called Dermot. "I don't want her hurt!"

Nessa was beyond caring, however. She was in the grip of a rage that would not be denied. As Alura staggered back a step, Nessa closed in, swinging the sword in a roundhouse blow that might take Alura's head off if it connected, even with a wooden blade.

Alura ducked under the blow at the last instant and whacked the flat of her sword against Nessa's shins. Nessa yelped in pain. Close now to her opponent, Alura lunged ahead, driving her right shoulder into Nessa's midsection. Nessa went over backward, and this time Alura took no chances. Summoning up the last of her strength, she swung her sword up one-handed and then brought it down against Nessa's right forearm. She heard the snap of bone breaking, and Nessa screamed. Alura swung the flat of the blade against the side of Nessa's head. The blow landed with a thud, and Nessa went limp as she lay on the ground. Alura knew she had not struck hard enough to kill, only to knock Nessa unconscious.

The battle was over, and a surprised hush had fallen over the clearing. None of the outlaws had expected Alura to win.

But she had, and she was ready to claim her prize. She let the sword slip from her fingers and bent to slide the bracelet off Nessa's left wrist. The ring came next, and as Alura straightened, she swung toward Dermot.

He must have read the triumph in her eyes, because he stared in sudden realization at the jewelry in her hand and shouted, "Kill her! Kill her now!"

But he was too late. Alura's fingertips were already gliding over the fire opals.

Arrows hissed through the air as Dermot's bowmen reacted hastily to follow his command. A billowing cloud of smoke was already enveloping Alura, however, and the arrows glanced off the smoke as if it had been a stone wall. Bolts of unnatural lightning lashed out from the cloud, striking men down where they stood. Ghostly shapes darted around the clearing, moving too fast for the eye to see anything save a blur of motion, but everywhere they went, outlaws cried out and flew through the air to crash against the stout trunks of the trees. Other men were lifted off the ground to dizzying heights, arms and legs flailing as they shrieked, only to come plummeting back to earth in bone-shattering falls.

Alura stumbled back toward the trees as the smoke began to thin around her. She had not yet seen Zahir and Radiya, but everywhere around her she saw the results of their terrible vengeance. She could imagine how furious the two djinn were, trapped as they had been in their gems but still able to see and hear everything going on around them. Now they had their opportunity to strike back at the outlaws, and they were wreaking havoc among the band.

She braced her back against a tree trunk and slipped the bracelet and ring on. Never again would they leave her hand, she vowed.

Suddenly, out of the chaos, she saw movement coming at her and ducked just as a sword whistled over her head and cut deeply into the tree trunk. Dermot wrenched the blade free and cried, "Witch! Meet your death now, woman!"

Alura twisted away from the tree and darted into the woods as Dermot slashed at her again. Where were Zahir and Radiya? she wondered wildly. Why were the djinn not protecting her?

Perhaps, caught up as they were in the destruction they were raining down on the outlaws, they had lost track of her.

She kept running as Dermot crashed through the underbrush after her, howling curses. She knew she could not outrun him, and fleeing through the forest like this in the darkness, she might run into a tree and dash her brains out. . . .

She ran into something, all right, but it was not a tree. Instead it had strong arms that wrapped around her, and a broad chest that comforted her, and a familiar voice that said urgently, "Alura! Are you all right? 'Tis—"

Connor. He had no need to say his name. She would have known him anywhere, even in the middle of a dark English forest with a sword-wielding madman hot on her heels.

"Look out, Connor!" she managed to gasp. "Behind me—"

She felt herself thrust aside and a heartbeat later heard the clash of steel against steel. It was too dark to see anything, but Alura could track the progress of the battle by the ringing of blades and the grunts of effort that came from the two men. She could tell that Connor was gradually forcing Dermot back toward the clearing, so she followed them, stumbling over roots and rough ground.

A moment later she saw them, silhouetted against the firelight. Connor was larger and no doubt stronger, but Dermot was quicker and was fighting with the frenzied strength of a man filled with rage and fear. They seemed evenly matched, and as they reached the edge of the clearing, they were exchanging a furious series of blows. Alura's eyes could not follow all the moves, but she saw that each time one of the men seemed to be on the verge of gaining an advantage, the other stalemated him.

Scattered around the clearing were the senseless forms of the outlaws. Alura knew not if they were dead or alive, nor did she care at the moment. With a rushing sound, as if of a great wind, Zahir and Radiya were suddenly beside her.

"Mistress!" cried Zahir. "Are you harmed?"

"I am fine," Alura told them.

"We are so sorry, mistress," said Radiya. "We were enjoying so much teaching a lesson to those horrible men that we failed to protect you."

"My protector was here," said Alura as she watched the battle between Connor and Dermot.

Zahir swung toward the two men. "I shall take care of that thieving, no-good—"

Alura reached out to him. "No! Not yet." She was unsure how she knew, but she was certain that Connor would not want anyone interfering in this combat.

Connor's right arm ached intolerably, but his rage drove him on and allowed him to ignore the pain. He knew not who this man was, other than the fact that he looked vaguely familiar, but the villain had been trying to hurt Alura, and that was all Connor needed to know. He fended off blow after blow, but his reactions were slowing as the muscles of his right arm and shoulder failed to answer his commands as quickly as they had before. The knowledge that he might well lose this fight loomed in the back of Connor's mind.

If he was going to emerge victorious, it might require some desperate action. . . .

Alura's pulse pounded loudly in her head as she watched. She could tell that Connor was slowing, and she gasped suddenly as a particularly vicious stroke of Dermot's drove Connor's blade far to the side, leaving Connor wide open for a disemboweling backhand.

But then, so fast that it appeared almost magical, Connor's right hand used his sword's own momentum to carry it behind his back, where he passed it smoothly into his left hand. The blade whipped around just as Dermot was starting his deadly backswing. Dermot's stroke was never finished, because before he knew what was happening to him, he was run through by Connor's sword. A hand's breadth of the blade protruded from his back.

Dermot gasped once, his eyes widening in the knowledge of his own death, and then Connor ripped the sword free. Dermot toppled to the ground and lay still.

Connor lowered his sword and rested the tip of the blade on the earth, leaning against it as he drew a great breath into his heaving chest. He looked up as Alura cried, "Connor!"

Then she was rushing toward him and into his arms, and for an instant he thought he caught a glimpse of two oddly attired figures at the edge of the clearing. But then they were gone, and at any rate, his arms were full of Alura and she was all he could think about. He let his sword fall from his left hand and lifted his right to stroke her hair. His right hand trembled slightly, but then it steadied as he rested it against the fiery tresses. He breathed deeply of her hair's scent and gloried in the warmth of her body pressed against his, scarcely able to believe that she was all right, that they were together again.

They were still standing there like that several moments later when the group of knights led by Sir Herve rode into the clearing. Sir Herve looked around at the scattered figures on the ground and exclaimed, "God's eyes! How did the lad do all *this*?"

Beside him, Jeremy smiled and, for some reason that not even he could fathom, said, "It must have been magic, mi-lord."

Twenty-two

~

Zahir leaned back against the pile of silk cushions on the inlaid tile floor of his fire-opal home and said with a sigh of great satisfaction, "Aaaahhh."

"Do not be so pleased with yourself," Radiya cautioned him from the other side of the red barrier between them.

"Why not? Alura is safe, she and Connor are together again, and as soon as they get back to the castle, they'll be married. That's one more happy couple for us. A few thousand more years and we'll be out of here for good, I tell you."

"How do we know they will be happy together?" insisted Radiya. "There are still secrets between them. Until they have told each other the truth . . ."

Zahir rolled his eyes and shook his head. "Always with the truth! Well, here we are back at the castle, so let's just watch what happens. You'll see that I'm right."

"That," Radiya said, "will be a cold day in the pit of the demons."

Alura rode in front of Connor on the golden sorrel, his cloak wrapped around her to cover the thin chemise. She leaned against him, enjoying the warmth and strength of his arm wrapped around her.

Jeremy rode beside them, along with Sir Herve and a couple of knights from Brynclair. The rest of the men-at-arms had been left back at the clearing to take care of the prisoners. Dermot and two of the other outlaws were dead, but the rest were still alive and would be brought back to Brynclair, then taken to London to stand trial before the king for their crimes; including Nessa, who had whimpered and wept from the pain of her broken arm. Alura almost felt sorry for her. Almost.

The djinn were back in the gems. Alura had stolen a moment alone before they'd left the outlaw camp, retreating behind some brush in order to tend to her needs. While she was there, the djinn had come to her and gone back into the fire opals at her command, but only after she had thanked them in a whisper for all they had done for her.

Now, as the riders were approaching Brynclair, Jeremy was still talking about the events of the evening. "Never saw the likes of it," he said. "And if you hadn't left a trail for us to follow by the light of our torches, we never would have found that hideaway, Sir Connor."

" 'Twas luck that led me there," said Connor. "Luck, and the smell of woodsmoke. Dermot must not have noticed that the wind had shifted."

As Connor said that, Alura found herself wondering if Zahir and Radiya could have had anything to do with the wind turning around. She had assumed that the djinn could not use their powers as long as they were confined inside the gems, but she suddenly recalled how the bracelet and ring had fallen off the table in her chamber at Welwynd, the night she had first met the two ancient spirits. Nothing had touched the jewelry to cause it to fall, so the djinn must have been responsible. And there was the mysterious phantom storm Zahir had brewed up while Alura was visiting Stavebrook, too. If the djinn could do things like that, it was certainly not beyond the realm of possibility that they could have caused the wind to carry the smell of smoke to Connor. . . .

There was no real point in speculating about such things, Alura told herself. Connor had been there when he was needed, and that was all that mattered.

One of the guards at the castle must have reported that riders were coming, because Katharine was waiting anxiously in the inner bailey when they rode in. She ran forward as Connor set Alura down from the back of the horse. Throwing her arms around her daughter, she cried, "Alura! Are you all right?"

"Yes, Mother," Alura told her. "I am unharmed, thanks to Connor and Father and the other men."

Katharine said a prayer of thanksgiving as she hugged Alura. Then, leaning back with her hands on Alura's shoulders, she said, "We must take you inside."

"Aye," said Alura. "So that I can dress for the wedding."

"Wedding!" exclaimed Sir Herve. "You mean to say you intend to go ahead and be married tonight?"

Alura looked up at Connor, who was still sitting on the charger. "If Connor will have me."

With a broad grin, he swung down from his saddle and drew her into his arms. "What do you think?"

Alura turned her head and looked at Sir Herve. "See that the priest is ready, please, Father."

Sir Herve shook his head, laughed, and said, "Aye. See to it I shall."

They all went into the castle, Alura flanked by Connor and her mother. Katharine took Alura upstairs, and Connor sat down at the table in the great hall with Jeremy. The squire hesitated, then said tentatively, "Milord, about what happened tonight in that clearing where the outlaws were camped . . ."

Connor grunted. "Reminded you of another time, did it?"

"Aye," said Jeremy, "when they waylaid us in the forest near Welwynd." He leaned toward Connor and lowered his voice. "I told Sir Herve it must have been magic. It was, wasn't it, milord?"

"I know not, and that is the God's truth, lad. I mean to speak to Lady Alura about it—but not tonight."

Jeremy blushed. "Oh, no, milord, I didn't mean that you should."

Connor clapped a hand on the squire's shoulder. "Worry not, Jeremy. If there is indeed magic loose in this world, it can do good as well as ill. Tonight is proof enough of that."

Jeremy nodded in agreement. Sir Connor was laughing and happy now, moreso than he had been in months, if not years, and for Jeremy, that was sufficient evidence of the good that magic could do.

Even if the magic was just the fact that Sir Connor was in love. . . .

After everything that had happened, the wedding seemed to pass by in the wink of an eye. Brynclair's bald-pated priest spoke the necessary words, and Alura, clad now in the elegant blue-and-silver gown that had been made for the wedding, was drawn into Connor's arms for the kiss that sealed their union— symbolically, at least. The true consummation would come later, after the feast.

The feast, too, seemed to go by quickly. Alura lolled in the chair next to Connor's, a glass of wine in one hand while the other was clasped in Connor's. She had eaten well, but lightly, and had drunk only a small amount. Connor had likewise seemed to lack much of an appetite—for food and drink, at least.

Not so the wedding guests, who were eating and drinking and laughing and roistering. The musicians were playing, and the air was filled with sounds of celebration. Sir Herve sat in his chair and looked out over the festivities with an expression of contentment on his face. Beside him, Katharine appeared equally pleased.

Finally, and not a moment too soon as far as Alura was concerned, Connor growled, "Enough of this," and came to his feet. His firm grip on her hand lifted her with him. He turned to her and swept her up in his arms, drawing a gasp of surprise from her and cheers from the crowd.

"Milord," she said, "what are you doing?"

The answer he spoke was utterly unnecessary, but hearing it thrilled her anyway. "Taking my wife to bed."

Hoots of laughter and shouts of encouragement came from the crowd as Connor carried Alura toward the stairs, followed by her parents, the priest, and several of the guests. Connor and Alura ignored the raucous display, caring only about each other at the moment. Alura worried a little that the strain of carrying her would be bad for Connor's shoulder, but at the

same time, she did not want him to put her down. Not until
they reached the bedchamber.

When they did, Alura saw that the bed had been strewn
with fresh, newly bloomed flowers. They smelled lovely. Connor lowered her amidst the colorful blooms as the others
crowded into the room behind them.

The priest blessed the marriage bed, stifling a yawn as he
did so. It was much later than he had intended to be up. Connor was slapped on the back and congratulated by Sir Herve
and the other guests, who then filed out of the room. Katharine
gave Alura one last hug, then followed her husband and the
others, leaving Connor and Alura alone at last.

Alura lay back on the flower-strewn bed. Connor leaned
over her to brush his lips against hers lightly. Alura lifted her
arms, locked them around his neck, and pulled him down harder. She knew she was being wanton, and she cared not a whit.

His hands skimmed her sides and slid down to her hips,
then back up to her breasts. Her nipples hardened as he cupped
and caressed. She wanted to go fast, but at the same time she
wanted this experience to last forever. When he finally took
his mouth away from hers, she was breathless, and she panted
quietly against his shoulder with her eyes closed.

When he abruptly pulled away from her, she cried out at
the feeling of loss.

Her eyes flew open as she sat up, and she saw that he had
rolled off the bed and stood up to go to the window, crushing
underfoot some of the blooms he had swept off the bed when
he'd placed her on it. He threw the shutters open and peered
out at the darkness, his back stiff and straight.

"Connor?" said Alura, her voice little more than a whisper.
"What is wrong?"

"You know," he said heavily without turning around to
face her. "You have married the Beast of Stavebrook. You
may believe that I am different now, but in my heart I am the
same man I always was."

"Oh," said Alura. "I know that. And I know as well that
you were *never* the Beast of Stavebrook. Morvyn was."

He stiffened even more, but at least he finally turned so that
he could look at her again. In the light from the candles on

the bedside table, his face might have been carved from stone. "What did you say?" he asked in a low, dangerous voice.

Alura felt a tingle of fear at the thought that she might have been wrong. But after everything she had faced, she was not going to allow fear to stand in the way of happiness.

"I said you were never the Beast of Stavebrook. All the evils that were ever laid at your feet were actually committed by your brother Morvyn."

Stubbornly, Connor shook his head. "You cannot know that. You cannot be certain. You know nothing of what happened years ago...."

Alura came to her feet to confront him, ignoring the fact that he towered over her, his face dark with emotion. Anger crept into her voice as she said, "I *do* know. Morvyn himself told me."

"Never!" exclaimed Connor. "He would never confess to what he really—" He stopped with a sharply indrawn breath.

"See? You admit it yourself. And no, Morvyn never actually told me that he had committed the crimes for which you took the blame. He never said that he pushed Elspeth Lyle from the tower of Stavebrook to her death because she irritated him by complaining that he had got her with child." The next words caught in Alura's throat, but she forced them out anyway. "I know what sort of man he was because he told me . . . he told me the plans he had for me, after we were married."

She had to turn away then so that Connor could not see her face as memories of the vile perversions that had spewed from Morvyn's mouth flooded back into her mind. When she had visited him at Stavebrook, not long before the wedding was to take place, he had drunk too much and grown careless in his talk with her when they were alone. He had spoken of the things he had done with other women and he had told her that when they were married she would be expected to join him in his twisted decadence. Alura had recoiled from him in horror and denial . . . and he had laughed at her.

She had thought then that being around his notorious brother must have had a terrible influence on him, even though Morvyn was the elder of the two. But as she had grown to

know Connor in these past weeks, she had come to see the
truth at last. Morvyn was the beast, the evil one, but for some
reason known only to him, Connor had assumed that yoke of
infamy.

As a shudder passed through her now, Connor's hands came
down on her shoulders, and he grated, "That bastard. Had I
been there . . . had I known you as I know you now . . . I
would have killed him myself, then and there, as I should have
years ago."

Alura let him turn her around so that he could embrace her.
She rested her tear-streaked cheeks against his chest. She had
not even been aware until now that she had started to cry.

"Why, Connor?" she asked. "Why did you allow everyone
to believe that you were so horrible?"

"Why should I not have?" he whispered as he held her
tightly to him. "I was the second son. I stood to inherit nothing. From the time I was a boy, first my father and then Morvyn told me that he was the only one who mattered, that he
had to be protected so that the barony would be safe. Then as
I grew older and the rumors began to make their way through
the district, I found that I no longer cared what people thought
of me. And when I decided to accompany King Richard to the
Holy Land, I expected that I would die there . . . and I almost
did."

"It must have been so lonely, having everyone hate you."

"Not everyone," Connor said softly. "There was one other
who knew the truth. . . ."

Alura lifted her head so that she could look up at him.
"Who?"

"One of my father's knights . . . a man named Sir William.
My only friend, really. He taught me much of what I know
about combat. When Elspeth Lyle . . . died . . . William was
the first one to reach her body. He looked up and saw Morvyn
watching from the tower window. I came running up a moment later from the stables."

"Then he knew you had nothing to do with her death, and
that Morvyn was responsible."

"Aye, but I made him swear not to reveal what he knew. I
had already decided to join Richard on his trek to the Holy

Land, so it mattered not to me that I might be blamed for Elspeth's death. Shortly after I left Stavebrook, William did, too, and caught up with the crusaders before we sailed." Connor smiled. "He brought his son with him."

"Jeremy!"

"Aye," Connor said with a nod. "I made the lad my squire and promised his father that I would always look after him, should anything happen to William." A sigh came from Connor's lips. "We fought side by side 'cross Palestine, but when Saladin's horde overran Al Sajihd"—he shook his head— "the last thing I saw before I passed out was a dozen of the devils surrounding William. I saw their scimitars flash red in the sun . . . then nothing."

Alura shivered. "You lost your best friend, and almost your life."

"Aye." He pressed his lips to her forehead. "But now I have my life back, thanks to you."

"And I have no reason to fear you."

"Never." Connor took a deep breath. "You know the truth now, Alura."

"And it will never come between us again." She found his mouth with hers, and her tongue darted lightly against his lips. He opened them and met her tongue with his own.

Connor turned with her in his arms and moved them toward the bed. He lowered her onto the flower-strewn sheets once more and covered her face with kisses. This time there would be no stopping, no uncertainties, no need to pull back. This time they would be joined, fully and completely.

Alura watched through heavy-lidded eyes as he undressed her, stripping off each garment one by one until she lay uncovered before him. The most incredible heat she had ever known surged through her veins like the flow of a mighty river. Connor lowered his head to each of her breasts in turn, sucking the nipples gently with his mouth and sending the tip of his tongue circling them in maddening swipes. His teeth caught at the sensitive flesh, tugging lightly on the delicate buds. Alura buried her fingers in his hair and held his head to her, moaning as his lips and tongue stoked the fire within her.

She would have almost been content to have him continue

what he was doing all night, but after a seeming eternity of pleasure, he moved his head down from her breasts and rested it for a moment on her stomach. He stroked the smooth skin in front of his face, feeling her tremble slightly under his touch. His fingers trailed down over her abdomen and into the triangle of finespun red hair at the juncture of her thighs. Alura gasped as he pressed the heel of his hand against her mound. Her thighs parted of their own accord, and a moment later his fingers found the slick folds of her core.

"Connor, I love you!" she cried softly as the tip of one finger probed delicately within her.

"And I love you, my lady Alura," he said.

She caught at his shoulders and pulled him back up to her, then began tugging at the tunic he wore. He obliged her by kneeling beside her on the bed and lifting the garment over his head. Her eyes feasted on his broad, lightly furred chest and the muscular arms and shoulders. Some women might have found the scarred shoulder distracting or even unappealing, but not Alura. It was part of Connor, and as such, she loved it as much as she loved the rest of him.

He stepped off the bed and kicked away his slippers, then peeled the hose and braies down his thighs and calves. When he tossed them aside he was utterly nude, and Alura rolled onto her side to look at him. The width of his chest tapered down to the slim hips of a man who had spent much of his life riding and fighting. The hair on his chest tapered as well, before flaring again into the thicket on his groin. His manhood was fully erect, long and heavy with need for her. As he moved closer to the bed, Alura reached out and closed her fingers lightly around his staff, marveling once again at the feel of it, like steel sheathed in velvet.

Connor tipped his head back and closed his eyes as she explored and caressed his body, seeking out the most sensitive spots with her questing fingertips. "I have dreamed of this," he said in a half-moan, drawing a look from Alura but no words. Best he continue to believe that what had happened between them before was naught but a dream, she thought.

Finally, when he could stand it no more, he reached down and captured her wrists in his hands. Holding her firmly, he pulled her up, and she came willingly, standing on the edge of the bed for an instant before she looped her arms around his neck and wrapped her legs around his waist. His fingers spread over the cheeks of her bottom, cupping them. Connor's arms around her supported her easily as they kissed, their bodies molded to each other. They swayed slightly, as if dancing to music that only they could hear.

Alura felt herself moving backward and down into softness, as if she was falling through a cloud. A part of her mind knew she was lying on a bed in a chamber of her father's castle, but she preferred to give herself over to the idea that she and Connor were alone in the universe, just the two of them, and that the two would soon become one. She felt him at the gates of her femininity, felt the gates parting as he surged into her and filled her. Tears of joy rolled down her face. Their joining was perfect and complete. She had given herself to him and him to her in total possession of each other. And as he launched into the timeless rhythm, Alura held him tightly to her. Their lips met, and she felt something amazing within, an opening of herself even more than she would have thought possible.

She cried out softly against his mouth as the culmination of their love shook them both.

Long moments later, bathed in the afterglow of their passion, Alura opened her eyes as she nestled there in Connor's arms. Her arms were still around his neck, and she could see the bracelet and the ring she still wore. As she had vowed, they had not left her wrist and finger. But as she looked at the fire opals, it suddenly occurred to her that she had not forbidden Radiya and Zahir to observe what had happened here tonight, and abruptly she stiffened in shame.

Connor had gone tense, too, and he abruptly rolled away from her and sat up on the edge of the bed. Startled, Alura reached out to him. "My love?"

"There is something you have not told me," he said heavily. "Did you lie with my brother?"

"No!" Alura exclaimed, horrified that he would even ask such a question.

"Then why were you not a virgin when you came to the marriage bed?"

Alura's hand went to her mouth as her horror deepened. With everything that had happened leading up to the wedding, it had never occurred to her that Connor would be able to tell they had made love before, even if he considered it naught but a dream.

"I swear to you, Connor, I have never lain with anyone save you," she said, hoping that he would believe her.

At least he swung around to look into her eyes. "But how is that possible?" She could tell that he was angry, but he was doing his best to control his emotions.

She looked again at the bracelet and the ring and took a deep breath. There was only one way to solve this problem and restore the wonderful loving feelings that had filled this room a few moments earlier.

"I have not told you the *entire* truth," she began. Even more anger flared in his eyes, and she quickly hurried on, "There is something you must see, but we should both get dressed first."

"I would have an answer now," he said, his voice low and dangerous once more.

"Well . . ." Alura looked at the bracelet and the ring and gave a weak smile. "If you insist."

She reached for the gems and stroked them lightly.

"You could have let me watch," grumbled Zahir. "Remember when we got back to the castle, you said we would watch."

"I said we would see whether or not they would be happy together," snapped Radiya.

"Well, you saw for yourself. They looked happy enough at the wedding feast. And when Connor picked Alura up to carry her upstairs . . ." Zahir rolled his eyes ". . . she was happy, let me tell you."

Radiya frowned as she paced back and forth in her sanctuary. "I am still not sure."

"Well, we could've been sure, if you hadn't made the gems opaque so that we couldn't see or hear anything!"

"Hush, you lecherous old fool."

Zahir reclined on his cushions. "You had no complaints about my lechery that night we were sailing on the gulf. Remember, the stars were so bright and looked so close to us I said I was going to reach up and pluck a handful of them for you to wear in your hair. . . . Of course, I could actually do things like that now, but it might upset the celestial balance—"

"Zahir," said Radiya through gritted teeth, "I truly wish this mystical wall was not between us."

He grinned at her and wiggled his bushy eyebrows. "So do I, my dear, so do I." He laced his fingers together behind his head. "Anyway, no need to worry now about Alura and Connor. They're going to be just fine."

"I hope you are right," said Radiya. "I really do hope you are right this time, Zahir . . . Zahir!"

He was fading away right before her eyes, and so, Radiya realized, was she.

They were being summoned.

Twenty-three

◠

The man in the hooded cloak moved as if he was either very old or incredibly tired or both as he walked down the gangplank from the ship. When he reached the dock he stopped and leaned on his walking stick and took a deep breath. "England," he said in a voice choked with emotion. He was home.

Well, not really, he thought. He still had a long way to go, and he might as well get started, he decided. He took one step, then another, then another . . .

Yes, indeed, a long way to go.

Summer lay gently on the land. The fields were green with crops, the days were warm and the nights were cool, and as Alura stood in the tower room at Stavebrook with her hand resting lightly on her belly, she looked out over the estate and tried to tell herself that she was content.

She should have been more than content, she knew. She should have been ecstatically happy. She had felt the faint stirrings of life within her and knew that she was carrying Connor's child. She had not told him yet; her belly was still flat and he had no way of knowing. But she would tell him soon, when the time was right.

But when would that be?

And this was certainly not the right place, thought Alura, this room where Elspeth Lyle had met her doom. Coming up here did not particularly bother her, since she knew that Connor had had nothing to do with Elspeth's tragic death. But with the bad memories that might lurk here, it was not the proper setting for delivering good news. Besides, the servants gossiped when she came up here too much. They did not know the truth about Connor as she did, and they probably thought she was up here brooding about her husband's sordid past.

In actuality, she liked the tower room simply because it provided such a good view of the estate. She was rapidly coming to love Stavebrook as much as Connor did. Oh, the castle was not particularly attractive—some might even call it grim and foreboding—but that was the way with many castles.

What she loved was the *land,* the trees and the fields and the flowers, the thickets and the streams and the hills. She and Connor would raise their children here, and those children would love Stavebrook and protect it as their parents did.

The door of the tower room slammed open behind her.

Alura gasped and jumped slightly. She turned and saw Connor stalking into the room. His tunic was wet with sweat, and strands of his dark hair were plastered to his forehead. He and Jeremy had been practicing with their swords down in the bailey. Alura had not been able to see them, but she had heard the frequent clang of steel against steel.

Connor's face was dark with anger. "I'm told it happened again," he said sharply.

" 'Twas naught, Connor," Alura began.

He stopped her with a slashing motion of his hand. "Naught, you say? Naught that my wife—my *wife*!—was insulted in mine own village?"

"The man was a traveling peddlar," explained Alura, "not one of your people, Connor. And what he said was not really so bad—"

"He called you the Whore of Stavebrook! Mossgrave told me! The man said only a trollop would have married a man like the Beast of Stavebrook—and he said it so that you could hear him! You should have summoned Zahir and had him blast the wretch off the face of the earth!"

"I had already walked past him," Alura said desperately. Her good mood had evaporated, as had her thoughts of telling Connor about the child. "I'm sure he did not mean for me to hear. Besides, 'tis bad enough I revealed the secret of the djinn to you without letting the entire village know about them."

"That is not the way Mossgrave told me it happened."

Alura suddenly exploded with anger. "Mossgrave is a meddling old fool! If he did not keep telling you when people say things about you, or about me—"

"Then someone else would," finished Connor. "The insults always find their way back to the ears of the one insulted. 'Tis the way of the world, Alura, and you should know that by now."

Truth to tell, she frequently *did* hear the comments, and they often hurt. It helped a bit that most of the insulting remarks came from travelers instead of the people of Stavebrook, but still . . .

She thrust aside the remembered pain and lifted her chin. "I am your wife, and proud of that fact. No matter what anyone says, I love you, and I always shall."

"And I love you," Connor raged, "which is why I should go down there and split that peddlar's skull with my sword!"

"Connor, nay!" More than once, she had been forced to restrain him from violence when he felt that her honor had been sullied by the vicious rumors and cutting remarks. One of these days, she thought, he was actually going to kill someone in his anger.

If only he was willing to reveal the truth . . .

But he had sworn an oath to his brother never to do that. With Morvyn dead and in his crypt half a year now, Alura saw no reason to keep such a vow, but Connor did. He would never break his pledge, not even to spare his wife from the insults of louts like the one today.

"I ought to kill him," said Connor. "I really ought."

Alura shook her head. "Nay. He shall be gone ere the day is over. I heard him say he is moving on to Brynclair."

"Where, mayhap, your father will kill him."

Alura frowned. She had not considered that possibility.

Connor paced angrily to the window. " 'Tis bad enough

when they insult you or me, Alura. What will happen the first time our son hears his father called a beast and his mother a whore?''

Alura's hand went instinctively to her belly again.

''Better to kill one or two of the varlets now, and put a stop to—'' Connor stopped short as he swung around to face her. His eyes dropped to her middle where her hand was resting, and somehow he recognized the meaning of the gesture. ''Alura?'' he whispered.

She made herself nod. No, this was not the right time or place, she told herself, but she could not lie to him. ''Aye.''

He held out his arms and she came into them, luxuriating as she always did in the combination of strength and tenderness with which he embraced her. He stroked her hair and lavished kisses on her eyes and nose and mouth, then hugged her tightly. ''A son,'' he said, his voice hushed with awe. ''I know it.''

Alura was about to remind him of the possibility that their child could be a girl, but she merely nodded instead. Somehow, she knew that he was right, that the child growing within her was a son.

''Now I *have* to kill that peddlar,'' said Connor.

She jerked back and said, ''Nay!''

He shook his head in determination and set her aside. ''Bad enough that the villain insults my wife, but to insult the mother of my son . . . !'' His hand went to the hilt of his sword.

''Connor!'' Alura cried as he stalked out of the room, moving with the wolfish speed and grace she knew so well. His footsteps echoed in the corridor outside.

Alura started to run after him, then stopped abruptly. Instead she lifted her left hand and quickly rubbed the gems on the jewelry she wore.

The familiar clouds of smoke billowed from the fire opals and formed themselves into human shapes. As soon as she was solid, Radiya threw her arms around Alura and hugged her. '' 'Tis true?'' she asked. ''You are really with child?''

''Of course she is,'' said Zahir. ''I could have told you that just from looking at her. See how she glows—''

''You must stop him!'' Alura broke in. ''Please!''

"Stop who?" asked Zahir. "You mean Connor?" He and Connor had become great friends since Alura had revealed the existence of the djinn to her husband on the night of their wedding.

"Yes!"

"You mean stop him from killing that buffoon who insulted you? I think that's a good idea, myself. I can tell you from experience, you lop off a few heads and people start paying attention—"

Alura let out a moan.

"We will do what we can," Radiya said quickly. "Come along, Zahir!"

The two of them vanished, and Alura hurried to the window. She knew that whatever the djinn did, they would do it invisibly.

From the window of the tower room, she could peer down past the walls of the castle into the village, and it took her only a moment to spot the peddlar. He had already packed up his cart and was making ready to depart for Brynclair. Not soon enough would he be gone, however, because Connor was already striding purposefully through the bailey, followed by a curious Jeremy. They passed through the gates and into the village, and Connor stepped in front of the peddlar with sword drawn.

The man stopped and cringed back against the poles of his cart. He snatched off the filthy cap he wore and said in a nervous voice, "Milord . . . ?"

"I am told," Connor said heavily, "that you spoke about my wife this day. You will repeat what you said to me."

"B-but, milord, I know n-naught of this—"

Connor lifted his sword slightly. "Lie to me and 'twill go harder with you. I want to hear the words on your lips so that all here will know why you are about to die."

The man cringed again. "Oh, milord, no! I swear I meant no harm—"

Suddenly, with loud cracking sounds, both wheels of the cart fell off, dumping the vehicle on the ground. The peddlar's trade goods, which had been piled high on the cart, fell forward, raining down around the frightened, unfortunate man.

He yelled in pain and fear and threw his arms up to protect his head as he collapsed under the shower of iron pots, crockery, bolts of cloth, wooden utensils, and pieces of dented, second-hand armor.

The whole thing happened so quickly that Connor had time to do naught but step back in surprise before gales of laughter were rolling over the village street. Connor had to admit that the peddlar did look ridiculous, half-buried as he was in the pile of his motley goods. The man was too ridiculous to kill, he realized.

That was the sort of thing Morvyn would have done.

Connor sheathed his sword and raised his voice to say, "Someone help this man repair his cart, then send him on his way. He is no longer welcome at Stavebrook, and if he shows his face again, you all have my permission—nay, my mandate—to pelt him with rotten vegetables until he goes away."

That brought more whoops of laughter from the villagers. Connor turned back toward the castle, and as he did so, Jeremy fell in step beside him and said, "I thought you were going to gut that man, milord."

"I came close, Jeremy. I might have, had he not made such a fool of himself."

Up in the tower, Alura heaved a sigh of relief as she watched Connor enter the castle. A moment later, Radiya and Zahir materialized, and Zahir said, "Pretty good, eh? I knew a man like Connor would never kill anybody who was rolling around on the ground with an iron pot stuck on his head!"

"So it was your idea, was it?" asked Radiya. "I seem to recall that *I* had something to do with it. . . ."

Alura's relief had already turned to gloom. "Connor was spared this time from becoming a murderer. But what about the next time? As long as people believe the worst of him, things like this will happen again and again."

Zahir frowned. "You're not happy, are you?"

"How could anyone be happy living with such a dark cloud of untruth hanging over them?"

"Do you wish us to do something about it?" asked Radiya.

Alura stared at her in surprise. "Can you?"

"Your wish is our command!" Zahir leered at Radiya in

triumph. She had not been able to stop him this time from voicing his favorite saying.

"Then I wish things were different," said Alura. "I wish Connor did not have to live the lie of his past."

"He made a vow," Radiya pointed out. "He cannot break it. That is who he is, and we can do nothing to change that."

"Then change something else!"

Radiya smiled and nodded toward the window. "Perhaps we will not have to. Look down the road."

Frowning in puzzlement, Alura turned to the window and did as Radiya suggested. She peered along the path that led away from Stavebrook toward London. She saw a figure in the distance, a man in some sort of hooded cloak from the looks of him. He was hobbling along the path toward the castle.

"I see an old cripple, but that is all."

"A visitor to Stavebrook," said Radiya. "Perhaps as the lady of this castle, you should go down and greet him."

Alura was confused, but she had trusted the djinn so far. She supposed she could trust them again, although Zahir seemed to have as little idea what was going on as she did. "Take us with you," he requested. "I want to see this, whatever it is."

Alura held out her left hand, and the djinn turned to smoke and entered the gems. Then she left the tower room and hurried down the stairs.

She met Connor and Jeremy in the great hall. "Where are you going?" Connor asked when he saw her striding toward the entrance.

"A visitor is coming," she said.

"What visitor?" he asked as he turned to follow her out of the castle. Jeremy came along as well.

"I know not," said Alura with a shake of her head. "Only that he is coming here."

It was clear from the expression on Connor's face that he was worried she had gone mad. For all she knew, she had, thought Alura.

She walked through the tunnel under the gatehouse and paused just outside the open barbican. The distant figure was closer now and was still approaching slowly. Connor frowned and asked, "Is that who you spoke of?"

Alura nodded. "Aye."

The three of them stood and waited as the man walked closer and closer. He entered the edge of the village and made his way along the street toward the castle gate. His head was lowered, his eyes downcast toward the ground, but he seemed to know where he was going. He did not veer from his path by as much as a hand's breadth, and his pace was stronger now, more sure.

Alura realized suddenly that she was having trouble breathing. Connor's hand was on her arm, and he was gripping it tightly as the same tension that Alura felt affected him as well. Even Jeremy was taut with anticipation.

Then the man came to a stop in front of them and raised his head. He had a walking stick clutched in his right hand, but he lifted his left and shoved back the hood that had shielded his face.

Alura gasped. She could not help herself. The stranger's face was a mass of scars, terrible scars that ran jaggedly up and down and across his rugged features. And yet, though he should have been hideous, he was not. As he looked at Alura and Connor and Jeremy through eyes that burned with courage and strength, he straightened, drawing dignity around him like the cloak he wore.

Connor said in a choked whisper, "William?"

The scarred man smiled. "Connor," he said. His voice was raspy. One of the scars went nearly all the way across his throat.

"F-Father?" said Jeremy.

"Jeremy, lad."

And Sir William opened his arms to his son.

Alura stood there, stunned, watching Jeremy and William embrace. They began pounding each other on the back and making loud whooping noises that were half-sobs and half-laughs of joy, and then Connor was with them, throwing his long, powerful arms around both of them, and all Alura could do was say to herself, "How . . . ?"

But the answer came to her even as she spoke. Connor had

survived the fighting at Al Sajihd, though he had been
wounded nearly unto death. He had been carried away from
that bloody castle in the desert and nursed back to health. Who
was to say the same thing could not have happened to Sir
William? And in the confusion following the massacre, no one
had thought to tell either man that the other was still alive.
Considering the scars on William's face, his survival was even
more of a miracle than Connor's. Their friends could have
considered it a kindness not to tell Connor that William had
lived through the battle, thinking that the older knight was sure
to die.

Alura glanced down at the bracelet and ring. Or perhaps Sir
William had had someone else looking after his welfare, so
that someday he could come home to his son and his best
friend. . . .

With tears shining on their faces, Connor, William, and Jeremy turned toward Alura. "Come inside," said Connor.
"There is much to talk about."

"Aye," rasped William. "For one thing, I was told in London that you are now Lord Ridglea, Connor. That murdering
brother of yours finally had the good grace to die, did he?"

Connor grimaced. "William," he hissed. "Speak not of—"

"The hell I'll not speak of it!" roared William, with more
strength than he should have possessed in his war-ravaged
body. He thrust a bony arm from his cloak and pointed at
Connor. "Morvyn is dead, and it matters not who hears the
truth now."

"But I swore a vow to him—"

"I never did! My promise was to you, lad, and I shall break
it now and hope you will forgive me for it. But 'tis time the
truth was known!"

Alura's heart leaped as a thrill of excitement went through
her.

"You there!" William said to one of the villagers. He
pointed to another of them. "And you! And you! Listen, all
of you! For years, you have known Connor Warrick as the
Beast of Stavebrook. Well, you are all wrong! The true beast
was his brother Morvyn! 'Twas Morvyn who pushed that poor

lass to her death! I saw it with my own eyes. 'Twas Morvyn who performed all the evil deeds ever laid at the feet of this boy!''

Connor simply stood there, breathing heavily, looking stricken.

One of the crowd called out, ''How do we know ye be tellin' the truth, old man?''

''Old man, is it?'' William practically snarled. He whipped his cloak aside and reached for his sword. ''I be Sir William of Stavebrook! Some of you remember me, and you know that I do not lie! What I have told you here today, I will swear to on the holy cross ... just as I swore on the cross when I told everyone who would listen in London, and on the road 'twixt here and there.'' He relaxed from his angry stance and grinned at Connor. ''You see, lad, you have no evil reputation to uphold any longer. The damage is already done.''

''William ...'' Connor threw his arms around the older knight again. ''Thank you. I would have taken the secret with me to my grave—''

''But now you need not,'' finished William. ''Now you can get on with your life.'' He smiled at Alura. ''And tell me who this beautiful damsel is.''

''My wife, the lady Alura,'' Connor said proudly.

William bowed to her. ''Milady. I am ever at your service, as I am at that of your lord.''

''You have already done me a great service, Sir William,'' Alura told him. She hugged him, then stepped back.

''Ah, with child, are you? I'll have to teach the youngster some tricks with the sword, when he is old enough.''

Alura laughed. ''How can everyone tell?''

'' 'Tis simple,'' Connor said as he took her left hand. ''They can see that the love in you has grown even stronger.'' He lifted her hand to his lips and kissed the back of it.

Alura looked at the fire opals and mouthed the words, *thank you.*

Connor still held her hand as he asked, ''Why are you thanking me?''

''For making my life complete,'' Alura said.

•   •   •

"See? I told you everything would work out just fine!"

"*You* told *me*? You had no idea Sir William was coming back. I have been watching over him for months now, just so he could save Connor from his own foolish pride."

"That does nothing to change the fact that I said Connor and Alura were going to be happy together, and you can see for yourself. They're happy! Only a few hundred more couples to go. I tell you, Radiya, we're going to be out of here before you know it!"

"Zahir . . ."

"Yes, my love?"

"The next time we are out of the gems . . . kiss me, you old fool."

About the Author

~

Elizabeth Hallam has been a professional writer for the past eighteen years and has authored dozens of novels and short stories. Her most recent book, *Spirit Catcher*, was published in July 1998. *Romantic Times* referred to *Spirit Catcher* as "An engaging, warm-hearted story." *Rendezvous* called it "... a glorious tale of past and present merging to give readers a few hours of spellbinding sensuality mixed with a tempting mystery that will keep you guessing until the end." Elizabeth has won awards for her novels and her work has been critically acclaimed in *Publishers Weekly*, *Booklist*, *Library Journal*, and the *Los Angeles Times*. You can write to Elizabeth Hallam at P.O. Box 931, Azle, Texas 76098 or e-mail her at livia@flash.net.

FRIENDS ROMANCE

Can a man come between friends?

__A TASTE OF HONEY
by DeWanna Pace   0-515-12387-0

__WHERE THE HEART IS
by Sheridon Smythe   0-515-12412-5

__LONG WAY HOME
by Wendy Corsi Staub   0-515-12440-0

All books $5.99

Prices slightly higher in Canada